My Lady Quicksilver

BEC MCMASTER

sourcebooks
casablanca

Published by Sourcebooks Casablanca, an imprint of Sourcebooks, Inc.
P.O. Box 4410, Naperville, Illinois 60567-4410
(630) 961-3900
Fax: (630) 961-2168
www.sourcebooks.com

Printed and bound in the United States of America.
VG 10 9 8 7 6 5 4 3 2 1

To Michelle, who loved it first.

and factory, where the mechs within were forced to work steel in repayment for their mechanical limbs. This particular enclave was responsible for manufacturing mech parts for the automaton army that protected the aristocratic Echelon.

In the distance, chimneys lurked in the smog like little watchtowers. A foghorn echoed mournfully as the boat slowly traversed the Thames. The world seemed unnaturally silent beneath its ethereal blanket, but for the faint whisper of movement in the shadows.

"Here," someone murmured in the alley below him. "Is that them? Someone give 'em the signal."

Lynch's head snapped up.

Tendrils of fog eddied around a man on the other rooftop, licking at his legs and cloak—Garrett. Making a sharp gesture with his fingers, Lynch silently directed his lieutenant. There were four other shapes in the dark, but he couldn't see them, only hear a faint scraping sound that whispered on the tiles through his aural communicator. Made of fine brass pieces and leather, it fit in his ear perfectly, a transmitter receiving every whisper that Garrett made. Garrett's matching piece could relay his commands no matter where they both were.

The sound of iron scraping over cobbles echoed in the still night. Someone hissed a warning and the sound cut off. Lynch leaned forward, cocking his head to listen.

"Quiet." This was a voice of command, cool and low. "D'you want the world to 'ear us? Remember, the friggin' bleeders can 'ear for miles."

Definitely humanists.

One

"You have three weeks to find Mercury...or I swear you'll share his fate..."

Smoke belched with a coughing roar from a distant furnace as Sir Jasper Lynch leaned against the edge of a chimney, staring through the smoky gloom, the echo of the prince consort's words ringing in his ears.

His gaze tracked the foggy streets below, hunting for any sign of movement as he slowly stretched cramped muscles. As Master of the Guild of Nighthawks—thief-catchers and trackers—he'd spent the last week hunting for leads on the mysterious revolutionary leader, Mercury, whose humanist movement was plaguing London.

And now he'd found one.

No mention of the name Mercury, but Lynch's instincts were on fire at the rumor of a shipment that was due to be smuggled out of the steamy enclaves on the edges of the city—a particular shipment that was received every month at this time, though his informant hadn't known what it was.

Easy enough to guess. The enclaves were both jail

Praise for *Kiss of Steel*

"Exquisitely imagined…McMaster's wildly inventive plot deftly blends elements of steampunk and vampire romance with brilliantly successful results. Darkly atmospheric and delectably sexy, *Kiss of Steel* is an extraordinary debut."

—*Booklist* Starred Review

"Dark, intense, and sexy… A stunning new series."

—*Library Journal*

"An enthralling debut… A leading man as wicked as he is irresistible… Heart-wrenching, redemptive, and stirringly passionate… A series opener to be read and savored."

—*RT Book Reviews*, 4.5 Stars

"An interesting twist on the vampire mythos and the brutal side of London high society."

—*Publishers Weekly*

"A stellar steampunk novel with an amazing world, complex characters, and action-packed plot. Steampunk fans will gobble this book up…an excellent example of how great steampunk can be."

—*The Romance Reviews* Best Book of 2012 Nominee, 5 Stars

Praise for *Heart of Iron*

"McMaster's second London steampunk book dazzles and seduces. She crafts complicated, damaged, and driven characters whose unlikely passion is unforgettably powerful...Will leave readers breathless. Though new readers will be enthralled, devotees will find enormous rewards."

—*RT Book Reviews* Top Pick of the Month, 4.5 Stars

"Deliciously atmospheric, completely enthralling...a sexy literary merger of Bram Stoker, Jules Verne, and Jane Austen."

—*Booklist*

"Edgy, dark, and shot through with a grim, gritty intensity, McMaster's latest title adds to her mesmerizing steampunk series with another gripping, inventive stunner."

—*Library Journal* Starred Review

"Intriguing... [readers will] love the sexy, action-packed narrative."

—*Publishers Weekly*

"*Heart of Iron* is so impressive, it deserves a seal of excellence! Like moths to a flame, readers will be drawn to the world and characters McMaster has created. Make room on your keeper shelves."

—*Fresh Fiction*

Lynch crouched low on the edge of the tiled roof, his heart fluttering in his chest with anticipation. Darkness swallowed him as he leaned over the edge, his eyes picking out his prey immediately. One of the benefits of the craving virus that afflicted him was superior senses. A blue blood could see on the darkest of nights and hear the faintest whisper, though that barely made up for the fierce hunger he could never quite assuage, the unrelenting craving for blood...

A trio of cloaked figures hovered in the alley, a phosphorescent flare stick shielded by one of their cloaks. One was a tall man, with broad shoulders beneath the concealing cloak and pockmarked cheeks. He knelt and dragged a heavy crate out of the open sewer grate in the cobbles.

Lynch's eyes narrowed. There were men within the sewers, but he couldn't tell if they were from the enclaves or more of this mysterious group.

Holding up a hand to counteract his previous command, Lynch melted back into the shadows to listen. If the mechs were using the nearby sewer systems to smuggle metalwork out of the enclaves, then the prince consort needed to know.

A month ago, the humanists had tried to bomb the Ivory Tower, the seat of the Echelon's power. The handling of the bombing had been a disaster, with half the aristocratic Echelon trampling through his evidence and only one witness, who sullenly refused to talk, in custody. The only piece of evidence Lynch had was in his pocket: a piece of leather that had torn from a woman's cloak in one of the antechambers. A humanist, he suspected, and one involved in the bombing. The scent of her was long faded from the worn leather, but if he closed his eyes, he knew he could bring her scent to mind. It filled him, branding his memory as if he could never escape her.

Maybe she would be below? His blood fired at the thought. He wanted to find her—he needed to. Though sometimes, in the dark of night, he wondered if his reasons for this madness were the same as the prince consort's.

Swallowing hard, Lynch forced the thought of the mysterious woman from his mind. He had a job to do.

What could the humanists be doing here? Were they after explosives? Or maybe a weapon to counteract the heavily armored metal automatons that patrolled the streets?

He needed to get his hands on that crate.

"Hurry," the leader snapped. "We're already behind schedule."

A man grunted. "'S bloody heavy, you know?"

"Steel often is," came the reply.

"What's that?" someone hissed.

Silence fell. Lynch faded back against the brickwork of a chimney.

"Thought I saw somethin' movin'," the same person murmured. "Up there. On the roof."

"Nighthawks?"

"'Urry it up," the leader snapped. "We need to move. Now."

Lynch scowled as one of the Nighthawks darted between chimneys. Too late. They'd been seen.

Lynch stepped onto the incline of the roof and rode it to the edge, leaping out over nothingness. He saw Garrett and the others moving at the edge of his vision, then he landed in the swirling fog that clung to the cobbles below, his knees bending to absorb the shock.

A man in a rough jerkin, with shoulders the size of a pugilist's, staggered to a halt in front of him, his mouth gaping in shock and both of his arms missing from the elbows down. He wore instead the heavy hydraulic arms of a mech, the work crude and rudimentary, without even the synthetic flesh the Echelon's master smiths could create. Enclave work.

"Nighthawks!" the man bellowed, the hydraulic hoses in his steel arm hissing in the night as he swung a blow at Lynch.

Grabbing the man by the wrist, Lynch kicked his feet out from under him and drove him onto his face on the cobbles.

A shadow shifted in the fog. Lynch caught a glimpse of a dark-hooded cloak and a pistol gleaming in the weak, phosphorescent light of a fallen flare stick. "Let 'im go," the leader commanded in a low voice. He thumbed the hammer on his pistol back.

Lynch could see little of his opponent beyond the cloak and a gaping blackness where his face should have been. A black satin mask covered his entire face and throat, leaving not an inch of skin visible. And he suddenly *knew*.

"Mercury," he said, staring down the barrel of the pistol. Hungry exhilaration leaped through him, shadows sweeping through his vision as the hunger of the craving momentarily overtook him. *The bastard was right in front of him.*

He heard the click a moment before the gun barrel coughed.

Lynch flung himself into a roll as the gun retorted with a hollow *thunk*. A Nighthawk appeared behind him and stiffened, a tiny blue-feathered dart sticking out of his chest. Lewis Hicks, one of the novices. He staggered forward, gave a little sigh, then crumpled at Lynch's feet.

Hicks's eyes remained open and he trembled on the cobbles, rigid as a board, momentarily paralyzed.

Lynch looked up. The new hemlock darts the humanists were using to bring down blue bloods made him wary. The poison paralyzed a blue blood for a good five to ten minutes, leaving them at the human's mercy. As a predator, the sudden sense of vulnerability unnerved him.

Mercury's shoulders stiffened but he wasted no breath. Instead, he turned and bolted down the alley, his cloak swirling the remnants of the fog and his shadow lengthening.

"Scatter!" someone yelled.

Men poured out of the sewers, scrambling past the Nighthawks. Garrett had a man shoved up against a wall and slapped cuffs on him. The humanists fled like mice, darting down alleys. There weren't enough Nighthawks to catch them all, but Lynch only needed one. Oh yes. Cut off the head of the snake and you had them all.

"He's mine," he snapped to Garrett, leaving his lieutenant with the rest of them. Sprinting down the alley, he swiftly gained on the revolutionary, making a snatch at the man's cloak. It tugged for a moment and Mercury spun with a vicious left hook that smashed Lynch across the face. Pain slashed through his cheekbone, leaving his vision white for a second. There must have been something in the revolutionary's hand. Brass knuckles perhaps.

Whirling, Mercury tore free of the cloak and bolted, leaving Lynch with a handful of fabric and the elusive scent of gunpowder.

Curse it. Lynch started after him with deadly focus.

The alleyway was running out, the stone walls that surrounded the enclaves rearing up into the night. Lynch slowed to a halt as Mercury spun, staring at him through the thin gauze of his eye slits.

"Don't come any closer," the revolutionary leader warned, lifting the pistol again.

"The problem with the new make of recoil dart gun is that it requires manual reloading. You appear to be out of darts. Or you would have used it on me already." He had no doubt of that.

Mercury's chin tipped up as the pistol lowered. "That don't make me no less dangerous."

Lynch rubbed at his jaw and the bruise that was no doubt starting to form. "I never expected it to. What did you hit me with?"

"A love tap, milord." The words were laced with sarcasm. "Come closer and I'll give you another."

They stared across the expanse of cobbles. Lynch frowned at his enemy's choice of words, something about the situation stirring unease through his gut. Behind him came shouts. He sensed Mercury's attention shift over Lynch's shoulder and then the revolutionary took a hesitant step backward, hitting the wall.

"Nowhere to run," Lynch said softly. "Nowhere to hide."

"There's always somewhere to run. *Au revoir*, sir." Tossing the steam pistol aside, Mercury whipped a heavier gun from the belt at his hip, with a sharp four-pronged hook at the end of it.

For a moment, Lynch thought the revolutionary was going to fire it at him, but then he pointed it into the sky above and pulled the trigger.

The grappling hook soared into the darkness with a hiss of rope trailing behind it. Metal clamored on stone far above, then the revolutionary jerked on the rope. It held and he pressed something on the side of the grappling gun.

"No——" Lynch snapped, leaping forward.

His fingers grazed the toe of Mercury's boot as the revolutionary sailed into the air. Laughter rang down through the darkness, thick with huskiness. Lynch snarled and slapped a palm against the stone. He'd had him. In the bloody palm of his hand and he'd lost him.

Looking up, he bared his teeth. It was risky for a blue blood to enter the enclaves. Recent mech riots had seen dozens of mechs trampled in the streets by the metal Trojan cavalry. There was no love lost for a blue blood—or a craver, as the mechs called them.

His eyes narrowed. He was dangerous too. And he'd spent over a year hunting the bastard, only to have Mercury slip through his fingers. The prince consort's warning rang dire in his ears. *Bring me his head. Or share his fate.*

Not bloody likely. Looking around, Lynch shoved his boot into a crack between the stones in the wall and hauled himself up through sheer strength, biceps straining.

It was the last thing Mercury would expect.

∽

Steam hissed as the enormous piston rolled through its rotation. The woman known as Mercury hurried past, her breath hot and moist against the silk mask over her face and her eyes darting.

Here in the enclaves, hot orange light lit the steel beams of the work sheds and enormous furnaces. The place was riddled with underground tunnels where the workers lived, but aboveground, the work sheds dominated. It wasn't quite a jail—mechs earned a half day off a fortnight—but it was close.

Metal ingots glowed cherry red and the air was thick with the smell of coal. Men worked even at night to keep the furnaces hot, silent shadows against the shimmering heat waves. Rosalind slipped past a mech in a pitted leather apron as he shoveled coal into the open mouth of a furnace, the blast of heat leaving a light sheen of perspiration on her skin. Droplets of sweat slid beneath her breasts and wet the insides of her right glove. She couldn't feel the left. Only a phantom ache where the limb used to be and where steel now stood.

Damn it. Rosalind tossed aside the spring-recoil grappling gun and started tugging at her right glove. Her heart wouldn't stop rabbiting in her chest, her body moving with a liquid anticipation she knew well. Foolish to relish such anticipation, but the danger, the edge of her nerves, were a drug she'd long been denied.

She couldn't believe her bad luck. The Nighthawk himself, in the flesh.

A man of shadow and myth. Rosalind hadn't gotten a good look at his face in the darkness, but the intensity of his expression was unmistakable and she'd felt the heavy caress of his gaze like a touch upon the skin. Her most formidable opponent, a man dedicated to capturing her and destroying the humanists. The shock of his arrival had thrown her, and Rosalind wasn't a woman who was surprised very often.

She slipped between rows of fan belts with heavy metal automaton limbs on them. The hairs on the back of her neck stood on end. She'd known it was risky, making this one last trip, but she didn't have any choice. Martial law had choked the city ever since the bombing of the Ivory Tower and she needed the parts the mechs had promised her.

The bombing had been a mighty blow for the aristocratic Echelon. Every major blue blood lord in the land, including the prince consort and his human queen had been gathered. If the attack had succeeded, it would have wiped out nearly all of the parasitic blue bloods, leaving the working classes—the humans—to cast off the yoke of slavery and servitude. No more blood taxes or blood slaves. No more armies of metal-jacket automatons to keep them suppressed.

A bold plan.

If it had succeeded.

For a moment Rosalind almost wished she'd thought of it, but the group of mechs she'd rescued from the steamy enclaves to work steel for her a year ago had gone behind her back. For the past six months, she'd urged for patience while the mechs had whispered that she was too soft, not merciless enough to lead the humanist movement. In the end, they'd taken matters into their own hands. Rosalind tried to stop the bombing attempt before it was too late, to try and save her younger brother, Jeremy. Instead, the mechanists had used him, seducing him with grand stories and sending him to deliver the bomb himself.

It had been a catastrophe. The Echelon now understood the threat the humanists posed. Rosalind had been forced to scatter those still under her command as martial law settled its heavy weight over the city and the Echelon put a bounty on their heads. She and her older brother, Jack, had gone into hiding while they tried desperately to discover any word of Jeremy.

Of the mechanists who'd betrayed her and the rest of the movement, there was no sign. All she had left of them was the rancid taste of guilt in her mouth. She knew Jeremy had been fond of their leader, Mendici, and his brother, Mordecai, but she hadn't stopped the hero worship. She'd been too busy with the cause and her own personal project to see what was happening within her family.

Steel screamed as it rang against stone. Rosalind spun on her heel and looked around, fists clenched protectively in front of her. Her gaze raked the shadows. He wouldn't have followed her here, would he? The enclaves were dangerous for a creature of his ilk.

Nothing but stillness greeted her questioning gaze. Sparks sprayed in the distance from a steam-driven welding rig, but there was no one in sight.

Didn't mean he wasn't there.

Easing a foot behind her, she stepped back slowly, watching the shadows. The feeling of danger was a familiar one. She'd been a child spy, an assassin, and years of such work had taught her when she was being watched and when she wasn't.

"You're clever," a cool voice said behind her.

Rosalind spun with her fist raised. The Nighthawk caught her arm in a brutal grip, barely flinching at the blow.

"But I expected that," he murmured, looking down at her from his great height. His fingers locked on her right arm in a cruel grip.

"I'd return the compliment," she snapped breathlessly, forcing her voice lower. Where the hell had he come from? "But I don't think it very clever for a man like you to 'ave ventured 'ere."

She jerked against his grip but it was immoveable. Harsh red light lit his face, highlighting the stark slash of his brows and his hawkish nose. He looked like the Devil's own, his lips hard and cruel and his eyes glaring straight through her. A hard black leather carapace protected his chest—the body armor of the Guild of Nighthawks.

"You and I both know I could kill any number of mechs if they come running." His voice was soft, she noticed, a low, gravelly pitch that one strained to listen to nonetheless. He'd be someone who didn't bother to raise it often. Someone who expected his word to be obeyed and wasn't often disappointed.

"Aye," she agreed, curling her middle finger and twisting the tip of it. The thin, six-inch blade concealed in the knuckle at the base of her hand slid through the glove silently, one of the many enhancements to the joint she'd received. Punch a man like this and she could skewer him. "But I weren't speakin' o' *them*. This is my world, not yours."

Rosalind stabbed hard, stepping forward with her body to give strength to the thrust. Lynch caught her wrist, jerking to the side so that the blade skittered across his ribs and not through them. Shoving away from her, his fingers came away from his side sticky with black blood. In daylight, there would be a faint bluish-red tinge to it—the color gave the blue bloods their name.

He looked up, his pale eyes burning with intensity and the promise of revenge. The blood in Rosalind's veins turned cold at the sight and she snatched the knife from her boot, feeling its familiar weight in her right hand.

Lynch sucked in a sharp breath and looked away from his bloodied fingers. "That wasn't very wise."

Shadows moved. Rosalind shifted, striking up with the knife to where she thought he would come at her. A hand caught hers, thumb digging into the nerve that ran along her thumb.

"Damn you," she swore, as the knife dropped from her suddenly useless hand. She knew a hundred ways to disarm a man. But her arm was yanked hard behind her, and as the Nighthawk spun her, shoving her face-first against a brick wall, she realized none of them would matter. For he knew them too.

His strength terrified her, even as it exhilarated. *Here was a match*, she thought with a shiver. An enemy she just might not be able to vanquish.

Shoving her between the shoulder blades, he jerked her arm up behind her back. Black spots appeared in her vision, but she didn't cry out. Instead, she relaxed into it, the pain slowly softening, much like digging a thumb into a hard knot of muscle. She knew pain; it was an old friend and she'd faced far worse than this in her time. Pain didn't scare her. No, indeed, she welcomed it. The physical ache was something that she could fight, unlike the gut-wrenching, hopeless fear that assailed her whenever she thought of her missing brother.

Lynch's firm body pressed against her, one knee driving into the back of hers. There was nowhere to move, nowhere to go. He had trapped her quite neatly. But then, she had a surprise up her sleeve, one last ace to play.

Lynch paused. Then he caught her wrist and peeled her mech hand off the wall, examining it. The useless fingers splayed wide as he touched a pressure point in the steel tendons, turning it this way and that. Hatred burned within her.

"Aye," she murmured. "I'm a mech."

His thumb ran over the shiv where it erupted through the glove, revealing just a hint of the gleaming steel of her hand. She hadn't bothered with the synthetic flesh some used to conceal their enhancements. They were never real enough, never the right color or consistency. And she didn't want to conform to the Echelon's demands. Damn them. She was human enough, with all the rights a human should have, no matter what they said about mechs.

Lynch found the catching mechanism and the

blade slid back within the steel. "Very clever, lad. No wonder you hit like Molineaux."

"Let me go and I'll give you another."

Silence hung between them. Then Lynch laughed, a short, barking cough of amusement that sounded as if it had been a long time since he'd found anything remotely amusing.

The laughter died as swiftly as it had appeared. His pressure on her arm relaxed, and Rosalind slumped against the brickwork as her injured shoulder protested.

"No doubt you would." Grabbing a handful of her coat, he spun her around, one fist clenching the shirt at her throat. "And perhaps you'd overwhelm me eventually, but I don't care to test the theory. You're bound for Chancery Lane."

The Nighthawk Guild Quarters. Once there, she'd never see the light of day again. Except for a brief view of it on her way to the scaffold.

"I've got a better idea," she said recklessly. *The ace up her sleeve...* "You and I...we could come at some sort o' arrangement."

Those cold gray eyes met hers. She could see them more clearly now that her sight had adjusted to the hellish red glow, but her perception hadn't altered. Lynch would give his mother to the law if she broke it.

There was always a way to manipulate a man though. Even Lynch had to want something, to desire it...She just had to work out what it was.

"You're trying to bribe the wrong man," he said coldly, shoving her arms out wide.

A cool, impersonal hand ran along each arm, under her armpits and lower, to her hips. His hard fingers found the small pouches attached to her belt—powders and poisons that specifically injured a blue blood. Their eyes met and Lynch jerked hard on her belt buckle. The belt slithered through the belt loops on her breeches with a leathery slap, and Rosalind sucked in a sharp breath.

"Every man can be bribed," she said. "What is it you want, Lynch? Money? Power?" She saw the contemptuous answer in his eyes as he discarded her belt with a jerking toss.

"Nothing you can give me. If you move your hands, I'll break them. Even the steel one."

With that, he knelt, sliding his hands down the inside of her legs. His palms were cool and impersonal, but Rosalind jerked at the touch. No man since her husband had touched her there and the feeling unnerved her.

There was another knife in her boot. He took it, tucking it behind his own belt as he started the return journey. Smooth hands slid behind her knees, the pressure just firm enough to make her breath catch. Higher…higher…then shying away just before he cupped her arse.

"You missed somewhat," Rosalind forced herself to say as he straightened. To escape, she would have to outwit him and for that she needed his senses dulled.

His fingers lingered on her hip. "Where?"

"'Igher," she whispered, tilting her head back to look at him. The smooth leather of his gloves slid over the rough linen of her shirt. "It's me greatest asset."

His thumb splayed over her ribs, beneath her breast. So close. Though she'd wanted to keep her sex a secret, men often underestimated a woman or were fooled by the flirtatious bat of her eyelashes. She had nothing but contempt for those who'd fallen to her knife for that mistake.

"'Igher," she dared him. Her stomach twisted in anticipation, unexpected heat spearing lower, between her thighs. Rosalind licked dry lips. *Don't think about what he is. Use him; use your body.*

Lynch's hand slid over the faint, unmistakable curve of her breast, his eyes widening. They were tightly bound, so as not to interfere with her movement, but he was a man. He knew what it meant.

"Surprise," she whispered.

"Bloody hell." He yanked his hand back as if burned. His eyes narrowed, but she could see thought racing behind them. "You! You were in the tower. With the bomb."

One hand curved around her skull and he grabbed a fistful of her hair. Rosalind snatched at his cloak as he dragged her head back, exposing her throat.

Stubble rasped against her cheek and Rosalind's gut turned to ash as his jaw brushed against the smooth skin just below her ear. *No!* She flailed wildly, her iron fingers wrapping around his wrist, knowing even as she grabbed him that she couldn't stop him. Not if he wanted her blood.

"You *are* her," he whispered.

And she realized that he was inhaling her scent.

He wasn't going for the vein after all. Rosalind's body trembled as it relaxed, her stomach quivering. *Lord have mercy.* She was safe from that particular violation.

Then her mind started racing. "Who?" How had he

known that she was in the Ivory Tower the day the
mechs had bombed it? The day the Duke of Lannister
had died? Did he suspect her hand in that?

Lynch lifted his head, his hand cradling her skull.
She saw his eyes and stilled. *Dangerous.*

He dragged a scrap of leather from his pocket and
held it between two fingers. "You left this behind. I
could smell you all over the leather. You, two other
people—and gunpowder."

A perfectly innocuous piece of leather, its absence
barely noticed. "And you've been carryin' it around all
this time? How touchin'."

"In case I forget the scent."

Rosalind stared into his eyes, her mind making one
of those insane leaps of intuition it sometimes did.
Lynch wanted her. His own personal obsession, she
realized. A mystery—one that appealed to his intellect
as well as his desire.

"And now?" she whispered, knowing she had him.
This was his weakness, right here. "Ain't there nothin'
I can bribe you with now?"

He understood her meaning, his pupils flaring as he
jerked away from her. Rosalind tumbled against the
bricks, her hand splayed to catch herself. If she were
a lesser woman, she might have known some prick
to her conscience at the rapid rejection. But she'd
searched his eyes as she said the words; this wasn't
repulsion. For a moment, interest had flared there.

"You shot the Duke of Lannister and tried to
blow up the court. If you think I'll make any sort of
arrangement with you, you're a fool."

"I shot the duke," she admitted. "A woundin'

blow only. 'E was tryin' to strangle an acquaintance of mine."

"You deny being behind the bombing attack?"

"I tried to stop it."

"Do you take me for a fool?"

She dared to take a step toward him. "If I thought it would 'ave worked, then I would 'ave led the action, but this were no plan of mine." *No, she'd gone to find Jeremy.*

"No?" Lynch loomed closer, his nostrils flaring. "Then what were you doing tonight? Just what are you up to?"

"You tell me." She looked up through the gauze of her mask's eye slits.

Lynch caught her chin, his finger stroking over the black satin. His thumb slipped beneath the edge of the mask, lifting it over her mouth and higher. "I want to see you."

Her hand caught his. "No." Rosalind took a chance and darted her tongue out, licking the edge of his thumb.

Lynch jerked his hand back, heat smoldering in his gaze. "You disappoint me. Nothing you say or do will change my mind. You're under arrest, petticoats or not."

He reached for her wrist and she twisted, capturing his own. The tendons in his arm tensed, but Rosalind slowly brought his hand up, keeping her gaze locked on his the whole time. She pressed the palm of his hand against her cheek, turning her lips into it. Lynch returned her stare with cool disinterest, but the pulse in his throat had quickened.

Rosalind licked his palm, tracing her tongue slowly

across the seam there. "Don't it excite you?" His gaze flickered to hers and she stepped closer, turning his hand over to trace her lips against the tender flesh between the back of his fingers. "You," she whispered. "Me. Two enemies finally come together." Palm out, she pressed her other hand flatly against the rippled abdomen of his body armor and flexed her fingers. The leather was polished with age and use. Impossibly smooth. *Like his skin.*

The thought took her by surprise. In all her years, she'd only ever felt such a curiosity stirring within her once, and that had been for her husband, a man she admired and respected. Lynch was worthy of neither in her eyes.

Or was he?

She'd learned enough about him in recent months. Testing his weaknesses, discovering what type of man he was—what type of enemy she faced. The answer made her nervous. Cold and implacable, people whispered. Ruthless. Even the Echelon called him Sir Iron Heart, but never to his face.

The man in front of her was hard. She could sense that innately. But the look in his eyes…Oh no, that was not cold. Not cold at all.

"All these months you've been chasin' me, Lynch." The words were a caress, but her mind raced. "And now you've caught me. Ain't you curious? Don't you want just a little taste before you turn me over to the prince consort?"

Her own trembling thoughts used against him.

"No." His head tilted toward her, his breath coming harshly.

Excitement thrilled through her. Anticipation. It was the only time she ever truly felt alive these days. As if she'd been sleepwalking for so long, Lynch's presence was like an icy dash of water to her face. Sliding her hand over each ripple of leather, Rosalind let her fingers pause on the edge of his belt and looked up, beneath her lashes. "Liar."

Furious color flushed the stark edges of his cheekbones. Lynch glared down at her, but the cool disinterest in his eyes had burned away. The blackness of his pupils overwhelmed his irises until she stared into a demon's eyes, his rational thoughts obliterated by hunger, by desire.

She had him.

Rosalind lifted onto her toes, sliding her iron fingers through the inky black strands of his hair. Her lashes half lowering, she dragged his head down with a fistful of his hair and guided his mouth to hers.

She'd kissed men in the line of duty, seduced them with a flirtatious smile that barely touched the cold, hard ball of emotion within her. It had never meant anything to her. Yet she trembled now, her hand stroking the hard, leather-clad body, feeling the buttery soft texture of his armor beneath her gloves. Her words hadn't only seduced him—she felt the truth of them herself. The excitement of something forbidden.

His cool breath brushed against her sensitive lips as they caressed her own. Lynch resisted. "Take off your mask," he said hoarsely, his own fingers stroking the trembling flesh of her jaw.

"No."

She could feel his body leaning away from her as

he fought for his senses. In desperation, she reached up and opened her mouth over his.

A shudder swept through the massive frame enveloping hers. He stiffened in shock and she drank of his mouth, her tongue caressing his with a dare and her hands sliding lower. That hard body melted against her and she felt the moment he stopped fighting his inclinations. Hands cupped her face and he kissed her as if he were a desperate man, passion rising up within him so swiftly that it shocked her. She tasted loneliness in his hunger, and something flared to life within her, something foreign and dangerous. A yearning that ached like a fist in her stomach, an echo.

Rosalind turned her face, gasping into his hair as she sought to pull herself back from that. The moment she could breathe the sensation lessened, but she didn't immediately kiss him again.

His hand cupped her nape and he grabbed a fistful of hair, dragging her head back. Cool lips slid over her chin and lower, across her throat. Rosalind clutched his shoulder, wary of her vulnerability but it didn't return. If she concentrated on the feel of him, on each delicate sensation as he licked at her throat, then she could manage to hold on to herself.

A blue blood. But he felt like a man beneath her questing hands, and he tasted like one as he returned to her lips, his breath sweet with his evening wine. The kiss deepened, his tongue forcing her lips apart, taking no prisoners. Hungry. Her body ached, the throb between her legs so long denied. Eight long years since Nathaniel died, and she'd never once regretted not taking a lover. Never found a man who even tempted her. But danger was its own addiction and a part of her thrilled at the man in her arms. The Nighthawk. Her dearest enemy. A shadowy entity she'd taken great pleasure in thwarting for the past six months.

A man she was about to thwart again.

Her back hit the brick wall. Lynch's mouth slid up her throat and claimed her lips again. She barely had time to snatch a breath or even a fistful of his shirt before his tongue rasped over her teeth. A thousand impressions leeched into her; the chafe of her nipples against the linen that bound them; the taste of his mouth; the drugging scent of him; and the gravely rasp of his knuckles on the brick as he caught her beneath the arse and dragged her legs around his hips.

Rosalind's nails curled into his shoulders, padded only by the single glove she wore. Sweet lord... She was losing herself again... She kissed him, biting at his mouth, drawing his lip between her teeth and nibbling on it. It would be so easy to forget herself, to let herself surrender until she was lost...

No.

Hands caught her own, pinned them to the wall. But she needed them free and she fought him.

Her head spun. "Let me—let me touch you. I want to touch you."

The words stilled the violence of his passion. Rosalind bit her lip, catching a glimpse of those dark eyes. She wasn't the only one fighting this attraction. And if she let him go—for just a second—then she'd lose him.

Never. Rosalind surrendered, rocking her hips against his, feeling the hard steel of his erection between her thighs. She let her body ride against his, her hands sliding over his shoulders and luring him closer as she threw her head back and gasped.

Lynch slammed one hand against the wall beside her head, shuddering. "Curse you," he whispered. Then his mouth bit at hers hungrily and he was lost in her again.

Rosalind slid her hands over the corded muscle of his throat, linking them behind his neck. It was a simple matter to tug the glove from her mech hand. Dropping it carelessly, she groaned into his mouth as his hand slid over her arse, tugging her against him hard.

A twist of the knuckle on her mech ring finger and a sharp needle slid from the interior. Rosalind tasted his breath and realized that she was stalling. She slid her hands over his shoulder, the rasp of his stubble scraping her jaw.

Just another moment.

One more…

Her hips rode his and she threw her head back, eyes glazed with passion. "I almost wish…" she gasped, "that I didn't 'ave to do this."

Then she slid the needle into his neck and injected the hemlock straight into his body.

Lynch stiffened, spasms racking him. "*No.*" Slumping against her, he clawed at the wall to hold himself up, his knees giving way.

Rosalind landed lightly on her feet, the hard body pinning her to the wall. It was a good thing, for she wasn't sure her own knees would support her right now. She caught Lynch under the arms as he gurgled something in his throat. Words she probably didn't want to hear.

Laying him on the ground, she stepped back, capping the needle neatly within her metal finger and twisting the knuckle back into place. A sensation almost like guilt licked at her.

A stupid thought. A dangerous one. Sentiment had no part in her world. Nor emotion. Either could get her killed in an instant.

Her knives were tucked behind his belt. Lynch's gaze locked on hers and she realized what he was thinking.

Cut his throat now and there'd be no more Nighthawks on her trail, no more martial law. This would be a devastating blow to the Echelon that they might not recover from.

Her fingers slid over the knife hilt as she took it, familiarity molding it into her hand. Rosalind's fingers clenched unconsciously as she stared at him. It wouldn't be the first blue blood she'd ever killed.

Come on, my little falcon. Do it. You are what you are, after all. What's one more death?

She could almost hear Balfour whispering in her ear. Lust died a quick death and bile rose in her throat. *No.* She wasn't his to command. Not anymore. She'd freed herself the moment she'd cut her hand off.

It doesn't matter. His whisper sickened her. *I made you what you are. And you can never escape that...*

"No," she whispered. Metal clanged and she realized she'd dropped the knife.

Lynch twitched, a gurgling snarl in his throat. She couldn't tear her gaze from his. He knew, she realized. Knew that she couldn't do it. No, not couldn't. Wouldn't.

Fool. She shook her head and took a step back, her boots crunching on old metal filings on the ground. She'd regret this. Tactically this wasn't the right choice. All of her training screamed at her to finish the job.

Lynch's fingers twitched. How long had he been down for? One minute? Two? The amount of time the hemlock would paralyze him depended on how high his craving virus levels were. If his CV levels were high, then he might begin to regain control of his body before she'd fled the scene. Not a thought to relish, especially with *that* look in his eyes.

Rosalind snatched her knife up again and sheathed it in her boot. Sparks sprayed off a welding rig nearby. She crouched low, looking to see if anyone had seen. If they had, then Lynch's life would be in danger.

You don't even have to wield the knife. Just walk away and leave him here. Defenseless.

One second of hesitation. It would be so easy…but something stopped her. A hitherto unknown sense of mercy. This was the second time in as many months where she'd allowed someone to live whom she probably shouldn't have. Rosalind cursed under her breath and bent low to grab his wrists. Dragging him behind a boiler, she hid him from sight.

"I want you to know that you were beaten," she murmured, kneeling beside him. His eyes glittered in the shadows, red furnace light flickering over their dark depths. A promise of vengeance. She nodded slowly, acknowledging it. This—what she had started here tonight—would not end until one of them had the upper hand.

"*I'll come...for you...*" He could barely speak, but the words sent a shiver down her spine.

A vow. A deadly promise.

Anticipation flared as she turned and walked away. The world was bright with color, her body still dancing with energy. *Awake.* "I'll watch for you then."

"*I'll watch for you then.*"

A hand curled around his shoulder and Lynch jerked awake, the shattered remnants of the dream slipping from his mind as his study came to life around him. Blinking, he looked down at the mess of paperwork he'd been leaning in and the ink that stained his hands. There was crusted blood under his fingernails, where he'd tended the wound in his side. Though it had already healed, courtesy of the blood-craving virus that made him a blue blood, the action had weakened him.

Garrett stepped back, arching a brow. "You need to go to bed."

Scraping a hand over his tired face, Lynch shook his head. "I need to find Mercury. The analysis on the crate?"

With a scowl, Garrett strode across the room and knelt by the fire. He teased the meager coals to life again with the bellows, then added a stick of kindling. "Where's Doyle? He should be looking after you better than this."

Lynch scraped his chair back from the desk and

stood. "He's already been in here nursemaiding me. I sent him away. The crate?"

"The steel within appears to be some sort of steam-driven part. A boiler pack, Fitz suspects. Could be used for all manner of machinery."

Fitz would know. The young genius had never met an invention that didn't fascinate him. Lynch's lips thinned. "Useless then?"

"Not quite. I've sent Byrnes to the enclaves with some men to inquire of the make."

"They'll find nothing," Lynch stated, turning toward the liquor cabinet. "The mechs in the enclaves are remarkably closemouthed these days."

"Ever since the prince consort set the Trojan cavalry on them two months ago," Garrett replied.

Lynch poured himself a snifter of blood, measuring it carefully. He screwed the lid of the flask back into place. "Be careful where you say such things."

"We're in the guild headquarters."

"And no doubt the Council has at least three spies in here." Lynch lifted the snifter and drained it, the cool blood igniting his senses. His vision swam, painting the world in black and gray for a moment. Slowly he put the glass down. He wanted more; he craved it. And just as certainly wouldn't allow it.

"You think they've got men inside the guild?"

"I'm certain of it." The Council knew too much of his affairs for it to be coincidence. Lynch swiftly changed topics, to one he wanted to pursue. "There's been no sign of the woman?"

Garrett leaned back against the desk, his arms crossed and his gaze neutral. Too neutral. Lynch hadn't asked how much he had heard through the aural communicator; its range was limited, but Garrett had found him quickly enough to have been in the vicinity.

"The men returned. No sign of her. The scent trail ended near Piccadilly Circus. One of those chemical bombs the humanists use to obliterate all scent had been dropped."

Clever girl. Lynch's eyes narrowed. He'd fallen for her ruse like a green schoolboy and the thought rankled. She was out there somewhere, no doubt laughing behind his back. The worst of it was that his men had found him before he'd recovered, lying on his back still partially paralyzed. Garrett had covered for him, sending them after the fleeing revolutionary, but they'd seen enough.

"I'm still not quite sure how she gulled you. You're no pigeon, ripe to be plucked." Though Garrett's manner of speech was so precise as to mimic the Echelon, sometimes his base roots showed in his language choice.

"That makes two of us." Lynch's voice was hard and dry. A warning for Garrett to drop the subject.

The encounter frustrated him. Sex and the female form were distractions he'd long since thought himself invulnerable to. That she'd gotten under his skin so quickly and easily chafed at him.

Sex was just another need, another form of hunger, and he thought he'd controlled those needs well. He strictly controlled the amount of blood his body required and bedded a woman when he felt the urge arise. Not once had either need ever overruled him. Until now.

And all it had taken was that little whisper of sin in his ear, her knuckles stroking down over the leather carapace of his abdomen. He'd barely seen her face, just her lips beneath the edge of the mask as she tempted him with her offer.

Sensory memory flooded through him: the faint hint of her breast in the cup of his hand, her long legs locking around his hips as she arched against him, the exhale of her breath burning against his lips...

Damn her. Even now his body stirred and he knew why.

A body was never enough. He'd seen and slept with some of the most beautiful women the Echelon had to offer and rarely remembered their names. But this one haunted him. A mystery. A challenge. A part of him hungered for the next encounter, longing to take it further. This time he'd have the upper hand and he intended to make full use of it, to pay back every ounce of humiliation on her flesh and leave her gasping for more.

He couldn't wait.

Closing his eyes, Lynch forced his body to cool. The thoughts were madness—the hunger speaking, his own personal demons. He was *the* Nighthawk, damn it, and when he got his hands on her, he'd arrest her and hand her over to the Council.

Case solved.

When he opened his eyes, Garrett was watching him, entirely too perceptive. Chestnut colored hair swept over his brow, a drawcard for women's eyes everywhere. Or perhaps that was the smile Garrett flashed at them. He had his uses, despite his weakness for anything in a petticoat. Put him in a room with a woman who refused to say a word, and before five minutes were out, he'd have her signed confession and every intimate detail of her life.

Garrett knew women inside and out. And he knew when a man had been bested by one.

"If you breathe a word of this…"

A slow, stealthy smile crept over Garrett's mouth. "I wouldn't dream of it, sir."

Two

THE CANDLE GUTTERED IN THE CHILL BREEZE AS
Rosalind climbed down the ancient stairwell. Once,
a long time ago, it had been designed as access from
an abandoned surface station to the underground train
platform below. Now it was boarded up and long
forgotten, except for the timber slats she'd carefully
broken and then forged into a slender gap—access to
her world, the musty caverns and dark tunnels they
called Undertown.

Water dripped in the distance. The only other
sounds were the faint shuffle of her flat-soled boots
and the echoing moan of a breeze stirring through
the abandoned rail tunnels. Rosalind reached up and
dragged the stifling mask over her head. Cool air met
her heated skin and she sighed in relief.

The taste of Lynch lingered. Or perhaps that was
the mocking burn of memory, taunting her with what
she'd done.

Or rather, how she'd reacted.

You liked it.

A horrible, gut-clenching thought. She'd never

cared for men, a deficit she'd thought of as a relief until Nathaniel had come into her life and awakened her to the joyous misery of lust. Her husband had been the brightest light in her life…and the greatest sorrow. If his death had taught her one thing, it was never to betray herself again. Never to let another man close.

And she'd succeeded. Until now.

Unclenching her hand around the satin mask, she shoved it into her pocket grimly. Tonight she'd played her game and she'd enjoyed it. It wouldn't happen again.

Stepping out onto the platform, she had only a second's warning before a breath of wind blew the candle out. The sudden darkness obliterated her vision but not her senses. She felt something move, and reacted, shoving her arm up in a block. Twisting her finger, she felt the hiss of vibration as the blade slid through her metal knuckle—

A hand hit her high in the chest and Rosalind gasped as her lungs emptied. Then she was smashed up against the brick wall, mortar crumbling around her.

"You're dead," a husky voice said in disgust.

Rosalind tilted her head back as her vision slowly adjusted to the darkness, and panted, trying to ease the vice around her lungs. She pressed her hand a fraction forward. The tip of the blade dug into the hard muscle of abdomen. "And you're gutted."

A grunt. Then Ingrid shoved away from her. "Wouldn't kill me."

Truth. Rosalind's face twisted in disgust at herself. A distracted revolutionary was a dead one. She eased the blade back into the mech hand, rubbing her thumb over the polished steel. "You're back early."

"You're late." The dark shadow materializing in the depths of the tunnel was starting to take shape. Ingrid towered over her at nearly six foot, with broad shoulders and shapely hips. She had a warrior's physique, courtesy of her Nordic ancestry, though she was smaller than many others of her kind. The loupe virus that made verwulfen what they were encouraged growth and muscular development. Or so the scientists said.

Though Ingrid's words were harshly spoken, Rosalind heard the gruff, underlying fear. "I'm back," she said, sliding a hand over Ingrid's forearm. The other woman was almost a sister to her. An overbearing, overprotective sister at times, but Rosalind found she appreciated it. "I had a run-in at the enclaves. The new boiler pack is lost."

"What happened?"

"I ran into the Nighthawk."

Silence. Then Ingrid slowly released a breath. "I hope it was with a sharp knife."

"Unfortunately not. Come. We need to meet with Jack, find out how his night went."

Ingrid followed as Rosalind leaped down onto the train tracks. A rat chattered in the dark and Rosalind smiled as her friend cursed.

"Bloody rats," Ingrid said in disgust. But she kept close to Rosalind's side, just in case.

"They won't bother you," Rosalind replied, disappearing into the dark silence of the tunnel.

They walked for several hundred feet, unerringly following the abandoned steel tracks. Ingrid could see in the dark, but Rosalind was forced to rely on memory, silently counting the steps. Her groping fingers found an ironbound door in the side of the tunnel just as a gust of wind blew through the emptiness, stirring her hair. It sounded like a faraway scream, no doubt one of the trains that ran in nearby underground systems.

Some of the locals who ventured down here thought the sounds were the cries of ghosts; those long-dead miners and engineers trapped down here when the Eastern line collapsed. Or those who had died three summers ago, slaughtered by the vampire that had haunted the depths until it was killed.

Rosalind was scared of neither. A vampire was just a blue blood gone wrong and she knew how to kill those. As for ghosts…well, she had plenty of her own.

Shimmying into the access tunnel, her hands and feet found the metal ladder and she scurried down it. Ingrid followed, shutting the iron door behind her with a clang.

A sickly green light burned below. Rosalind slid the last few feet to the bottom of an old ventilation shaft. An enormous fan stirred lazy circles in the wall, casting flickering shadows through the phosphorescent light. A man leaned against the pitted brickwork, his arms crossed over his chest and a scowl on his face. He saw her and relaxed, pushing off the wall toward her.

"Jack," she said, letting out her own breath of relief. Her brother looked tired, what little she could see of his face. A heavy monocular eyepiece was strapped over one eye to help him see in the dark and a leather half mask obscured his lower face. The eerie green tint of the phosphor light-amplifying lens unnerved her. With it, he could see almost as well as Ingrid.

Rosalind lifted a hand to touch him, then paused when he flinched. Jack didn't like to be touched anymore, even through the heavy layers of his coat and gloves. Rosalind's fingers curled into a hard fist. That was one of the things she missed so much about Jeremy—the way he'd wrap an arm around her shoulders and drag her close, taunting her about the fact that he'd outgrown her. The way she'd kick his feet out from under him and take him to the ground with a laugh. "*You might be taller,*" she'd say, "*but I'll always be your older sister.*"

Jack's hard gray gaze ran over Ingrid. "No trouble?"

"Not for me," Ingrid replied.

Rosalind found herself the recipient of that stare. She shot her friend a hard look. "Nothing I couldn't handle."

"Well, I'm curious," Ingrid said, stalking past. "Just how did you get away from the Nighthawk?"

Gritting her teeth together, Rosalind ducked past her brother's startled gaze and hurried after Ingrid. "I seduced him."

"Rosalind!" Jack snapped, trailing in her wake. Three long strides and he was close enough to fall in beside her, the phosphorescent flare stick in his hand highlighting the harsh planes of his face. "Tell me you two are jesting."

Ingrid laughed under her breath.

"Unfortunately not," Rosalind replied. "I lost the shipment and five men."

"Steel can be replaced," Jack replied.

"So can men," Ingrid called back.

But not the money for either. Rosalind ground her teeth. The money was filtered through the Humans First political party, along with information from several sources in the Echelon. The humanist network had already been in place before she stepped into her husband's shoes and tried to fulfill his dream; it was only lately that she'd begun to wonder where so much money was coming from.

Ahead of them, a rectangle of darkness was limned by bright yellow light. Home. Rosalind's shoulders drooped, starting to feel the exertion of the night. The excitement with Lynch had driven her through the streets on the run from his men, but now, in the shadowy darkness of safety, her energy began to flag.

Beyond the door a single candle sputtered on the table at their entrance. The furnishings were sparse and mostly scavenged. They didn't need much for their purpose and everything could be left behind in a hurry.

Jack shut the door behind them as Rosalind sank into one of the stuffed armchairs. A spring dug into her hip and she shifted.

Jack crossed his arms again. "Talk."

"You haven't told me about your night," she said as Ingrid lit the gas boiler to make tea.

"I'm more interested in yours."

There would be no shaking him in this mood. "We were ambushed as we left the enclaves. Lynch and his men were waiting for us, no doubt given the tip by somebody." Rosalind frowned. "I need to discover who—that could be costly."

"What's he like?" Ingrid asked, looking up from the kettle.

Intense. Rosalind stilled as unwelcome memory flooded through her body. "Exactly as they say. Hard and cold. And very determined." The way he'd looked at her—as if he'd tear apart the world to get his hands on her again. She shivered. "I don't think I've seen the last of him."

"You should have put a bullet in him," Jack said.

"I wasn't in the position," she lied, dropping her gaze. "The best I could do was paralyze him with hemlock. His men came while I was getting away and I had to flee."

Rosalind could feel Jack's gaze boring into the top of her head. Looking up, she smoothed the expression from her face. "So tell me about your night. Any luck?"

Tension lingered in his shoulders, then he blew out a breath and glanced at Ingrid. "We intercepted the coach carrying the *London Standard*'s editor toward the Ivory Tower. The escape went as planned and one of our men got him out. Unfortunately, a group of metaljackets came and we were forced to separate."

Another avenue lost tonight. The editor had printed a caricature in the *London Standard* of the prince consort with a monstrously deformed head, dangling puppet strings over a wan image of his human wife, the queen. He wouldn't be doing that again.

"No casualties?"

"Not on our side." Though she couldn't see it, she could sense the vicious smile behind the mask.

"And no word of Jeremy?" she asked, looking toward Ingrid with deceptive casualness. Though it rankled, there was no use in her looking for Jeremy when Ingrid's senses were far better suited. She'd spent the entire month blundering along behind Ingrid, no doubt hindering her. Tonight had been the first night she'd forced herself to let go, to let Ingrid do what she did best.

This time it was Ingrid's turn to drop her gaze. "Nothing. No sightings, no scent trail." Ingrid took a deep breath then looked up, her bronze eyes gleaming. "He's not outside the city walls, Rosa. If there's any hope that he survived—"

"He survived," she snapped. There could be no other option, for if there was, then she had failed him. Her baby brother, the one she'd practically raised. The world blurred, a haze of heat sweeping behind her eyes.

Jack's hand slid over hers and Rosalind looked up in shock as he squeezed her fingers gently, then let go.

"It's not your fault," he murmured, then turned to Ingrid. "And nor is it yours. If you can't find him, then he's not there."

It *was* her fault though. Rosalind had been too wrapped up in her cause to pay attention to her brother. Jeremy had fallen in with the mechs, lured by their rough talk and bawdy laughter. He was almost a man, and she couldn't blame him for wanting the company of other men. It was only when he went missing that she realized how much she'd been ignoring him lately.

"So he's not outside the city walls," she murmured, rubbing her eyes. *So tired.* "That leaves the city."

"No," Ingrid snapped. "You can't even think it."

The thick wall that circled the city borough kept the riffraff out and the blue bloods in. Inside it was their territory. Their stalking grounds. A world of glittering carriages, fancy mansions, silk, and steel.

Rosalind slowly lowered her hand. "Where else do I look, Ingrid? He was last seen in the Ivory Tower during the bombing and the bodies were all accounted for. I'd hoped he'd escaped with the few mechs that got away but we've hunted some of them down and nobody knows where Jeremy is."

"Which leaves the blue bloods," Jack murmured.

"Or the bloody Nighthawks," Ingrid snapped. She shoved to her feet. "And none of us can get near the Guild Headquarters."

Nighthawks. Rosalind stilled. The very men who were hunting the mechs—and Mercury. Why hadn't she thought of it before? "If anyone knows what happened to the mechs who blew up the tower," she said quietly, "it would be the Nighthawks."

Sensing trouble, Jack shot her a sharp look. "What are you planning?"

Rosalind looked around. "Where's my file on my lord Nighthawk?" She spotted it on a pile on the table and pushed out of her chair eagerly. "There was an advertisement," she said recklessly, tearing open the file and hunting through it. Pages and pages of notes on Lynch and his comings and goings scrawled across the page. *Know your enemy.* "Several weeks back in the *London Standard*." Her fingers closed over the piece. "An advertisement for a secretarial position—"

"No," Jack snapped, knowing precisely where her mind was going.

Ingrid looked between the two of them, then frowned. "The position might be filled."

"Then we'll have to ensure it's vacant again," Rosalind said flippantly, not averse to kidnapping anyone temporarily for her needs.

"Roz, this is insane," Ingrid said. "We don't have anyone to play the part. I can't do it, not with these eyes."

"But I can."

Her words fell into an abrupt silence. Ingrid's jaw dropped and Jack took a menacing step toward her.

"No," he said.

"This is what I do," Rosalind replied, knowing where the trouble was going to come from. "This is what Balfour trained me to do." And perhaps the only thing she was truly good at. Though she hated him, the prince consort's spymaster had recognized her talents and nurtured them early on. He knew her in a way even Jack did not. The only thing he had ever misunderstood were her limits, what even she could not be coaxed to do.

Like the day he had asked her to kill her husband.

The only time she had ever disobeyed him—the cost of which still haunted her at night. Her hand sacrificed to save the man she'd betrayed. And Nathaniel lying dead at Balfour's hand in punishment.

"You were too late, mon petit faucon," Balfour murmured, cleaning the blood from his hands with a rag and eyeing her dispassionately as she'd slumped to the floor from the blood loss. "I gave you five minutes to prove your loyalty." A furious glance at the bloodied stump with its rough tourniquet. "And so it is proven." Throwing the rag aside.

She could barely see him or Nathaniel. Her vision was bleeding black around the edges.

"Come," he whispered, *lifting the wrist and making her scream as her vision went white. "I shall make you a new hand. And you will serve me again."*

But she hadn't. It had been Jack who broke her out of the healing ward where she lay delirious, his own skin acid-burned and bloody from the cost of her betrayal. And Ingrid, the young verwulfen girl from Balfour's menagerie whom she'd always felt sorry for.

Because she too knew how it felt to be trapped in a cage.

"I don't give a damn," Jack snapped, his hand slicing the air in a sharp gesture. "Balfour used you. And me. He didn't care whether we came back from our missions alive or dead, Rosa. Well, I do. I can't find my brother and I'm damned well not going to watch my sister walk into such a dangerous situation."

She couldn't bear the cost of Jeremy's loss on top of what she already owed those she loved. "You can't stop me," she said simply. "And I can manage Lynch. I know I can."

"I'll chain you to the bloody—"

"Why are you so certain you can manage the Nighthawk?" Ingrid asked.

Rosalind backed away from her brother. *Avoid rather than fight.* "He's attracted to me—to Mercury rather. I can manipulate that. Lynch might be a blue blood but he's still a man."

"Christ, are you listening to yourself?"

She ignored Jack. "It's perfect. Almost too perfect. As his secretary, I'll be given free rein to examine his paperwork at my leisure. If he knows anything about the mechs and Jeremy, then I'll be able to find it. If not, then I walk away and he never sees me again."

"That's if he offers you the position," Ingrid replied.

"He will." Jack shot her a cutting look. "Rosa always gets what she wants, doesn't she?"

Rosalind curled her hands over the back of the chair and stared at him. Hard. He didn't realize it, but that was capitulation in his voice. "Then that means I'll find Jeremy."

"If he's there. If he's still alive." One last parting shot.

Rosalind hid her flinch. She felt better now that she had a plan. "True. But I need to find out if he is. It's the only way I'll ever be able to move forward."

Ingrid frowned. "You'll need to disguise yourself."

"It's one of my talents."

"Even your height and scent," Ingrid muttered.

"Find someone roughly my height. 'Mercury' can make an appearance while I'm with Lynch. He'll never suspect me."

Jack's face tightened. "So be it. But we do this the way we were trained—and you get out the moment you find the Nighthawk doesn't have him."

"Deal," she said softly, knowing that she had won.

❧

Fog swirled at his feet as Sir Jasper Lynch strode through the narrow alleyway, his great cloak flapping around his ankles and his cane echoing on the cobbles. Each slap of his boot soles seemed to echo the frustration beating in his chest.

Crossing Chancery Lane, he caught sight of the grim building that housed his men. Almost all of them were

blue bloods, but their infections had been by chance
or accident, rather than intention. Only a son from the
best bloodlines of the Echelon was offered the blood
rites when they turned fifteen. Any chance infections
were considered rogues, and they were offered either
a place in the Nighthawks or the Coldrush Guards that
served the Ivory Tower. Or death.

Lynch had been the original Nighthawk, but over
time the entire guild had come to represent his name.
The Nighthawks were legendary in the city, a threat
used to cow criminals and revolutionaries alike.

They'd never once been unable to track their prey.

Until now...

The streets were starting to bustle with pre-dawn
traffic. A young paperboy with ruddy cheeks from the
cold shoved a copy of the *London Standard* in front of
him. "Murders in Kensington! Read all about it! Blue
blood gone mad!"

Lynch slipped him a shilling. The Haversham
massacre was being investigated by his man Byrnes, a
task he'd usually save for himself but for the importance
of capturing Mercury. It had been an effort to keep it
out of the papers so far. "Any other news, Billy?"

The lad wasn't the only one he used for information. Though they stood in plain sight, the paperboys
were almost invisible in the city. "The Coldrush
Guards arrested the *London Standard* editor yest'day,
sir. Found 'im in a cellar with a printing press and a
pair of 'umanists."

"A shame."

Billy's eyes gleamed. "Not really. They was escortin'
'im back to the Ivory Tower when they was attacked

last night. Bunch o' lads swarmed the metaljackets guardin' 'em and knocked the Coldrush Guards out some'ow. Them 'umanists, they says."

Hemlock darts no doubt. But the interesting thing was that they'd taken out the metaljackets. He'd have to look into how they did that. Slipping Billy another coin, he took a paper for show and hurried across the street.

The guild loomed over Chancery Lane, an alley running along both sides, as though the row houses on each side feared to touch it. Leering gargoyles kept watch on the roof; inside each gaping mouth was a spyglass that—by use of a clever mirror system he'd designed—transmitted inside images of the street so that his men could keep watch without being seen. Stepping through the pair of glossy black double doors, he found himself in the main entry. It looked like the typical London manor and it was easy to penetrate—not so easy to escape. If he pressed the security breach button a chain-and-lever system would drop heavy iron bars over every opening.

A faint creak on the floor above drew his eyes upward. From the faint hint of bay rum in the air, he recognized Garrett. Nobody else wore bloody aftershave.

Lynch took a step forward, then froze as the scent of something else caught his attention. Warm flesh. Linen and the mouthwatering tang of lemon. Just a hint of woman.

His hunger stirred. He was overdue for his allotted measure of blood. That had to be the problem.

Garrett appeared at the top of the stairs, lean and stark in his black leather body armor.

"There's a woman here," Lynch stated. "Who is

she?" His men knew the rules. All assignations were to be on their own time and not in the guild.

Garrett sauntered down the stairs. "She's here for you."

"Me?" He paused.

"For the secretarial position. To interview with you."

"Bloody hell," he muttered, stripping his great cloak off. He tossed it on the hatstand. "I forgot. I thought I said no more women? I want someone with a stronger constitution and more fortitude."

"She insisted."

"It's the nature of a woman."

"Aye." Garrett grinned. "That brutal sense of honesty is why you keep a lonely bed."

Lynch scraped a weary hand over the stubble on his jaw. That hadn't always been the case. "It could have something to do with the fact I've not *been* to bed for two...possibly three days." He considered it. "Definitely three."

"I'll have some coffee and blood sent up. And a plate of biscuits for the lady."

Lynch gave an abrupt shake of the head. "Don't bother. She's not staying. Blood however...blood would be much appreciated."

Climbing the stairs, he paced toward his study on cat-silent feet. All the better to observe. The door to his secretary's study cracked open an inch. The scent of her was much stronger here. The heavy overlaying perfume of lemon verbena and linen lingered in the air. Some scent she'd dabbed on her wrists and throat he imagined.

The narrow slice of door presented him with a view of dark blue skirts, the bustle hooked up in a style fashionable almost five years ago. A thick velvet wrap the color of midnight covered slim shoulders and her hat disguised her features. He couldn't tell whether she was young or old, pretty or plain.

He *could* tell, however, that she was examining the enormous map of London that covered the far wall. Red pins dotted the map, carving out a large swathe of East London and red string ran between each pin, creating an incomprehensible spider web for those who didn't know what it meant—sightings of Mercury that he'd been able to verify or the location of several humanists he'd uncovered. Some he'd left in place. It was enough to know who they were. He had larger prey to catch.

Lynch's hand slid inside his waistcoat pocket and the small scrap of leather inside. No perfume there. His fingers had long since rubbed away any trace of scent. But close his eyes and it would be a simple matter to recall the hot scent of *her*, laced with the burning smell of iron slag in the enclaves and the choking pall of coal. Mercury wore no perfume. His cock throbbed at the thought and Lynch ground his teeth together. *Devil take her.*

The woman in his study ran her fingers along the map, the jaunty hat swiveling to survey the room. Searching for something? Or merely bored? He hadn't asked how long she'd been waiting, though since it was but morning, it couldn't have been too long. Nobody was allowed out at night between the hours of nine and six during martial law.

Easing the door open, Lynch slipped inside without a sound. The woman froze, as if she sensed him immediately. Her head tilted to the side, revealing the fine line of her pale jaw and a pair of rosy lips. From the prickling uneasiness in her stance and the stiffening between her shoulder blades, she hadn't been around a blue blood often. No doubt she was one of the working class, her ears full of rumors and superstitions about how a blue blood lusted for blood, their hungers insatiable. Or how the Echelon kept factories filled with human slaves.

"Sir Jasper." She turned slowly, the light striking over her fine features. Eyes the color of polished obsidian met his. Lynch stopped in his tracks. She was just past the first blush of youth, but…no…He looked closer. Her tip-tilted nose and fragile features gave the impression that she was younger than she was. Her sense of poise told another story.

Thirty perhaps.

Lynch raked his gaze over her. Skin like porcelain, so pale and creamy it almost glowed in the soft dawn light through the windows. Her eyebrows were coppery wings, arching delightfully as she examined him back. He couldn't see her hair for the hat and netting, but he imagined it was the same fierce copper of her brows. She was slender enough through the torso that her heavy skirts swamped her and her hands were hidden by kid-leather gloves that she hadn't bothered to remove, as etiquette demanded. To present the wrists or the throat to a blue blood was tantamount to exposing a breast.

So she did have some experience with blue bloods. Interesting. Lynch had to amend his previous assessment of her. She was wary enough that the experience had not been a good one, he suspected.

"How do you do?" she asked, pasting a smile on her rosy lips and offering him her right hand.

Lynch stared at it. "Let us get to the point, Miss—?"

"Mrs. Marberry." Slight emphasis on the first word.

"Married?"

"A widow."

He frowned. "I'm afraid your services are not required. There was a mix-up with the advertisement. The position has already been filled." His eye caught a letter on the desk, the address written in gold ink. From the Council of Dukes then. He started toward it. "Garrett will see you to the—"

"Obviously not by a woman," she replied tartly. "With their weak constitutions and all."

Lynch stopped and looked at her. She'd overheard him in the entry. Cool brown eyes met his. A challenge. If she thought he would be embarrassed, then she didn't know him very well.

Opening her reticule, she tugged out a sheaf of papers. "I have references from my last two places of employ. I worked for Lord Hamilton in the War Office, and then for Lady Shipton as her personal secretary. I assure you"—her voice became a drawl—"after that, nothing could shock me or turn my stomach."

Lynch crossed his arms over his chest. He'd dealt with the Shipton case. A jealous blue blood husband and an adulterous consort whose predilections had surprised even him. He'd thought he'd seen it all by now. "You are aware that both your previous employees are dead?"

"Not by my hand, I assure you."

A bold piece. He straightened in interest. "I meant that I would be unable to check your references."

"Let me be bold…I assume that is your preference anyway?"

Lynch gave a brisk nod. She was observant at least.

"My previous employers are dead, as you noted, which means I have nothing but two pieces of paper to prove my aptitude for employment. This leaves me in somewhat of a quandary. I need to earn a respectable living, Sir Jasper. I have a brother…" And here she faltered, showing perhaps the first lack of composure. "He's young. And assorting with certain types of people I don't approve of. I should like to let an apartment in the city, away from these influences, but at the moment I am unable."

She needed a steady job and a good wage. Lynch's eyes narrowed. "I'm not unmoved," he told her, leaning his hip against the desk. "But I've had five secretaries in the last three months. My work involves certain grisly details and long hours, and nobody seems able to keep up with me. I've spent more time in the past three months training new secretaries than working, and I haven't the inclination to waste any more of it."

Mrs. Marberry squared her shoulders. "I'm aware of that. Garrett informed me of the nature of the job. He said you would work me into the ground, forgetting human needs such as sustenance and sleep, squire me all around the city to take your notes and examine dead bodies. You told your last secretary to hold someone's head, so you could examine the angle of the cut that decapitated the body and that was why they resigned."

For a moment Lynch was taken aback. "And you're still here?"

"It's all correct then?"

"There are some matters I believe he forgot to mention, but mostly yes. The men call me 'that uncompromising bastard,' though they're not aware that I know that. It's not the worst thing I've been called. Still want the job?"

"Sir Jasper." Mrs. Marberry leaned toward him, completely unaware of the fact that her bodice gaped. He, however, noticed everything. Smooth skin, the veins tracing their way beneath her flesh, blue and pulsing with blood. Shifting slightly, Lynch glanced away. She would be trouble. He shouldn't hire her. With her pretty little mouth and stubborn chin, the men would be all over her.

"You can't frighten me nor can you drive me away," she said. "You need someone who's not afraid of you."

Lynch's gaze locked on hers. Her eyes were truly fascinating—dark pools that seemed to hint at infinite depths. He wondered briefly if they echoed her personality; were there hidden depths there too? Then he shook the thought off as foolish. One had only to observe to understand the true measure of a man—or a woman. He'd not met one yet whom he'd been unable to decipher down to the last iota of their soul. People were predictable. "And that person is you?"

She didn't look away. Instead, she looked right through him, as though she could see inside him. Not once had he been on the receiving end of a stare like that. "That person is me."

By gods, she would be trouble. And yet he was strangely tempted. The girl had gumption, glaring at

him as if daring him to employ her. Not even a hint of
the vapors, though she was clever enough to be wary.
He was what he was, after all.

Perhaps she *could* manage to deal with him? Perhaps
she might last longer than a week, unlike the previous
Mrs. Eltham, she of the decapitated-head incident.

Mrs. Marberry glanced away, her fathomless eyes
hidden beneath thick, dark lashes. Lynch's breath
caught. Devil a bit.

"You're too pretty," he growled.

"I beg your pardon?"

Lynch gestured at her, striding away from the desk.
"This…" He made a curving motion in the air to
indicate her. "This won't work. I hire ugly women.
Ones with moustaches. Ones my men wouldn't look
twice at."

"I hardly think I'm the sort of woman to inspire
riots in your guild quarters."

"That's because you're a woman," he said. "We're
speaking of four hundred and fifty men I work into
the ground. They barely have time to speak to women
and now you want me to place a pretty one in the
middle of them all?"

Her gaze hardened. "Should I be concerned?"

"Concerned?" Then he realized she was speaking of
assault. "Good God, no. They wouldn't dare. I'd have
them eviscerated. And they know it."

"Then your objection stems from the fact you think
I'd be a distraction?"

A distraction? A damned catastrophe. Lynch
scowled, turning toward the window with ground-
eating strides. He'd never been a man to stand still

for long. It helped him to think. "I *know* you'd be a distraction."

"But shouldn't I be at your side at all times?" she asked, following him in a swish of skirts and perfume. "I daresay your men wouldn't dare risk such foolery in front of you."

"They wouldn't."

Lynch spun on his heel and found her in his path. Acres and acres of navy skirts with that tight cinched in waist and…the breasts. The dress was modest, but at his great height, he couldn't help that the angle gave him a certain view.

Perhaps I wasn't speaking of the men?

Heat tightened in his abdomen and he clasped his hands behind his back. Damn her, this would be a mistake. He had a thousand things to think of and a revolutionary leader to find. He couldn't afford to have a buxom, determined redhead under his nose. Especially one who smelled like lemons and soft, freshly laundered sheets.

The thought conjured to mind the image of her upon his own sheets, that pale, flawless skin laid bare for his inspection. Her pretty little mouth parted in a gasp as he ground his hips down upon hers.

Lynch's cock stirred, reminding him of what it felt like to be a man. Damn it. She was already affecting him. This should be evidence that this would be a bad idea.

But he needed a secretary. One who wasn't scared of him.

A faint hint of color rose in Mrs. Marberry's cheeks but she refused to look away. He was staring, he realized.

"Are you going to employ me or not?" she asked.

Instinct told him to say no. But as he opened his mouth, the words changed. "Yes," he found himself saying. "On a trial basis. I'm desperate."

"And a charmer," she noted with an arched brow. A little smile toyed over her lips. Relief. "I shall have to watch myself with you, I see."

I shall have to watch myself.

After the disastrous encounter with Mercury and now this, it was becoming clear that he needed a woman to take the edge off. Mercury had done this to him, left him on edge, and now his body hungered for release.

"What's your given name?" he asked bluntly.

"That's highly informal, sir."

"You'll find I rarely bother with formalities. I'm not going to bark 'Mrs. Marberry' whenever I want you. It's a mouthful."

A slight hesitation. "Rosa," she said, her full lips forming the word softly. "My name is Rosa. And you?"

He'd already turned toward the desk, determined to get away from that lingering scent. "Me?"

"What should I call you?"

"Sir Jasper will be perfectly fine."

⁓

Lynch gave her his back and Rosalind finally had a chance to take as deep a breath as she could in the unfamiliar corset. The other night hadn't done him justice, with the darkness and the red glow of the enclaves. She'd realized then his great height and cold, penetrating stare. They said fully grown men broke into confessions when he looked at them and women quivered at the knees.

What she hadn't expected to find was a coldly handsome man, his dark hair cropped neatly and raked back out of his face with an impatient gesture. His jaw was darkened with stubble and a pinched line swept his dark brows together in what seemed a permanent frown.

Rosalind examined him, little goose bumps prickling over her skin. The other night had left its mark on her body. She'd long since thought herself impervious to men, especially dangerous ones, but she'd dismissed Lynch as merely another blue blood and that had been foolish.

Her gaze slid over his broad shoulders as he clasped his hands behind his back. Shoulders she'd dug her nails into, her lips caressing the smooth skin of his throat. A little flutter of excitement started low in her belly, tempting her. She sucked in a breath, her fingernails digging into her palms. This was what she hadn't dared admit to her brother or Ingrid. Lynch might be attracted to Mercury against his will, but the truth was a delicious irony, for she too had been caught in the trap.

Rosalind stole a calculating glance at the room as she took a step forward. Tonight, she'd be able to recall almost every little detail. Her gaze slid to the wall with that damning map. She wasn't stupid. She knew what all those little pins meant, because they were the location of dozens of humanists hidden in the general populace. Some had been discovered and arrested, but a great deal of those pins were humanists who were blissfully unaware that their identity had been compromised.

The map told her a great deal about the Nighthawk. He was patient, for one thing. He was also clever enough not to flush them out of their holes. The red string became a spider web, and Rosalind had the feeling that he was the one who'd woven it.

Just waiting for a little fly, a certain revolutionary, to get caught in its sticky web.

Thank goodness she'd decided to risk infiltrating the guild. Now she knew the trap was there and could warn people, or perhaps use it for her own gains.

"Sir Jasper," she forced herself to say. "That is rather a mouthful too."

The Nighthawk shot her a hard look over his shoulder as if surprised she'd spoken up. Those icy gray eyes stole her breath, leaving her feeling as if the room had faded away and there was nothing beyond the two of them.

A horrible, uncomfortable feeling for it gave her the impression that he could see every little secret she was hiding. And she was damned good at hiding her secrets.

Light played over the straight, hawkish slant of his nose. "Lynch, then."

"When would you like me to start?" Rosalind toyed with her gloves, a habit she'd never broken herself of.

"Would you like to discuss your wages first?" His gaze dropped to the fiddling of her fingers and Rosalind forced them to stillness.

"I already asked your man, Garrett."

"Then as soon—" His head lifted, stark, gray gaze

tracking something beyond the door. A hint of dark shadows flashed through his eyes, signs of the hunger within, the voracious predator that lurked beneath the sophisticated skin of every blue blood. The craving.

Rosalind stilled. There was a gun strapped to her thigh fitted with firebolt bullets that exploded on impact, and a sheath of needles at her wrist that were dipped in hemlock. But the creeping fear still prickled at her skin.

Lynch might look and act like a gentleman, albeit a brusque one, but she would never forget what he truly was.

The door slammed open and an older man with a bald head and leather jerkin stormed in. He saw her and stopped, ruddy color infusing his cheeks. "Beg pardon, miss." A faint Irish accent. His blue eyes shot to Lynch. "Didn't know you 'ad anyone 'ere."

"Doyle, this is my new secretary," Lynch replied, stillness emanating from him. "Mrs. Marberry."

"Another one?" Doyle arched a brow. A brisk nod in her direction, then he returned his attention to his master. "This just came in. More bad news." He tugged a letter from within his jerkin and tossed it at Lynch.

Lynch snatched the missive out of the air. "You'll have to be more specific."

"Park Lane," Doyle replied. "It's a bloodbath. Lord Falcone slaughtered 'is entire family. Women, children, thralls…all of the servants. Lord Barrons wants you there now."

As the Duke of Caine's heir, Barrons would be reporting directly to the ruling Council of Dukes, despite their friendship. Lynch frowned. "This is the second incident in a week. Byrnes has barely begun to go over the facts of the Haversham case."

"Seems it weren't an isolated incident after all." Doyle shrugged.

"Curse it." Lynch spun on his heel, pacing the rug. "I don't have time for this."

"I don't think that excuse will suit 'is Royal Pastiness," Doyle replied bluntly. "Not with nob's gettin' their hands all bloodied. Might be different if it were just us rogues."

Interesting. Rosalind's gaze flickered between the men, wondering if Lynch would chastise his man for the insubordination, but his expression remained coolly neutral.

Division in the blue blood world? She went very still, her mind racing. All along she'd thought the enemy was one, but if she could use this information to somehow turn the Nighthawks against the Echelon then she would have a powerful weapon on her hands.

The men seemed to have forgotten her for the moment. "Excuse me," Rosalind asked. "But what is going on?"

Lynch shot her a piercing look that went straight through her. "A murder scene, Rosa. Now we'll see whether you are suited for the job. Fetch that writing case and follow me. I'll need to see the bodies while they're fresh."

Three

Rosalind ground her teeth together as the carriage shot around another corner. The strap dug into her hand and she clutched the writing case to her chest so as not to lose it.

Lynch rolled with the sway, his long legs eating up the interior. He sat opposite her, rifling through a sheaf of papers and frowning occasionally. Though he largely ignored her, the occasional quick glance scoured her like fire. She didn't like being in here, trapped so closely together. He was too large, the force of his presence dominating the space.

It didn't help that, in the dark confines of the carriage, all she could remember was what that hard body felt like pressed against her own. The taste of his mouth and the depth of his longing as he had kissed her startled something into life deep within her. Hunger. Newly awakened and barely sated. A desire for flesh, for sin, for wet kisses and the hard stroke of his body over hers.

She'd told herself to forget the memory, but it lingered on her skin like some textural apparition.

She'd been a fool to kiss him. A fool—even now—to want more.

"Who were the Havershams?" she asked.

Lynch barely glanced up. "Lord Haversham, his consort Lady Amelia, and their three children. A minor branch of the House of Goethe. They were found on Monday morning by the eldest son, who'd returned from a gaming club. The entire household was torn apart, humans included, and Haversham had shot himself in the head."

"*He* tore them apart?"

"We suspect so. There were two quarts of blood in his stomach and his consort had pieces of his skin under her fingernails from where she'd tried to fight. The man's bloodletting knife was on his person and the blade matches the marks found on the servants and…the children."

Rosalind absorbed that. The tone of his voice had sounded as though he repeated the facts by rote, but at the end… He didn't like the part about the children, she thought.

"Why would he do such a thing?" Despite her personal feelings about blue bloods, it was an odd thing. Haversham was a minor lord. No doubt he kept enough thralls to satisfy the bloodlust, unless he was close to the Fade, when a blue blood lost all trace of color and began to evolve into a mindless, blood-driven predator. "It wasn't the Fade, was it?" The thought unnerved her. She knew what happened when a vampire stalked the city.

Lynch shook his head. "His craving virus levels were holding at sixty percent."

Not the Fade then. The craving virus made a blue blood what they were, but most of the Echelon kept a careful monitor on their CV levels. It was law. A spate of vampires a century ago had forced the ruling Council of Dukes to make it compulsory. Any blue blood whose levels began to hit seventy-five or even eighty were closely monitored.

Any higher and an ax was sent for.

"Doyle said there'd be children here." As a child she'd seen enough gruesome sights to consider her nerves steel—indeed, she'd been the cause of some of them. But children...children were always bad.

"Yes," Lynch said in a deadly soft voice. "Falcone had two. A boy and a girl." He considered her for a long moment. "If you wish, you can wait outside."

"That's not necessary." She needed to make herself useful to him.

"I won't think less of you." The stark gray of his eyes became shadowed with something else, something haunted. "Nobody should have to see children like that."

"What about your last secretary?"

"That was different. The victim was a grown man, a blood addict. He'd beaten his thrall one too many times and so she cut his throat when he was asleep."

"Cut his throat? I thought he was decapitated." A blue blood could heal from almost anything but that.

"She used a large knife," he replied, "with great force and a considerable amount of times."

Rosalind considered his words, slowly drawing her own conclusions. She needed to know more about this man—her adversary. Yet she couldn't deny the slight tingle of genuine curiosity. "Children unnerve you then?"

"You might be surprised to find that I do occasionally display and feel emotion. I'm not a machine."

He might have been asking if she'd like some tea. Rosalind looked out the window, at the fog-laden streets. She didn't want to empathize with him. Lynch was the enemy. But she'd heard whispers of how even the Echelon thought him cold and mechanical. A steel heart. Virtually a mech, they laughed.

Evidently he'd heard those rumors too.

"How do you do it?" she asked, despite her intentions. "How do you do this job?"

Lynch lowered the papers into his lap. "Because I'm good at what I do. I'm the best. For every woman I find assaulted, every child murdered, I know that I can find the culprit, perhaps even stop them before they get at someone else.

"And I can...switch it off. It's a gift I have," he replied softly. "I try not to think of them as human. They're gone by the time I get to them. Bodies. Nothing but bodies. All I can do is offer them justice."

That she certainly understood. Emotion had been burned out of her long ago. It was easy to simply... push it to the side. To not think of it. To focus on her cause.

The mystery of Lynch deepened. Who was this man? He was her opponent, the shadowy entity on the other side of the metaphorical chess game they played. She needed to know him, and yet, each answer humanized him in a way she didn't like.

He was nothing like the Echelon. Like Lord Balfour.

Not a steel heart, she thought, *but steel walls.* Built to protect him. And that would be how she would bring him down, she realized. The man was not impervious, which meant he had a weakness. Rosalind simply had to find it.

Lynch's gaze dropped. "You toy with your gloves. Do I make you nervous?"

Rosalind stopped playing with the fingertip of her glove immediately. "No." *Perhaps.* It was that damnable stare of his. She'd faced many an adversary, often at knifepoint, but there was something about Lynch that itched at her skin, along her nerves. It wasn't fear. She'd killed enough blue bloods to know they weren't infallible. But...something... She couldn't yet identify the reason for it. "It's a habit."

Folding her hands in her lap, she peered through the window. The streets raced past, an endless tapestry of brick, mortar, and fog. Gas lamps still gleamed on the street corners. And the touch of his gaze was almost a physical pressure. She found herself shifting in her seat and forced her body to still. It had been easier as Mercury, when the mask hid her from him. "Perhaps it's the thought of what lies ahead. What we'll see."

There was a flash of movement in her peripheral vision. Rosalind jerked her hand back as he reached for it.

Lynch froze, his face hardening. "I was only seeking to offer comfort."

Her left hand. Her iron hand. Rosalind's heart thundered in her chest. "I'm sorry." She put it back in her lap. One touch and he might feel the iron, feel the joins. It was only luck that etiquette demanded she keep her gloves on at all times in front of him, except while dining, though she intended to take her repast in private or not at all.

"I don't like my hands being touched," she replied. "Anywhere else is fine."

For a moment his gaze flickered to her décolletage. Then away. It might not have even happened but suddenly her nerves were on fire again.

He'd looked at her as a man would eye a woman. And suddenly Rosalind realized what she'd said. Her mind took a swift detour, imagining those hands on her, and her body reacted, nipples hardening beneath the stiff taffeta of the gown, a shiver of feeling edging its way down her spine.

"I won't touch you again then," Lynch replied. "You have my word."

Rosalind didn't want to drive him away. She needed to get under his skin, learn his secrets, the manner of man he was. "It's not personal," she said, her mind racing through a list of plausible lies and finding one that was almost real. "My father..." She looked down at her lap. "I have a bad association with the gesture."

Lynch's stark features softened. "I see. I apologize then."

The carriage lurched into another corner. Rosalind hung on for dear life. Lynch merely braced himself, his powerful thighs clenching as they cleared the corner. The butter-soft leather of his trousers creaked.

"This is madness," she said. "We'll be lucky to arrive at the crime scene alive."

"I assure you, Perry drives like this all the time.

I prefer speed over caution. I need to see what happened before the Echelon's men step all over my evidence and destroy it."

Her fist tightened on the carriage strap. "Some of the Echelon will be there?"

"Barrons perhaps, the Duke of Caine's heir. The summons came from him and he has an inquiring mind." Lynch picked up his papers again. "And no doubt the prince consort's Coldrush Guards will be there, to report back to him."

The place would be swarming with blue bloods. But not Lord Balfour. She breathed a sigh of relief. She was much changed from the child and young woman he'd known, but though he expected her to be dead, he would still recognize her.

"What—"

The world suddenly slammed to a halt, tires squealing and people cursing. Rosalind lost her grip on the carriage strap and plummeted forward.

A firm grip caught at her as she tumbled onto the carriage floor between Lynch's legs. There was a moment of hard muscle beneath her hands, then she realized exactly where her hands were and wrenched them back.

Lynch's fingers dug into her arms, his large body stiff as they both realized the suggestiveness of her position. The color leeched out of his irises, his black pupils swallowing them whole.

The demon inside him.

Rosalind froze. The gun strapped to her thigh suddenly chafed, as if reminding her how difficult it would be to get at it. She'd cut through the pockets in her skirts, leaving a clear path to the weapon, but her skirts were hopelessly tangled around her legs.

With a jerk he tore his hands away, his fingers clenching in the seat.

"I'm not going to hurt you." Lynch's voice was hard, almost metallic, completely lacking inflection. He took a deep breath and looked away, closing his eyes. "Just move slowly." A muscle jumped in his jaw. "I would help you, but I don't believe I should touch you just now."

There was nowhere to put her hands. Rosalind eyed his knee grimly and forced herself to lay her right hand on his thigh. The steam carriage jerked into motion and her fingers dug into the clenched steel of his muscle.

"I'm sorry," she murmured.

He hadn't opened his eyes, his breathing slow and steady. Controlled. Forcing himself to reign in his hungers, his desires. "As am I." A tight smile. As if he could only permit himself this.

Rosalind pushed herself to her knees, her eyes level with his chest. The hard carapace of his breastplate molded to fit his body, the musculature defined in an almost vulgar way. Beneath it he wore a black shirt with a long, leather coat over the top.

The only thing she could smell was leather. A blue blood had no personal scent, but some liked to disguise that fact with perfumes or aftershave. Indeed, Garrett reeked of it, though from her impression of the man, she wasn't surprised. Lynch however…No scents, no perfumes. Only a faint lingering hint of coffee and something else, something almost coppery.

Blood.

His eyes opened, as if wondering what was taking her so long. Rosalind's breath caught and she surged to her feet, practically throwing herself back into the seat. The black had faded, his demons well and truly leashed. The sight was impressive. She'd rarely ever seen a blue blood control himself like this.

"It doesn't happen often. But I've not been to sleep for several days and I didn't have time to…partake of nourishment before we left."

His entire body was rigid, his words so quiet she might not have heard them. A hint of embarrassment? Of shame? Rosalind stared at him, the breath slowly leaving her lungs. She felt almost unnerved, her body primed to fight or flee. But the danger had passed. Why then did the feeling persist?

"Perhaps you should carry a flask," she suggested, her voice rough and low.

"An excellent suggestion."

The murmur of his voice shivered over her skin, and she tore her gaze away, forced it to the window. The world beyond was a foggy haze, gas lamps flickering past in rapid succession. The brickwork on the houses was fancier, and iron-scrolled fences appeared, often with small gardens.

They were nearly there. Suddenly Rosalind couldn't wait. She wanted to get out of this damned carriage, away from him. And it wasn't fear that motivated her desire, but rather the uncomfortable turmoil he left her thoughts in.

The carriage slowed, the rumble of the steam engine softening to a hiss as the furnace exhaled.

Rosalind pressed her hand to the window, peering through the glass. He watched her, she knew. She could feel it on her skin, shivering down her spine. The thought almost tore a laugh from her lips, sharp-edged with panic.

Think of Nate. She pressed her lashes tightly together, desperately trying to picture her husband. For years he'd haunted her thoughts, but she couldn't find him now—only a vague outline, a hint of the smile that had won her heart.

"I would never hurt you," Lynch said.

No doubt he could smell her nervousness, read it in the still lines of her body. But he misconstrued the reason behind it.

Opening her eyes, she noticed her breath fogging the glass. "I know." She wouldn't allow him to hurt her. Taking a slow breath, her corset digging into her ribs, Rosalind pasted a smile on her lips. "It's the carriage. I'm not fond of small spaces. Not for too long anyway."

His penetrating gaze bore into her. "Don't touch your hands. Don't lock you up." A slow nod. "I shall remember."

Finally the carriage eased to a halt. The door jerked open and Rosalind could barely contain herself. She wanted to get out with a desperation that bordered on anxiety. The walls were pressing in on her.

Garrett appeared, surprised to find her in the doorway so suddenly. He offered his arm in reflex, that insincere smile edging over his lips. A dangerously handsome man but far too pretty for her tastes. No her tastes ran darker, or so it seemed.

Rosalind ignored his arm and stepped down,

pleased to be free of the carriage. The lack of its constraint lightened her soul. Her skirts spilled around her and she straightened them.

Garrett looked down beneath his lashes, as if considering his arm. He'd made it clear he considered this a hunt and she the prey. Every affront only seemed to heighten his intensity, though it merely frustrated her.

"She doesn't like being touched." Lynch alighted with dangerous grace. "On the hands anyway."

Their eyes met. Was it her imagination, or was there actually a play of amusement around the hard line of his lips? A softening perhaps or hint of smoldering warmth in those glacial eyes?

"Of course." Garrett stepped aside with a smile that almost gleamed.

One punch with her metal hand and all those pretty white teeth would be scattered across the cobbles. Rosalind smiled at the thought and he smiled back, no doubt thinking he was winning her over.

The warmth faded out of Lynch as if it had never been there.

"Come." Lynch snapped his fingers and strode toward the house. "Stop trying to seduce my secretary, Garrett, and get your mind on the job. Mrs. Marberry, if you would kindly do what I'm paying you to do. Feminine wiles are almost as teeth-grating as the vapors."

No softening there.

Rosalind stared after him with narrowed eyes, then grabbed her skirts in her fist and scurried after him. "You haven't paid me anything yet. And believe me, I have no interest in plying my 'feminine wiles.'"

He stopped abruptly at the front door of a large mansion, well lit from within. Rosalind nearly ran into him. Turning, he said, "Garrett likes women, Mrs. Marberry. Don't think you'll be the only one."

"Why thank you, Sir Jasper." She fluttered her eyelashes at him, goaded into sarcasm. "I hadn't figured that out at all."

Lynch's eyes narrowed. "You're mocking me."

"You're mistaking me for a fool."

Another hot glare that unnerved her. "I dislike women who think they're smarter than I am."

"I don't think I'm smarter." To her own credit she didn't emphasize the word "think." "And it seems you dislike women in general."

"That's not true. I simply find little use for them."

This time she *could* feel her cheeks heating. "Beyond the obvious."

His gaze traced her mouth. "Mrs. Marberry. This is precisely what I wished to avoid with my men."

"I thought it was Rosa? Now I am Mrs. Marberry?"

A long, steady look. "You are always Mrs. Marberry. To me. For convenience sake, you are Rosa."

She looked around. "And we're alone, Sir Jasper." On the stoop of a Georgian town house, the wind whipping his great cloak around her in a cocoon of intimacy. Rosalind took a shallow breath. But this was what she wanted, she decided—to discover the man's weakness. And it seemed, from the way he was looking at her, that he did find some use for women. Or perhaps for redheads in particular.

It was easy to smile, to play at being Rosa Marberry, now she was out of that carriage. She slipped into the role as if it were a second skin. All of the disquieting thoughts she simply shoved aside. "I don't believe my supposed wicked tendencies are bothering *your men* at all."

But bothering him. Ah, yes. She smiled, let her gaze drop beneath her heavy lashes. It helped to think of him as a man, not a blue blood, to pretend that he was only human.

If she pretended he was only a man, then she could admit that he was quite a fine figure of one. It was no wonder she felt this odd attraction. The thought eased her nervousness. It meant nothing. Lynch's silence was troubling. Expression flickered over his face when she looked up, but so minutely that she could not decipher it. He was an observer, she realized. Always watching, always thinking. She wondered what conclusions he drew as he examined her. Wondered if he could see right through her.

"I'll say this once," he said quietly. "If I suspect you are having inappropriate relations with any of my men, the position will be forfeit immediately."

"So I'm not allowed to smile at any of them?"

Stillness. Then: "Of course you are."

"For that is all it was," she replied tersely. "Garrett holds no interest for me as a man. He laughs too much and he wears far too much cologne." She gathered her skirts. "Now, if that is settled, shall we?"

Lynch's lips thinned. "Follow me then, Rosa. If you feel the urge to cast up your accounts, please don't do it on the bodies."

With that he strode past her, his broad shoulders framed by the elegant chandelier in the entry. Rosalind licked her lips and gave a frustrated sigh as she hurried after him. The man was infuriating.

Four

"Bloody hell," Garrett muttered, standing in the middle of the foyer and turning in circles as he examined the scene.

Lynch moved slowly, cataloging each inch of room and analyzing it. One of the servants lay on the grand staircase. She'd obviously tried to flee before Lord Falcone got to her. The woman lay sprawled across the carpeted stairs in her mobcap and apron, blood dripping from the torn gash in her throat. It was messy—made with blunt teeth and not a blade.

The butler had almost made it to the door before he too was cut down. A spreading pool of blood beneath his crumpled body soaked into the carpet. Lynch's brows drew together. "It's the same as the Haversham case," he murmured. "Falcone was more interested in killing them by this stage. No doubt he glutted himself upstairs." Kneeling down, he touched the sticky pool beneath the butler. His vision blurred momentarily, his sense of smell heightening even as his mouth watered. He wanted to touch his fingertip to his tongue but years of control had taught him better.

Behind him, Rosa scribbled furiously in her notepad, taking down his words. Her skin was pale, her lips compressed, but she gave no other sign that this scene bothered her—or she was determined not to.

Rubbing his fingertips together, he looked up the stairs. Golden lamplight bathed the walls. Falcone had not bothered to update to modern conveniences like gaslight. Some of the older blue bloods were like that.

Perry slipped silently into the room, her dark hair slicked back beneath a cap. "A bloodbath," she murmured, exchanging an uneasy glance with Garrett. Her nostrils flared, scenting the air, the blood. As one of the five who made up Lynch's Hand—his best—she needed to be on scene. Perry had gifts of her own, beyond driving a steam carriage through hairpin turns at breakneck speed. With one sniff she could place a man to the London borough he came from.

"Find Falcone," Lynch commanded. "I want a full CV count by morning." If Falcone had been close to the Fade, Lynch needed to know.

Barrons appeared at the top of the stairs, lean and moving with a swordsman's grace. Dressed in black velvet, the only sign of color was a ruby stickpin in the stark white cravat at his throat.

"Barrons." Lynch nodded, a sign of respect to the young lord. Barrons was often involved in matters requiring an inquisitive mind. Their paths crossed regularly at these events; no doubt the prince consort wished to be kept apprised.

"Falcone's up here," Barrons called, his voice carrying the inflection of the well bred. "He's still alive."

"Still alive?" Lynch hurried up the stairs. Behind

him came the swish of skirts and the lemon-and-linen smell he couldn't quite escape.

The two men exchanged a look.

"If you can call it that. I've managed to subdue him in the study. I'll warn you, it's not pretty," Barrons said, his gaze drifting over Lynch's shoulder toward Rosa.

"It rarely is," Lynch replied. He had the brief instinct to step in front of her, his shoulders bristling.

Barrons didn't have the look of a man eyeing a fine woman, but something about his perusal chilled Lynch to the core. He turned and offered his hand to Rosa to help her up the last three steps.

She eyed it for a moment, then reached out with her right hand and accepted it. Too late, he recalled her aversion to being touched there. But then her warm, slim fingers were sliding over his, the kid leather beneath his touch smooth and well-worn.

"Barrons, this is Mrs. Marberry, my new secretary," he introduced.

"A pleasure." Barrons nodded.

Rosa smiled, but Lynch had the feeling it wasn't genuine. "The pleasure is mine, my lord. I never expected to be rubbing shoulders with someone from the Council of Dukes itself."

Barrons studied her, then glanced away. "An honorary member, my dear. I stand in my father's place until he recovers."

Lynch said nothing. The Duke of Caine had been afflicted with a mysterious illness for years. The chances of him recovering were slim and Barrons knew it.

The fact that the craving virus was a possessive disease was not unknown. It tolerated no other viruses or illnesses in its host's body. Yet few dared tell Barrons that to his face. He knew it. The man was no fool, after all.

Whatever illness afflicted his father, he kept rumors of it under lock and key.

Barrons gestured toward the study. "Perhaps we'd best view Falcone first. Your men can deal with the bodies. They're through there." He gestured behind him, at the library and the bedrooms.

Though Lynch wanted to see the bodies himself, Falcone was of the greater interest to him. "I was unable to examine Haversham properly. He'd killed himself before we arrived. I thought it guilt at the time."

Barrons shot him a sober look. "I don't believe so. I don't believe Haversham had enough control of his senses to suffer such an emotion."

"Then you think he was murdered? I examined the body myself. The entry and exit wounds seemed consistent with suicide and powder burn was found on his hands and jaw. I could smell other people on his skin, but I assumed they were his victims."

"Like I said, I don't believe Haversham had the faculty to kill himself."

They strode along the carpeted hall. It was darker here, a single candle burning in the sconce.

"What should I expect?" he asked. "Was Falcone close to the Fade?"

"Falcone's barely forty."

"There's neither rhyme nor reason to the Fade," Lynch argued. "Sometimes the virus colonizes a man swifter than it does others. I've seen an eighty-year-old with a CV count as low as twenty-three."

"There's no sign of albinism," Barrons countered. "His skin carries a healthy glow, his hair is still light brown, and his eyes are hazel. If his CV count were higher, his color would have begun to fade before now."

Muffled screams began to penetrate. Lynch's gaze locked on the closed study. "How precisely did you subdue him?"

"I shot him with a dart of hemlock," Barrons replied. "It paralyzed him for barely a minute."

"A minute?" Rosa blurted.

Lynch had almost forgotten her. Almost.

The two men looked back.

"My apologies," she said. "I've read of these new hemlock concoctions in a scientific journal. I thought they paralyzed a blue blood for nearly ten minutes?"

No scientific journal would dare speak of such a thing. Lynch's lashes lowered in consideration, running over her. The propaganda pamphlets the humanists printed, however, were a different story. Did his secretary have humanist tendencies? Or was she simply one of the many curious in London who read the pamphlets when they were distributed?

He knew a man, an informant who was emphatically loyal to the Echelon, who liked to read the pamphlets, regardless of his loyalties. Jovan thought the caricatures of the prince consort as a pale, bloated vulture hovering over the queen were humorous.

"The amount of time the concoction paralyzes depends upon the amount of craving virus in the blood," Barrons explained. "The higher the CV levels, the quicker paralysis wears off. I've tested it on myself, actually. It takes me four and a half minutes to begin regaining control of my limbs."

Which meant Barrons had a high CV count. Lynch filed that away for future thought.

"Then if Lord Falcone doesn't have a high CV count, how on earth did he manage to recover so swiftly?" Rosa frowned.

"That is the question," Barrons said. "There's no explanation. In fact, there's no explanation for his state at all."

The three of them stopped in front of the study door. From within came the muffled sounds of a thud. Then something splintered.

Barrons reached grimly for the dart gun at his side. "I tied him to the chair," he admitted. "I believe he's just broken it. Be prepared for anything."

Reaching for the door, he eased it open and slipped inside. Lynch clutched his cane-sword and glanced at Rosa. "Stay there," he snapped, and hurried after Barrons. If he allowed the Duke of Caine's heir to get killed, then his own head would be forfeit.

The room was silent and dark, a breeze blowing through the gauzy curtains. The splintered remains of the chair littered a rug in front of the desk, with rope discarded in bloodied pools.

Barrons hurried to the window and looked out. "Bloody hell," he swore. "He must have gone through it."

The hair along the back of Lynch's neck lifted.

"This is a catastrophe. If he gets loose in the city, it'll cause mass hysteria," Barrons said. "We have to capture him before he goes too far."

"What are we dealing with here?" Lynch asked, aware of everything the young lord had not said in front of Rosa.

"A blue blood acting like he's in the Fade when he isn't. Presume you're facing a vampire, Lynch, and you might come close to the truth."

Lynch stilled. Becoming such a creature was the only fear a blue blood had. A vampire could kill hundreds before he was brought down—and had in the past. But the Echelon had become adept at controlling such matters. If a lord somehow managed to alter his CV readings, then the telltale signs of the Fade began to show in his flesh. He began to stink of rot, his body slowly deforming into a wiry, maggot-pale quadrupedal creature.

The hair along his spine tickled. Lynch scrubbed at the back of his neck. Barrons strode past him toward the door but Lynch hesitated. He could smell something now. Something sweet, like flavored ices or sugared buns.

Blood dripped.

"Barrons," he said slowly. "I don't think he went out the window."

The lord reached for the door, his gaze snapping back over his shoulder. Lynch slowly rolled his eyes up and Barrons's head lifted. He didn't need to see what had caught the lord's attention to know where Falcone was.

Barrons jerked his pistol up and Lynch dove out of the way as the man who'd once been Falcone dropped from the plaster ceiling. It landed where he'd been standing and as Lynch rolled to his feet, it sprang for Barrons.

Gunfire spat in the dark room, momentarily singeing Lynch's vision. All he could see were a pair of dark forms grappling and then Barrons's yelp as the young lord went down.

Lynch had his own pistol up, but the center of his vision was a mess of glittering lights. Leaping forward, he reached for Falcone and yanked with all his strength, tearing the creature off the fallen lord. Blood stained the air. He could taste it in his mouth, smell it thick in his nostrils. There was no time to see the damage however. Falcone twisted in a way not even a blue blood should be able to and leaped for him.

A blow smashed into his hand and the pistol skittered across the floor. Lynch ground his teeth as his arm was nearly wrenched clean out of the socket. He twisted back, avoiding another blow, and finally caught a good look at his adversary.

Falcone's face twisted in an expression of rage, his eyes bloodshot and wild. Nothing human lurked there. Blood matted his hair and clothes, and the nails on his hand were sharp. Lynch had a split second to examine him before they raked toward his face.

Parrying with the cane-sword, he barely managed to block the first blow, then the next one, let alone use it to his advantage. Falcone was monstrously fast and each blow echoed up the muscle in Lynch's forearm. Lynch ripped the sword free of the cane, but Falcone lashed out, nails screaming on steel as he knocked it out of Lynch's hand.

"Help!" Barrons yelled, scrambling upright. Blood bubbled on his lips and his chest was a raw mess. He clutched at the stained velvet, trying to drag himself into a sitting position against the wall.

Falcone's head turned at the sound and Lynch seized his chance. He leaped forward, tackling the man to the floor and using his own considerable strength to force Falcone onto his face. Yanking on an arm, he wrenched it up, putting a shoulder lock on the creature.

Light flooded into the room as the door opened.

Lynch recoiled from the bright glare just as Falcone gave a mighty heave beneath him. Rosa rushed inside, backlit by the light, a pistol in her hands and her face grim as her eyes locked on him.

"Get out!" he bellowed. "Get out of the house!"

Falcone strained, the tendons in his shoulder tearing. Lynch could feel his grip slipping, and horror sank its cold claws into his gut as he saw Rosa's jaw drop in surprise.

"Run!" he screamed as Falcone rolled and threw him aside.

Lynch hit the wall, the breath whooshing out of him. He landed on hands and knees, just in time to see Rosa flee down the corridor. Falcone went after her in a blur.

"Perry! Garrett!" He shoved off the wall and lurched toward the door. Something hurt in his side. Maybe a cracked rib. No time though. He had to stop Falcone—before the creature tore Rosa's throat out.

That thought burned through his chest like fire. Tearing through the door, he saw the flap of Falcone's coattails as the lord bounded down the stairs. Rosa screamed out of sight and a gun barked.

"Bloody hell!" Garrett's voice echoed through the entry.

Lynch sprinted along the corridor as shouts broke out. He didn't know what was happening. More gunfire coughed. Perry screamed Garrett's name and then the gunfire fell silent.

Vaulting over the rail of the staircase, Lynch leaped through the air, raking the scene with a sharp glance. Rosa tripped on the bottom step and went sprawling. Garrett was down, clawing at his chest. He was perhaps the only reason Rosa was still alive. Falcone had stopped to attack him first.

Lynch landed hard on the marble foyer below, the vibration shivering up his legs. Falcone ignored him, leaping on Rosa and riding her to the ground. Her head cracked on the marble tiles and the gun in her hand tumbled free.

No!

Blind rage turned his vision to shadows. The demon in him—the hungry, darker side of him—rose with a choking grip until he could barely see. The next thing he knew, he was hauling the creature off Rosa and throwing it into the wall. Falcone gathered his feet under him as he hit and rebounded off it with athletic grace.

Lynch had a knife in his hand before he knew it. Falcone hit him hard, blunt teeth sinking into his throat. Lynch drove the knife up, deep into the creature's chest. As if realizing his intentions, Falcone jerked, his jaw opening. Lynch grabbed him and yanked him over his shoulder, slamming the lord flat on the ground. His bone handled knife hilt gleamed in the golden light, and he knelt down, using his knee to shove it home as he grabbed Falcone by the head and snapped his neck.

Silence fell, broken only by the gasping wheeze from Garrett's throat.

Lynch staggered off the body, the shadows draining from his vision. He felt light-headed all of a sudden. Rosa was on her feet, her mouth parted in shock as she stared at him.

"Stay there," he snarled, stabbing a finger toward her. One last glance at Falcone—he wasn't getting up again—and he staggered toward Garrett.

Perry was on her knees, hands clamped over the wound on Garrett's chest.

"How bad is it?" Lynch demanded. Not Garrett. He'd been only a boy when Lynch took him on, streetwise and full of an insincere charm he used to protect himself, running along at Lynch's heels, emulating him, driving him insane with a thousand and one questions.

He reached out and tilted Garrett's head to the side. Garrett winced. "I'll live," he gasped. With a bloody smile, he added, "Can't leave so many bereft women behind. They'll be...crying for days."

Perry shrugged out of her coat and pressed it over the mess in Garrett's chest. Lynch saw blood pumping through an artery and felt the iron grip of those icy fingers rake his gut again. The heart. Falcone had hit the heart. There was no surer way to kill a blue blood.

"He needs a physician," Perry said in an emotion-less tone, but that didn't mean she felt nothing. When she looked up, light gleamed off her eyes, suspiciously bright. "Fast."

Lynch straightened and looked around. "Where the bloody hell are the Coldrush Guards Barrons brought with him?"

Nobody could answer that.

"Rosa, I need you to fetch help," he said, trying to prioritize needs in his mind. Lynch liked Barrons enough that he didn't wish to see the lord die—but more than that, he knew losing the Duke of Caine's heir would be a monumental catastrophe. Garrett however...Garrett was personal.

"I've got him, sir," Perry said softly, seeing the dilemma in his face.

He nodded shortly. "Barrons is down. I need to see if he's going to survive. Rosa, send for a physician or a doctor. Even a bloody midwife will do."

Rosa's gloved hands were clenched in her navy skirts as she stared at him with those liquid-dark eyes. She made no move to obey.

Had the fright shocked her insensible? "What?" he snapped.

"You're bleeding." Her lips compressed, a hint of defiance glinting in her eyes. "Quite badly."

He slapped a hand to his throat and felt the wetness there. The room stank of blood—most of it not his, thank goodness. But the smell of it... Lynch almost groaned, his tongue darting out to wet his lips. That was the only sign of his discomposure, but she saw it.

"I've had worse," Lynch said, tugging the collar of his leather coat up. Gesturing toward the door, he added, "Hurry. Before the others bleed to death.

And then make sure you stay outside until this is dealt with."

Lynch needed her out of here. He'd not risk her life again and right now, with the way she was looking at him and the intoxicating scent of blood, *he* just might be the one who lost control.

∾

Rosalind shivered on the doorstep of the mansion, tucking her cape-jacket tight about her shoulders. More of the Nighthawks had arrived in the last hour, as well as a pair of physicians and enough Coldrush Guards to secure the mansion. Crowds of curious onlookers loomed beyond their impassive forms, desperate to know more of what had happened.

"Was it them humanists?" a blue blood lord called, his top hat bobbing in the crowd.

"A vampire?" another cried, waving his walking stick.

Panic edged their voices and the crowd murmured. Rosalind edged back into the concealment of the trailing roses that cascaded over the entrance and tugged her bonnet up around her face. Nobody would know her here, yet vulnerability rode her. She was surrounded by too many blue bloods—half the Echelon it seemed, clad in their flamboyant velvets and silks. Even at this time of the day, gaudy feathers bobbed in ladies' bonnets and Rosalind caught a glimpse of several white wigs and powdered faces in the crowd—older blue bloods, by the look of it, those still mired in fashions from the past. Or perhaps seeking to hide the effects of the Fade. Who knew?

"Rosa?"

Lynch's voice cut through her scrutiny. Rosalind turned swiftly, her skirts slithering over the tiled portico and her heart leaping into her throat. She was used to keeping a cool head in moments of stress, but once the excitement had settled, she couldn't seem to stop her heart from pounding. *So close.* Falcone's eyes had been full of madness and hunger. She'd heard his harsh panting as he chased her down the hall, knowing that she'd never make it in time, knowing that he would have her... And then Garrett had looked up, his eyes widening in shock before he smoothly drew his pistol and put a bullet into Falcone's chest.

He'd saved her life. A second more and Falcone would have had her. As it was, the shot had barely slowed him. Rosalind had stumbled down the stairs, Garrett launching himself past her to meet the maddened lord—another action that saved her.

It was easy to despise the blue bloods after everything they'd done to her, but Garrett had risked his life for hers without a thought. She didn't like that. It didn't fit her view of the world.

Lynch had tried to hastily wash the blood from his skin and rake his hair back into place, but the same feverish glow that burned in her chest lit his eyes. "I need you. Come."

Tugging her notebook and pencil out of her reticule, Rosalind followed him inside. The stale scent of death seemed to permeate the air in the grim afternoon light and two of the Coldrush Guards were stationed inside. Her gaze went immediately to where Lynch had launched himself over the railing of the banister. He'd landed lightly, the edges of his long leather coat flaring around him, his eyes cold with purpose, before he'd thrown himself at Falcone. Killed him in fact, with grim, efficient purpose. She hadn't missed the way he'd moved; someone had taught him a brutal fighting style. Falcone had been stronger and faster, but Lynch knew how to disable a man with a few swift chops of the hand.

Rosalind looked up, light gleaming through the facets of the chandelier above. A good twenty-foot drop and he'd handled it like it were a step off the porch. A shiver worked its way along her spine.

Dangerous.

Blue bloods were superior in strength and speed to a human, but that didn't always mean the balance was uneven. A trained assassin could cut down an untrained blue blood in hand-to-hand combat. Someone like Lynch though? Impossible.

If he ever realized who she was, Rosalind had no intentions of getting close enough to him to find out who would win.

"Here," Lynch said, gesturing to the body by the stairs. Someone had draped a sheet over the corpse, but it clung wetly to Falcone, drenched in blood. "Write this down. We've taken an analysis of Falcone's CV levels with the portable brass spectrometer. They came in at fifty-three percent. Note: Request Haversham's CV levels when we return."

The butler was covered with a coat someone had found. Rosalind frowned. "Do you usually cover the bodies?"

"No."

He'd done it for her then. Her pencil paused,

scratching to a halt. Then she hastily wrote the rest of
his words.

"From what I can determine, Falcone was in the
dining room with his family when the…seizure…took
him," he continued, starting up the stairs. "His cup
was nearly full, but the decanter levels indicate he'd
partaken of a quart of blood. He shouldn't have been
driven by the craving. His CV levels indicate he was
far from close to the Fade. Something caused this then.
An outside influence? A toxin? Was the blood he was
drinking tampered with? Or some hitherto unknown
disease that afflicts blue bloods—"

"Wait," she called, trying to scribble furiously in
her writing pad as she followed him up the stairs.

Lynch waited. "This way." He started down the
corridor, barely giving her pause. "What—"

"What happened to Garrett?" she asked, inter-
rupting him. "And the duke's son?"

"Barrons is recovering in Falcone's room with the
physicians. Thankfully his wounds are already healing,
though they were serious enough at the time. As for
Garrett, he's in the kitchen. Doyle arrived through the
back with the rest of my men and he's trying to stitch
him up."

"Will he recover?" The thought shouldn't have
bothered her. One less blue blood for the world to
worry about.

Lynch's dark lashes shuttered his eyes. "Garrett's
stronger than he appears, but he's lost a lot of blood.
Perry had to give him some of hers."

He strode through the doors ahead of him. Rosalind
followed, a fistful of skirts in her hand. He might not

have cared, she thought. Truly, for all the emotion he showed, Garrett could have been any man off the street.

"Here," he said, gesturing to the dining room. Two bodies lay beneath the bloodied linens of the tablecloth. "This is where he was dining."

Rosalind stumbled on the doorstep, her gaze narrowing on the small shapes beneath the table cloth. So small… Her throat tightened, the blood draining out of her face. Shards of porcelain littered the floor, a spilled decanter flooding the mahogany tabletop with a pool of spreading red wine. It dripped from the edge in a steady, monotonous plummet.

"It smells like…a bakery," she murmured, swallowing hard against the flood of bile in the back of her throat. She couldn't look at them again. How could anyone slaughter their own children? What manner of monster could do that?

A blue blood, a voice whispered in her mind.

Lynch stared at the scene as though absorbing it. "So it does. As did Falcone." He turned to her to speak, then paused. "Rosa?"

She looked up and saw something that almost looked like concern on his face. "I'm—" The words dried up and she clapped a gloved hand to her lips. She wasn't all right. All she could see were those tiny, twisted shapes beneath the bloodied linen.

Movement blurred. A hand wrapped around her elbow, Lynch's large body stepping between her and the bodies. Then he was pushing her through the door, into the blinding light of well-lit corridor. The walls staggered by, a door opening in front of her. She moved like a puppet in his grasp, acid burning her throat.

Lynch pushed a window up and shoved her toward it. Fresh air swept that sickly sweet scent out of her nostrils and she clutched the window ledge, sucking in a choked breath. His hand settled in the small of her back tentatively, as if he wasn't sure how welcome his touch would be.

"I shouldn't have taken you in there." Soft words. "My apologies."

Rosalind shook her head, swallowing hard. "I'm sorry." No matter how much she tried to shove the image away—into that small dark recess of her mind where lurked unimaginable memories—she couldn't. It was tattooed on the back of her eyelids, burning its way into her stomach and throat.

A cool hand rubbed small circles against the curve of her spine. Rosalind gripped the sill and leaned out, drawing the coal-laden air of London into her lungs. Anything to rid herself of that bakery scent.

As if to distract herself, she focused on his touch. Her breath caught.

"You have nothing to be sorry for," he replied, his cool exhale stirring the curls at the nape of her neck.

For the first time Rosalind realized how closely he stood, his legs pressing against her bustle and skirts. Nervousness etched its way down her spine. She hadn't forgotten the look in his eyes when he killed Falcone—he'd enjoyed it, licking the taste of blood from his lips. It should have sickened her further, yet she found she couldn't quite equate that monster with the man who stood behind her, his hand rubbing soothing circles against her skin.

Rosalind's body responded to his nearness, but not

with lust, not with the way the previous scene still haunted her. Instead, she relaxed back into his touch, her head bowing low as she took some small, guilty comfort from his closeness. She didn't want to think about why his presence made her feel...*safe*?

She'd stood alone for so long, walling herself off from others after her husband's death. She didn't need the softening of a man's touch or his presence to comfort her. She was strong enough without it.

Rosalind stiffened. He had to stop touching her. She didn't like it. "I'm fine, sir."

His touch hesitated, his fingertips skating over the smooth taffeta of her gown. "Very well."

The sudden screaming absence of his touch made her feel almost cold. But no, that was nothing more than the chill breeze through the window. A shiver worked its way across her skin and she looked for anything to take her mind off the frozen melee of emotion that stirred her.

"What shall you tell the crowd?" she asked, examining the assembled blue bloods below.

"That we are investigating." His voice was hard again. "They don't need to be made aware of the full facts of the case."

Rosalind's fingers tightened on the windowsill. "If you don't tell them, they'll suspect worse. They're already crying 'vampire.'" She shook her head. "There've been too many people through the house: the Coldrush Guards, Lord Barrons, the physicians... You cannot keep all of them quiet. I would imagine it would be better to give the press some details, enough to still the fear."

"You're right," he murmured. "Very wise of you, Rosa."

"People fear what they don't understand," she said with a glance over her shoulder, then abruptly regretted the words.

Lynch stared back at her, his hands clasped behind his back. His gaze was hauntingly intense in the chill afternoon light. "So they do." Slowly he bowed his head. "Take your time. I shall wait for you in the foyer when I'm done speaking to the journalists."

She waited until she heard the door click behind her before letting out the breath she'd been holding. A glance outside showed the crowd baying at the iron-scrolled fence, fury and fear etched in stark emotion across their faces. For a moment they looked almost human, then she pursed her lips, her eyes narrowing.

There was nothing human about a blue blood, nothing at all. No matter what she thought of Lynch, she could never forget that.

As she turned away, her eye caught on a solitary figure leaning against the corner across the street, his arms crossed over his chest.

With his cap pulled low over his face and a heavy coat obscuring his throat and jaw, she shouldn't have recognized him but she did. Mordecai. The leader of the mechs who'd tried to bomb the tower.

The satisfaction curling over his lips was unmistakably his—the smug grin that had always made her hackles rise. What was he doing here? Surveying his handiwork? Or simply enjoying the sight of the blue blood's distress?

Her iron fingers jerked inside her glove

unconsciously. He'd done something, she was certain
of it. Somehow he'd been the cause of this, the reason
those two small bodies lay still and silent beneath the
white table cloth.

The reason she couldn't find her brother Jeremy.

Rosalind was moving before she thought about
it, the house a blur around her as she darted down
the stairs to the foyer, her boot heels ringing on the
polished tiles as she shoved the front door open.

Stopping on the edge of the portico, Rosalind
caught her skirts in her hand in frustration. He was
gone. The corner was empty, the crowd swallowing
up any sign of him and trapping her here. There was
no way she could push through them and the thought
of being surrounded by so many of the enemy made
her throat tighten.

I'll find you. Her eyes narrowed. Then she'd make
him regret ever sending her brother in to deliver
the bomb.

Five

FOG LINGERED IN THE ALLEYWAYS, SEEMING TO LURK IN the still corners and doorways where no breeze stirred. Rosalind dragged her shawl tight around her shoulders and moved swiftly through the evening crowd. The hairs on the back of her neck lifted. It was the silence, she decided, the way everybody's voices were muted and nobody would meet each other's gaze. Martial law had choked the city since the bombing, with metaljackets on every corner and rumors of humanists in every whisper. The unease was universal. Even she felt it, despite nerves that should have turned to steel long ago.

A quick glance at her pocket watch told her she'd best hurry. It was almost half eight and she had to be home before nine. If she were caught out, she'd be arrested.

Fifteen minutes later, she took out her key in front of the door that led to her leased apartment. The door jerked open.

Rosalind slapped a hand to her chest as Ingrid glared at her over the threshold. "Damn it, Ingrid. Are you trying to give me a fit of the nerves?"

"Nerves?" Ingrid asked in a smoky voice. "You?"

Rosalind pushed past. The door slammed and then the lock clicked behind her as she tugged at her gloves, each finger at a time. She hated wearing them; they made her right hand sweat and it was difficult to grip a pistol with them. But if anyone caught a glimpse of her bio-mech hand, they'd alert the authorities. It was clearly not enclave work.

Mech limbs never came cheaply and it sometimes took as many as fifteen years in the enclaves for a mech to pay off his debt. After they had worked off their bond, they often returned to the enclaves as free men—or women. The streets of London weren't the same for a person with a mech enhancement. The Echelon saw them as less than human and, therefore, without even the punitive rights most humans lived by.

Sometimes Rosalind wondered if it would be better if she'd not had the replacement, not that she'd had the choice. It made her stand out and that was dangerous in her world. But it also gave her two working limbs and that was invaluable for an assassin.

Rosalind tossed the gloves aside, flexing her steel fingers. *You're not an assassin anymore.* But sometimes it still felt like it. Sometimes in the night she woke sweating, seeing a victim's face flash through her mind. It was the only time she couldn't protect herself from the memories.

There'd been five of them in total. Balfour's enemies. At least she had the satisfaction of knowing they'd been blue bloods. Still…

Shoving them aside, into that little mental compartment in her mind that she kept locked, she turned toward the sitting room and the decanter there. The fire was stoked, casting a merry light over the stuffed armchairs, with their wilted lace doilies clinging to the backs and a mahogany table between them. Sparse accommodations, but then she didn't truly live here. This was just a facade for her little game.

Silence lingered and she cast a distracted glance over her shoulder. Ingrid leaned against the doorjamb, a frown drawing her dark brows together. "You *are* nervous. I can smell it."

The problem with living with a verwulfen—their enhanced senses could smell anything. Rosalind shrugged out of her cape and feathered hat, discarding them on an armchair. "I'm tired. I've been dragged to Kensington and back, upstairs, downstairs, and then home again, with no luncheon or refreshment to speak of. The man's a machine—a well-oiled machine that runs on fumes."

She sank into the remaining armchair and slumped in an unladylike manner. Lynch had been an unstoppable force today, his mind making leaps of logic that even she struggled to follow. He questioned everything, checking over every inch of the house. The only aberrance they'd found had been a pair of small metal balls in the dining room that looked somewhat like the clockwork tumbler balls children played with in the streets. The sickly sweet smell lingered around them, though undoubtedly the children had been behind their presence.

Ingrid stepped closer, dragging a footstool forward and tugging Rosalind's boots up before straddling the edge of the footstool herself. "Got something for you."

Slipping a slim, rectangular box out of her waist-coat, she handed it to Rosalind. From the weightless-ness, the box might have been empty.

Rosalind opened it. A thin, pale glove of almost translucent material lay on crumpled tissue paper. The artistry was exquisite, with fine blue veins of cotton barely showing through the outer layer of synthetic skin and slick scars that looked like ancient burn marks marring the back of the hand. Small oval scales were embedded into the fingertips with painted half-moons and a rosy hue.

"Synthetic skin," she murmured. "Where did you get this?"

"There's a man in Clerkenwell who knows someone who does this sort of thing. I asked him for it."

"This must have cost a fortune." Rosalind looked up. "Ingrid, how did you pay for this?"

Their eyes locked, the burnished gold of Ingrid's irises flaring. "Made some money in the Pits," she admitted.

"Ingrid!" The Pits were notorious dens in the East End where men pitted themselves against other men—or even beasts. Sometimes the fights stopped when a contestant was unconscious. Sometimes not.

Forbidding it wouldn't stop the other woman. Indeed, quite the opposite. Still, she had to say some-thing. "You're not invulnerable."

"The fighting helps to keep me temper under control. And I don't like you being unprepared. If the Nighthawk asks to see your hands," Ingrid said, "then what shall you do?"

Rosalind slowly closed the lid over the glove. "It won't hold up under scrutiny."

"No. But all you got to do is let him catch a glimpse so he don't start getting suspicious."

"Thank you," Rosalind murmured.

Ingrid nodded gruffly. She'd never say how worried she was, but she was fretting and that would put her on edge. They'd first met when Ingrid had been just a little girl, trapped in a cage in Balfour's menagerie. Rosalind had been well fed and cared for, but she had been a pawn-in-training, just as alone in some ways as Ingrid. The pair of them had struck up a friendship and eventually Balfour had let Ingrid out of the cage at times to duel with her. Of course, pitting her against an opponent who was stronger and faster than her, but untrained, had been nothing more than a test of her skills.

He'd underestimated the bond the two girls had struck however.

Ingrid cleared her throat "No word of Jeremy?"

"I haven't had a chance to look. There was a massacre." Rosalind didn't know what else to call it. "Lord Falcone tore his household apart then tried to do the same to us." She swiftly relayed the day's events as Ingrid tugged off her boots. The woman dug her thumb into Rosalind's heels and her eyes glazed. She was half tempted to shut them, but the memory of Mordecai's face flashed through her mind. She'd been trained to always finish her report, no matter what state she was in. "I saw Mordecai there. He was outside, watching the house."

Ingrid froze, then her thumbs slowly resumed their massage. "Did he have anything to do with it?"

"I don't know." Rosalind rubbed at her forehead.

"I'm beginning to suspect they had some plan up their sleeve when they broke with us, something they didn't deem fit to share with the rest of us."

"A weapon?"

"Something that drives a blue blood into blood-lust." She'd considered the thought many times today. "I've never heard of the like. But why else would he be there? And how did he do it? Is it a poison? A toxin in the air or in Falcone's cup of blood? An injection perhaps?" She shook her head. "No, not an injection. Lynch had the body examined thoroughly this after-noon, back at headquarters. He wouldn't have missed something like that."

"He might have."

Rosalind laughed mirthlessly. "You don't know the man. He's painstakingly thorough." Her eyes narrowed. "I don't believe I'm aware of half of his thought processes. There's nothing on his face, but I know he's thinking. Always thinking."

"Does he suspect you?"

"I don't believe so," she replied. "He was distracted by the case." Rosalind considered the day's events and the way Lynch had glanced at her. "And he would never suspect his pretty young secretary is his adver-sary. He's attracted to me."

Why had she blurted that out?

Ingrid's eyes narrowed. "You smell nervous again."

Rosalind shoved to her feet, her skirts swishing around her stockinged ankles. "Of course I'm nervous. The man's a blue blood."

"As long as you don't forget that," Ingrid said.

"I never forget." Nathaniel's face swam into her

mind and a pang of grief soured Rosalind's embarrassment. She still felt his loss each night, when she
slid into her blankets and he wasn't there. The days
weren't so bad, but the nights... She had nothing to
distract herself then.

The blue bloods had taken him away from her
forever. It might have been Balfour's hand, but it was
by the Council's edict. The threat of the humanist
movement had been so terrifying to them that they'd
had a harmless dreamer of a man murdered.

She was not harmless however. Their mistake.
For Nathaniel had been an orator, not a fighter. His
war would have been fought in courts and in rallies.
Hers would be fought in the streets, metaljackets
against the enormous metal Cyclops army she'd been
building in Undertown.

"I'm going to find Jeremy," she said hollowly.
"Then I'm going to finish the Cyclops project and
destroy the Echelon. I will never, ever forget how
much they've taken from me."

"And Lynch?"

Rosalind clasped her hands behind her back and
stared unseeing at the wall. This time a new image
overtook Nathaniel's. One of carved features with the
sharp aquiline nose and piercing gaze.

"I'll deal with him," she said quietly. "One way
or another."

Lynch eased open the door and slipped inside the
room. The surgery was small with only the most basic
of operating facilities. The craving virus healed almost

anything short of decapitation, hence there was no need for more, and the Council funds barely covered the men's wages and upkeep.

The sound of rasped breathing filled the air. It wasn't loud, and yet in the midnight silence of the room, it seemed as if every man in the place should hear it.

A phosphorescent glimmer ball turned the room a sickly green. Tucked in the narrow bed, the stark sheets pulled up underneath his chin, Garrett slept restlessly. There was no sweat on his forehead—a blue blood couldn't perspire—but the sickly pallor of his skin spoke of fever.

Perry slumped in the chair beside the bed, her head resting in her hand as she dozed. Lynch let the door click shut behind him and her eyes blinked open, her hand straying to the knife at her side.

"Sir."

Lynch gestured for her to relax, then crossed to the bed, staring down at the wounded man. He'd had frequent reports from Doctor Gibson all evening, but he still had to ask. "How is he?"

"He asked for you," she said, a touch of reproof in her voice.

Lynch nodded. He came because he had to—and because the not coming would haunt him all night—but he didn't want to be here. Any blue blood that was so injured as to be bedridden was unlikely to get up again. And Garrett... Damn him, Garrett was one of his.

"I should have..." His words trailed off. He didn't know what to say. *I should have taken one of the others. I should have stopped Falcone. I should have been faster...*

The truth was hard to admit. "I failed."

"No more than I did. I was right there, sir. I saw Falcone coming and—I didn't expect it. I froze. Garrett didn't. If I'd been one second faster he wouldn't—"

"You'd be lying there instead," Lynch said. "Has his breathing changed?"

Perry shook her head, her dark hair curling around her face. She'd clipped it short enough that no one could get a handful of it, and he'd seen hints of blond at the roots over the years to know she dyed it.

"No, sir." The words were soft. Broken.

Lynch looked at her sharply and saw her dark gray eyes were gleaming. He went still, his stomach clenching. Bloody hell. He rarely thought of her as a woman. He'd never needed to. Perry always did her job, rarely voicing a word of dissent. Rarely voicing anything, as a matter of fact.

She'd come to him nine years ago, a trembling waif in the rain, her dyed hair tumbling around her shoulders and the hunger burning in her eyes. The clip of an aristocratic accent had flavored her words and though he knew some of her secrets, he never mentioned it. Perry wasn't the only Nighthawk hiding from her past.

Perry was an accident, he guessed. Women were never offered the Blood Rites for fear that the hunger would overwhelm their delicate sensibilities. The only other exception was the Duchess of Casavian, and she had the power of a great house behind her.

She'd shorn her hair that first night and swathed herself in the uniform he'd presented to her—having a shortage of any other garments—and that was how she'd stayed.

"I'm sorry, sir." Perry took a deep, shuddering breath. "Garrett's my partner. I just feel...so helpless."

"I know." He squeezed Perry's shoulder. "If anyone could survive, it'd be him, the stubborn bastard." Then he winced as he heard what he'd said.

"I know," she said, with a weak smile. "I just hate seeing him like this."

"I hate seeing any of them like this."

Forty years since he'd formed the Nighthawks. A lot of good men had died in that time. The Council didn't care. They were only rogues. But they were his, each and every one of them. Lynch frowned, feeling the steady muscle of Perry's shoulder beneath his palm. It grounded him and he realized he rarely touched anyone anymore.

He had once. He'd shared his meals with his men, even laughed with them, but that had died over the years, as they had. And slowly he'd stopped taking his meals with them. He'd buried himself in the job, until the names of the dead meant another strike, another failure on his behalf—but nothing more.

So why did Garrett lying here like this affect him so much?

He knew the answer immediately. Garrett refused to keep his distance, his humor wearing away at even Lynch's determination to keep his distance.

Cor, sir, don't you look dapper this evening. Why, put a smile on your face and half the gentry morts from here to the city would be lining up.

Perry leaned her head against his hand, as if she took some solace from his touch. "I can't believe he did it. Garrett always said heroics are for fools."

"Perhaps he was trying to impress someone."

"Mrs. Marberry," Perry said with a frown.

The thought of Garrett and Mrs. Marberry together darkened Lynch's mood. To hide it, he said, "Well, the only other option is you or I—and I don't think he wants to get either of us into bed."

Perry stilled. "No, sir. I believe not." She drew her knees up to her chest and rested her chin on them. The motion jerked her shoulder out of his grasp.

"I'm sorry."

"Don't be, sir. You're right, after all." A smile edged her lips, as if she were trying to make him feel better, but her gray eyes were still lost. "You're not his type in the least."

Lynch almost choked. "Hell, I should hope not."

She patted his hand. "You should go and get some sleep. I'll keep watch."

It was the opening he needed. Lynch pushed himself to his feet, though sleep was the last thing on his mind. He desperately needed it, but there was too much to do. And guilt was ever a harsh mistress. He snuck a glance at Garrett. No. No sleep tonight.

"Send word," he said quietly. "If the situation changes."

"I will." Perry knew precisely what he spoke of. Her hand slid over Garrett's, as if she unconsciously sought to keep him from death's door, through pure persistence if nothing else.

Lynch took his leave with quiet efficiency. Through the door he could still hear the faint rasp as Garrett's abused lungs sucked in another tortured breath.

His chest constricted and Lynch shoved away from the door. Sickrooms. Bloody sickrooms. He hated them.

Six

LYNCH WRENCHED HIS HEAD OUT OF HIS HANDS AS THE door to his study burst open, pain flaring behind his eyes. His vision slowly adjusted and he blinked, looking at the scattered paper strewn across his desk. Messy handwritten notes covered half of them— scrawled ramblings he'd made last night as he let his mind sort through the previous day's events. *The tumbler balls. A sticky residue on the sill. Some sort of sweet smell that lingered on Falcone's body.* And underlined three times. *Mrs. Marberry: Why does she have a pistol?*

Doyle went straight to the fire and stoked it, sending a gush of smoke through the room. "You look like you've been three solid nights in a gin 'ouse. Smell like it too."

"Hardly," Lynch replied, scraping his hair back out of his face. He must have dozed off. "I know what a gin house smells like."

Pushing to his feet, he staggered toward the liquor cabinet in the corner. Thick, viscous blood pooled in one of the decanters. For a moment his vision sharpened, the color leaching out of his sight. His hand shook as he unstoppered the decanter and poured himself a short glass.

Staring out through the windows at the gray morning, he drained the blood. The taste of it burned through him, igniting desire in his belly like the hot stroke of a woman's touch. Lynch forced himself to put the glass aside and stoppered the decanter again. He rationed himself strictly—a necessary evil. No matter how much he thirsted for more, he never allowed it. It was one of the few methods he used to control his unnatural hungers. Meditation was another.

"How's Garrett?" he asked quietly.

"Still breathin'," Doyle replied, wiping his hands on his trousers as he turned. His own expression was inscrutable. They never spoke of it amongst themselves, but every Nighthawk knew the risks of the job.

Every hour Garrett survived meant increased hope that the craving virus was healing him. He might survive. Might.

"Here," Doyle muttered, tugging a letter out of his pocket. "It's got the gold seal on it."

The Council then. Lynch snatched it and broke the seal with his thumbnail. His gaze raked over the words, any warmth draining from his face.

"What is it?" Doyle asked bluntly.

"A summons," he replied, striding toward the set of rooms he kept off his study. "At eleven at the tower."

Doyle followed him into the bedroom. "Aye, its not good news then?"

"I'm not sure." The last time he'd received a summons, it had come with a threat. This reeked of the prince consort's touch. A reminder of his absolute power? Or something far more sinister? He was growing bloody tired of being jerked around like a puppet.

"Send for my horse to be saddled."

"Done," Doyle replied.

"Then I'll need a pair of lads to escort me—"

"They'll be waitin' at the stables." Doyle restrained himself from giving Lynch a telling look. He knew his job. "A pair of the latest recruits. Still so new they piss their pants at the sound o' your name."

"Preferably not in the Council chambers."

Lynch poured a pitcher of warm water into his shaving bowl and made short work of the task. Doyle wasn't far wrong. With his bloodshot eyes and the thick, dark stubble along his jaw, he looked rather more like a miscreant than the respectable Guild Master.

Doyle yanked open his closet and fetched the black velvet coat Lynch wore to court and a crisp, white shirt that had been starched to within an inch of its life. "We'd best get you ready then. The gray waistcoat? Or the black checked one?"

"Black." Lynch dragged the heavy leather carapace of the breastplate off over his head, then shrugged out of his undershirt. He stripped completely and gave himself a brisk wash.

"I want last night's reports on my desk by the time I return," he instructed. "And Doctor Gibson's final autopsy results on Lord Falcone. If you can, have his blood run through the brass spectrometer again. I know his CV count came in normal, but I want to see if it's changed at all. The craving virus tends to survive in the tissues after death for several days. Let's see if it's still within its normal ranges. And send Byrnes to question the Haversham heir again."

Doyle threw the shirt at him. Lynch toweled himself off, then dressed quickly. The stark white of the shirt was the only sign of color. Doyle tossed him a black silk cravat and Lynch tied it swiftly.

"Oh," Lynch said, on his way out the door. "Mrs. Marberry is due at nine. Show her to my study and instruct her to begin transcribing my notes into the formal case file." He paused. "See that somebody sends her some tea or...something."

He'd realized last evening that he'd barely fed her the previous day.

Doyle nodded. "Will do."

Lynch opened his mouth. Then shut it again. Doyle was giving him a long-suffering look. The man had been with him for forty years, as evidenced by the gray in his hair. He might be only human, but he knew his job.

"Very well then," he replied. "I'll be back as soon as I can."

Lynch entered the atrium of the Ivory Tower, bowing his head to the seated Council members.

Two chairs remained empty. Barrons was most likely still indisposed from Falcone's attack and the chair of the Duke of Lannister had been shrouded in black since his murder.

The sign of mourning was a mockery. Lynch had proved that the duke had known of the bombing before it occurred and still said nothing. If the duke hadn't died in the assault, then the prince consort would have had him executed regardless. Even now the Council seat stood empty, the prince consort obliterating the House of Lannister in his rage.

Lynch's fingers dipped into his pocket, automatically fingering the scrap of leather there. *Hers.* There'd been three other people in the same room as the duke when he died, and Mercury had been one of them.

Ignoring the man in the center of the brass circle that was cut into the tiles—Sir Richard Maitland, that lickspittle—Lynch strode to his side and turned to face the Council. The enmity between the Nighthawks and the Coldrush Guards had always boiled under the surface and Lynch would have liked nothing better than to drop the Master of the Guards off the top of the tower.

The prince consort's face was expressionless, the queen's hand resting on his shoulder as she stood beside him and stared distantly over Lynch's shoulder. None of the other councilors showed so much as a glimmer of their intentions.

"Sir Jasper, Sir Richard." It was the young Duke of Malloryn who stepped forward. Despite his youth, Malloryn had been duke for ten years, since the moment he'd reached his majority. The House had been nearly annihilated with his father's assassination, but Malloryn had hauled it back from obscurity with an almost-aggressive determination. "The Council has decided that this situation with the humanists in the city must be given priority, most particularly the capture of the revolutionary leader, Mercury. Since little headway seems to be made and you don't have a single humanist in your grasp, we have decided to set the pair of you on the case."

Lynch's jaw tightened. That was not precisely true, but they didn't need to know that. Not yet. Not until he had all the pieces of the puzzle.

Having more men on the street did not guarantee success. Indeed, it only made the task more difficult. No doubt it looked appealing from their precious Ivory Tower, so far removed from the streets Lynch walked.

"Do you have anything to say, Sir Jasper?" The prince consort's colorless eyes locked on him.

"No, Your Grace." He gave a curt nod. "Why would I argue with your infinite wisdom?" *Make of that what you will.*

The prince consort's eyes narrowed minutely.

"It has also been recommended that we provide some incentive for this capture," Malloryn continued. "As such, whoever brings us Mercury shall be rewarded most suitably. Your rogue status shall be revoked and you will be granted the privileges of one of the Echelon."

Sir Richard sucked in a sharp hiss of air beside him. Lynch's gaze jerked to the dais. He knew who to thank for this piece of news—Barrons's hand, working behind the scenes.

His mind raced. Enticement indeed. Maitland was almost quivering in anticipation beside him. He'd have every single available man he had on the streets, flooding them with guards. The populace would be in an uproar, men and woman too afraid to venture out.

And Mercury... Lynch stopped breathing. If Maitland got his hands on her, Lynch would kill him. His vision darkened, bleeding into shadows at the thought.

"Don't think my former command has been rescinded, Lynch," the prince consort said coldly. "It stands."

"Of course," he said, battling to control himself. He knew his eyes had darkened as the hunger sank its claws through him. They'd notice his state—and wonder. "I still have almost two weeks." His voice sounded as though it came from miles away, a rushing sound filling his ears.

"Is there a time limit I'm not aware of?" Maitland's voice sounded like an echo as he took a smooth step forward.

A foolish move to present his back to his enemy. Lynch eyed him. It would be ridiculously easy to snap his neck. Not even a blue blood could recover from such an injury.

He was letting the hunger rule his thoughts, his emotions. He ached to rip Sir Richard's smirking head from his shoulders—to stop him before he ever got a chance to look for Mercury.

Making a supreme effort, Lynch reined in his impulses, forcing his mind to empty of all thought, most particularly the revolutionary he had a score to settle with. Three shallow, controlled breaths and the shadows dropped from his vision, though they lingered at the edges as though he'd not quite banished them. That had never happened before.

Sound snapped back in upon him, the world suddenly gleaming with too much light. The Duke of Bleight watched him closely. He wore barely any fripperies and disdained to powder his hair the way most of the court did. It was white enough as it was and heavy creases lined his predator eyes.

They'd never been allies. When Lynch had pleaded his case before the council forty years ago, Bleight had been the only duke to vote no to his proposal to form the Nighthawks. "*Let the rogue die,*" he'd said bluntly. "*I see no use in him.*"

Of course he hadn't. Lynch had been a threat and Bleight didn't like to leave an enemy alive, despite the fact he'd been all of fifteen.

"Shall we make it fair?" Bleight intoned with a malicious little smile. No doubt he was hoping Lynch would fail. "Two weeks for both of them?"

"Sporting odds," the Duke of Goethe replied seriously. He was one of the few dukes that Lynch admired; indeed, they'd once been contemporaries, before the death of his cousin catapulted Goethe to power. Now his close-cropped black beard was salted with silver and his eyes, once as dark as obsidian, had begun to lighten—faint signs of the Fade. Goethe had only ten years or so left in him before the color drained out of him completely.

"Two weeks." An oily smile spread over Maitland's face. "I'll have Mercury in half that time." He saluted briskly. "By your leave, Your Grace?"

The prince consort nodded and Maitland strode past Lynch, his pale gaze fired with ambition.

"It's good to see a man so enthusiastic about his task," the prince consort said.

"He needs the head start. Is that all you wished of me? I have work to do."

"No doubt," the prince consort replied. "The Falcone attack?"

The way he said the words, as if testing them, made Lynch alert. The prince consort wasn't the only one with an interested gleam in his eyes. Each of the Council had stilled, resembling a painting of heightened anticipation.

Or fear.

"I believe both the Falcone and Haversham cases to be connected. I have no information on the agent that drove them into bloodlust, but witness statements and my own conclusions draw a parallel between them."

"So it's true?" the flame-haired Duchess of Casavian murmured. "They were both in a state of uncontrollable bloodlust?"

"They acted as if the Fade were upon them," he replied. "However, both their CV counts came in quite low. I believe something exacerbated the condition."

"Reports state that your hand killed Falcone," the prince consort stated. "He was a distant cousin of mine."

"He'd slaughtered his entire household. I had no choice. If he got loose in the city, we'd be awash in panic-fueled riots this morning."

The prince consort dropped his gaze. With relations between the Echelon and the working classes as they were, it wouldn't take much to set off a riot and he knew it.

"I want a report on the case," the prince consort demanded. "Mercury must be your priority, but I can't allow this madness to become an epidemic. You don't think it some disease that afflicts blue bloods, do you?"

"No." He'd considered that. "The attacks came on too swiftly. By all accounts, Lord Haversham enjoyed a night at the opera with his consort before ripping her to pieces. There were no symptoms of disease, no sign that he was out of sorts. I believe it to be influenced by some sort of toxin or poison, though I have no conclusive evidence."

"You'll find it."

"I will."

Both men slowly nodded at each other.

"Then you're dismissed. I want your report by tomorrow morning."

"As you wish."

Seven

FIRE BURNED IN A BARREL ON THE STREET CORNER, though not even a single soul gathered around it. Night had fallen and with it the brutal choke of martial law. Metaljackets prowled the city in troops, their iron-booted feet ringing on distant cobbles.

Lynch ignored the biting cold, striding through the night with his cloak swirling around his ankles. Three nights with no sign of Mercury. After the council meeting, he'd increased the flood of Nighthawks he had on the streets to counteract the sea of Coldrush Guards. A part of him was almost thankful that Mercury had gone to ground. He'd rather cut his own throat than see the woman in Maitland's hands.

Hearing the heavy tread of a metaljacket legion nearby, Lynch cursed under his breath. Grabbing hold of the edge of a drainpipe, he hauled himself up, hand over hand, onto the roof of the nearest house. The vantage gave him a good view of the city and would keep him hidden from most eyes. He didn't want Maitland breathing down his neck, trying to find out what leads Lynch had on Mercury.

No doubt there'd be one or two Nighthawks who reported back to the Council or even Maitland; that was the way of the world. But if they hoped to find anything in the guild, they'd be sorely mistaken. He kept everything important in his head, where no one could decipher it.

Hurrying across the rooftops, he saw the wall of the enclaves looming ahead. The last time he'd been here, he'd had his whole world shaken by a slip of a woman in a mask. Desire ran its smoky hand through him. How he burned. He wanted her desperately, wanted to get his hands on her and exact his revenge.

Leaping off the roof, he landed lightly in the street and started toward the gatehouse. A heavy-set guard with the sleeves cut off his vest stepped forward, a dark look in his eye. "Here now, you ain't s'posed to be out at night—"

Lynch opened his cloak, flashing the stark black leather of his body armor.

The man bowed, mutiny flashing in his eyes before his lowered gaze hid it. "My apologies, me lord—"

"I'm not a lord." Lynch stepped past him, toward the gatehouse. "I need access to your records."

At that the guard's head shot up. "Now, sir, I ain't s'posed to give that without Council orders."

Lynch stared at him. "The key," he said softly.

Lips thinning, the guard muttered under his breath and looked around. "I don't want no trouble from this." He dragged a key chain over his head and held it out flat, in his palm.

Lynch took it and turned toward the gatehouse. "I was never here."

Inside the gatehouse, the stench of stale coffee and long congealed ham struck him. The room was dark but he traversed the shadows easily until he reached into his pocket and struck the flare stick he carried with him.

The records chamber was just past the main room. It was a long room, filled with filing cabinets. Inside each were files, all of them listing names, descriptions, and each mech's serial number along with a grainy photograph. Lynch ignored the men's files and stopped in front of the women's. He discarded the flare stick on top of the filing cabinet, then unlocked the first drawer.

By law, each mech had to be registered with the city. Mercury would be in here somewhere. All he needed was to find a woman of around 5'8" with an enhancement to her left hand. A specialty order, fitted with blade and needle, and no doubt more.

Then he would have her.

If only to figure out what to do with her.

❧

The door to Lynch's inner sanctum was locked.

Rosalind glanced at the door to the hallway as her fingers meticulously folded a letter and sealed it inside its envelope. There'd been no sign of Lynch for the last two days. The room reeked of his presence; the maelstrom of untidy paperwork, a brass spectrometer in the corner for his CV count, the liquor stand with its vile flasks of blood, and that ever-damning map on the wall, but the man was as elusive as the wind.

She didn't know if that were blessing or curse. While it had given her ample time to search through his papers for word of her brother—or even the mechs—frustration filled her.

The part of her that played at Mercury—that dangerous, thrill-seeking part—itched over her skin like a hair shirt. She was growing restless with the inactivity. Forced to keep her head down due to Lynch's increased efforts to find Mercury, she had sat at home each night playing at the good widow. Without him here during the day, there wasn't even the challenge of matching wits with him.

Rosalind put aside the pair of letters she'd been preparing and crossed to the window, tapping the letter opener against her skirts. Late afternoon sunshine struggled through the gray clouds, washing the world with a melancholy tint.

She lasted barely a minute. Slowly her head turned toward the door to Lynch's private study. There'd been no mention of Jeremy here, but perhaps she hadn't looked hard enough?

Or perhaps she was simply that restless.

The guild was quiet this time of the day, most of the Nighthawks seeking their beds in preparation for the night ahead. Rosalind crossed to the door and pressed her ear against it. Lynch's rooms were accessible through his private study only, so there was no risk of him entering through that door. Her fingertips twitched and with one last glance around, she eased the letter opener inside the lock.

The thin stiletto tip rasped over iron. Rosalind cocked her head and listened to each click, feeling her way like a blind man with a whore. The tip caught and she held her breath, easing it, carefully, *carefully…*

A click.

The lock tumbled open.

A shiver ran down her spine and she licked her lips with one last look at the door to the hallway. The rush of heat that swept through her veins was almost dizzying.

Moving swiftly, she slipped inside. The room was dark, the heavy swag curtains drawn over the casings. Rosalind dragged one of them back and brightness spilled into the room, dust motes swirling through the stark spotlight that flood-lit the Turkish rug.

As her eyes adjusted, she glanced around, absently flipping the letter opener over and under her fingers. Lynch's private study was larger than she'd expected from the size of her study outside. She had to move quickly, yet despite her resolve, her gaze was drawn directly to the door on the other side of the room. *His* bedchambers. Curiosity bit at her. She knew he wasn't there. He never slept, it seemed. The lock to his rooms tempted her but that was surely madness.

Don't. Rosalind closed her eyes and took a deep breath, feeling that same restless urge sweep over her.

Sliding the letter opener between her breasts and into the stiff-boned fabric of her corset, she hurried to the other window and wrenched the curtains back, forcing herself not to think. He would scent her in here surely, but she could explain that away, protesting an unlocked door and the desire to tidy things up a bit for him. After the ruthless way she'd filed his paper-work in her study, he'd believe her.

But the trace of her scent in his private rooms could not be explained away.

Why, sir, I wanted to see where you sleep—if you ever do…to see your bed, your sheets, your coat discarded over a chair. To touch the fine fabrics of his cloak and breeches, and run her fingers over the slick leather of his body armor.

To leave Mercury's mask in the center of his pillow.

Rosalind bit back a nervous laugh. She didn't dare. The thought was foolish—stupid. But the idea made her skin tingle.

Keep your mind on the job. The smile on her lips died and she forced herself to remember the way Balfour had taught her to discipline herself as a child. Every last flicker of humor vanished and she hurried to Lynch's desk.

The monstrosity dominated the room, smothered in piles of paperwork. Honestly, the man had not met a piece of paper he could part with, though she'd swiftly learned that he could set hands on anything he wanted within a minute. Sometimes she found herself shifting things just to aggravate him—another unnatural urge. She shouldn't be playing such games, but she couldn't help herself.

Running her gaze over each sheet of paper, Rosalind rifled through the piles on his desk. The range of subjects fascinated her: scientific theories, what appeared to be treatises on rare plants and distillations of poisons, beautiful watercolor leaflets of exotic blooms she'd never even heard of, and anatomy sketches that would have made Ingrid feel ill just to look at.

There was, however, nothing on his desk that had anything to do with his work.

Rosalind tapped her fingers on the mahogany. An orchid dozed on the windowsill, its bonneted white head dripping with a florid pink tongue. She began to truly look around. One wall was nothing but bookshelves and Rosalind stepped closer.

"What type of books would you read?" The tips of her gloves rustled over the linen-bound spines and Rosalind's eyes tracked the titles.

Dull, dry scientific treatises. More plants. Dusty monologues of foreign places and ancient wars. An entire shelf dedicated to the Chinese Empire—that would be an interest in his blue blood origins, she presumed. And at the far end an entire wall of mysteries. How predictable. A smile touched her lips and she dragged one out, examining the cover. No doubt he solved the mystery a good ten chapters before the protagonist.

Sensation crawled across the back of her neck, lifting the hairs there. Rosalind's fingers froze on the book. She knew, without looking around, that he was watching her.

The restless urge slid through her veins like molten honey, the thrill of being caught. Her lips parted and she eased the book back between its neighbors, listening for any betraying sound from him, to try and place him in the room.

There was none.

Rosalind turned slowly, pressing her back to the bookshelf. Lynch leaned against the door to her study, his arms crossed over his broad chest and his eyes narrowed with a considering expression. She couldn't read him. Her blood fired at the thought, urging her to run, to fight, but she forced it down, lifting her eyes to his.

"I do believe that this is my study," he said in a cool, emotionless tone. "The door of which was locked this morning."

"You must be mistaken," she replied. "The knob turned in my hand the first time."

Not even a hint of doubt flickered on his face. "You often test my…doorknobs?" Easing away from the door, he started to shrug out of his coat. The stark black velvet slid from his shoulders, revealing a crisp white shirt that dazzled her for a moment. Braces rode over his powerful chest, tugging the shirt taut against his shoulders.

With a careless toss, he discarded the beautiful coat over a dusty armchair strewn with newspapers. Rosalind's gaze followed it for a moment, her lips thinning. "Locked doors make for tempting targets." Picking up his coat, she crossed to the hatstand by the door, her gloved hands kneading the luxurious velvet. There was no body heat in the soft folds. His skin would be cool, she thought, like smooth silk. "And I've sorted all of the papers in my study."

"*Your* study?" His brow arched.

She ignored the gibe, smoothing out the folds in his coat with absent fingers. "I wanted to tidy up in here."

"Destroy my carefully disordered sanctum, you mean?"

A smile edged over her lips. "I'm a woman, it's what I do."

"If I wanted someone manipulating my life, I'd have married." Shaking his head, he crossed to the liquor stand near the window.

"If you learned some charm, you might have found someone willing to take on such a role." She eyed the flask in his hand. Blood. She'd seen the way the thirst for it fired Balfour's eyes, and the other blue bloods' around him. Humanity drained away, leaving them little more than monsters, their eyes flooded with a demonic black.

Lynch poured himself a measured shot and threw it back with cool efficiency. Rosa couldn't look away. His throat muscles worked, the fingers of his hand curling around the glass in a betraying motion. Then he slammed the glass down and swiftly capped the flask.

Barely enough to keep his hunger at bay. Yet he turned as if the action had never occurred, dragging at the crisp white cravat at his throat with an absent scowl on his face.

Some semblance of her discomfort must have shown. He paused before his desk, his shirt open at the throat and the cravat dangling from his fingers. "My apologies. I didn't think to restrain myself."

Rosalind forced herself to stir. "You never have before. I don't see the point now."

With a guarded look, he tossed the cravat on the desk. "I've restrained myself greatly." Resting against the desk, he crossed his arms once more, a familiar pose. "Tell me... Did you find anything of interest?"

"Interest?"

"When you were rifling through my things."

For a moment she thought he'd caught her out. Then she realized that there were faint creases at the corner of his gray eyes and just a hint of a smile edging his harsh lips. Her heart started beating again, thundering in her veins.

And she liked the feeling.

"There were many things of interest," Rosalind said, circling the desk behind him. His head turned to the side then stopped, and she knew he was tracking her by sound now. His thick dark hair was cut brutally short, barely edging against the stiff starched cut of his collar. Rosalind eyed the broad span of his shoulders. "You're an interesting man."

"Yet you're afraid of me," he murmured.

"No, I'm not—"

"I can sense it. In your scent, in your voice, the soft catch of your breath." He looked over his shoulder then, his gaze smoky. "You cannot hide anything from me, Mrs. Marberry."

Lie. She smiled and kept moving, her skirts swishing against her legs. "Mrs. Marberry?" she mocked. "I wonder why you call me that at times."

He was good. His body didn't even stiffen, his eyes watching her dangerously. "It is your name," he reminded her, in that rough-as-velvet voice.

Rosalind edged closer. Dangerous. So dangerous. But that old thrill was there again, tempting her to madness. She trailed her fingers across the desk, close to his thigh. "I like it when you call me Rosa."

This time she called his bluff. The black breeches tightened over his thighs minutely. Rosalind's gaze lifted and she smiled up at him.

Lynch stared back, his body unnaturally still. The stillness of a predator, eyeing its prey. The bunching of muscle, the shortness of breath. Rosalind took another step and her skirts brushed innocuously against his calves.

"Why did you come in here?" he asked.

"To drive you mad." Shock drove his gaze to hers and Rosalind's smile grew. "With your paperwork," she elaborated. "I wanted to put it all away while you weren't here. You have an obsession with paper."

"Some might argue that so do you."

"I like things to be tidy."

"I like things to be where I put them," he replied, a slight hint of huskiness in his voice.

She was slowly coming to understand him. Though desire roughened his voice, he'd not make a single move toward her.

Their gazes met. All of a sudden she could remember the cool exhale of his breath against her throat and the feel of his fingers cupping her arse. A part of her wanted to shatter that icy control, to drive him panting to the edge of desire, the way she'd done in the enclaves.

A troubling thought.

Rosalind graced him with a smile to hide her inner turmoil and turned away, the hem of her skirts swishing over his boots. The smile slid off her face as soon as her back was turned.

"How is Garrett this morning?" she asked, pretending that nothing had just happened.

"Recovering." Behind her, Lynch let out a low exhale she almost didn't hear. "Thank goodness. I thought for a moment…" His voice trailed off, then strengthened. "But Doctor Gibson tells me he should recover, if somewhat more slowly than usual."

She wouldn't have expected it, but she was honestly grateful. "That is good news. And the rest of your morning? I thought you gone for the day."

"Evidently. You've written those letters?"

Rosalind rested her hands against the back of the settee and glanced over her shoulder. "On my desk."

"Excellent. There are some files there too. Can you bring them to me? I need you to take some notes."

When she turned, she found him bent over his desk, rifling through the stacks of papers as if to see what she'd done. The weak sunlight fell across his pale skin and the roughened stubble of his jaw. Dark shadows smudged his eyes, making the gray almost crystalline. He'd been out all night, she'd bet. Searching for her. Or for Mercury.

The thought should have made her smile, but instead she frowned. "Have you slept at all?"

A quirk of those dark brows. He didn't bother to look up. "Are you still interviewing for the role of wife?"

Rosalind bit back her initial retort. "I was concerned, sir. You look like hell, but I'll refrain from acknowledging such in the future. My apologies." Sweeping past him, she headed into her own smaller study and immediately saw the files on her desk. He must have sat them there when he realized she was in his own study.

When she returned, Lynch eased back in his chair and looked at her. "I'm sorry," he said. "You've caught me at a bad time. I'm out of sorts and exhausted."

Rosalind sat the files on his desk. She'd not have expected an apology. The force of his control, his exquisite manners, and his cool politeness were all things she'd not expected. He was an enigma and she enjoyed trying to understand him.

Far too much.

"That's quite all right," she found herself saying. "You've made no progress with the case?"

"Either of them." He closed his eyes and leaned back in the chair, raking tired hands through his hair. For a second his expression was unguarded; frustration warred with exhaustion, and she found herself almost tempted to reach out and touch him. To cup his cheek in her palm and turn his face to hers.

The moment shook her. To forsake it, she asked tartly, "Either of them? Lord Haversham, do you mean?"

At that his eyes opened. The light struck them, rendering them almost blue-gray and something tightened in her chest. An ache. A longing. She turned away, fussing with her skirts.

"Not Haversham, no," he replied quietly. "Have you heard of the humanists?"

Rosalind schooled her features. "It seems to be all anyone speaks of these days. People are concerned about what the Echelon intend to do about them and whether it will spill over into their world."

"I have to find them first," he said bleakly. "Before anything can be done."

"I have no doubt you will," she said, though she meant not a word of it—not if she had anything to do about it.

"You're right, of course. It just takes time and that is something I don't have." Lips thinning, Lynch pushed to his feet. "Here. Sit. I need you to take dictation. My own writing is appalling."

"I've noticed."

He circled her as she crossed to the chair, his head turning as she passed. That prickling awareness between them shivered over her skin and Rosalind took refuge in the chair, picking up the spring pen. Lynch crossed to the hearth and stared into the cold fireplace, his hands clasped behind his back. The pose drew attention to the long, smooth muscles of his spine and the way his trousers caressed the taut curve of his buttocks. Rosalind nibbled on the end of the pen and looked her fill. There was no point in not admiring him after all. *Searching for weaknesses*, she told herself with a self-deprecating smile.

And finding none.

"Annie Burke. Serial number 1097638," he said briskly. "Missing her entire left arm. The arm has been replaced with a hydraulic bio-mech piece manufactured by Craven's. The hand is standard issue—"

There was more, but her pen paused and Rosalind stared down at the piece of paper, her mind going blank as his words droned on.

Clever man. Looking for a mech, was he? In all the wrong places, of course, but still, the tenacity of the man bothered her.

"Rosa?"

She looked up and found him watching her over his shoulder. He'd evidently heard the pen trail off.

"I'm sorry," she murmured, hastily scrawling down the last of his words. "I wondered how you can remember all of this."

"I remember nearly everything," he replied. "I trained myself to do so years ago after a fire swept through the first building and took all of my notes. Now I rarely put anything important to paper."

The pen nib pressed hard on the paper, leaving an ink blot she silently cursed. *Damn him.* She'd spent days hunting through his files for naught. She'd wondered where he kept the important information. Now she knew. It was in that head of his. And she had no way of getting at it.

Unless... He would have to tell her of it. And if she played her game well, he might just take Rosa Marberry into his confidence.

"Why now?" she asked boldly.

"I've examined the files of all of the mech women in the enclaves and after viewing them, found that none of them match the one I seek. Which means she must be elsewhere." The hard note in his voice took her aback. "Once you've taken down my thoughts, I'll compile them into a description of the woman and what I know of her bio-mech hand. Then I'll send Byrnes through the enclaves to question all of the blacksmiths."

"Woman?" she asked lightly.

That steady gaze flickered to hers, as if he'd just realized she was still in the room. "The humanist leader, Mercury."

"You sound quite...enamored of her." She idly traced several letters on the paper, concentrating hard.

"She made a fool of me. I won't suffer to be made a fool of. That is all."

It wasn't all. Not by a long shot. Rosalind looked up beneath her lashes and saw the intensity of his gaze drift past her, out the window. He was thinking of

Mercury. She could see it in the sudden tension of his hands and shoulders.

A faint smile touched the edges of her lips and she dropped her gaze again. "Shall we continue?"

☙

Candlelight flickered in the night, lighting up the ceiling of his room. Lynch stretched his arms back and pillowed his head in his hands, staring up at the dancing shadows. He needed sleep desperately, but it wouldn't come. Instead, all he could think about was the taste of his revolutionary's mouth and the way she'd writhed against him, her legs locked around his hips.

His cock swelled, the end of his nightshirt riding over the sensitive flesh tormentingly. *Fuck it*. He bared his teeth, jerking his hand out from under his head. He'd never get to sleep if he didn't take care of this. It was bad enough during the day, the encounter with Mercury whipping him into a lather of frustration and desire and now Mrs. Marberry flirting with him. If he didn't control this, he'd break apart, torn by hunger and need, when he most needed his senses in place.

His hand wrapped around his cock in a brutal grip and he hissed as pleasure tightened his balls. Closing his eyes, he threw back his head and thought of that moment in the alley when Mercury had kissed him. Driving her lithe little body against him, her tongue darting into his mouth. And then, once the shock of it had left him, how she'd rubbed her body against his as he shoved her against the wall and possessed her with his mouth.

He came with a gasp, all too quickly. Collapsing

back on the sheets, he groaned as his body trembled, his need barely sated. *Witch*. Licking his lips, he cursed her name. His body was half-hard again, desire a raging inferno that couldn't be quenched. No woman had ever left him so undone before, not even Annabelle.

Slowly, he touched himself again, stroking his sex-slick skin. He would rid himself of this hunger, this need. No matter what it took.

Then he would hunt her down and do what needed to be done.

Eight

"You're certain the woman wasn't in the archives?" Caleb Byrnes asked, his arms folded across his chest as he leaned back against the laboratory bench. Sunlight from the high windows bleached the tips of his brown hair and sparked off his very blue eyes. A cold bastard. And dangerous too. But at least Lynch knew he could trust him to do his job; Byrnes was a force of nature when it came to tracking his prey. Intense and furiously focused. Indeed, he liked it a little too much.

"Certain," Lynch replied absently, slowly turning the page on one of Fitz's books. *A History of Biomechanics*. Horrendously dull reading, but the diagrams were what he was interested in.

There was a distinct smoky flavor to the air, no doubt a previous experiment of Fitz's that had gone awry. Scars and frequent little burn marks covered the battered workbench he leaned against. The rest of the men referred to this as the dungeon, and it was the frequent epicenter of explosions and small fires.

"You ever known 'is lordship to be wrong?" Doyle snorted.

Lynch flipped a page and then paused. He lifted the book and turned. "I only glimpsed her hand, but she had something like this designed into the mechanics." He showed it to Fitz.

"A Carillion blade? That will help to narrow it down. There's only a handful of craftsmen in the city who know how to forge one correctly." Fitz's thick eyebrows shot into his hairline and he smiled in rare anticipation. Burn marks turned the center of his left brow into a stubbly mess and the tweed suit he wore was acid-stained at the cuffs. A young rogue blue blood who had found his calling here, working with strange devices and inventions.

A fluttering started in Lynch's gut. He was getting closer to finding Mercury. He knew it. "I want their names."

"The problem is…" Fitz murmured, taking the book and peering at the diagram. "They belong to the Council."

"How the devil docs a revolutionary get work created by one of the master smiths?" Byrnes asked.

How indeed? Lynch's mind raced. "What makes a woman hate a blue blood so much that she wants to destroy them all?" This was his forte, his genius, predicting his adversary's moves and motives. "She's come into contact with the Echelon, I'm certain of it. Perhaps the loss of her hand itself is key?" He frowned. He could have his men question the members of the Echelon about a young human woman who'd lost her hand, but that would start people asking questions he didn't want them to. *He* needed to find her, not deliver her straight into someone else's hands.

"You think one of 'em took her 'and?" Doyle frowned. "That don't seem a strong enough motive to want to destroy 'em."

"Who knows how people perceive such things? To some, such a loss might be reason indeed," he retorted, pacing the small laboratory.

"If one of the Echelon cost her the hand, then someone helped her get a mech replacement," Byrnes said. "I'm thinking a blue blood again. Master smiths don't come cheaply and the only merchant's who might be able to afford one wouldn't have contact with them."

"Maybe they weren't *asked* to create it," Lynch suggested.

"Again, that brings me back to a blue blood," Byrnes frowned. "And it would have had to be done quietly or some rumor of it would have reached our ears. The master smiths don't create mech parts, not for mere humans anyway."

"No missing or kidnapped master smiths in the past twenty years?"

"I'll look," Byrnes promised.

A knock started at the door. All four of them turned.

Perry bumped the door open with her hip and dragged a wheeled chair into the room. Garrett slumped in the seat, looking completely indignant with the contraption.

"Here we are, sir. It took me a little longer than anticipated to fetch him," Perry said.

"She practically wrestled me into it," Garrett snapped. "I *can* walk."

"Not until Doc says you can," Doyle replied bluntly. "How's your breathin' been?"

"I'm fine." Black heat swam through Garrett's eyes. After such a grievous injury, his craving virus levels had increased dramatically, as if his body hadn't been able to fight the virus off while it tried to heal.

Lynch exchanged a glance with Doyle. He'd have to keep a close eye on his second. Garrett's CV levels were now around the sixty percent margin, but such an increase in a short amount of time might lead to brief losses of control. Garrett wasn't used to fighting off such increased hungers.

"And your stitches?" Doyle asked.

"Itching like a sailor with the pox."

"I cut them out this morning," Perry replied, ignoring his glare as she wheeled him into place beside Lynch. "Are you cold? Do you want a blanket?"

"I'm going to bury you in the garden if you don't leave off." Garrett clapped a hand to his forehead in frustration, scraping his hair out of the way.

Perry snorted. "As if you could. Even when you're at your best, I can have you facedown in the dirt nine times out of ten."

"I only need once—"

"That's enough," Lynch said quietly.

Both of them fell silent.

"I need you on your feet," he told Garrett. "If that means suffering through Perry's ministrations, then so be it."

"Besides…" A slow smile crept over Byrnes's mouth. "She can't help fussing, its part of her nature."

"Was that an oblique reference to my gender?" Perry asked, her eyes narrowing to thin slits.

If he left them at this, they'd be at each other's

throats within a minute. Lynch held up a hand, staring them all down. "Concentrate," he said, stabbing a finger toward the book. "Fitz, what's the difference between enclave work and the master smiths?"

"Enclave work doesn't have synthetic flesh," the young scientist frowned. "It tends to tear in their line of employment."

"She didn't bother with it."

"However the addition of the Carillion blade argues for master smith work. We all know a blue blood's saliva has chemical components in it that can heal a cut—or the slash of a blood-letting knife—without transmitting the virus," Fitz said. "That's what they use to create bio-mech limbs. They can meld steel tendons or muscle sheeting with flesh by using a blue blood's saliva. The interior of the bio-mech limb is grafted to a man's body as if it belongs, each contraction of muscle creating flex in the steel hand. It's truly an extension of the body."

"And enclave work?" he asked.

"Far rougher. They don't have access to a blue blood's saliva. A hand relies on clockwork pieces inside it to drive the mechanism and hydraulic hoses in the arm to lift it. Mech—not bio-mech. Far less accurate."

Lynch scratched at his mouth. "Its master smith work, I'm sure of it. She had full use of her fingers and hand."

"Looks like we've got some smiths to question," Byrnes said with a heated smile.

"You and Perry work together on that," Lynch directed.

Perry shot him a look. She and Garrett always worked as partners; Byrnes preferred to work alone.

"You're entering Echelon territory," he said, though he rarely bothered to explain his orders. "You need someone to watch your backs. Keep it quiet—but I want to know if any master smith created something like this within…the last ten or fifteen years. The hand's fully sized, so she had to be an adult by the time it was melded to her flesh."

And keeping Perry away from Garrett would stop them being at each other's throats. His head was pounding as it was. Lynch nodded sharply. "Dismissed."

Later that afternoon, Lynch stripped his coat off and tossed it on the armchair in his study, which was now free of debris. Pausing, he looked around the room. Evidence of Mrs. Marberry's meddling existed everywhere. Ever since he'd found her in here two days prior, she'd been making her presence known in myriad, subtle ways.

He'd been too busy to take her to task for it, but now he paused, taking a good hard look around the room.

The bookshelves were spotless and dust free, the orchid on the windowsill shifted to a warmer location. By the fireplace, all of the translations of an old Tibetan document he'd been making were gone and the desk was entirely clear of paperwork.

He turned on his heel and strode back through the door into her cheery, sunlit study. Steam drifted off the teapot on her desk and her head was bent as she carefully wrote something. Sunlight gilded the burning copper of her hair, tracing the fine downy hairs at her nape.

"Mrs. Marberry." He leaned on the desk, looming over her.

The pen stilled. Rosa looked up slowly, as if she'd heard the very controlled way in which he spoke. Those solemn brown eyes locked on his. "Sir Jasper," she replied in that composed manner that drove him beyond endurance. "What may I do for you?"

Shoving away from the desk—before he strangled her—he stabbed a finger toward his study. "Where is it?"

"Where is what?"

"Everything. My papers, my treatises, that bloody Tibetan document that is worth more than your life! All of it!"

She put the pen down. "The filing cabinet behind you is empty. I put all of your papers in there. If you look, you'll find them all in order. As for the Tibetan document, I have no idea what you speak of."

"The papers in front of the fireplace."

"That pile of chicken scratchings that was spread all over the settee, two armchairs and the rug?"

"Yes." The words came out between clenched teeth.

Her eyes widened. "Oh," she said. "I didn't think it was important."

The blood pumped through his veins. He shut his eyes and pressed his tongue to the roof of his mouth, silently counting to ten. "That document was written in blood," he said, "by an ancient Tibetan scholar. It is *irreplaceable*. They say the origins to the craving virus are hidden within its transcriptions. What did you do with it?"

When he opened his eyes, hers were as wide as

saucers. Her lips trembled and a sharp stab of guilt threatened him, before the slight twitching at the corners of her mouth made him realize she wasn't scared. She was trying not to laugh.

"Mrs. Marberry!"

"I'm sorry. I shouldn't be so wicked. I placed them very carefully on one of the remaining bookshelves, out of the light." Laughter erupted from her and she tried to restrain it with a slender, gloved hand. "I'm sorry, but I've never seen you in such a…such a state!" The laughter broke free and she bent over the desk, several coppery curls tumbling from her chignon.

The sound swept through him. Lynch froze, his mouth half open and his finger still pointing. She was laughing at him. The damned woman was laughing!

Looking up, Rosa dissolved into a fresh wave of giggles at the look on his face. The anger faded out of him as abruptly as it had come and he shook his head. Bloody woman. Lynch swore under his breath, marching toward his study. He slammed the door shut behind him, then paced to the bookshelf. She'd been right. The document had been here all along, neatly tucked beside his histories of the Chinese empire.

He could still hear her laughter through the door. Transfixed by the sound, he cocked his head and listened. Despite the situation, he couldn't stop a smile from edging his lips. She was tempting the wolf every day and she well knew it. His prim little secretary had a wicked side.

You wanted someone who wasn't scared of you.

With a sigh, he turned toward his desk and sat down. The polished mahogany gleamed in the late afternoon shadows. Lynch stared at it. He didn't think he could recall the last time he'd seen it. The neatness disturbed him. The presence of its perpetrator disturbed him even more. He shot another heated look toward the door. The low-cut, dark green gown she wore hadn't escaped his notice.

Seducing his secretary was completely beyond the pale, but damned if he wasn't considering it. Scraping a shaking hand over his jaw, Lynch forced his body to behave. The brief, frenzied way he took himself in hand at night wasn't helping. Mercury had ignited his dormant sexual desire and now he was even considering Mrs. Marberry as substitute.

Or not quite. Mrs. Marberry had her own unique effect; she was no woman's substitute.

A commotion caught his attention and he stilled, turning with predatory interest toward Rosa's study.

"Lynch!"

A rap came at the door, then Byrnes stuck his head in. The swarthy features were strained and spattered with blood. "There's been another massacre in Kensington."

"Where?" The mirth faded from Lynch completely as his third-in-command opened the door farther. Behind him Mrs. Marberry watched with wide eyes.

"It's…75 Holland Park Avenue," Byrnes replied grimly. He knew, as well as the others, what the address meant.

Cold spiraled through Lynch, taking him off guard. *No.* "Alistair?"

"I had to kill him, sir. I couldn't…I couldn't get him off her."

No. The thought was the merest whisper. The

world narrowed around him and he swallowed hard. "And Lady Arrondale?" Somehow his voice came out low and cool. Emotionless. When inside he felt as if the world had exploded.

A short shake of the head. "I'm sorry, sir."

❧

"You should have gone home," Lynch told her, staring up at the mansion with simmering reluctance in his eyes. Every light along the street was lit and dozens of Nighthawks flooded the scene as early evening settled its mantle over the city.

Going home was out of the question. Rosalind needed to find the mechs behind these massacres as much as Lynch did.

Lord Arrondale was the Duke of Bleight's heir, but she suspected there was more to this story than there seemed. Lynch had been icily composed on the way here, but he carried himself even more stiffly than usual. He'd checked his pocket watch several times in the carriage and spoken not a word. Grim tension rode his shoulders like a well-cut coat and the bleak, oh-so-expressionless look on his face made her instincts twitch.

"I'm quite all right, sir," she replied, watching him with assessing eyes. They'd argued briefly about her coming with him, but he'd been too distracted to force his will on her. Rosalind had promised to make herself useful taking his notes, when in truth she was desperate to see if this was another mech attack. Her voice lowered. "Did you know Lord Arrondale?"

Lynch shot her a harsh, raw look, his pupils

swallowing his irises and shadows carving deep planes beneath his cheekbones. For a moment she stared into the face of the demon within, and her breath caught behind the stiff boning of her corset.

"He was my cousin," Lynch stated, turning back to look at the house once more.

The absence of that black-eyed gaze made it easier for her to breathe. Rosalind rubbed her knuckles self-consciously against her skirts. She knew he'd been born of the Echelon once, but she hadn't bothered to search for more detail. As far as the world was concerned, Lynch had been cast aside as a rogue and made his own place in the world as a Nighthawk. There was never any mention of family or of his House, because none of it was important anymore.

The man he'd called Byrnes strode toward them, his dark features obscured by the shadows of early evening. He moved with a sinuous and deadly grace, the coldness in his blue eyes rivaling Lynch's. Around his throat a red kerchief lingered and a long sword was strapped over his back. "The house is secure. I've had word sent to the Duke of Bleight."

"When he arrives, have the men stall him and send word," Lynch said. "Don't tell him anything he doesn't need to know at this point." Lynch shot her a fierce look. "If I tell you to get out, then don't argue. Go straight out the back and find one of my men. Instruct them to get you back to Chancery Lane and protect you with their life."

"What aren't you telling me?" Rosalind grabbed a handful of skirts and followed him, the synthetic skin that covered her mech hand pulling against the soft kid-leather insides of her gloves. Tonight she'd planned to let him catch a glimpse of it—just enough to make him think her hand was real. It wouldn't stand up to intense scrutiny, but in the dark and at a distance…

Of course, he had other matters on his mind. Tonight might not be the best opportunity. Lynch held the door open for her. "Bleight despises me. There was some business when I was named rogue concerning Alistair and me. If he's stricken by grief, I find it highly likely he'll make some move against me—or go so far as to blame me. This could become quite a scene."

Rosalind stared up at him, the hard body but a breath away from hers. She could scent the coppery wash of blood through the open door. No doubt Lynch could too. His jaw was tight with strain.

"Do you have your pistol?" he asked quietly.

She nodded.

"Don't use it unless I tell you to." Then he pressed his hand to the small of her back and propelled her through the door.

Inside, the hall was charged with silence. It almost felt as if the house were listening. Each creak of timber beneath her boot heel made her wince. Lynch's presence behind her was almost comforting.

The firm hand in the small of her back directed her through another door. "This way," Lynch murmured and she knew he could smell the death within.

As soon as she saw what lay on the floor, Rosalind stopped in her tracks. Her mind struggled to make sense of the mess, of the red pool that bloated the carpets and the frozen, screaming visage of the elderly woman dead on the floor. Half her throat had been torn out and gashes marred her lavender skirts. From the dark blue-red blood that covered her fingers, it was clear she'd tried to protect herself.

Firm hands slid over Rosalind's shoulders and she relaxed into the touch. Death had never frightened her; she'd dealt it with little remorse, but that had been out of a sense of duty. Not personal. Not murder. This... this had been a woman just sitting down to her white soup, perhaps a smile on her face as she listened to her consort's account of his day. Most consort agreements in the Echelon were business items, nothing more, but the woman had worn her good pearls and the scent of perfume lingered in the air. The silvery-blonde hair had been curled artfully over her shoulder, as if for a beau, and from the roses spilled out of the vase on the table, they'd perhaps been celebrating something.

Rosalind melted into the hard body behind her, feeling numb all over.

"Wait outside," Lynch instructed quietly.

Rosalind turned, tripping on the carpet. Her worst fear—to be bloodied like that, torn apart by a rampaging blue blood. Pausing by the door, she held on to the frame and glanced over her shoulder.

Lynch knelt by the woman's side, his gaze hooded and his mouth a stark line. With a sigh, he reached out and held his palm over the woman's face, then slowly closed her eyes. His hand hovered there, as though to hide the dead woman's face. Then he clenched his fist and dragged it tight against his chest.

The privacy of the moment struck Rosalind. She hesitated at the edge of the dining room. He knew the woman. There was so little in his expression she might have thought him uncaring, but something about the aura of grief around him almost physically hurt.

A clatter of sound as he scraped the plates out of the way and dragged the white tablecloth from the table. Kneeling down, he folded the woman's hands over her chest and then carefully draped the tablecloth over her. It stained with red immediately, the edges soaking up the pool of blood beneath the woman's hair. Lynch slowly turned, emotionless once more.

"Lady Arrondale," he said, as if in explanation. Brushing past her, he strode along the hall, ignoring each door and tributary. Little spatters of dark blood trailed along the checkerboard floor and paintings hung haphazardly as if something had smashed up against the wall. By the stairs, a large smear of blood puddled on the marble tiles and the carved mahogany railing had been destroyed, splinters littering the floor.

Byrnes appeared at the top of the stairs. "He's up here. I didn't think it appropriate to leave him like that. Not with Bleight on his way."

Lynch nodded, taking the stairs two at a time. "How did you kill him?"

Byrnes peered over the rail. His cerulean eyes were almost bright with hunger, as if they saw something she didn't. Long dried blood clung to his right hand and his black sleeve was wet with it. "I couldn't get him off Lady Arrondale. She was still screaming by that stage—somehow she'd locked herself in the dining room and someone heard her cries for help. I was coming back from interviewing the head of the master smith guild and overheard the commotion.

From the look of the house, Arrondale killed everyone else, then went for her." His lips thinned. "I put my gun to the back of his shoulder and pulled the trigger to get his attention. Unfortunately, it was too late for Lady Arrondale."

Lynch glanced over the rail, assessing the bloody marks on the floor and the shattered paintings along the hall. "Just once?"

"I didn't have time for a second shot. He turned on me and I went down. Somehow we ended up there—" Byrnes pointed at the spot below. "I'd lost the pistol by then." He looked up, hard gaze locking on Lynch's. "I had to rip his heart out of his chest. He was trying to gut me." A shudder. "Christ, he was strong."

Lynch surveyed the scene one last time then turned. "Show him to me."

They'd taken the body to the main bedroom upstairs. The cloying scent of blood stained the air and Rosalind swallowed hard as she stepped inside. Someone had dragged a sheet over the body and Lynch strode to it, twitching it aside. His large body blocked her view and for that she was grateful. She'd seen enough macabre sights tonight.

Dropping the sheet, he turned, candlelight washing over his too-smooth features. "I want your report on my desk by morning. You'd best leave. If Bleight sees you, he'll want your head—"

A shout sounded outside. They all spun toward the window and Lynch pushed past, twitching aside the curtains. "Go," he said. "Out the back and return to the guild. Take a small guard."

"Surely the duke wouldn't attack anyone," Rosalind

murmured. Bleight was a vulture who sat on the council and circled for prey, but her dossier said he was once of the most cautious of the Council, choosing to pick his fights and rarely proclaiming them.

Lynch shot her a hard look as Byrnes left the room. "Don't leave my side. Try to be inconspicuous." He swore under his breath, grabbing her arm. "I should never have brought you here."

"Lynch!" someone roared. The sound came from inside the house.

Lynch's grip tightened, then he cursed again and started toward the door.

"Get your goddamned hands off me, you cur!" The voice was sodden with rage. "Lynch! You bastard, where's my son? Where's my bloody son?!"

Lynch stepped up to the rail by the stairs. "Release him." His voice rang through the entry.

Rosalind hovered in the shadows as much as possible. Below her, the old Duke of Bleight threw off the restraining grip of two Nighthawks. His own men, in their dashing red livery, had followed him in and the hallway looked like a sea of red and black. The black outnumbered the red, but not by much.

Dozens of blue bloods. Rosa's eyes narrowed fractionally, her gaze raking the hall. No faces she recognized. Her shoulders relaxed.

"You bastard!" Bleight bellowed. "You vengeful prick! You're behind this! You wanted everything he ever had!"

Lynch stepped forward, tugging at the soft leather gloves he wore. "Your Grace," he said sharply, "perhaps you'd care to discuss this in private? Your son's body has been removed to the bedroom. If you'd like—"

"I'll discuss nothing with you," Bleight hissed, starting up the stairs. "Get out. Get out before I kill you." The old duke's hand lowered to rest on the hilt of his sword. His pale face was even whiter with stress, his eyes glittering with malice.

Below them a half dozen men stiffened at the implied threat. Rosalind straightened as her vision narrowed on the duke. She could almost feel the cool ring of sweat around her garter, where it held her pistol in place.

The sword hissed as it cleared its scabbard. Below, a pair of Nighthawks leaped toward the stairs but Lynch took a commanding step forward, holding up his hand. "I'll leave, Your Grace. But if you would consider having some of my men remain, to examine the—"

"Get out!" Bleight swung the sword, cool gaslight glimmering off the razor edge of the blade.

Lynch ducked and the sword sheared through the elegant railing at the top of the stairs and stuck. Bleight snarled, yanking it free with a force that belied his evident age.

Lips thinning, Lynch stepped back, his hands held in a placating manner in front of him.

What the devil was he doing? Why did he not fight back? Rosalind had seen him in action; the duke didn't stand a chance.

Swinging wildly, the duke slashed forward as Lynch stepped out of the way, his back hitting the wall. Lynch's gaze met hers for a moment and narrowed in warning. Rosalind just had time to realize she'd stepped forward, her hand dipping automatically into her pocket when Bleight followed the direction of Lynch's gaze.

"Is she yours?" the duke asked in a soft, threatening voice.

This close, Rosalind could see the darkness of his pupils threatening to overtake his irises. Her corset tightened and her fingers clamped around the smooth grip of her pistol through the slit in the bottom of her pocket. If he made one move toward her, she'd blow his head off.

"Don't," Lynch warned. For a moment, she thought he referred to the duke, then she realized that his stark gaze was locked on hers.

Reality flooded in. Kill the duke and she'd be executed by dawn. Rosalind's finger rubbed the trigger hesitantly. Trust that Lynch knew what he was doing? Or take action? She hovered on the precipice, staring into the mad duke's eyes. She'd never stop him in time if he attacked her; a blue blood was simply too fast.

Her hand slowly withdrew and she took a shaky breath. Trusting Lynch went against all of her instincts, but she had no choice.

Bleight turned on her with a snarl, the sword cutting through the air. Rosalind threw herself backward, tripping over her skirts and tumbling to the floor. The sword gleamed eerily in the bluish light as it arced toward her.

Then Lynch was between them, slamming his body hard against the duke's. A sharp hiss of pain filled the air and blood spattered her face. The pair staggered into the railing, which gave with a sharp crack.

"*No!*" She snatched at Lynch's cloak, her fingers closing over air, and then they were gone.

The dull smack as they landed dragged her to the edge. She peered through the broken gap of rail as Lynch smashed his elbow into the duke's face. Somehow he'd gotten the upper hand and forced the duke's sword hand to the floor. Grabbing Bleight by the throat, he crouched over him with a snarl.

Around them, both the Nighthawks and the duke's men had danced back, clearing a circle. One of the red-clad guards stepped forward and Lynch looked up, baring his teeth. "Enough!"

Looking down, he smashed the duke's hand to the tiles. The sword clattered free, and as he stood, Lynch kicked it away. He staggered back, clapping a hand to his side.

Blood dripped on the floor.

Rosalind shoved to her feet, hurrying for the stairs. The moment when he'd leaped in front of her flashed before her eyes. He'd taken the blow meant for her.

She couldn't quite name the emotion that gripped her. Lynch shot her a quelling look and Rosalind slowed, her steps flagging. She couldn't see how badly he was bleeding against the black of his leather body armor. Nor could she ask him, not now, in front of the duke and his men. Any sign of weakness and Bleight would be on them.

"We're going," Lynch commanded. He nodded sharply to his men. "I want all preliminary reports completed by morning." Gesturing her to his side, he put his free hand in the small of her back—an almost protective gesture—and ushered her close to his body.

Bleight struggled into a sitting position, spitting blood. "I'll have your head for that—"

Lynch turned swiftly and the duke flinched, some of his men stepping forward with their hands dropping to their weapons. All eyes were upon him as he glared down at the duke. "If you ever make a move against one of mine again, you'll face me in the atrium. I swear it." Then Lynch shoved free and, taking Rosalind by the arm, ushered her to the door.

Nine

"HOW BADLY ARE YOU BLEEDING?"

Lynch pressed back against the carriage seat as the door closed, locking them in darkness. He could hear Perry outside, snapping at the men to get out of her way as she clambered up onto the driver's seat. A rumble started beneath him as Perry kicked the boilers into gear.

"Lynch?"

He dragged his attention back inside as Mrs. Marberry knelt on the seat beside him, her skirts tumbling across his legs. He shouldn't be feeling this weak—damn Bleight. Taking a shuddery breath, he peeled his hand away from the wound in his side and winced. The scent of blood flooded his nose, saliva springing into his mouth. His world was spinning slightly, the warm press of the body beside him his only anchor.

So hot. So tempting. The color drained out of his vision, leaving him with the silvery patina of moonlight across the pale skin of Rosa's throat. Instantly the demon within him leaped to the surface, threatening to drown him. Desire was a sharp ache that cut like a knife, his gut clenching in need. *Christ.*

He grabbed her upper arm, intending to push her away. The muscle beneath his touch tightened but Rosa didn't withdraw. Lynch loomed over her, the subtler scent of lemon and linen washing through him.

He shuddered. "Devil take you, leave me be!" The words were a harsh croak as he clung to sanity by the finest of threads.

"Here," she said grimly, withdrawing something from her reticule. Silver flashed in the moonlight as the steam carriage lurched into motion with a teakettle hiss. The sound of a flask being unscrewed drew his focus and then Rosa was pressing it to his lips.

Blood washed over his tongue. Lynch caught her wrist in surprise, then tipped the flask up. He needed blood. Lots of it—anything to focus his mind and leash the demon within.

Draining the flask, he collapsed back against the plush carriage seats, panting. Rosa took it from him and neatly screwed the lid back on.

He could feel her watching him. The world seemed to fade until it was just the pair of them, breathing softly in the dark interior. Even the pain in his side ebbed to a dull throb as the craving virus began to heal him. Come morning there wouldn't even be a scar, courtesy of his high CV levels.

"Thank you," he said.

Rosa let out a low breath. "I should be thanking *you*. That blade was meant for me. Here." Leaning closer, she fumbled at his chest. "Let me have a look at it."

"It will heal."

Tugging at her gloves, she eased them off, her pale hands finding the buckles to his body armor and snapping one open. Even in the faint moonlight, he caught a glimpse of the scarred back of her left hand and the paler skin. *My father...* He suddenly wanted to know what the man had done to her but he didn't ask. This was the first time she'd ever removed her gloves in front of him and as he glanced up, he realized that she knew he'd been staring at her slightly thickened fingers.

Rosa swiftly glanced down, tugging at another buckle. Heat darkened her cheeks as if embarrassed by his attention. Lynch didn't give a damn about the deformity, but he would respect her wishes in the matter and not mention it.

He winced as the leather breastplate gave way. Built to stop a knife or a blow, it had been poor defense against Bleight's sword.

"Why did he do it?" she asked softly. Taking hold of his undershirt in both hands, she ripped it up the side, baring his skin to her gaze.

Lynch shivered at the chill, feeling the cool blood pulsing down his hip. The blade had taken him high, just beneath the ribs. "Do what?"

Gentle fingertips probed the slash. "Attack you. Why did he think you had something to do with his son's death?"

"I told you, Alistair and I were cousins." Lynch bared his teeth in a silent hiss as she touched a particularly tender spot. "Bleight has long held the position that I desired Alistair's place as heir of the House."

"That couldn't be further from the truth."

"It was the truth," he told her, watching her expression in the flickering light from the passing gaslights. "Once."

Her silence was almost unbearable. A hungry, curious yearning filled her expression. "Of course. You were Lord Arrondale's cousin—which makes you the duke's nephew."

"Third in line to the duchy," he said with a bleak smile. "My father and Bleight were never friends. My father was born an hour after Bleight and he never forgot it."

Her gloved thumb stroked against the bare flesh of his side. "He wanted you to be duke?"

"He pushed me to compete with Alistair in all things, to prove myself. Alistair was heir by right of birth, but I could overthrow him if I chose. All I had to do was duel him in front of the court when we came of age. And kill him." Memory was a sharp stab. He would have done anything for his father, but not that.

Lynch looked down beneath his lashes at the soft fingers that unconsciously stroked his hip. "I don't know why I'm telling you this."

"You're weak," she said, her white teeth flashing a quick smile. "And I'm taking advantage of the moment." Sitting back with a sigh, she tugged her skirts up.

The sight stilled him. Acres of frothy white petticoats gleamed in the weak moonlight, revealing smooth, stocking-clad calves. Taking hold of the hem of her petticoats, she tore them with a sharp rip that made his gut clench.

"What are you doing?" he asked sharply.

"I'm not taking advantage of you in that way. You may relax." Wadding the fine linen into a ball, she tore another long strip, yanking sharply on the material with little care to the fact that his eyes were locked on her ankles.

Tossing her skirts down, Rosa knelt on the seat, bending forward. Shadows enveloped her upper body, but he could still see the faint outline of her breasts as she pressed her makeshift pad to his side. Sliding her arms around his waist, she tugged the long piece of linen around his back and dragged it clear with a determined expression.

Her teeth worried at her lip as she worked. Lynch watched, entirely frozen. He could feel the heat off her body and sense the scant inch between them. She was nothing but darkness and warmth, a shadow of a woman who ignited his desire, his dreams. And instantly he knew that when he was finally alone, he'd dream of her like this.

The thought shocked him. It had been Mercury on his mind, night after night, but there was something about the shadow-wreathed woman in front of him that drew him. A sense of...tenderness.

His own secretary. Bloody hell. If he was one of his men, he'd have strung himself up by the heels.

A tendril of hair brushed his cheek in the dark interior of the carriage, silky-smooth and lemon-scented. With Rosa busy tending his wound, she barely noticed as he turned his head and breathed in the scent of her. Whatever perfume she used, it bathed her skin and drenched her hair as if she'd washed in it.

He could barely discern her natural scent. His mouth went dry at the thought. He yearned to press his face to her throat, to drink in that scent, his body reacting with swift need.

"There," she murmured, tying off the ends of the piece of petticoat. The instant she was done, she tugged her gloves back on as if the lack of them left her vulnerable. "That should hold until we get to the guild."

Lynch sucked in a shaky breath. "Thank you. You're most efficient."

"In all matters." She shot him a soft smile, her dark eyes flashing in the silvery moonlight. Her gaze slowly lowered as she sobered. "You knew Lady Arrondale."

The words were no question.

"Annabelle?" The thought sheared through his desire like a knife.

"You were very gentle with her body."

He sucked in a sharp breath and dragged himself upright. *Annabelle.* Guilt was a sour taste in his mouth. "She was my cousin's consort."

He knew she heard the sharpness in his voice and cursed himself for a fool. He despised speaking of himself; the story had been all through the papers at the time, with every journalist taking it upon himself to form an opinion on the circumstances. Few of them had come close to the truth, but that didn't matter. He'd suspected Bleight behind half of the damned stories, and truth was but a varnish to the duke.

He'd never given a damn before, but something about the close nature of the carriage and Mrs. Marberry's curiosity bit at him.

"Why do you want to know?" he asked her.

"Because…" She floundered for words, a flush of color darkening her skin. His gaze charted the path of it, across her throat and cheeks.

"Idle curiosity is not something I encourage."

The words might have been a slap. Her magnificent eyes jerked to his. "Because I suspect you took more than one wound today. I wanted… I was offering comfort, nothing else." Shoving away from him, she leaned against the door of the carriage and peered out, limned by soft shadows and moonlight.

"You're not curious?"

Lashes fluttered against her pale cheeks as she gazed down at her lap. The line of her nape drew his eyes. He wanted to press his lips there, to lick the lemon scent from her skin and taste her body's salt.

Lynch stilled, arrested by his hunger again. The roar of it surged through his veins. *Just one little taste…to have her beneath him, the knife to her throat, hot blood in his mouth as she struggled weakly.* She was a temptation he never should have brought beneath his roof. For forty years he'd contained his blood urges, and she stomped all over his control as if it were worth nothing. The thought was troubling.

I will beat this.

"I'm curious," she admitted. "Of course I am. But the motivation is not vulgar."

"So your curiosity is personal?"

Silence. It lingered for long moments, during which he found himself examining her again, his fingers tightening their grip on the carriage seat.

"Yes, it's personal." A sharp look away.

He wasn't the only one afflicted by this madness. Fighting his body, he forced himself to think of Annabelle, lying on the floor with betrayal written all over her face.

It worked, like a splash of ice water to the face.

"I told you," he said simply, "Alistair and I competed in all things."

"You loved her?"

"I don't know. I was fifteen." He breathed a harsh laugh. "I was consumed by her with all the rabid fascination of a young man. And I wanted to win her. Neither Alistair nor I wished to push our rivalry so far as a duel, so Annabelle became the prize."

"And he won?"

Silence. This time of his own making. Lynch slowly shut his eyes, the image of Annabelle painted behind his eyeballs. He hadn't seen her in years. The shadow of age had surprised him, but he could recognize her still, in the elegant lines of her cheekbones and those lips that had been made to laugh. Guilt was a twisting sensation within his chest. Guilt, regret, and sorrow...

"My apologies," she murmured. "I didn't realize how strongly you still cared."

"I've not seen her in more than thirty years," he replied. An old wound, but this had only seemed to knock the scab off it. "They tell me he was kind to her."

Rosa seemed to wrestle with something. Slowly she reached out, her hand sliding over his. A gentling touch, but still a tentative one, as though she had to force herself to do it.

"My husband..." she began, and faltered. "It wasn't...wasn't love for me. Not at first. Indeed, I set

about luring him into the marriage quite purposely."
At this, she darted a glance at him, as if to see how he
took this revelation. "I hate that now that he's gone.
He loved me so much and I regret…so many things."

Lynch stroked her thumb through the kid leather,
simply listening.

"The guilt never goes away but the feeling fades,"
she admitted bleakly. "At the end, when he realized
what I'd done… I saw it in his face, you know? He
hated me in that moment. But if he had survived, I
wouldn't care if he still hated me. As long as he were
alive. That's all that matters."

Her voice trailed off, and he listened to the sound
of her breathing, the feel of her hand anchoring him.

"What do you think happened?" Rosa whispered.
"If your cousin cared for his wife, as you say, what
could have made him kill her?"

"I don't know." Lynch's gaze drifted to the
window. He squeezed her fingers, feeling strangely
vulnerable. "But I intend to find out."

Rows of gaslights gleamed in the night as the
carriage rolled past a park. Something caught his eye
as his gaze lowered to Rosa's hand and Lynch's head
snapped back to the window. There, standing by a
grove of trees was a familiar figure smothered in a
black silk cloak.

Mercury.

His heart leaped into his throat, throwing off the
pall of grief. Exhilaration flooded through him. "Stop
the carriage!" he bellowed, yanking at the door and
dropping Rosa's hand.

The masked figure blew him a kiss, then stepped

back into the grove. Lynch opened the door while the carriage was still moving and leaped out, staggering as he landed. He clapped a hand to his ribs. *Cursed weakness.* Of all the times for his body to give out on him.

"Sir?" Perry shut off the boilers and knelt on the edge of the driving seat, peering into the darkness intently.

"Mercury," he snapped, gesturing to the park. "I saw her in the trees. Get after her." He drew sticky fingers away from his side. No point running after her himself. Frustration soared through him.

Perry leaped down into the street and sprinted toward the park.

Skirts rustled and then Rosa was sliding under his arm to help hold him up, her dark eyes raking his face. "What's going on?" She looked down and paled. "You've torn your wound open."

"It will heal." He stared after Perry. On the other side of the park an engine hissed to life as a steam carriage pulled away from the curb. "Damn it." He'd bet his last penny that Mercury was in that carriage. Perry would lose her and he didn't know how to drive the carriage himself in order to give chase.

Rosa pressed her gloved hand against his side. "You need to sit back down and rest—"

"It won't kill me," he said absently.

"No, but you'll end up bedridden for days at this rate," she replied tartly.

That caught his attention. Lynch looked down in bemusement as his secretary clucked and scolded him back into the carriage. Her expression was furious as she tugged his undershirt back up and reexamined her bandaging.

"Of all the rotten timing," she muttered under her breath. "It doesn't look too bad. The bleeding is slowing. However, if you move suddenly again, I shall be most put out with you. Sit there and don't move until we reach the guild."

One didn't argue with a woman with that kind of tone. Lynch sank back into the leather seats.

Perry arrived at the door, breathing hard. "Lost them, sir. They had a driver waiting—a man wearing similar cologne to what Garrett prefers. Looked like he was wearing some sort of half mask over his lower face. And a tall woman on the back of the carriage, like a footman. She helped hustle the masked woman into the carriage."

"Not your fault." Lynch's eyes narrowed in the direction Mercury had disappeared into. "They planned this meeting."

But why? Nothing had come of it. Mercury had meant to be seen. Was she sending him a message? A taunt? Or was her presence in connection to the death of Alistair?

"Do you want me to track them?" Perry asked.

"You can do that?" Rosa's head jerked up.

"Perry can trace scents even I can't," he admitted, then turned back to Perry and shook his head. Most of the men would be returning to the guild. There was no way he was sending Perry after the revolutionaries on her own—not so soon after nearly losing Garrett.

"When we return to the guild, I want you to take three of the men and see if the scent trail's still alive," he murmured, easing back in the seat. "Don't confront them and don't be caught alone. You can give me your report in the morning."

Whatever Mercury's purpose, for tonight he had other concerns he was forced to prioritize.

∽◆∾

Lynch hadn't been able to examine the body or the house and knew Bleight would never allow either now.

Fitz had stitched the wound in his side and they'd propped him here hours ago. Staring across the dark shadows of his study, Lynch silently ran through what he knew of the case. He'd examined both Haversham and Falcone himself. There'd been no sign of needle marks, no toxins or poisons in either of their cups and no evidence in the house to suggest a reason behind this insanity.

Just that sticky sweet smell he'd noticed in both houses.

He could only assume that Alistair's bout of insanity would be the same.

Scraping his hair out of his face, he stared at the desktop. His mind felt dull tonight—grief, most likely. He could barely think. Every time he chased a thought, it skittered away, dissolving into mist. The confrontation with Mercury kept leaping to the forefront of his mind, despite the need to focus on Alistair.

Why had she appeared tonight? Had she tracked him from Alistair's house? Was she involved with his death? If she was... His fist clenched. There would be no mercy if she was.

A sharp rap at the door sounded.

Perry. He could tell by the way she waited for his

response. "Yes?" he called, glancing at the clock. She'd been gone only three hours. This wouldn't be good news.

Perry slipped in through the door, a light rain misting her hair and eyelashes. "Lost them," she said. "I got a trail on them for several streets, then it started to rain."

"Which direction were they heading?"

"The docks by the East End."

Lynch sat back in his chair and eyed the way she clasped her hands behind her back. "You have something else to report."

Perry sighed. "When I lost the trail, I went back to Holland Park Avenue. I managed to pick up a scent from the man wearing cologne in the opposite alley. He never approached the house, but I assume he was watching for you."

"Not involved in the attack then," Lynch muttered. "Which means their interest was in me. But why?"

"I couldn't say, sir." She took a deep breath. "There's something else. The taller woman is verwulfen. I'll swear it."

Interesting.

"I've sent two of the men out to check the registry, to see if they can identify a woman," she said.

The treaty with Scandinavia had introduced a change in the laws, freeing all of the verwulfen in the Empire from slavery. Yet, all newly freed verwulfen were required to register at each city and town they passed through.

"Excellent." The pieces were starting to fall into place. Lynch had always been patient; the spider's web was starting to tingle, the trap slowly drawing in on Mercury. A flutter of anticipation stirred in his gut.

"You look exhausted," he said. "Clock off and get some rest. You did well tonight."

Perry didn't quite smile at the rare praise, but she nodded and took her leave.

Slowly his gaze focused on the desk in front of him and he realized there was a piece of folded vellum popped beside his inkwell.

Scent wafted off the paper—Rosa's scent, reminding him of spring days and sunshine, of laughter and linen sheets. Despite his mood, he felt his shoulders ease. He'd wanted a secretary who wasn't afraid of him, though he had no idea what to do with her.

Be careful what you wish for.

Well, she certainly didn't fear him, and he had to admire her ingenuity with the flask of blood. He also admired certain other aspects of her person but those were better left unthought of.

Flicking open the letter with his thumbnail, he ran his gaze across the sheet. Moonlight glanced over his shoulder, giving him just enough light to understand the slanting script.

Dear Sir,

They say that cleanliness is next to godliness, which explains your lack of reverence. I have therefore taken it upon myself to save you from sinning. You'll find your papers filed in my office; sorted, alphabetized, and ironed flat.

I would appreciate it if you could keep them this way, though I have low hopes. With all due respect...

Your servant,
Mrs. Marberry

She must have written it prior to this afternoon. And he in his blustering state had not noticed it.

Lynch traced the curl of her name, his lips softening. Blasted woman. She had an audacity that astounded him.

She had also managed to distract, if only momentarily.

Lack of reverence indeed. He knew precisely who lacked reverence, whether he and his kind had been excommunicated or not. The admission spoke of her middle-class upbringing; the Echelon had long since turned its back on a church that disavowed them for being demons. As if in retaliation, faith was becoming a surprisingly strong counterpoint amongst the poor and middle classes these days. They had no churches—the Echelon had torn them down—but he'd heard of secret gatherings in shadowy places.

Lack of reverence. His eyes narrowed and he put the letter down, reaching for his drawer to try and find where she'd put his paper.

Bloody woman.

⁓

"You didn't think to ask me if you should make an appearance tonight?" Rosalind snarled, striding along the dark, damp passage.

"Finding someone of your height to play Mercury were your suggestion," Ingrid reminded her. "Keep his lordship from suspecting you, eh?"

Rosalind's lips compressed. "He was injured."

"Exactly. I could smell the blood on him when he come out of that mansion." There was a long moment of silence and Rosalind realized that Ingrid was wondering why she would care. "Knew he couldn't give chase," the other woman muttered. "Perfect opportunity to dress Molly up in a cape and mask. We just took advantage of the situation."

Which was precisely what she would have done in Ingrid's situation. Rosalind slowed as she neared a door. What the hell was wrong with her? Lynch hadn't been injured, not badly... Though she felt an odd discomfort at the thought of his blood on her fingers. The ruse with Molly would assuage any doubts he might own if she slipped up by accident. *Act. Don't react*, Balfour had always said.

Holding the flickering gas lamp high, Rosalind slipped through the door. "I just wish you'd have given me some warning," she murmured.

Shadows melted away from the encroaching light, revealing enormous man-shaped statues in the dark. Light gleamed on steel, reflecting back off the empty glass eye slit of the creature in front of her.

"One hundred and twelve," Rosalind said, staring down the rows of automatons. "And not enough."

"Calculations indicate each of our Cyclops are worth four of the Echelon's metaljackets," Ingrid said with a shrug. She tucked a cheroot between her full lips and struck a match. Red phosphorus burned in the cold, dark cellars, then Ingrid shook it out.

The other woman disdained the chill, wearing naught more than a gentleman's shirt rolled up to the elbows and a pair of tight, men's breeches. Her thick, dark hair was pulled back tight into a chignon that left her high cheekbones bare. Sucking back on the cheroot, she blew the sweet-scented smoke through the room, running a bare hand over the steel-plated arm of the Cyclops.

Rosalind sighed. "And they have over a thousand of those."

"We'll make enough."

"Eventually." At that, her lips thinned. Ever since the mechs had abandoned the humanist cause and vanished, the secret production of the Cyclops had ground to a halt. She could be patient—she would be—but she was fast running out of options. And now that Lynch had discovered her supply smuggling route out of the enclaves, she had even fewer. "Have you finished inquiring in the enclaves for a blacksmith?"

"Mordecai's evidently beaten us to it. Not a mech amongst them will offer us help."

"Then we look elsewhere. Kidnap one of the Echelon's master smiths."

Ingrid choked on her cheroot. "Are you insane? The Echelon has them locked up tighter than a virgin's drawers."

"Then where?" she snapped, spinning on her heel and staring at the silent, motionless giants. Based on the metaljackets' blueprint, they'd been designed so that each heavy breastplate opened wide for a human to haul themself inside and manipulate the metal monster from within. It gave them a greater dexterity and manipulation, with a human's reactions safely guarded behind the thick steel body armor. Coupled with the cannons that were fitted to each arm, they could belch Greek fire accurately up to twenty feet.

"I need men to wield them," she continued. "And men to build them. I don't have either at the moment."

"You've always been patient enough to wait."

"That was before Jeremy vanished!" Cursing under her breath, Rosalind slapped her hand against the nearest Cyclops. Pain stung her palm, bringing with it a clarity she knew she needed. She was failing—failing her brother, failing Jack and Ingrid by this odd softening toward her enemy, and failing Nate's final dream to restore human rights in Britain. Somehow, speaking of him tonight to Lynch had stirred her guilt to tormenting levels. "Did you circle the guild?"

"Aye. No sign of Jeremy's scent. I've been in the city too—"

"Ingrid!" she snapped, turning on her friend. "You take too many risks. One look at your eyes and every blue blood in the city would know precisely what you are."

As if to spite her, Ingrid lifted her gaze, those metallic golden irises catching the light. "The laws against verwulfen have been revoked. And there's enough trickling in from Manchester and the Pits for one more not to be noticed."

"That doesn't mean you're safe." A blue blood was a verwulfen's natural enemy. Even Ingrid's berserker-fueled strength wouldn't help her if there were enough of them. "Promise me you won't take any more risks. Don't go near the city again—don't show your eyes."

Ingrid's shoulders swelled, a look of burning indignation narrowing her eyes. "I've as much a right as you," she growled softly. "I've hidden these bloody eyes half my life, down here in the dark. Now that the blue bloods have signed a truce with the Scandinavian verwulfen clans, I don't have to hide anymore." Her expression turned stubborn. "I won't. It kills me to be cooped up down here, in these bloody tunnels."

Rosalind clasped Ingrid's hand between her own—one of the few who would dare when Ingrid was in this mood. The skin beneath her right palm was burning hot. The loupe virus that made Ingrid what she was had done more than just make her super-humanly strong. "I know." Rosalind's voice softened. "I'm just worried that the truce is still too new. The blue bloods have long memories and some of them are so old they still live in the past." She squeezed her friend's hand. "If you go above, take several of the men. Or Jack, even."

Ingrid tossed the cheroot to the floor and ground it beneath her heel, expressionless. The very blankness of her face told Rosalind how upset she was. Ingrid had long since learned to keep her temper leashed for fear of hurting someone, and her control showed in the stiff line of her shoulders.

"Truce?"

Ingrid glared at her moodily, then nodded. Rosalind grabbed her hand in a rough shake, squeezing with her iron fingers. Ingrid's nostrils flared, but she squeezed back. The seconds dragged out, then Ingrid shoved her away, cursing under her breath.

Rosalind hit the wall and laughed—an old ritual that never failed to soothe Ingrid's savage temper. She flexed the metal fingers, feeling the muscle grab through her forearm where the steel cables met tendon.

"If you've broken my hand, you'll have to pay for it," Rosalind warned with a smile.

Ingrid rolled her eyes. "I'll kidnap a master smith."

Rosalind's mirth faded at the reminder. She pushed away from the wall. "Come. We'd best get going after these mechs. I'll need some sleep tonight if I'm going to manage my lord Nighthawk on the morrow." The thought tightened something within her—a feeling of shivery anticipation.

She was so distracted she didn't even notice the sharp look her friend gave her.

Ten

ROSALIND YAWNED AS SHE ENTERED HER STUDY AT THE guild. She'd spent half the night searching for the missing mechs. There was no sign of them anywhere in the blacksmiths, the iron foundries, or the enclaves, where they might be working steel. There were plenty of whispers about the massacres in the city, however.

Closing the door, she blinked. Something seemed out of place.

The sense of wrongness became immediately evident. Her desk was piled with a mishmash of folders, abandoned paperwork hanging precariously from the top of the pile.

The culprit was nowhere in sight.

He'd found her note. Rosalind took a step forward, surveying the scene of devastation. In the wake of all that had occurred last night, she'd quite forgotten it.

Poor timing on her behalf perhaps, though she'd been unable to help herself at the time—that rash, impulsive feeling she could never quite escape.

Control helps, she told herself, eyeing the massive pile and trying to smother her first instinct, which was retaliation. Balfour had taught her that, and while she hated him, she would use the lessons he'd given her to master her own impulses.

Finding order in this chaos, however... She sighed and reached for the top sheaf of paper. The writing was barely legible, an impatient type of script, as if Lynch couldn't get the words out swiftly enough.

> *Mrs. Marberry,*
> *Since you evidently have so little to do, I have found some old case files for you to sort. Some of them—the 1863 files, I think—refer to a rash of odd poisonings in the city. I want those files on my desk by noon. There are also lists of the blacksmiths in the city. I want them all cross-referenced against the metalworking guild's records to see who is capable of creating bio-mech parts. The guild records are...somewhere in the pile.*
> > *Sincerely,*
> > *Lynch*
> *P.S. I rarely sin, and when I do, it is completely intentional. I have no need of saving.*

Rosalind's lips parted as she stared at the enormous mess in front of her and then curved up in a rare smile. If he thought this was the end of it, he was wrong. Eyes narrowing, she reached for a piece of paper and her pen.

❦

The clock on the mantel ticked twelve.

Rosalind put down the last of the files and stared at

it. There'd been no sign of Lynch all morning, which should have been a good thing. It left her with time enough to dwell on her next move regarding the mechs and Jeremy's continued absence.

Jeremy. There had to be some sign of him somewhere, some word. She couldn't believe he'd perished in the bombing. She'd know. Wouldn't she? He'd practically been hers to raise.

It was the first time she'd ever considered that possibility. All the bodies had been accounted for, according to the newspapers. But what if the newspapers hadn't been allowed to know the full body count? What if, for some reason, the true body count had been kept quiet?

Her breath quickened. The unfamiliar corset clamped around her ribs like an enormous fist, slowly squeezing, and heat sprang up behind her eyes. *Don't.* She shoved away from the desk, moving unconsciously toward the soft afternoon light that streamed through the window. *Don't think about it. Keep moving. Keep hunting him. You'll find him.*

Rosalind rubbed at the knuckles of her false hand, feeling the smooth join of each ball and socket through the thin satin gloves that stretched to her elbows. It ached sometimes, as if the limb were still there. Now was one of those times.

Below her, the world came and went, tiny little men in caps and coats, the ladies sporting sober bonnets and dark dresses. This wasn't the heart of the city where the Echelon roamed in all their peacock finery. The people below her were staid, middle class, human. Her kind of people. Those she fought for. Those she'd sacrificed for.

To the point where she'd forgotten her impressionable little brother, guilt whispered. So focused on the Cyclops plan that she'd barely had time for him, focused on what she owed Nate.

Why couldn't she find him? The ache in her chest was so fierce she could barely breathe.

Action. Take action.

Emotion crippled a man—or woman. If you couldn't lock it away, then it was best to distract oneself with affirmative action.

Rosalind took a slow, steady breath. Lynch was the answer. She needed to get inside his head and find out what he knew about Jeremy and the bombing of the tower.

No matter what she had to do to get that information.

❧

The observatory was cool, despite the warmth of the autumn sun outside. Lynch crossed to the north wall, with its map of the stars and the crank that opened up the roof to the skies above. Grabbing the shaft, he unlocked it with a swift flick of the finger and pulled the lever that would open it. The process had been a laborious one, featuring crank and handle, until Fitz had taken one look at the system ten years ago and mechanized it.

Probably a good thing, as the newly knit wound in his side gave a warning pull as he released the lever. Though he'd protested his fitness to his men, Doyle had taken one look at him and instructed a day of rest. Frustration had no handle on the feeling that ran through him.

His gaze narrowed on the beakers across the room and the steady drip of distillation. The observatory wasn't only used to stargaze; indeed, with London's smog he rarely used it for that purpose at all anymore. Instead, it had become part laboratory, part retreat. It was only here that he could force himself to stop thinking about work.

The brass dome opened with a steely rasp, like a flower revealing its petals to the sun. A fresh breeze stirred the lapel on his coat and sunlight spilled across the stone floor of the observatory, cutting off just before it reached him. Lynch skirted its edges and peered into the first beaker and the pale, tasteless liquid within. A rare poison he'd been working with for months, which could create a catatonic, almost deathlike trance.

No sign of Mercury, either on the streets or in his dreams. No, last night had been a torment of its own making, featuring the temptation that was currently sorting out his folders and keeping him from his rooms—fever dreams full of all manners of sin.

Lynch's mouth firmed and he turned on the distillator Fitz had designed for him. The small boiler pack shuddered to life, the water within vibrating quietly. He'd give it five minutes and then steam would be filling this small corner of the observatory, quietly distilling his poisons.

Quiet footsteps caught his attention. Almost too soft to be any of the men. The first light traces of lemon perfume caught his nose.

Not yet. He wasn't ready yet. He growled a curse under his breath and turned just as Mrs. Marberry carried a tray into the room. Sunlight spilled over her and she looked up, her eyes widening in shy surprise as she took in the open roof. The expression on her face was muted and yet struck him as more real than any other he'd seen from her.

Genuine, he thought, and wondered why that felt so right.

"Good morning," he said, noting that the gray gown she wore fit like a glove. Black velvet buttons ran from her throat to her waist, but the fabric there curved over her hips tightly before spilling to the floor. Her bustle hinted at the soft curves of her bottom as she turned in a slow circle, looking up, and his mouth went dry at the long slope of neck revealed by the action. Coppery red hair trailed in loose tendrils from her chignon, caressing her throat. In the sunlight she was a creature of fire, her porcelain skin almost ethereal.

He wanted to put his hands on that fabric, to tear at it until he'd stripped her naked. The color slowly drained from his vision and Lynch took a sharp breath, jerking his eyes away. His pulse ticked heavily in his ears, a dull throbbing beat that should serve as warning to any blue blood.

"It's afternoon I believe," she said, placing the tray on a messy desk. "Doyle said you asked me to bring a tray to your observatory." Her voice faded as she evidently turned her back on him, examining the contents of the room with interest. "What the devil is—"

Lynch looked up just as she reached for a curious spiked object on one of his workbenches. "Don't!" he snapped, leaping across the room toward her.

His arms locked around her waist as her gloved

finger brushed over the steel tips on the back of the mechanical hedgehog. Once activated, the pressure build-up caused each spine to explode outward.

Lynch ended up with a soft, warm armful of serge and velvet that gasped against his chest. Rosa caught a handful of his cravat, a steely, frightened expression on her face before it suddenly smoothed out.

"Goodness," she said, her breath catching. "You startled me."

The fingers of her left hand were locked around the crisp white linen of his cravat. Lynch cleared his throat. "You're strangling me."

Instantly she let him go.

Lynch reached for her right hand then paused. "May I?"

She considered his outstretched hand dubiously, then slowly placed her fingers within his grasp. "What is it? What's wrong?"

He tilted her hand over, reaching for the tips of her gloves. Rosalind sucked in a sharp breath and Lynch stilled, his gaze lifting to hers. "The tips are poisoned with curare, a very dangerous poison from South America." He slowly tugged at the glove, sliding it over her hand. "I need to make sure you didn't break the skin."

Reluctance made her spine steel. He could feel her body trembling beneath the hand that stroked the small of her back as he dragged the glove free.

"I barely touched it," she whispered.

"Please."

Her hand was small and pale, the skin soft against his. Lynch slowly turned it over, examining the unmarked pads of her fingertips. Relief spread through his chest, and his thumb stroked the indentation across her palm. "No cuts."

"I could have told you that." The tremble was gone from her voice, but something about her tone caught his attention.

She was watching his thumb through half-lidded, wary eyes. Lynch stopped the movement, suddenly aware of how intimate this was. The blue veins of her wrist were splayed vulnerably in front of him—a temptation and a mockery. As if she were aware of where his gaze had dropped, she stiffened.

He let her go. "I don't take my blood directly from the source," he said, putting a step between them.

Rosa jerked her hand to her chest, meeting his gaze with smoky, dark eyes. "You don't?"

He shook his head and crossed to the tray on his desk, heart still thundering in his ears. The world was gray, but somehow Mrs. Marberry seemed like a shining light within it, the sound of her own rapid heartbeat drawing his attention like the predator he was.

Someone—Doyle, no doubt—had seen fit to provide him with blud-wein. He poured a shot of it and threw it back, so aware of her that he could almost feel her gaze on the back of his neck.

"I'm a rogue, Mrs. Marberry. I buy my blood from the draining factories—or what's left of them." Blood that was taken in the blood taxes the Echelon had forced upon the populace for years. He slowly stoppered the decanter. "I don't have the kind of living to support a thrall."

"But surely—"

"No," he replied firmly. "I've never taken from the vein."

Silence settled heavily over the room. Lynch gathered himself and turned to face her. Rosa still clutched her arm, staring at him with that burning curiosity he often saw in her gaze.

"You want to know why," he said, and the gray washed out of his vision suddenly.

Color flooded into her cheeks. "Of course not."

"Surprising," he noted, almost to himself. "You've shown little restraint in the past, unless it happens to involve yourself or unless you're referring to me directly as a blue blood." He saw the little flinch she couldn't hide and refused to give in to guilt. "You don't like to think of me as a blue blood." No shock this time, but he knew he'd hit a nerve. "You make me very curious about your history, Rosa. And your humanist tendencies."

The blood drained out of her face. "My what?"

Interesting. He picked up the glass he'd used and grabbed the decanter. Taking a seat on the settee, he cocked his boots on the table and poured himself another. Rosa still hadn't moved, but tension radiated through her frame, as though she were prepared to flee at any moment. Her bare hand clutched the glove as if it were a lifeline.

"You read the pamphlets," he said, taking pity on her. "You know enough to make me think you sympathize with the humanist cause if nothing else. Very few humans have an understanding of hemlock and its applications. I would also suspect an incident in your past involving a blue blood."

Some color had returned to her cheeks. "And why would you suspect that?"

"The pistol," he replied bluntly. "Your fear of me and my men, the way you don't like to be touched or locked in a small space with me. The only time you weren't frightened to be in the carriage together was when I was wounded and therefore, in your mind, vulnerable."

She stared at him like a cornered animal. "I'm not afraid of you."

Lynch cocked a brow.

"I'm not," she snapped, her fists clenching.

"Then you are wary. And that makes me suspect you have run afoul of a blue blood."

She dragged her glove back on as if it were armor. "My father was a blue blood," she told him. "My mother had been his thrall but she fled when...when my younger brother was born. Unfortunately, she passed away; the streets were not kind to her and we had to learn to make do, which should explain the pistol. Old habits die hard." Dark lashes closed over her eyes. "My father found us when I was ten, so I have...a healthy respect for blue bloods and what they can do. That is all."

The truth perhaps, but far from the whole of it. If her father was a blue blood, that meant she had genteel origins. *Who?* He forced the thought away; time for that later. He could be patient, and everything he knew about her said he would need to be.

Lynch sipped at his blud-wein, knowing that the sight of it disturbed her. "Your father hurt you—?"

"My lord," she replied icily, "I believe this is

completely outside conventional conversation. You have no right—"

"To poke and pry? Perhaps I share your curiosity, but instead of breaking into locked rooms—the means of which interests me, by the way—I am asking you."

The look she shot him was by no means friendly. "I didn't break in; the door wasn't locked."

Lynch sat forward, putting his glass down. "Now that," he said, "is a lie. Though you do it so well I almost cannot tell." Another sobering silence. He gestured to the seat opposite him. "Sit. Why do we not dispense with this dancing around?"

"I have work to do."

"I'll very generously grant you a lunch hour."

Still she hesitated.

"And I shall offer you a truth in exchange for one," he said, knowing that curiosity was her downfall. He reached out and lifted the lid off the tray in front of him, revealing a spread of small cucumber sandwiches, a plate of spiced cake, and a platter of biscuits. A pot of tea steamed beside it. "Besides, I didn't request this food for myself, obviously. I have been remiss in feeding you since you started."

"I don't mind."

"You mean," he said, looking up over the tray, "that you do not wish to tell me your truths." He watched the mutinous flare in her eyes. "I have four hundred and fifty Nighthawks, Mrs. Marberry. Don't make me too curious. And I'll warn you that you are most certainly stirring my interest, though I doubt that was your intention."

She sat, though the stiff way she perched across

from him indicated her mood. Lynch leaned back in the chair, his long legs stretched out in front of him. He had dozens of questions and not nearly enough answers about her, and every evasive response only gave him more questions.

"Eat."

"I'm not hungry."

He observed her. "Yes, you are."

"Are you always so accurate, my lord?"

"I have had a lot of years to learn when someone is lying to me." He leaned forward and poured her tea. "Lemon," he murmured. "And one sugar, I believe?"

Mrs. Marberry stared at him. "You know how I take my tea."

"I observe everything, Rosa." The use of her name was entirely deliberate. This wasn't an interrogation—not yet—but there were certain questions about her that he needed to know the answer to. Certain... doubts. And while he had the time—enforced rest, so to speak—he might as well satisfy his curiosity.

"Thank you," she murmured, accepting the cup and saucer. She sat it on her lap, as if it were a barrier between them.

Good. He wanted her uncomfortable. He wanted her to spill her secrets.

Rosa's hands curled around the teacup as if seeking its warmth. "May I go first then? Since I have given you many truths already."

He spread his arms over the back of the chair and inclined his head. "I believe only some of them were truths, but as a gentleman I'll allow my lady to go first."

"Too kind." She sipped her tea, consideration

warming her eyes. "You loved Annabelle. Have you ever loved another woman?"

A direct volley. She was seeking to put him on the back foot. Lynch smiled lazily. "No. I learned my lesson once, Rosa. I am not so eager to repeat the experience."

Her eyes narrowed. "But its—"

"My turn," he cut her off. "You never denied my suggestion that you have humanist tendencies. I find that very curious."

"Hmm." She took refuge in her tea. "I don't believe that's a question."

"Do you have humanist sympathies?"

Porcelain chimed as she put her cup down and examined the tray of sandwiches. "I'm human, sir. Of course I have humanist tendencies." Her eyes met his, flashing with an emotion he couldn't quite name. "You wouldn't understand. You have rights. I don't. Every man and woman in the city secretly wonders if it might be better if the humanists succeeded."

"I have rights, do I?" Lynch mused, half to himself. "I might have to explain that to the prince consort the next time we meet."

Rosa selected a sandwich for her plate, her black satin glove hovering over them. "I don't forget that you're a rogue. But you're certainly in no fear of being molested in the street for your blood." Her fingers dipped and swooped, filling her plate. "I'm not strong enough to fight a blue blood off. They could leave me to bleed to death in a gutter and no one would dare say a thing. So yes, I do have humanist sympathies."

Nibbling at her sandwich, she looked completely at ease. But she'd put her glove back on. Sitting down to eat was considered the only respectable time a woman could show her wrists to a blue blood and she hadn't.

He filed that thought away, wondering why she thought she was safe with her gloves on. Did she not consider her bare throat, with the edging of black lace that taunted him?

"I wish you wouldn't watch me eat," she murmured, wiping her lips with a napkin.

I wasn't. He dropped his gaze. There was a chessboard seated on the lamp table beside him. He gestured to it. "Do you play?"

"A little."

She was toying with him. Lynch dragged it across to the table between them and cleared a space. "It will give you some sense of privacy." And himself further insight into the mystery of her character. He swiftly set it up, placing the pieces on the smooth lacquered board.

"Not black, sir?"

He glanced down at the white pieces in front of him. "White moves first." A flashing of his teeth, perhaps a smile. "I'm a man. I attack."

"Far too blatant a proposition," she shot back, watching as he placed his first piece. "That is an aggressive move—but there are others that are more aggressive. I think you're trying to screen me from your true purpose. And that"—she eyed him with a dangerous little smile—"is far more like your nature than such a bland assessment."

Lynch actually smiled. "Touché."

"So I must presume you have another strategy in mind," she replied, examining the board with interest.

Her dainty little hand hovered over her knight, then back to a pawn. She placed it directly in front of his. A challenge to see if he would take the bait.

He moved his knight to a threatening location, giving her a bland look. She'd wanted to attack first but had restrained herself. Interesting. "I always have another strategy."

"Mmm." She dragged her chair closer, leaning over the board with her chin cupped in her hand. "My turn: What did you mean when you told the Duke of Bleight you'd see him in the atrium if he moved against you and yours again?"

"He's always feared my ambition," Lynch replied, watching her fingers hawkishly. Knight to the center. "And he's getting older, with no direct heir except for a tangle of distant cousins. The thought that I might challenge him for the duchy is the only thing that can keep him in check."

"Would you ever consider challenging him?"

"I'm a rogue, Rosa." He ignored the fact that this was a second question and moved his knight to counteract her. "I can't hold titles or any position in society. He should realize that, but he's too blinded by his fear of me."

She slipped a pawn across the board as if the move were inconsequential. "And if he does break the pact, will you challenge him?"

"Yes," he said firmly, capturing her pawn. She was playing almost recklessly. He frowned. Recklessly or trying to lull him? "I told him I would; therefore, I will. I can't afford to go back on my word, though. It would gain me nothing."

"You wouldn't break your word, even if you could, would you?" she asked, looking up. The sight of her eyes arrested him for a moment; they glittered with an intense emotion he couldn't name. "I admire that, my lord. You're not the man I expected to find."

"Lynch," he corrected, holding her gaze. "I am no lord."

"But you could have been." Her gaze softened. "You must hate them for what they took from you."

A tight little smile crossed his lips. "Took from me? Whatever makes you think the choice wasn't mine?"

She knocked over her own rook in surprise. "I—I don't understand."

"No? You haven't heard the story? You must be one of the few who haven't." He reached forward and picked up her rook, his fingers brushing her glove. Rosa flinched but she allowed the touch. "Allow me," he murmured.

Some devil took hold of him. He set the rook upright and slid his little finger around hers, linking them. The satin was delicious and warm, so smooth against his skin. His lids lowered, thinking of that small hand on other parts of his body, stroking, soothing. Her gloves still on but nothing else as she knelt before him. All of that gorgeous red hair tumbling down her naked spine, caressing the tops of her thighs. His mouth went dry at the thought.

Their gazes locked.

Rosa's lips parted breathlessly, as if she could see exactly what he was picturing. The room felt thick with silence, each slow tick of the clock on the mantel striking loudly in the background. The air between them was charged with tension. He could have let her go. He should have, but the tiny interlocking of their fingers seemed so innocuous. So innocent.

Hardly dangerous at all.

He looked down and soothed his thumb over the backs of her knuckles. Why the fascination with her hands? Perhaps because she hid them from him? He was tempted to peel the glove off and press his lips to the smooth skin of her wrist, to feel the kick of her pulse against his tongue. Blood pounded through his temples. For once, he understood why a woman's hands should always be gloved.

Rosa sucked in a sharp breath, as if she hadn't taken one since he'd touched her. "My lord?" A whisper, tight with need.

Damnation. He let her go, digging his fingers into the hard muscle of his thigh. His erection strained against the tight leather of his breeches, the muscles in his abdomen clenched. "My turn," he said hoarsely.

He raked through questions in his mind. *Why don't you like having your hands touched? What did your father do to them? Who taught you to use a pistol?* All of them sensible questions he wanted answers to. Instead, another arrested him.

"You said you didn't love your husband at first. Did you ever love him?"

Rosa yanked her hand back to her side and pressed them both into her skirts. "That's very forward."

"I told you about Annabelle," he replied. "And let's not pretend you are shy or retiring. Tell me what he was like."

Silence. "Nathaniel was a good man. Ambitious

but kind. I thought it a fault at first, for he was always looking for the good in people, even when it wasn't there. So different from myself." She stilled. "I never realized what I felt for him until he was gone."

Finally, some truth from her. Though it bothered him in a way he wouldn't have expected. Lynch eyed the chessboard and realized he'd lost his entire strategy—with just one touch of her hand. He shoved a knight forward and leaned back.

"Now tell me what you meant about the choice of becoming a rogue being yours," she said. Hot color stained her throat. The question about her husband had somehow touched a nerve.

"I hadn't finished yet. I answered three questions in a row before. You owe me another two."

A flare of temper in her eyes. Swiftly concealed. "Very well."

"How long ago did your husband pass?"

"Eight years," she said too quickly.

"And you never married again?"

"As you never loved again, neither did I," she retorted.

"Do you ever get lonely?" The soft words were a mistake as soon as he said them.

Rosa stilled. She glanced his way, and despite himself, his treacherous mind chose to replay the image of her on her knees, sliding those satin gloves up the naked muscle of his thighs.

"That's three," she replied, her tongue wetting her lips.

"Answer it."

"I have my brothers."

"That's not what I meant."

Fury and desire vibrated through her. The dichotomy of character intrigued him; Mrs. Marberry had been calm and flirtatious in all situations, except now, when he pushed her. He wanted to push more, to break that cool control and find out just how far the depths of her passion ran.

Such a move was dangerous though, for he was not immune to her. Not at all. The flush of blood through his body only served to remind him that she was scant inches away, a flimsy table between the pair of them. It would be a simple matter to kick the table aside and drag her into his arms.

If he were a lesser man.

She glared at him, the heat of her gaze cutting through him like a knife. "Of course I get lonely. I'm a widow, not a virgin." Jerking her gaze away, she grabbed her knight and took his rook. "The question is," she said, tossing the rook carelessly beside his captured pieces, "whether you do?"

"I'm a man. There are other avenues open to me," he replied, trying to examine the board to see where the play had moved.

"True." He could feel her hot little gaze on him. "That's not an answer though, but an evasion. Which you are quite skilled at, I notice. Don't you like being under the microscope, my lord?"

A faint tightening of the muscle in his jaw. He took a pawn and began to outline a campaign that would see her swiftly finished. "I'm too busy to think about female companionship."

"Now that," she murmured, "is a lie."

Taking her rook, she smashed his pawn off the board. As he'd intended.

Their eyes met.

"You think about me," she challenged, leaning back in the chair and rolling the captured pawn between the black satin of her fingers. A slight smile curled over her lips; whatever advantage he thought he'd taken, she'd evidently recovered. The tip of the pawn brushed against her lips, then back again, tracing that enigmatic smile.

Lynch forced himself to shrug. "Of course I do. You're a handsome woman of a certain age, and I am forced to spend a great deal of time in your company. I'm only a man."

"How…passionate a declaration." Her smile deepened, eyes shining bright. "Do you know what I think sometimes when you're around?"

Danger. He accepted the challenge with a cool look. "What?"

She curled the pawn in her palm, slowly dragging it down over the lace at her throat and across the gray French serge. It dipped over each curve and his gaze went with it. "I think about all these buttons I want to unlatch." Her small pink tongue darted out and wet her lips. "Starting perhaps with this one?" The pawn was gone; he hadn't even noticed the sleight-of-hand. Instead her gloves found the velvet button directly beneath her chin. One deft move and it popped open.

Not even a hint of skin revealed, but suddenly the room felt far too small. He swallowed hard, leather creaking as his thighs clenched. What the hell had happened? How had he lost control of this entire situation?

"I love how fiercely you control yourself," she murmured. Her smile was entirely coy, her gaze watchful. She felt safe now, when it was he who was so evidently distressed. "Another button, sir?"

His lips thinned and he leaned back in the chair. Curse her, but he wouldn't cry foul. "As you wish."

"Mmm, not even a hint of concern. You're very good, my lord." The second button gave. This time skin gleamed through, warm with her body heat.

The scent of her perfume grew stronger. Everything in him wanted to shove that fucking table out of the way and drag her into his lap. A vein in his temple throbbed. But he hadn't learned control over all these years for nothing.

"It's very tempting," he said. "Would you like more tea?"

"I would like," she purred, "to undo all of these wretched buttons."

"If you start this game," he warned her, "I will finish it."

Their gazes locked. Dueled. The damned woman smiled. "I dare you, sir."

Leaning forward, he poured her another cup of tea, anything to keep his mind and body busy. The knuckles of his hands tightened as he heard her fingers whisper over another button. He didn't dare look up.

"I would like to undo all of your buttons too, my lord—"

His hand shook and tea spilled across the polished silver tray. *Fuck.* He shot her a dark look and then froze at the sight of her bare décolletage. It barely revealed more than her green dress the other day, but the way she was sitting there, calmly unbuttoning her gown nearly did him in.

"I don't have buttons," he replied sharply, cursing the hoarseness of his voice.

"Not on your coat, no." Her gaze dipped, dark lashes fluttering against her smooth cheeks. Leaning forward, her bodice gaping, she took the teapot from him and accepted her cup and saucer. "But then, I wasn't speaking of your coat."

The only buttons he had were on his trousers. Mercy. His cock swelled and he shifted to hide the sight.

"I'm more interested in yours." He smiled tightly, determined to regain the upper hand. "Another button, my dear?"

She sipped her tea, holding the saucer elegantly. "What will you give me?"

Anything you wish. "What would you like?"

Those vibrant brown eyes warmed in victory before she looked down demurely. "Tell me, why would you choose to become a rogue?"

"You hate not knowing, don't you?"

"My affliction." She smiled, fingers trembling over the next button. "How much would you like to see more?"

"Very much."

"Then answer me."

His eyes hooded. "The year I turned fifteen, I told my father I had no intentions of dueling Alistair. He was furious, but no matter how much he raged, I would not give in. So he forced my hand. He orchestrated it so that when it came time for the blood rites, the Council offered me a choice: duel Alistair for the right of heir or be denied the rites."

Her fingers tensed on the button, as if surprised. "You chose to deny yourself your birthright?"

"It wasn't worth it. Not if I had to kill my cousin." He gestured. "Now, I believe that has answered your question."

His hot gaze devoured her. Mrs. Marberry gave him a coy smile and slowly, slowly undid the next button. "Satisfied?"

His body burned. "Hardly."

That earned another smile. They were almost as devastating as her slow manner of undressing.

"Now," she murmured, "your turn."

He stared at her. "I thought you didn't like being questioned."

"I mean to play fair, sir."

"I doubt that."

Another enigmatic little smile that made his cock clench. She sipped her tea.

Where to begin? Hell, what had he even asked her so far? He raked a hand through his hair. "How long were you married to your husband?"

"Five months." Shadows flickered through her gaze, then vanished. She stared at him, her gaze cutting right through him. "A button, my lord. That is the forfeit, is it not?"

It took him moments longer than it should have to understand what she meant. Heat flushed into his cheeks and he pinned her ruthlessly with his gaze.

Rosa sipped her tea. Patient. Waiting. Practically daring him.

If he wanted to know more, he had to indulge her—even if indulging her was the worst mistake he could ever make.

I can control this. He gave her a brief nod, acknowledging her victory, then dropped his hands to the top button of his breeches. His coat was long enough to cover himself decently, though any sense of decency had long since left this room.

Yet slipping the button free felt like the first step to the hangman's noose. His vision was swimming again, dipping between gray tones and color, his entire body on edge. He grabbed the decanter and poured himself more blud-wein—anything to take the edge off.

"How did you become a blue blood then, if you were denied the rites?" she asked.

"It was Alistair's idea. He said he felt guilty for what had happened to me and suggested a plan. He would infect me with his blood and we would both be blue bloods, free of our father's influences."

"A curious choice of words," she murmured. "'He said he felt guilty...'"

"I have always wondered," he replied. "To go against Council edict was foolish and I knew that."

"But?"

"Annabelle came to me that night professing her... her feelings for me. We could be together, but only if I were a blue blood. Her father would never allow her to forge a consort contract with a human."

"Do you think they were working together?"

"I think the duke wanted to make sure that I could never overthrow his son," he replied. "What had occurred with me was unusual, and there were members of the Council querying it. If I were named rogue, however, my chances were forever lost."

Rosa sipped her tea, thoughtful. "So Annabelle gets to become duchess, Alistair remains heir—and by all means pleases a father I suspect was rather forceful—and the duke gets everything he wants. They trapped you very neatly."

"Yes, I suspect they did."

Rosa frowned. "You seem very calm about it all. I would be furious."

"What good would it have done? I was very fond of Annabelle, no matter whether she lied to me or not. I had no wish to hurt her, nor Alistair. You're right in your assessment of his father. In truth, Alistair might have gotten what he deserved—he still had to live with that monster."

Her gaze dropped, her frown deepening. "You're a better person than I."

"I've seen revenge, Rosa. So many times and in so many different ways. I've pulled the bodies out of the Thames and arrested hysterical wives or husbands. Revenge is a cold, lonely place, and it consumes a person until there is nothing else left but bitterness and ashes. And it always affects so many more than the people involved." He scratched at his jaw. "I don't think I was ever furious. Hurt, yes. Frustrated and afraid. I'll even admit to the odd vengeful thought against the duke, though I never took action on it." He took a deep breath. "My father was a brutal man, and the world I walked in was a cesspit of ambition and game playing. When I walked out of the Ivory Tower, with only the clothes on my back and a rough plan of what I would do, I felt free, for the first time in my life. I could be the man I wanted to be, and I could fight them, find some sense of justice in the world."

Rosa stared at him, the teacup forgotten in her hands.

"And now," he said, sitting back in his chair, "I do believe you owe me some buttons. Three to be precise, for you asked three direct questions." He smiled hawkishly, letting his gaze drop to the inch of chemise that beckoned him. "You're going to be half naked if you keep this up."

Eleven

"I've changed my mind. I don't want buttons. I want hooks."

"Hooks?" Her corset. Rosalind's hands stilled.

"Hooks," he repeated firmly.

"Playing for high stakes now, sir." The words were breathless. She couldn't believe that he was doing this. What on earth had she been thinking, to ever call him cold?

And why the devil had she started this?

If you start this game...I will finish it. A shiver went through her. She'd never felt so excited in her life.

What are you doing? He's a blue blood. But her thoughts on what constituted an enemy were beginning to fracture. She couldn't look at this man, with his rare smiles and his icily controlled hungers, and call him what she called the others. Lynch was nothing like the Echelon.

As if of their own resolve, her fingers slipped the first hook on her corset. Then the second and the third. Lace parted with a soft whisper; it was the palest of pinks, so creamy it was almost white. Smooth white flesh swelled over the top, tempting the straining hooks to part. A dangerous path she walked, but the rashness in her was overwhelming. She couldn't control this. She wanted him so desperately, her thighs were wet with it.

"My turn," he said, shifting in his chair. "How did you meet your husband?"

The equivalent of a dash of cool water to the face. Guilt was a marvelous method in controlling the baser side of one's nature. "Nathaniel worked for the *London Standard*. He interviewed me for an article on one of my previous employers and asked me to dinner. We were married a week later by special license."

"How rash of you."

"Why are you so fascinated with my husband?"

He couldn't answer that; Rosalind saw the truth in his eyes though and her heart dipped. Lynch wanted her. And not just in his bed. He was beginning to soften toward her, his emotions engaged. It should have been a triumphant moment, but instead she froze, staring at him breathlessly.

For she herself had forgotten one of the cardinal rules in manipulation. *Don't ever fall for your opponent.* She stood on the edge of the precipice; she couldn't stay cold against the onslaught of this.

Yes, I can. I will. Her lips compressed.

"Another button, I believe," Lynch said, jolting her out of her shock. His hands dropped, and she stared hungrily as the second button on his pants emancipated itself.

Concentrate. She was here for a damned reason.

"My turn," she said, taking a deep enough breath for her breasts to heave. Those gray eyes locked on her.

"Indeed."

Rosalind licked her lips. "You said you were on the hunt for humanists. Have you ever caught any, sir?"

Though he'd been staring at her breasts, his eyes leaped to hers and she wondered if she'd taken that one step too far. This was not the type of man to lose himself so completely in staring at her. He might forget himself, but he was no fool.

"One or two," he said.

Curse him. She couldn't ask more, not with him looking at her like that. But at least the answer gave her hope. Summoning a smile, she set another hook loose. Her nipples strained against the tight corset, the dusky tops of them peeking over the frill of lace.

Their eyes locked. He swallowed. Hard.

"Your turn," she prompted.

"I can't think of a damned thing to ask." Scrubbing a hand over his mouth, he shifted in his seat again. "What's your favorite color?"

Rosalind smiled, unable to take her eyes from his. "Right now, I believe it is gray." Her lips parted... Did she dare? *Yes.* "I'm having some trouble with my hooks, sir. Would you help me?"

Lynch went still, his eyes softening dangerously. "Rosa," he warned.

"You did say you would finish it," she whispered.

One long, drawn-out moment where she thought she'd pushed him too far. Then he erupted, shoving the small table with its chess pieces out of the way and coming for her.

Black and white pawns spilled everywhere and Rosalind sucked in a sharp breath as he parted her knees with his, kneeling on the edge of her chair. His knee trapped her skirts, pinning her. "I think you want me to finish it," he said, cupping her jaw and tilting her face to his. "You are a devil of a woman."

"The hook, sir," she whispered innocently.

"So I see." His gaze dropped, his spread hand sliding over the curve of her breast. "Such a difficult task. I understand why you couldn't manage it yourself." One deft flick of his fingers and the corset gaped.

Her nipple slid free of the lace edging. Lynch sucked in a sharp breath. Rosalind couldn't move. The knee between hers was dangerously alluring.

"Ask me a question," he demanded.

She looked up. "Do you dream of me?"

"Yes," he hissed through clenched teeth. His hands dropped, but hers were quicker.

She caught his wrist. "Allow me."

Lynch's hands dropped to his sides. "I dream of you with your gloves on my thighs." The pulse in his temple throbbed. "Your fucking gloves. I can't stop thinking about them."

Heat spilled through her. Wetness. Rosalind slid the palms of her hands lightly up his thighs, staring up at him daringly. The bulge in his pants was hot and hard. She couldn't stop her fingers from brushing over it, then again, stroking harder, her right hand clenching over his heavy length.

"My apologies," she breathed. "I can't quite seem to find the button."

Lynch speared a hand into her hair with a sharp hiss.

"I should take my belt to you for this." He spilled her back into the chair, his body driving hers into the soft cushions. His eyes were black again but she wasn't afraid. Not this time. She knew exactly what sort of hunger she'd roused in him.

She was winning.

"Would you like that, my lord?" She arched her back, sliding her hands up his chest. "Would you like me to bend over your desk and remove my drawers?"

He groaned, tilting her head back sharply. "*Fuck.*" His other fingers traced her lips. "You'll pay for that. I want to kiss you, Rosa."

"Then do it," she whispered, her hot breath on his mouth.

Those hawkish eyes met hers, his cruel fingers cupping her jaw. "I shouldn't."

Dangerous eyes. Had it been so long ago that she'd thought him cold and merciless? Rosalind sucked in a breath. How wrong she'd been. There was such heat in him, such passion.

"Do it," she whispered.

His gaze dropped to her lips. "Not on your pretty little mouth." Lifting his knee, he shoved her skirts up. Capturing her right hand, he slid it low, between her legs. "Part your drawers."

Shock sliced through her. Then heat, stirring between her thighs, wetting the linen between her legs. She almost died at the thought of what he intended. "My lord!" she whispered.

"Not so amusing when the shoe is on the other foot. I told you I would finish it. Now do it."

His hand slid over hers, pressing her fingers against

her damp drawers. A shiver trailed down her spine and Rosalind gasped, the sensation shooting all the way through her.

The coolness of his palm was rough and demanding. Rosalind's thighs tightened, trapped by his knee. She could barely see their hands, her frothy skirts tumbling over them, but she could feel it, feel the pressure of his fingers, guiding her own to a secret part of herself.

"You surprise me," she whispered, her mouth but an inch from his. A desperate part of her wanted to press her lips to his, to lick his own, to captivate him. But she held. This was a new game, with new rules, and the shiver of delight at the thought of his mastery almost undid her.

Closing her eyes, she parted her drawers, cool air stirring against her sensitive flesh. "It's done."

"Is it?" Lynch's lips brushed her own, feather light.

She almost cried out then, half reaching for him, but his mouth trailed lower, his lips dancing over the lace of her dress, roughening it against her skin—darting over her nipple. Then lower still, brushing the smooth silk of her corset, tasting her, touching her, as if it were bare skin and not clothing. She shivered, wishing she were naked, wishing it *was* his mouth on her body, wreaking such delicious torment.

Lynch's hand fisted in the spill of skirts, dragging them up and Rosalind lost her breath on a gasp. She couldn't believe this was happening. "Oh God," she whispered, her iron fingers digging into the soft cushion beneath her bottom.

A knock sounded on the door.

No! Rosalind lifted her head, trying to recapture

her breath. Lynch stilled, her skirts almost baring her completely to his gaze.

"Tell them to go away," she whispered.

He looked at her then, harsh desire burning in his gray eyes. Swallowing visibly, he glanced over his shoulder, fist clenching and unclenching in her skirts. "Who the hell is it?" he called, in a tone of voice that threatened dire consequences on the knocker.

"Garrett, sir." A faint cough. "I understand you're busy, but there's a lad at the front gate, insisting he speak with you. One of your game boys, sir."

"Fuck," he muttered, his gaze locking on hers. "*Fuck*." He lifted his voice. "Which one?"

"Meriwether."

Lynch closed his eyes, a muscle in his jaw jumping. "I have to go." His voice was rough and low. "Don't go anywhere."

Rosalind caught his wrist as he drew his hand away. "Stay," she whispered. "Let Garrett deal with it."

He shot her a helpless look, and she realized then just how much he wanted to stay. "I can't." Lips thinning, he shoved her skirts down. "I've been waiting over a month for this message." Capturing her face, he tilted it ruthlessly toward his own. "Stay here. We have unfinished business."

"I might just finish it myself," she said, pushing herself upright. Her thighs quivered with thwarted desire.

Lynch was in the process of standing, but at her words he caught her wrist and drew her close to him. "No," he said. A quick brutal kiss, then he pushed away from her. "Wait for me."

Rosalind tumbled back against the armchair as he

strode for the door, tugging the buttons on his pants into place. He looked almost unmoved, while she sat in a puddle of skirts and the gaping sway of her bodice, her entire body seemingly melted.

He'd destroyed her. Torn all sense of control from her with one move. A dangerous man, for she wanted more desperately.

Oh God, what had she done? She needed to win back her control and desperately too, before she lost all sense of her purpose here.

"Check," she whispered.

The game was afoot.

∽

"What the hell are you doing out of your sickbed?" Lynch demanded as he shut the door behind him.

Garrett's face was pale and almost waxen. Those perceptive eyes met his. "Fitz says I need to walk around the building at least three times a day. So I volunteered to deliver the message."

"You look like hell. You'd best get back to bed."

Garrett grimaced. "Perry's driving me insane, fluffing my damned pillows and offering to fetch something for me at every second moment."

"She nearly lost you. It frightened her." It had frightened him, though he didn't speak of it. Men generally didn't.

Garrett fell into step beside him, or tried to, his breath coming harshly. "Probably a good thing it *was* me, sir."

Lynch stopped in his tracks and cut a glare toward his second. "Why?"

Garrett arched a brow. "You smell like lemon verbena. If you want some advice, I'd wash before you see anyone else. Unless I assume wrong; unless you don't want to keep this quiet."

His jaw clenched. "I'll take your advice then. But breathe a word of this and you'll be back in the infirmary."

Garrett's mouth curled in a slow smile. "It's about bloody time you had a woman." A hint of his old humor surfaced. "Besides, if she takes the edge off you, maybe you'll let up on the rest of us."

"I wouldn't presume so."

"We'll see, sir."

Twelve

LYNCH SIGHTED HIS PREY AS SHE STEPPED OUT OF THE jewelry shop, clutching a package in her mink-gloved hands. Her brisk steps swished her burgundy skirts around her ankles as she darted into the stream of pedestrians. A young mother pushing her perambulator glanced up, saw the woman's eyes, and then jerked her child out of the way.

She was alone. Perfect.

"Thanks," he murmured, passing a five-pound note to Meriwether, the young boy he paid to watch Mrs. Carver's house. Shoving away from the corner of the building he was leaning against, he cut directly into the oncoming traffic. Striding in front of an omnibus, he ignored the blaring horn and curse as a pneumatic rickshaw tried to veer aside. The woman in front of him glanced over her shoulder just as he reached the curb and Lynch ducked behind a tall gentleman in a top hat.

He stalked her for several streets, keeping an eye out for her husband. Mrs. Carver might be dangerous, but at five and a half feet she was manageable. Her husband however was another matter. This was the closest Lynch had come to getting his hands on Mrs. Carver since her transformation a month ago.

It didn't help matters that she'd once been Barrons's ward. Taking on the newly minted verwulfen ambassador was one thing; going up against Barrons another. But she'd been in the tower the day the Duke of Lannister was murdered and the bomb went off, as had her husband. Of the two of them, he knew which one was more likely to talk to him about the identity of Mercury.

A steam coach idled by the curb ahead with the distinctive snarling wolf sigil of the new ambassador. A coachman lingered beside it, his hands cupped around a cheroot as he lit it. Towering over the crowd, his blond hair brushing the collar of his great coat, he bore faint traces of his Nordic ancestry. As he slowly shook out the flame on his match, his golden eyes watched the crowd with a hungry, cold look. One of the newly released verwulfen, no doubt. Trying to fit back into society and failing badly.

Lynch surged forward. If Mrs. Carver reached the coach, he'd not get his chance. And time was running out for him.

Sidestepping through curious onlookers, he grabbed her by the upper arm, his fingers sinking into the soft velvet of her coat. The muscle of her arm tightened and he bent low before she could react.

"Walk with me," he murmured. His gaze met the coachman's over the top of her head and the man stiffened. "I mean you no harm."

Lena Carver shot him a lowered lash look, the

bronze ring around her eyes catching the sunlight. The slightly flirtatious glance was entirely at odds with the tension running through her slight frame. "You wouldn't want to, Sir Jasper. Max is recently come from the Manchester Pits. He made his living killing men in the ring."

"Smile at him then. Before I'm forced to cut short his newly freed circumstances."

She considered his entreaty, then graced the burly coachman with a smile that would have shaken any normal man's wits. Sliding her hand over Lynch's, she made as if they were any other couple, out for a stroll.

The bodyguard's shoulders relaxed but his eyes never left them. Lynch turned her down a side street, toward a park.

"My husband will not approve of this," she said. "He's...protective."

"He's verwulfen," Lynch replied, which meant everything. He let her go as they reached the park. Leaning back against the iron rails of the park fence, he stared at her. "I have questions for you."

Those pretty brown eyes with their newly minted gleam widened slightly. "Questions? I'm afraid I know little of my husband's work—"

He ignored her. "Questions about the package in your hands perhaps? No doubt if I look I'll find a half dozen ruby rings filled with hemlock."

The smile slid off her face as if it had never been. "I don't know what you're talking about."

"And I don't care if you *are* carrying poison rings." In a way, he approved. Mrs. Carver had once been a debutante, and as such, prey to the blue bloods that prowled the Echelon. Gossip had it that certain members of the younger generation thought it old-fashioned to take a debutante as their thralls, when they could take their blood by force. Only rumor of course and Lynch hadn't had time to look into it, but if so, the sudden rash of poison rings on every debutante's finger was something he was willing to turn a blind eye to.

"Firstly, I want to know if there are any verwulfen women in London," he said. "There are none listed in the registry. I know. My men checked."

Mrs. Carver's anxiety faded a little, as he had intended. "Only myself. The rest returned to Scandinavia once the treaty was signed."

Then where had Mercury's verwulfen companion come from?

"Anything else?" she asked, fluttering her lashes.

"A month ago the Duke of Lannister was stabbed, shot, and partially decapitated in the Ivory Tower," he stated, watching her reaction. Her sudden pallor took all the warmth from her pretty features. "I don't care who stabbed him or tried to tear his head off—and mind you I have suspicions, considering the scent trail left in the room—what I'm interested in is the woman who shot him."

"I'm afraid I know nothing about it," she said quickly.

"I could make it my business to discover who decapitated the duke," he replied. Mrs. Carver, he suspected, would run straight home to her husband if he made a threat against her. But if the threat were against her husband... It was all simply a matter of applying the right pressure points.

Of course, he could never follow through with the

threat. Mrs. Carver had once been Barrons's ward and he'd sworn an oath to the man that he wouldn't reveal who'd been in the room that day.

She didn't need to know that however.

Mrs. Carver's lips thinned. "Why do you want to know?"

Relaxing slightly, he offered her his arm as a pair of elderly gentlemen strolled their way. Mrs. Carver took it, the unnatural heat of her skin permeating even through her gloves. He led her along the path, skirting a pair of squirrels chattering at each other near a park bench. "The explosion during the treaty signing was an attack by a group called humanists." The lack of surprise on her face made his mind race, but he didn't think she was involved. Will Carver wouldn't have allowed that. Still... Thought for later. "They are led by a woman who calls herself Mercury. She is always masked and her identity is unknown. I need to find her."

"For what purpose?"

"The prince consort has tasked me with delivering the revolutionary to him."

"Where she'll be executed."

"The bombing cannot go unpunished, Mrs. Carver."

Nibbling on her lip, she paused. "What if she had nothing to do with the bombing?"

Interesting. The precise same statement his masked nemesis had made in the enclaves. Lynch's gaze sharpened on her. "Why would you say such a thing?"

"Keeping in mind that this is all supposition," she replied, "perhaps you're hunting for the wrong group? Perhaps there were humanists who broke from the revolution and decided to take matters into their own hands? Suppose she tried to stop them?"

The breath went out of him. "Dangerous supposition, Mrs. Carver."

"Arresting the wife of the verwulfen ambassador is bound to incite tension between Scandinavia and Britain. I'm trying to cooperate as much as I can."

She knew the rules of society well. The prince consort wouldn't stand to have his new treaty smashed apart by Lynch. He wanted Mercury, but there were some prices he wouldn't pay.

"You're trying to protect someone. The interesting question is who. And why."

"You know who," she replied. "I'm prepared to reveal certain sensitive information, as long as I have your word not to move against me or my husband."

"That depends on the information revealed."

"Then I'm not inclined to be obliging."

Lynch stepped in front of her. "I like your husband. Don't force me to do something I don't wish to."

Mrs. Carver stared up at him for a long moment, searching his gaze. "You smell like desperation, sir," she finally said. "Why?"

Lynch took a deep breath, trying to still the tension radiating off him. If Mrs. Carver—newly a verwulfen— could recognize his distress, then it must be evident indeed. "If I don't get my hands on Mercury soon, then I fear the prince consort will resort to desperate measures."

"You don't think he'd send out the metaljackets in force?"

"I don't know." Blunt words but true. "He's not acting entirely rational at the moment."

Mrs. Carver sighed. "If I knew anything at all, I might suspect that what you were searching for can be found in Undertown." She looked up. "I can't say any more than that. I won't."

Lynch grabbed her arm as she turned to go, desperation driving him. "You know who she is."

"She's no friend of mine, though I wouldn't wish her ill." Mrs. Carver's fingers curled over his own, the strength of her grip belying her small stature. "I have told you what I can, Sir Jasper. Though I fear you are hunting for the wrong person. You should be hunting for a group of escaped mechs."

"The woman," he snapped. "Who is she? Give me something, anything... A name?"

Mrs. Carver pried one of his fingers loose. The sudden blaze of bronze in her eyes warned him. "I am terribly sorry for your predicament, sir. But I have given my word and I won't betray it. That is all I can tell you. Now get your hands off me before I am forced to call Max."

Lynch stared through her for a second more then let her go. She staggered slightly, gave him a curt look, then straightened her skirts.

"War is coming, Mrs. Carver."

"War's already here," she replied bluntly, then turned toward the park gate and hurried away.

Thirteen

ROSALIND PACED THE HALLWAY, CLENCHING AND unclenching her fists. The longer she'd waited for Lynch, the more she'd begun to question herself. In the heat of the moment, all she'd wanted was him. It was only after, as her body slowly cooled, that she realized how dangerous events had become.

Losing her head like that, losing control of the game… If she wasn't careful she would find herself in deep water.

She'd had to get away.

Twitching aside the curtains, she glanced into the street. No one had followed her home. Not that she expected them to, but still… Today's sudden inter- rogation made her wary. Did he suspect something?

I have four hundred and fifty Nighthawks, Mrs. Marberry. Don't make me too curious.

Was his curiosity satisfied? She knew hers wasn't.

"Have we got a problem?" Ingrid's husky voice startled her.

Rosalind's gaze jerked up as the other woman took a stealthy step into the room. "Are you trying to catch me unawares?"

"It's been remarkably easy of late. You need to get your mind off whatever's distracting you before Jack notices."

She stared at her friend.

"You smell like a man's cologne." Ingrid folded her arms across her chest as if daring Rosalind to reply.

"Of course I do. I work in a whole building full of them." Lifting her arm she sniffed at herself. "It's most likely Garrett." She ignored the way Ingrid's expression didn't change. Not fooled one bit. "No news?"

"No sign of Jeremy," Ingrid replied.

Restlessness itched down her spine. Rosalind started working on her gloves, frowning worriedly. "I need to push plans. Lynch has nothing in his study about Jeremy or the mechs—the dratted man keeps it all in his head."

"Then you may as well abort the mission."

"No." She dropped her glove on one of the frilly little table covers that haunted the room. Every inch of space was taken up with knickknacks and lamps and lace doilies. "I'm learning too much and I'm in the perfect position to hear the latest news from the Echelon."

"And if he discovers you?"

"He won't," Rosalind affirmed.

Ingrid growled under her breath. "So what next?"

Rosalind paused by the liquor cabinet and unstoppered a decanter of whiskey. She poured the pair of them a generous shot. "Lynch needs to find the humanists who bombed the tower."

"Hardly news."

"So I'm going to point him toward the mechs. I think it's time Mordecai had a taste of what it's like to look over your shoulder."

Ingrid took her glass and clinked it against Rosalind's. "I'll drink to that." She threw the glass back. "How do you propose to do that without blowing your cover?"

Rosalind swirled the contents of her glass in the lamplight, watching the play of light. Exhilaration beat in her breast and lower—a longing unfulfilled. "I'm not. Mercury is."

Time to take a risk.

And time to assuage the restless ache inside her. She threw the whiskey back, feeling it burn all the way through her.

⁓

Feeling thwarted, Lynch sank under the waters in the pump room, the biting hot bringing a flush of warmth to his flesh. Scraping his hands over his tired face, he surfaced, blinking through the water droplets.

Steam lingered on the surface of the bathing pool and clung to the stone pillars that supported the heavy domed ceiling. The drone of the enormous furnaces and the pumps that drove water throughout the building echoed in the walls. Years ago, Fitz had taken one look at the plumbing and devised a system of hot water that not only supplied the entire guild but ran heated pipes through the stone floors too; the by-product of that bit of genius was this. The heat from the furnaces had to go somewhere, Fitz had said. Why not use it for a bathing room, much like the ones the Romans built centuries ago?

If there was one indulgence Lynch owned, it was this.

Easing against the edge of the pool, he shut his eyes and let his body float. His cold blood made him crave the heat like one of the mythical dragons the Chinese Empire spoke of.

The steady throb of the pump engines filled the room, vibrating against his skin. Lynch let his mind float free, trying to forget about the afternoon and the incident with Mrs. Marberry. She hadn't been here when he returned and guilt added a sour flavor to his mouth. Did she regret what had happened? Perhaps it was for the best. He couldn't imagine what he was going to say to her on the morrow. Seducing his own employee...

Water rippled against his chest, gentle little waves that lapped at his skin. Lynch scraped his wet hair back and then froze.

There was nothing to stir the water but his own body.

He cracked his eyes open and stared at the shadow-wreathed figure on the other side of the pool. She knelt at the tiled edge, steam obscuring her face as she traced her fingers through the water.

His body screamed its awareness as Mercury smiled at him. Her eyes were covered, this time with a leather half mask that reminded him of Carnevale. Brass studs curled up one side in decoration and the thin gleam of her eyes watched him through the cat-slit eye holes.

"Why look," she drawled huskily, "it's me Lord Nighthawk...in the flesh."

The double entendre stirred through his gut with hot fingers. Lynch lowered his hands slowly, relaxing his arms back on the edge of the pool. A muscle ticked in his jaw. She'd come here on purpose, no doubt to disarm him.

She would learn. He was never disarmed, never

anything short of lethal and right now his temper was roused.

Barely eight feet of water separated them. He could cover that distance in a second, but from the way she edged onto the balls of her feet, she was expecting that. No doubt there were more than a few weapons hiding under that overwhelming brown coat.

And she wouldn't have come here without reason. His curiosity was aroused.

Lynch forced his body to relax, though it was hard. Mrs. Marberry had destroyed him this afternoon and he could barely gather his thoughts—or his rampant lust—long enough to deal with the revolutionary. "You do realize there are over a hundred Nighthawks in this building?"

"And yet not one of them noticed me." Her smile taunted him. "Not even you." Pointing a forefinger at him, she made a shooting gesture that wasn't lost on him.

His gaze hooded. "If you wanted me dead, I would be." He'd give her that. "I just didn't realize you wanted me naked."

"All the better to seduce you, me lord."

That made him laugh. "So you can overwhelm me again? I think not. I make mistakes, my dear, but only once and only rarely."

"So I'm a mistake, am I?"

"I don't precisely know what you are. But I will." He let his own smile edge over his lips. "I never intended it to be difficult to get into the guild. Getting out is another matter."

Mercury slowly unfolded herself, revealing dark

red skirts hooked up just enough to reveal a flirtatious froth of petticoat and a bronze corset-style bodice that thrust her pale breasts high. The same brass studs that decorated her mask ran along a heavy belt that held her pistol and her dark hair curled over her shoulder. It wasn't coincidence that her coat had fallen back, barely clinging to her pale shoulders.

His throat went dry. He'd never seen a woman dressed like that before. It was indecent. Scandalous. And he wanted her more than ever.

His dreams lately had been of another woman, but right now, temptation roared. His slender secretary who liked to drive him wild, or a woman he barely knew, his sweetest obsession?

"You'll lemme go," she said with a careless shrug. The coat slipped a fraction more, revealing her rounded shoulder. "The alternative's the Echelon's dungeons and I ain't thinkin' you want that."

"What I want doesn't always matter."

"Don't you ever give into your urges, me lord?"

"Rarely."

"You should." Another slow suggestive smile that sunk through his gut with iron-tipped claws. "Why don't you come out of the water?" She kicked the toe of her boot through the surface, sending a shower of droplets toward him.

"Why don't you come in?"

"I wouldn't want to get meself wet."

Lynch pushed away from the edge. He kept his eyes on her, not trusting her an inch. Steam curled around him as he stood, shaking off the water.

Mercury took a wary step back. "I'll get your

towel," she said, dragging it off the hook it hung on. Turning, she held it out, staying a good five feet away from the water.

Lynch found the steps that led out of the bathing pool and ascended with cool disregard for his nakedness. Water sluiced down his skin, steam rising from his bare arms as he lifted his hands and raked his wet hair back. When he glanced at her, the little smile had died, replaced by something far more watchful.

He took his time, flicking off water droplets before holding his hand out. "The towel?"

A husky laugh greeted him. "Now, why would I want to do that?" Another slow, heated look that caressed his body. "Me lord Nighthawk, imagination does you no justice at all."

"I would like to be able to say the same." He stepped closer.

Her smile remained, but he sensed the coiling of muscle within her at his abrupt nearness. So she was not so certain of his intentions? Good.

"I'd like to indulge," Mercury replied, her iron hand clenching in the toweling. "But I think we'd both prefer it if I kept me mask. Adds a little, what's them Frenchies say? Jay nay say—"

"*Je ne sais quoi.*" A certain little indescribable something. An edge. For the first time, he had the impression that she was toying with him. She knew exactly what she meant to say. He frowned slightly. The cockney was distracting, which was precisely the point, he imagined.

Who was she? His hands ached to remove the mask, to reveal her identity to him. He could do it too, before she even knew he'd moved.

And then?

She was right. He liked the mask, the mystery. It drove him to distraction and yet he was not quite prepared to solve the puzzle of her identity. To do so would mean he had to act on it and reluctance sat heavily on his shoulders.

Lynch grabbed her hands where they clenched the towel and dragged them around his waist. The soft toweling brushed against his groin as Mercury landed flush against him, her sharp intake of breath telling him he'd succeeded in disarming her.

"Desire cuts both ways, my dear."

She looked up, her corset pressed flush against his chest. The angle thrust her breasts into smooth globes he ached to touch. "So it does."

Letting go of her hands, he drew the ends of the towel tight and tucked one edge into the other. Mercury's hands trailed over his hips, her head lowering in curious exploration and Lynch suddenly understood her. Whatever had happened between them in the enclaves—whatever he thought he had lost—she had lost too.

"So what makes you think I won't just hand you over to the Echelon?" he asked.

Her fingertip trailed down the smooth trail of hair beneath his navel, tangling in the dark strands. It brushed the edge of the towel and hooked against the fabric as she tugged, just gently enough to be suggestive. Lynch sucked in a sharp breath.

"I think you want me for yourself."

"That's a dangerous assumption to make considering where you are." She seemed so certain he wouldn't hurt her.

Could he? That shadowed gaze met his behind the mask. He couldn't see her eyes, but he felt the connection as their gazes locked. It ran a hot hand through his body, wrapping tightly around his cock. His erection stirred against the toweling and Mercury noticed. She wet her lips, her finger sliding more securely behind the towel.

"Did I presume wrong?" The mask challenged him; he desperately wanted to see behind it.

And just as desperately did not. A hollow feeling pooled in his gut. Instinct. Whatever her secret was, a part of him didn't want to know it.

Why? His expression turned hard. He'd learned to trust that instinct over the years, but what was it telling him?

"No," he said softly. "You didn't presume wrong."

The air between them changed. Stillness radiated through her as if he'd surprised her. Lynch's gaze dropped to her mouth. He knew he was going to do it. Call it madness or insanity, he couldn't help himself.

One hand slid around the curve of her nape, cradling the stark line of her skull. The edge of a wig cut into his hand and his mind filed that away for future pondering, even as his mouth descended on hers.

The moment their lips touched he felt the spark of it all the way through him. He wanted her. Not to capture her, not to turn her over to the prince consort, but just to *have* her. As his.

The thought was madness. There could be no future in this, nothing behind the heat of sex and hunger. Mercury was a shadow; he knew nothing about her. But she was his shadow, his challenge, his obsession. Mrs. Marberry was a temptation he couldn't afford, a dream of something he'd long since thought gone, but this…this was safe enough to risk.

Violent need swept through him, ignited by passion and frustration. He growled deep in his throat and slid a hand down the smooth curve of her back to the full flesh of her arse. Pressing her against him, he sucked in a sharp breath as his hips rode against the soft juncture of her thighs.

Lynch squeezed his eyes shut, sensation spearing through his groin with white-hot abandon. Her tongue darted into his mouth and he crushed her against him, trying to drink her all in, to take everything he could of her. Lifting her against him, he drove her back against one of the marble columns, her thighs locking around his hips and her skirts riding up between them. A little gasp drove from her throat, then she was kissing him again, her iron hand sliding over his nape as she rolled her hips, straining against him.

Lynch tore his mouth free, gasping as his hips pinned her to the column. He didn't think. Couldn't. Need was a vicious beast within him, so hungry for release that he could barely see through the gray haze of his vision. Somehow his hunger had risen and he grabbed her wig and wrenched her head back, his lips sliding over the smooth skin of her throat. The heady kick of her pulse vibrated against his tongue and Lynch bit down, his teeth sinking into the soft flesh with a warning.

Mercury stilled, her iron fingers curling in his hair, just this side of painful. Her heart thundered like a panicked animal in her chest, her breath coming in little gasps that punctuated the air.

"Don't you trust me?" he whispered, pressing his lips gently to the area he'd just bitten. He licked her, suckling gently to soothe the hurt. "Do you think I'd do it?" The words were reckless. That was precisely what he wanted to do. To put a knife to her throat and spill the sweet blood beneath her skin. To drink it down, to assuage the hungry ache that never completely left him.

His hands quivered as he cupped her backside, lips brushing temptingly over the smooth muscle of her trapezius. He wanted it so badly, the scent of her fear sending hunger cramping through him with iron claws. But he was better than that. He could control this. He would.

Mercury's hand slid over his throat and down his chest. "I don't know," she whispered. "Would you?"

Lynch pulled away with a gasp, pressing his forehead to hers. Swallowing hard, he fought to rein himself in. He'd never been this tempted, never come so close to losing control. It was his greatest fear and his own secret agony. "I want to," he admitted. "But it frightens you."

"I ain't food," she snapped.

"That's got nothing to do with it." He shook his head and dragged his hands up to cup her face. "I want you. I want to claim you as mine, and this…this is part of it." He breathed hard, biting her lip, her chin. Lower. Pressing his face to her cheek as he moaned. "I want to own you."

Mercury's iron fingers locked around his wrist. "Like a thrall."

"No." He trailed his mouth down her throat and felt her head drop back stiffly. She was clinging to him, as if to hold on to some semblance of control. Lynch's lips rasped over the bite mark, feeling the imprint of his own teeth. "As mine."

"You barely know me."

"Then tell me something about yourself," he demanded, bringing his drugged gaze back to her flushed face.

Mercury's hands slid down his chest, one warm, the other cool iron. They trembled. "You scare me," she whispered, and he didn't think she was referring to what he could do to her.

His hands stilled. Her full mouth was parted and swollen, her breasts heaving with her breath.

Slowly, he stroked a thumb over her mouth, feeling the wetness on her lips. "You scare me," he admitted.

Lynch almost caught a shadowed glimpse of her eyes as they darted to his. Then she turned her face away, shutting them. A shudder ran through her. A reckless laugh. "I never expected this." Slowly her hands ran over his shoulders, fingertips trailing over his skin. "I should ne'er 'ave kissed you."

"But you did."

"Aye." She leaned forward and kissed his chest. Opening her mouth she licked his skin, her small blunt teeth sinking into the muscle of his pectoral.

Lynch sucked in a sharp gasp at the flare of pain, his hands clenching into fists beside her face. His hips gave an involuntary flex, and heat flared through his mouth. *Need.*

Mercury's hips slowly unlocked and then she

was sliding down him with sinuous grace, her lips trailing over the smooth skin of his abdomen. Muscle clenched and Lynch shoved a hand against the marble column to hold himself up, his gaze locking on her. Mercury slid to her knees, her palms gliding over his thighs and her lips grazing the roughness of the towel, dangerously close to his groin.

She looked up and Lynch's knees almost gave at the heated look on her face. "Do you trust me?" she whispered, a slow smile spreading over her lips. Slowly she kissed him through the towel, the touch spearing through his engorged member.

Lynch's other hand hit the column as he shuddered. "Not even an inch," he told her on a rough laugh, almost an exhale.

"What about"—her eyes ran over him—"a good ten inches?"

His breath caught. Slowly, she reached up and hooked her fingers in the towel. The tucked end came loose and the rough toweling rasped over his erection as it dragged free.

He knew what she intended. Still, he could barely breathe as she slid her palms up his thighs, her tongue darting out to wet her lips.

The shock of her hot mouth almost drove him out of his skin. His hand speared down through her hair and he thrust against her, feeling the wet glide of her mouth over his cock. Her teeth scraped against him as if in warning and behind the mask he saw the gleam of light off her eyes.

Yes. His head bowed in defeat, a guttural groan tearing through his throat. She had the upper hand for the moment, but for once he didn't give a damn. She was his unholy fascination, simply his in a way that he couldn't yet comprehend and he needed this so damned much. The week's torment had driven him out of his mind. He still didn't know what he would do about Mercury, but luckily this didn't require thinking at all.

That hot little mouth worked him wetly, stealing his breath and the few wits he had left. Lynch's mouth parted on a gasp, his eyes hooding as his fist clenched in the wig she wore.

"Stop," he groaned.

A smile widened over her full mouth and her iron hand fisted around the base of his cock, making him suck in a sharp breath. Hell, that felt so fucking good. He was so close, he needed her to stop, but somehow his lips wouldn't say the words and she knew it.

She'd put a spell on him. One kiss in the enclaves like a bullet to the chest and now he couldn't stop feeling it, no matter what the consequences were.

Mercury took him deep, her tongue stroking his shaft with wet abandon and he was lost.

Lynch's fist clenched and he gasped, thrusting hard against her mouth as he came with a guttural groan. Those pink, swollen lips suckled the sensitive head of his cock and he collapsed against the column, breathing hard.

Mercury pressed a kiss against his thigh, stirring the fine hairs against his skin so that he shivered. "Well," she whispered, licking her lips. "Me lord Nighthawk, you do impress." She smiled up at him, cool and mysterious, then slowly slid up his body, pressing herself between him and the column.

If she thought that would undo him, then she was mistaken. And if she thought that was the end of what lay between them… He watched her with cool eyes, stroking the back of his fingers against her swollen mouth.

"I have barely begun," he murmured, leaning closer and breathing in the sweet taste of her breath. A smile curled over his mouth as he looked down, his fingers trailing lower, brushing over the smooth curve of her up thrust breast. "You, my love, are no lady."

Her breath quickened at the teasing stir of his touch. "Do you want me to be one?"

"No." He slid his hand over her nape and spun her around, pressing her hands against the column. She tensed, then stilled as he smoothed the long, dark tail of her hair out of the way and pressed his open mouth against the back of her neck. Suckling hard, he brought the blood to the surface in a red bruise then nipped at the damning mark. Mercury shivered, a soft little gasp of surrender crossing her lips, and Lynch smiled.

He ran his lips down the soft curve of her shoulder, biting her just enough to leave a mark, then soothing the sting with his tongue. Slowly his hands slid up beneath her coat, tracing the curve of the corset she wore. The feel of it stirred desire through him and he pressed his hips against her bottom, letting her know just how much he wanted her.

Mercury sucked in a sharp breath, half turning. "Me lord—"

He caught her hands and shoved them against the column. "Don't let go." Then his hands were cupping her breasts, holding the plump weight in his palms.

Mercury's head tilted back with a groan. "Mercy," she moaned. "We need to speak."

"Do we?" He edged the lip of the corset down and her nipple sprang free, hard and tight. Sliding his other hand against her abdomen, he drew her hips back against him, rolling the turgid peak of her nipple between his fingers. "I thought you came here for this?"

Mercury arched into him, her head falling forward with a helpless gasp. He could feel the surrender in her body and the shaking in her knees.

"No. Yes." She shook her head and moaned. "You want to know who blew up the tower?"

Lynch's hand tightened on her hip. The words cut through him like a knife. To hide it, he pressed a kiss against the tender skin below her ear and was rewarded with another shiver. She liked this. "You still claim you didn't do it?"

"Nor did I burn the draining factories." Her hand splayed over the column, her iron fingers flexing unconsciously. The other hand slid between them, wrapping around his growing erection. "A year ago," she gasped, "I set a group o' mechs free o' the enclaves. They wanted vengeance and I…I needed 'em for somewhat."

His lashes lowered and he thrust into the grip of her palm. *The steel boiler pack he'd taken from her at the enclaves.* "I'm listening."

"There were a power struggle. They broke from me leadership and burned the factories. I were tryin' to stop 'em when they 'it the Tower."

"Why?" he asked. Her tight fist made the vein in his temple throb but he could contain the fierce need now. Her clever ministrations had seen to that. She, however, was not so satisfied. "That explosion nearly killed half the blue bloods of the court. I thought that was what you wanted."

"Personal reasons," she replied, tilting her head to the side to glance back over her shoulder. "And it didn't succeed, did it? Now I've got every blasted Coldrush Guard and Nighthawk on me trail. You think I wanted that?"

"I think you're in a lot of danger."

She laughed under her breath, an almost sad sound. "I chose this path. I knew the risks."

His lips thinned. Damn her, but he was starting to soften toward her. Was she telling the truth? "Give yourself up," he said, edging his hand down her abdomen, "and I'll demand a lenient sentence."

The stiffness in her body was almost anticipatory. Tension radiated through her and she dragged her iron hand to his, urging it lower. "You can't make the prince consort do anythin' 'e don't wanna."

"There are ways to play the game," he replied, his fingers sliding between the heat of her legs, bunching up her skirts. "If you tell me everything you know about the mechs, I'm inclined to be lenient."

She was tempted. Gasping hard, she pressed her lips to the column, her hips driving back into his groin as his fingers dipped into the wet heat between her thighs. She wasn't wearing drawers. "Mordecai," she gasped. "'Is name's Mordecai. I don't know where 'e is, but I do know this: 'e's got somethin' to do with the massacres in the Echelon. I seen 'im near the second crime scene."

"How convenient that you were nearby," he murmured, his mind racing. The mechs had something to do with the madness sweeping the Echelon? That meant it had to be a toxin or a poison. It was man-made and that meant he could catch them.

If she wasn't lying.

Grabbing her wrists, he spun her around and shoved her against the marble column, holding her hands over her head.

Slowly his hands relaxed on hers, sliding down over the betraying pulse of her right wrist. "Tell me," he demanded, "that you had nothing to do with the massacres. With Lord Arrondale's death."

Mercury pulled against his grip but didn't fight him. "I 'ad nought to do wit' it."

Her pulse ticked through her wrist, as steady as before. She was telling the truth. Either that or she was such a good liar she could control her body's reflexes.

"I believe you," he said.

His thumb stroked the soft skin of her wrist. The other one was cool metal, woven so seamlessly into skin that he recognized it as a master-smith job. No wonder her reactions were so exquisite; metal hydraulics had been linked to flesh tendons, and muscle sewn to the thin fibrous sheeting of the interior of her gauntleted wrist. The limb worked almost as naturally as her right hand.

"You want me, don't you?" she asked. "You've been chasin' me for months."

Lynch's gaze hooded. He let her go, hands sliding down her arms. "I don't need to chase you," he whispered in his ear. "Because you'll come back to me."

"What do you mean?"

Lynch pushed away from the column and dragged the towel around his hips. "I won't be played for a fool twice. But you...you're burning for it." He backed away, watching her shocked expression as she realized he had no intentions of finishing this.

"I thought I'd 'ave to fight me way free," she whispered, her pupils dilated with desire.

He *should* capture her. Lock her up now. But what to do with her? He was certain the prince consort had spies in the guild, and although he'd managed to keep one or two humanists quietly guarded in his time, the possibility of the prince consort getting his hands on Mercury made him feel physically ill. He couldn't guarantee her safety. Not at the guild and not anywhere in his little hidey-holes in the city.

Lynch took a step away. "Go via the south wing and wait until the clock tower chimes ten. The guards will be changing their shift." He tucked the towel into itself, uncertain whether he was doing the right thing. A thought flashed into mind: if he couldn't hand her over to the prince consort now, how was he going to do it in when the time came?

Mercury's head. Or his.

"Go," he said, before he changed his mind. "Get out of here."

⤎⤏

It was a long, slow climb to his rooms and he barely noticed any of it. Once he'd left the warm steamy chamber, his mind had started working again.

What the hell was he doing? Lynch knew what she

was doing and doing well—testing his resolve, slowly turning him away from his purpose. He hadn't missed her words about a challenge to her leadership. She'd meant to set him upon the mechs tonight and they both knew it.

But had she meant anything else she'd said? Or was seducing him just a way to soften him? His fist clenched. He highly suspected she was playing him, though whether he'd managed to inflict some damage on her own psyche, he didn't know.

This had to stop. He had less than a week to "find" Mercury and deliver her to the Echelon. The first part seemingly the easier of the two tasks. He needed to focus himself and think about what he was going to do before he found himself played for a fool.

Lynch stopped in front of the door to Mrs. Marberry's study, the scent of lemon-infused perfume flavoring the air. Here was another reason his footsteps dragged. Guilt suffused him. He'd left Rosa this afternoon only to find her gone when he returned. After his actions in the observatory, it was little wonder.

When he was in her presence, he hadn't once thought of Mercury. Rosa eclipsed all thoughts of any other woman. Yet one steamy encounter in the bathhouse had proven him as susceptible as any other man.

Both women intrigued him in their ways. Mercury was a mystery, designed to be solved. A challenge. Sex.

And Rosa? His stomach clenched. He wasn't quite sure what she meant to him. Her slightly bawdy humor intrigued him and he found himself seeking her out increasingly. The shocking truth was that he *liked* spending time with her. She drove him insane with her little games, but the thought of them made him smile—a feeling of lightness when she was around, as if the sun shone just that little bit brighter.

So why then had he betrayed her in such a way? Each step away from the steam room only made him feel more uneasy with his actions. He'd lost his head for a moment, taken pleasure for pleasure's sake. The agony of it speared through him. He wasn't the sort of man who could bed two women at the same time. His actions tonight had taken the choice from him, and for a moment he almost hated Mercury for taking Rosa from him. It wasn't a fair thought though—he'd been the one at blame. The one who hadn't been able to deny himself.

And it damn well shouldn't matter. Today had beguiled him in ways he had to turn his back on. He had a job to do and a week to do it in. If he didn't wall himself off from these distractions, then none of this would matter. He'd be executed in the atrium.

Rubbing at his chest, he pushed into Rosa's study. She'd gone home long ago, but the ghost of her remained in her fragrance and the meticulous neatness of the room. A vein in Lynch's temple throbbed. He had to forget her. She appealed to a future that didn't exist for him.

The heady trail of her perfume, however, wouldn't let him forget. He followed it through his study, to the previously locked door of his private rooms. Warm candlelight filled his bedroom, the candle sitting in a puddle of wax. She'd evidently expected him long before.

There was a note on his pillow and something small

and black beside it. Lynch frowned before realizing what it was.

He crossed slowly to the bed. The letter tempted him. His fingers almost itched to touch it, but he'd made his decision. Mrs. Marberry needed to be forgotten—for her own sake as much as his. No matter how much he longed to see her again.

Pull yourself together. Focus. He crumpled the letter in his fist and threw it in the cold grate where it landed with a soft exhale of white ash. The velvet button however…that he kept, slipping into his pocket as a reminder of what could have been.

Then he turned and headed for his armoire and the stark leather body armor that awaited him. He had work to do.

Fourteen

FOG BOILED THROUGH THE EAST END, FILLING THE close-knit streets and obscuring the houses below. Lynch peered across the disembodied rooftops, rubbing at his knuckles absently. This was a dangerous part of town, ruled by cutthroat human gangs and the Devil of Whitechapel himself, one of the few rogue blue bloods who'd fought free of his fate and carved his own living outside of Echelon power.

The city walls loomed in the distance, keeping the Echelon in and the human rabble out. Both groups seemed to prefer it that way, and it was an easy way of distinguishing who belonged where.

Sound skittered off the tiles behind him and a half glance alerted him to the arrival of Byrnes. The other man moved with catlike grace along the ridge of the house, fog stirring around his boots as he silently surveyed the world. The taste of coal was thick in the air, like the exhale of a pipe-smoker's breath.

"Well?" Lynch asked.

"I found an entrance to Undertown," Byrnes murmured, kneeling beside him. His cold gaze raked the fog. Garrett was a leader of men, but Byrnes was the only choice when it came to hunting in dark spaces. He liked to be alone, liked the shadows. "I wish you'd brought more men."

"I've had that lecture from Doyle already. I want to observe tonight, not attack." Lynch scratched at his jaw. He'd let her go but that meant nothing. He needed Mercury's secrets, to discover if what she had said about the mechs was true. "Where's the entrance to Undertown?"

"Behind a whorehouse in Limey," Byrnes replied. "Trapdoor around the back that looks like it leads to a cellar. Someone's cut a hole down into the ELU tunnels."

No doubt the brothel fronted as a smuggling den then. Undertown existed for enterprising types. Lynch's eyes narrowed. "A guard?"

"I slipped him," Byrnes replied. "He's too busy fondling the merchandise."

"Let's move, then."

The tiles were slick beneath Lynch's boots, but he moved like liquid through the night, knowing that Byrnes followed. Fierce joy arose in him as he leaped across a narrow alley and landed on a nearby roof, his feet barely touching before he raced up the steep slope of the roof. This was the only time he felt truly free, unhindered by responsibility and duty. Byrnes might frown on him taking such an active role in the hunt, but Lynch needed it, now more than ever.

With a sharp gesture, he indicated Byrnes to take the lead once they reached Jamaica Street. The silence of the world was strangely eerie now that martial law had descended. People no doubt prowled the streets—there weren't enough guards to police every rookery—but they kept their outings quiet.

A whispered argument caught his ear, ghosting through the fog. He ignored it, trying to stay low on the roofline and out of the stark moonlight.

And then something about the words caught his ear. A voice he knew only too well. "You must be mistaken," Mrs. Marberry said quite clearly, her voice echoing through the reaches. "I've paid my lease for the month."

Lynch stopped in his tracks. What the hell was she doing out? One glance showed Byrnes vanishing into the shadows. Lynch ought to move on; duty beckoned. He'd made his decision earlier about Mrs. Marberry and he intended to stick with it.

Then a man's low-laughed reply made every hair on the back of his neck lift, the world muting down to gray shadows tinged with red. Lynch knew that sort of laugh. He was moving before he could think.

∽

Rosalind leaned against the brick wall, trying not to breathe too deeply. Her temporary landlord reeked of gin.

The butcher leered down her bodice, not even making pretense at decency. "I don't recall that transaction."

"Would you like me to fetch the receipt?" she replied through her teeth. She knew precisely what he was up to. A widow was considered fair game here in the East End and she'd been lucky to be unmolested for so long. Of course, if he knew what she was planning—how easy it would be to slit his throat—then he might not be so interested.

She stilled her impulses. A body in the streets would raise questions that she didn't need right now. Someone like Mrs. Marberry would deal with this in other ways.

"I shall look for it," she said. "Perhaps you would prefer to speak to my brother Jack about the misunderstanding?" It rankled to involve a man, but sometimes it was quicker. Rosalind wasn't above using whatever tool was needed for the task.

Taking a step to the side, she jerked back as the butcher slammed a meaty hand against the wall beside her face. "Let's not cause trouble we don't need," he said, looking around. "You and I, we can come at some sort of arrangement."

The press of his body almost made her gag. She was half tempted to trigger the blade in her iron hand and shove it up underneath his fat chin, just to see the piggish gleam in his eyes disappear.

"Listen here—" she began, when a shadow swooped down from above.

The butcher disappeared. One moment, his gap-toothed smirk was in her face and the next he was slammed up against the wall by a cloaked figure. The stranger held the butcher by one hand, his fingers digging into the man's throat with ease. Rosalind's mouth parted in shock as she recognized the harsh, aquiline features and cold burning gleam of Lynch's eyes.

What was he doing here? Her stomach twisted itself in knots as she mentally raked her attire. She wore nothing of Mercury's and she'd liberally sprayed herself with perfume before leaving her home. Unless the imprint of what had happened in the steamy bathing room beneath the guild had left some sort of invisible mark—a scarlet letter painted against her forehead.

Had he followed her from the guild? She was rarely careless, but she knew her head had not been in a clear space of mind. Instead, frustration and sexual desire had raked through her, driving her half-mad with impatience. She'd had to get out of there before she marched back in and demanded her dues. This was twice now he'd left her on the edge, her body thrumming with unfulfilled need.

I don't need to chase you... You'll come back to me.

He was right. Even now her body betrayed her, fierce hunger beating in her breast as she eyed that hard, muscular frame—a body she knew almost every inch of now.

"Do you know who I am?" Lynch asked quietly.

"Ye-es." A hoarse reply. The scent of urine filled the air. "Please—"

"Keep your mouth shut." Lynch's voice was almost unrecognizable, almost metallic. A knife appeared in his other hand and he pressed the sharp edge to the man's throat and leaned on it just enough to break the skin. "This woman is under my protection, do you understand?"

Those piggy eyes widened and the butcher made a whimpering sound that could have been assent. Rosalind took a nervous step back. The demon rode him hard tonight. Her hand slid into her pocket and gripped the hilt of the pistol strapped to her thigh. Then let go. She didn't quite know what to do.

"If you ever come near her again, I'll cut your throat," Lynch whispered. "And nobody will ever find the body." His gaze dropped as the knife moved an inch, slicing through skin like it was paper. Blood slid between the rolls of the butcher's chin. "Her lease is free for six months, do you understand? And all the other women who rent off you—you don't touch them either." He leaned close, menace radiating from him. "Don't ever think I won't have someone watching."

"No, sir," the butcher gasped, swallowing against the blade.

Another rasp of the knife. Rosalind watched in morbid fascination as Lynch sliced the man from ear to ear, the pressure just firm enough to part the skin. The butcher was barely even bleeding but he'd remember it. And when he looked in the mirror in the morning to shave, he'd see evidence of this night.

Lynch shoved away from him and the man tumbled to the cobbles, crying in great, racking sobs. "Go," he said coldly, wiping the edge of the knife against his breeches. "Before I change my mind and have you arrested for breaking curfew."

A quick scramble on the cobbles, then the butcher staggered past her, so frightened he didn't even seem to see her. Rosalind pressed back against the bricks to avoid him, then slowly looked up.

Lynch breathed hard, staring down at his gloved hands. He closed his eyes, his entire body trembling.

Something was wrong. Rosalind wet her lips and pushed away from the building.

"Are you all right?" she whispered. He hadn't followed her. He couldn't have—or else he wouldn't have stayed his hand with just the butcher. This was pure chance that their paths had crossed.

"No." Hoarse words. He reached out and splayed a hand over the pitted brickwork. The very preciseness of his movements made her still, the hairs on the back of her neck lifting. She'd seen this before in Balfour.

This wasn't the man she knew; his hunger was in ascendancy, Lynch holding on to it by the thinnest of leashes.

"What are you doing out?" he asked harshly. "It's martial law. I should damned well arrest you."

"I was looking for my brother," she said, a pang of sadness twisting through her. "He's not come home yet."

The words almost bought tears to her eyes. She was holding on to sanity herself by the slightest grip. Every day only tightened the knot inside her heart, where Jeremy belonged. No matter how busy she kept herself, the quiet moments still crept up, where she couldn't help but dwell on her growing sense of loss.

Still no sign of him... She couldn't give up. She wouldn't... But why couldn't she find him?

Lynch turned black eyes on her, the irises completely obliterated by darkness. "How often has that man harassed you? Has he ever—"

"No," she hastened to assure him. "He hasn't dared before. I came across him on the way home and he'd been drinking—" She shook her head. "And I have my pistol. For men like that."

Lynch pushed away from the wall. "Then why didn't you draw it?"

Rosalind was tempted to back away but didn't dare. "I didn't think I needed to. I was in control."

"It didn't sound like it."

She gaped for words, not understanding the change in him. His anger was so fierce she could almost feel it on her skin. "Well. I don't think I shall have to be concerned in the future. Word will spread after that little performance."

He grabbed her arm. "I would force you to stay at the guild, but I don't think that wise. I'll set a man to watch over you instead."

The closeness of his body set her on fire, her heart hammering in her chest. She couldn't quite forget the feel of those clever fingers between her thighs and the rasp of his teeth against her throat. Concentrating was hard, but she would not be undone like she had been in the bathing room. "No," she blurted. *The worst thing possible.* "That's quite all right. I don't need a Nighthawk on my doorstep." Then she frowned. "And why don't you want me staying at the guild? I thought…after this afternoon—?"

His gaze lowered, but he wasn't staring at her breasts as the butcher had. "This afternoon was a mistake," he said gently but firmly. "I should never have taken such liberties and I beg your forgiveness." He met her gaze then. The black was fading, but the implacability of his resolve was not. "It won't happen again, Rosa. It can't."

She should never have provoked it in the first place. Yet her heart clenched at his words, a dangerous sense of…*something*…filling her. Disappointment?

"Why?" she blurted recklessly.

Lynch seemed to withdraw into himself as if he

were putting up walls. "You're my secretary," he said, "and I your employer. I would be taking advantage."

"I didn't mind," she murmured. "I wanted what happened—"

"I kissed another woman tonight," he said bluntly. "You should know that."

She'd known. Of course she'd known. Yet the way he threw it in her face actually hurt. She could feel the heat draining from her skin, her heart suddenly pounding sharply in her ears. How ridiculous... To feel such jealousy over what was essentially herself.

"Why?" she whispered.

Lynch drew away, raking a hand through his hair. "I don't know," he snapped. "It's a complicated situation."

"Is she... Is she someone you know?" It seemed ridiculous to ask, but she was suddenly desperate to know what he truly thought about her. Or about Rosa Marberry.

Anger filled her. She *wasn't* Rosa Marberry. The woman was just a role. Yet it felt real. A tiny little part of her wanted to be Rosa Marberry. Someone without the crushing burden of her past or the pressure of a missing brother. Someone that Jasper Lynch had wanted, even for a second.

Lynch's bleakness surprised her. "No," he said. "She's no one I know, no one...important."

That made the ache fiercer. "I see."

"I should never have touched you. The shame is all mine," he replied. A faint hesitation. "Come, I'll walk you home."

"No." She jerked away. "It's fine. I can find my own way."

"Rosa." A hand caught her upper arm.

She lashed out then, balling her right hand into a fist and driving it into his gut. "Don't touch me! Just leave me alone!"

He exhaled sharply but the ribbed padding of his armor deflected the blow and she was left clutching at her hand, heat bubbling up behind her eyes.

The shock of it took her by surprise. Then she was crying and she couldn't stop, wet messy tears sliding down her cheeks and a sob catching in her throat. She jammed her fist against her teeth to stop it from escaping, a hot flare of pain sliding through the wounded limb.

"Damn it," Lynch cursed. He stepped closer, the toes of his boots coming into her watery vision. "Damn it, Rosa. Please don't cry." His hands slid over her upper arms and she stiffened, but he was only rubbing them. Her metal hand was far from his touch.

Then his arms wrapped around her, crushing her close. Rosalind fought for a second, hot angry tears scoring her cheeks, then collapsed into his arms. Hesitantly, she put her hand against his chest. Sexual desire she could fight, but not this... She wanted to be held as if someone cared, just this once.

Hurt bubbled up inside her at the thought. A sudden lurching wave of grief went through her; she missed her husband so dreadfully. Or perhaps simply the touch of a man, the warm companionship, the feeling that someone would look after *her*, instead of always being the one to look after everyone else.

"What's wrong?"

Rosalind curled into Lynch's arms, silently pleading

with him to hold her. Shaking her head, she buried her face against his chest and let the tears come.

She'd thought she was strong enough to deal with this but she was coming apart at the seams, fracturing, her entire world shattering like a stained-glass window.

"I'm trying to be strong," she blurted, not knowing where the words were coming from.

"You are strong—"

"No, I'm not," she cried. "Everything is going wrong. Everything!"

"I don't understand," he replied, frustration edging his voice. He rubbed her back, his hand curling protectively against her spine. "What's wrong, Rosa? What is 'everything'? Is it the butcher? Or…me?"

Longing filled her. Rosalind wanted to tell him, to blurt out all of her troubles and stay here in his arms. To have someone else deal with the problem for once. As if someone cared, as if someone would look after *her*. What a mess. She dragged strands of wet hair off her cheeks and shook her head. If she told him the truth, the caring tone would leech out of his voice immediately. He wasn't her ally nor even her friend. Not truly. She had to forget this feeling and forge ahead on the path she'd set herself.

You are alone. That's how it had to be—or had been since Nate's death.

Dragging in a breath, she wiped her eyes, her cheeks. The tears slid silently now. "I'm sorry."

"Rosa," he whispered, cupping her face. An echo of her pain lingered in his expression, as if it actually hurt him to see this. "Tell me what's wrong. I can help you."

She shook her head. "It's just——" Her breath caught again. "I can't find my brother. I haven't seen him... for a long time. I don't even know if he's still alive." Her mouth kept saying the words even as her horrified brain screamed at her to shut up.

Lynch's hands cupped her face and tilted it up. "I can help you, Rosa. I can find him. It's what I do."

"You can't. Nobody can help me."

His gaze turned watchful. "Are you afraid of what might happen if I do find him? Rosa, you said once he'd fallen in with a bad crowd. Is he... Is he a humanist?"

Her fingers tightened on his sleeve in fear and she looked up, a swift denial on her lips.

Lynch pressed his finger against her mouth, stilling the words. "Don't," he demanded in a silky-harsh voice. "Don't lie to me, please." The backs of his fingers brushed against her cheek, tracing the path of her tears. "I'm not a monster, Rosa. I wouldn't hurt him. It's not the first time I've turned a blind eye."

Disbelief shivered through her. "You lied to the Echelon?"

His hands were almost hypnotic, tracing over the curve of her lip. "Sometimes the Council misreads a situation." His fingers hesitated. "I'm not the enemy, Rosa. I never have been."

She closed her eyes, taking a deep, trembling breath. Did she dare trust him? It was so tempting, but she'd had her lessons beaten into her over the years with brutal efficiency. Could she go against everything she'd ever learned?

"Please, Rosa."

It broke something inside her. She trembled beneath

his touch, another hot tear sliding down her cheek. "I wanted to try and find him. That's why I took the job as your secretary," she whispered. She needed this, she realized. Needed some sense of honesty between them. "I thought you might have word of him. That's why I went through all your papers. That's why I picked the lock on your study. I've...lied to you several times."

He was so still. She looked up, catching his wrist as if he sought to draw away.

"Go on."

"He's a humanist," she replied. The words almost shriveled on her tongue. "Just a boy though. I tried to protect him..."

"But boys will do as they will." Lynch frowned. "What's his name?"

Again she couldn't speak the words. This went against everything she believed in. Lynch watched her silently until she finally tore her gaze away. "Jeremy," she murmured. "Jeremy Fairchild." Her voice dropped wistfully. "I call him Jem. He's so much younger than I. My mother died when he was two, so I had the raising of him."

"How old is he?"

"Seventeen."

Another grim silence. "That's old enough to be tried in the tower."

"No." She shook her head desperately. "He's just a boy."

"What does he look like?"

The words were starting to come easier now. "He has red hair, like me." She fingered a strand of hair that hung over her face. "And freckles, though they're fading now. He's perhaps six foot, although it seems like he grows an inch each time I look at him."

Lynch sucked in a sharp breath as if she'd struck him. "And how long has it been since you've seen him?" he demanded.

Another hard question to answer. "August 24th."

They both knew what it meant. The date the Echelon signed the treaty with the Scandinavian verwulfen clans. The date the mechs had tried to blow up the tower.

"Did he have anything to do with the bombing?"

She shook her head. Then hesitated. It was so terribly difficult to answer this question. Did she trust him? Truly trust him? He had said this wasn't the first time he'd turned a blind eye to events, but she was playing with Jeremy's life here. "Yes." A whisper. A plea. "I think so. The men he was involved with…"

Lynch sucked in a sharp breath. "Bloody hell." He looked at her, then scraped a hand over his jaw. "You realize what this means? A humanist is one thing, but an act of such magnitude?" His voice broke. "Rosa, do you know what you're asking of me?"

Hope deflated, her chest squeezing tight. Of course she'd asked too much. He couldn't help her. Nobody could. "Yes."

Lynch swore under his breath. "I'll do my best," he promised. "But I need more facts than this. I need to know that if I found him and set him free for you, he wouldn't hurt anyone. I can't—I can't promise you anything."

That he was even willing to help her was so much more than she would have ever suspected. On impulse, she reached out and took his hand, sliding her fingers through his. "I know you'll do what you must."

As would she. But the weight that had been dragging at her for weeks seemed to have lifted. A flood of feeling swept through her, as alien and uncomfortable as a knife itching against her skin. She didn't understand it; or perhaps she understood it all too much. This was what had almost destroyed her so many years ago, when she'd slammed the door open on the cell and staggered inside, only to watch Balfour drag the blade across her husband's throat.

A cold chill swept through her, her eyes swimming with tears again. Balfour had ripped her heart from her chest in one move, destroying her entire world. She'd sworn then that she would never weaken herself ever again, never place another man in such a situation.

Lynch's head lowered, his lashes falling half-closed over those glacial blue eyes. Rosalind's heart stuttered in her chest as she realized his intentions. It was one thing to kiss him as Mercury, to tease him as Rosa Marberry, but now she was neither. She had bared part of her soul to him, the first time she had done so in many years. The feeling left her surprisingly vulnerable. This, more than anything, was her truth. Not the words she had just spoken, but her own admittance that she had growing feelings for him.

A blue blood.

Abruptly she tugged her fingers from his grasp. Panic curled through her abdomen and she turned away, almost tripping on her skirts. Balfour had taught her to fear neither pain nor death. But...this... And the devastation it left in its wake...

"I'm sorry," he said curtly. "I did not mean to do that."

Rosalind nodded, tucking her hands into each other. What was she thinking? Maybe Ingrid was right. Perhaps it was time to cut her losses… But then he had just promised to help her try and find Jeremy.

She needed to see this through to the end.

If she could. For the first time, Rosa had serious doubts about her ability to remain cool and unaffected.

"You were right," she whispered. "I don't think it wise to pursue this… this…" She had no name for it, as if in the giving of a name, she gave the weakness power over her. "I think perhaps we should remain as we were. Employer and employee."

She waited for his answer, her head tilting to the side to see him. Uncertainty filled her, she who was never uncertain. What was he doing to her? She had to keep her distance.

"Of course," he murmured. "But I must insist on walking you home. I hate to think of you out here on the streets."

She could handle almost anything she found on these streets. The irony was that her one weakness was him. Rosalind took a slow breath, collecting herself. "If you must."

She turned to accept his sleeve. Lynch staggered into her, his hands clutching at hers before she could stop him.

Horror filled her. His hand closed over the hard metal of her left wrist. She couldn't feel the touch of course, though she felt as though she should. She felt as though it should burn right through her.

"Oh God," she whispered.

Then his knees went out from under him and he slumped against her, his hand catching at her skirt, her fingers, anything to stop himself from falling.

That was when she saw the dart sticking out of the back of his neck.

Fifteen

A MOCKING LAUGH FILLED THE ALLEY.

Rosalind looked up as a shadow separated itself from the rest. A tall man wearing a heavy leather seaman's coat lumbered forward. He didn't bother to hide the sharp hook he wore instead of a left hand, his heavy-lidded gaze sliding over her.

"Well, now. Look what we got, boys. A Nighthawk by the looks of it. And a well-rounded tart." A smile split his broad face. "The craver for Mordecai, and the bitch for me."

She watched the hook, her gaze following its hypnotic motions. Years ago, seeing a glimpse of that would have been any East-Ender's worst nightmare. The slasher gangs that had roamed these parts used whatever scrap metal they could find to enhance themselves. Some said they even cut the limbs from their own flesh to replace with cruel hooks and sharp blades in order to join the gangs. The better to drag a body to Undertown, where they'd strap it to a gurney and drain it of blood for profit.

Three years ago, a vampire had taken care of most

of them, with the Devil of Whitechapel cleaning up the rest. Obviously some few had escaped.

And Mordecai must have allied himself with them, giving them the secret of hemlock.

"I'm afraid I've got a prior engagement." Rosalind watched the shadows. Slashers used to run in packs, hunting their prey like wild dogs. There'd be more of them.

A second man slid free of the encroaching fog. Then a third. Rosalind glanced up as something shifted in her peripheral vision and saw more on the roof.

At her feet Lynch made a helpless noise in his throat. A sudden burning fierceness in her chest took her by surprise. They weren't going to get their hands on him. She'd make sure of that.

"Don't worry," she said softly. "I won't leave you."

"Get her," the slasher said with a contemptuous wave of his hook. "And tie that bleeder up before he comes to."

Rosalind's hand dipped to her pocket and came out with the pistol. She took a step away from Lynch to give herself room to work. "Don't move," she said coldly, aiming the pistol at the lead slasher's forehead. "Or all the metal in the world won't fill this hole."

He grinned slowly. "That's a pretty little toy, lass. You know how to use it?"

"Would you care for a demonstration?" Rosalind pulled the trigger.

The slasher staggered back, his eyes rolling up in his head and a red dot blooming in the middle of his forehead. His body hit the ground hard and Rosalind was moving, leaning low to take the knife from her boot.

She preferred a pistol but in these streets it wasn't wise to draw too much attention.

The two remaining men stepped forward, expressions blunt and hard. One of them took the lead, his ugly face marred by what looked like a half dozen scars.

"I'm going to keep you alive for that," he promised. "For a very long time."

"I have no such compunctions." She leaped over Lynch's broad back, grateful that he was lying face-first and couldn't see.

The man met her blade with one of his own; a knife grafted to his forearm, no doubt drilled into the bone. Rosalind swirled, the skirts barely hampering her as she released the Carillion blade in her iron hand. It slipped between his ribs with a surgeon's ease, then she slashed down with her other knife, dragging it across the inside of his thigh. Blood sprayed across her skirts, hot and coppery as she hit the femoral artery.

He went down with a scream and she spun low, hooking the toe of her boot behind the other man's heel with feral grace. Anger burned hot in her throat. She wanted this, needed it. Anything to drive away that helpless feeling and unleash the tide of hopelessness within her.

As he hit the ground, she was upon him, slamming her heel into the vulnerable bones of his throat. A satisfying crunch filled the air.

Noise whistled in the eerie fog. Rosalind spun, knife held flat. Then something heavy dropped over her and she went to her knees under a net, the ends weighted with lead.

Damn her skirts! She tried to kick, but the net was

tangled hopelessly with her bustle and she'd dropped the bloody knife. A pair of boots landed in front of her, then the sound of another. Rosalind slashed desperately at the net with her Carillion blade. It sawed through the thick hemp with ease, but then hands caught her by the upper arms and she was dragged upright, the net wrapped round and round her ankles.

"No!" She jerked hard, the first hint of unease seeping insidiously through her veins. "What are you doing? Get your hands off me!"

The world upended as someone dragged her over their shoulder. Through the net, she glimpsed a pair of men kneeling over Lynch and something flared white-hot within her.

"What are you doing to him?" She kicked desperately.

"Take her down below," someone snapped. "Throw the bitch in a cell while we get the bleeder contained."

The giant beneath her turned around and Rosalind lost her view of Lynch. "No! Help! Someone help!" she screamed, feeling dread for the first time in years.

If they hurt him… She shook her head. He was invincible. A blue blood. Surely he could get free and save himself.

But they'd paralyzed him with hemlock. She of all people knew only too well how to incapacitate blue bloods—and keep them that way.

"No!"

❦

They strapped him into a set of manacles and dragged him high using a winch. Lynch jerked into the air, unable to do a damned thing to stop himself from being hung like a slab of beef. He hated this, hated the vulnerability.

The cell was deep in Undertown. They'd blind-folded him and wrapped him tight with chains, but that didn't mean he hadn't been able to make some sense of where they'd taken them. The smell of tar and rope lingered in the air as they entered the tunnels—somewhere near Sailmaker's Lane if he wasn't mistaken. From there, it had been a brief journey down through the chilly tunnels to this godforsaken cell where they'd ripped the blindfold off.

The leader strode through the door with a scowl of frustration. "String 'er up too."

"Get your hands off me!"

Lynch fought to lift his heavy head, trying to see what they were doing to Rosa. Red flared through his vision as two men dragged her into the cell. Her hands were bound behind her, blood sprayed across her skirts, but she squirmed in their grasp as if she thought to free herself.

One of them balled his fist and smashed her in the abdomen. Rosa gasped, crumpling over the man's arm with a soft cry. *Kill them...* Lynch stirred, his leg kicking faintly. The muscles in his shoulders ached as he strained to get some movement into his body. Anything other than hanging here uselessly.

Where the hell was Byrnes? He should have doubled back once he noticed Lynch was missing.

The leader stepped back as they dragged Rosa's gloved hands into another set of manacles and yanked her high. The toe of her boots dragged on the ground, then she cried out as they winched her into the air. Whatever sort of operation they were running here, they knew what they were doing.

The barest light gleamed through the heavy cell door. Lynch caught Rosa's gaze and saw the frustration and pain echoed there. She stopped kicking when she saw him, taking a deep, shuddering breath, her dark eyes rich with fear.

"Did...they hurt you...?" he managed to rasp.

Rosa shook her head. "No."

With a laugh, the leader slapped Lynch's thigh, sending him swinging, the toes of his boots dragging over the cold stone floors. "Don't need to." A broad smile lit his ugly face. "That's what you're 'ere for."

Words. Just words. But ice ran down his spine at the thought. He looked at Rosa, her coppery hair bedraggled and tumbling around her pale face. She bit her lip and shifted against the weight dragging on her shoulders. Lynch's gaze raked over the cell. It was bare, but he could see faint splashes of darkness against the walls. Blood. Sprayed across the walls as if someone had torn a man's throat out.

He went cold.

That's what you're 'ere for...

They wouldn't have to hurt Rosa. He would. He knew it as certainly as he knew his own name. These men were involved with the massacres somehow. The mechs that Mercury spoke of.

He didn't know what they'd done to Haversham, Falcone, and Alistair, but he had a suspicion he was about to find out.

No. He jerked—or tried to. Every muscle in his

body felt sluggish, as if they'd weighted his bones down with steel implants.

"All right, boys," the leader called. "Let's leave 'em to their fate." He met Lynch's eyes with a leer. "I'll be seein' you in an hour or so, Sir Nighthawk."

Then the cell door clanged shut behind them.

"Rosa."

She kicked uselessly. The muscles in her abdomen ached and she still hadn't quite gotten her breath back, or else she'd have protested more.

"Rosa." Lynch's voice was cool, but something warned her—some underlying hint of tension.

She looked across at him. Bars of light striped his face from the small barred window in the cell door. Movement stirred in his limbs, signs that the hemlock was finally wearing off. They must have hit him with a huge dose in order to keep him down for so long.

"What?" she whispered.

For a moment, an unknown emotion crossed his face, there and gone so swiftly she didn't recognize it. Her breath caught and she stilled, staring across the shadowed expanse at him.

"They took your pistol, didn't they?" he asked. "Do you have anything at all that might be used as a weapon?"

Only herself and her training, but he could not be allowed to know that. "No. I'm sorry. I've got nothing to fight them with."

His expression tightened. He cursed under his breath and looked around. "Are your manacles fastened tight? Can you get free?"

His urgency burned through her. "What aren't you telling me?"

"Just answer the damned question!" he snapped.

It shocked her. He'd never once been frightened. And that was what she recognized in his clenching fists as he strained against the manacles.

Rosalind licked her lips and looked up. "Maybe," she admitted. "I have several pins in my hair. I might be able to pick the lock on these."

"Do it."

Pressing her lips tightly together, she put all her weight onto her right wrist and reached up to grab a loop of chain with her left. Her iron hand clutched tight around the links and she hauled herself up, high enough to dig her right hand into her hair. Her fingers finally locked around the edge of a pin and she tugged it free with a gasp, her body weight tumbling back against the manacles. This would have been easy ten years ago, but she no longer trained every day as she had under Balfour's care. Then she'd been fit and limber and far stronger than she was now.

"Got it," she gasped, her shoulders aching against the swing of the manacles.

Voices sounded in the corridor outside the cell. Their eyes met.

"You need to get out, Rosa," he said. "Pick the lock and get out. Get as far away from here as you can."

A laugh outside. Her gaze jerked that way as someone yanked open an iron trapdoor in the door.

"Give 'er me regards, Sir Nighthawk."

Rosalind flinched as something was thrown into the room. The iron ball was barely the size of Lynch's closed fist and it rattled across the stone floors, bouncing off the far wall before spinning to a halt in the center of the room. It looked almost like the clockwork tumbler balls that children played with in the alleys aboveground, chasing them until they finally wound down. Like one of the balls they'd found in Falcone's dining room.

She stared, cold sweat lining her lip. What the devil was it? And why was Lynch staring at it as one would eye a live snake? He strained against the manacles, a silent snarl on his lips as he jerked and twisted.

"I'd love to stay and watch the final test," the stranger called. "But you cravers don't take kindly to being locked up. We'll be nearby...for when it's over."

The iron trapdoor slammed shut and then the laughter was edging away.

"Lynch," she whispered, fear knifing through her. "What's going on?"

The iron ball quivered, a thin line becoming apparent around its circumference as though some internal pressure fought to force it open.

"This is what they did to Falcone," Lynch snarled. He fought furiously, twisting his body up to try and wrench the manacles from the ceiling. "I'm sure of it. You have to get out."

What they did to Falcone... She stared at him for a long moment as his words penetrated. He'd known. Somehow he'd known what was to come—just as he knew he wouldn't be able to stop himself from hurting her.

She saw the truth in his eyes as he flailed helplessly, then fell still, panting hard. He couldn't free himself. He had been weakened by the hemlock until he was almost human in strength, but if the bloodlust hit him the way it had done to Haversham or Falcone or his cousin…he would be unstoppable. That's why he'd asked her if she had anything on her that might be a weapon. It wasn't to use against the mechs. No, it was to use against him.

The heat drained from her face, her hand tingling with numbness.

"I'm sorry."

"Don't be." She looked away, frightened by the defeat in his eyes. "I'm not going to let you kill me." She sucked in a deep breath and let it out slowly. *Think, damn you.* She'd survived worse than this. If there was one gift that Balfour had ever given her, it was this—the urge to survive against all odds.

The ball started shaking so hard it quivered across the floor. Almost open.

"I want you," she said slowly, "to think of buttons."

Lynch's gaze shot to hers. "What?"

"My buttons, to be more specific."

"Rosa!"

"I'm going to escape," she added. "But I've heard that a blue blood has strong… urges. Strong hungers."

He caught her meaning. "The bloodlust is stronger."

"We'll test that theory as a last resort," Rosalind replied, her fingers tightening around the pin in her hand. "You want me, my lord. So think about my breasts, which you can never quite take your eyes off, and that afternoon in the library where you left me quite unsatisfied." Kicking her legs up, she locked an ankle around one of the chains, her skirts falling over her head.

The iron ball popped apart with a hiss, steam pouring through small vents around its middle.

Lynch coughed. "Hurry!"

A sweet scent caught her nose as the cloud of steam drifted across the cobbles, hanging low for the moment. It wound around Lynch's dangling legs and for a second she saw his fear again.

He couldn't give into the fear. If he did, then he would be lost completely.

Rosalind swallowed, her pin sliding into the lock. *Success.* She let out her breath. "You never asked," she said, forcing her voice to remain calm.

"Never asked what?"

"Whether I obeyed your final instruction in the observatory that day. Whether I waited for you."

For a moment Lynch's gaze locked on hers. Shadows flickered through his eyes, stealing the color from them. He shut them tight. "This isn't helping."

"You're going to lose control," she said bluntly. "Try and think—"

"I am *not* going to lose control," he snapped, a muscle in his jaw tightening. "I can't. I won't."

The steam writhed around him with hungry tendrils. And Rosalind finally understood him. The reason he had never taken from the vein and strictly controlled his intake of blood. This was his greatest fear—the loss of control, the bloodlust. For the first time, she realized what it would be like to be stricken with the craving, to fight against instinct and need, when it would be so much easier to give into it.

"I know you can fight this."

"Don't trust me," he gasped. "Get your hands on a weapon—anything—and don't be afraid to use it."

The steam rose, obscuring her view of his body. Lynch strained, trying to lift himself above it.

Rosalind turned her attention to the lock. She slid the pin inside it, fumbling blindly in the near dark.

The lock finally clicked.

Wrenching the manacle open, she flexed her steel fingers, then gripped the chain above her right hand. She didn't have time for finesse. Instead, she yanked hard, her bio-mech hand breaking the links of the manacle.

"Bollocks!" Her eyes flew wide as she started to fall. Hitting the ground hard, she lay for one panicked, breathless moment.

"Rosa? Are you free?"

"I'm free." She rolled onto her hands and knees with a wince. Steam obscured the room and she coughed as the cloying, sticky-sweet smell of it clotted her lungs.

"Can you… get out?"

Feeling along the wall, she saw the bright bands of light against the foggy darkness. The door!

Lynch was a dark shadow in the mist. Rosa kicked the iron ball away into the corner, stilling when she saw his gleaming eyes lock on her. Like prey.

"Did you?" he gasped, clenching and unclenching his fists. A shudder ran through his body.

"Did I what?"

"Did you wait?"

She backed away from him as his eyes turned black

with fierce need. He clenched them tight, trying to hold on to himself.

"I waited," she whispered. "I'm still waiting."

Slowly, she reached out behind her for the door, feeling for the lock in the darkness. Her pin had twisted. She'd need another. But she couldn't, for the moment, take her eyes off him. Steam obscured him completely and he jerked, still fighting, even now, not to lose control of himself.

Rosalind could barely see him. But she heard a low hiss of breath, a sound that terrified her, despite her intentions. And then the sound of metal straining as he tore at his manacles.

"Run," he pleaded. Another strained laugh, as if he fought to hold it back. "For God's sake, run!"

Rosalind turned and jammed another pin into the lock, her heart rabbiting in her chest in terror.

He'd just lost the battle.

Sixteen

THE DOOR OPENED AND ROSALIND DIDN'T WASTE TIME to see if he'd gotten himself free. She could hear him straining, a low growl of frustration echoing in his throat as he fought the manacles. The steel wouldn't hold him in this state. Not for long.

Shoving her shoulder against the door, she staggered into the tunnel—looked like an old maintenance tunnel of some sort, with a pair of torches burning steadily in their niches.

Grabbing a handful of skirts, she started running.

Behind her, a thwarted roar echoed as she escaped. The sound sent a chill down her spine, her footsteps lengthening in response. Had to get away. If he caught her—

The door at the end of the tunnel was locked. Rosalind jerked at the knob, then slapped her steel hand against it in frustration. "Damn you!"

Behind her silence fell.

Rosalind turned slowly, the hairs on the back of her neck lifting. At the end of the tunnel, a dark figure stepped free of the cell, moving with an eerie, predator grace. He stopped and stared at her, his eyes black with fury and need and hunger.

Rosalind yanked a pin from her hair and spun around, jamming it in the lock. "Come on," she murmured, jiggling it until she felt it catch. "Come on!" A glance over her shoulder showed him stalking toward her, taking his time, knowing she couldn't escape. Rosalind slammed her fist against the door, dinting it. By some stroke of luck the lock clicked. She yanked at the door, sucking in a frightened hiss of breath between her teeth as it opened.

"NO!!!"

Lynch's scream of rage echoed in the tunnel and Rosalind barreled through the door, slamming it behind her. There was a key on a hook beside the door and she thrust it into the lock and twisted it, staring through the thin window slit as Lynch thundered toward her.

"Damn you, come on!" The lock snicked and Rosalind staggered away from the door as he hit it.

The hinges screamed in protest, dust shaking off the stone walls. Rosalind met his eyes and saw nothing human there. Not the man she knew. Not the man she cared for. Here was her own secret fear, staring at her with cold, hungry eyes.

His fists wrapped around the bars and he wrenched. The iron screamed, bending like Indian rubber. Rosalind turned and ran up a flight of stairs.

Behind her, an enormous crash echoed.

Faster, her lungs screaming for air. She threw a glance over her shoulder and saw something move in the shadows behind her.

A door appeared in the wall. Rosalind crashed through it, slamming it shut behind her and locking it before she turned and collapsed against something in the dark. Her fumbling fingers found a smuggler's lantern and a packet of matches. Striking one, she lit the lantern's wick with shaking fingers.

Something hit the door. Rosalind jumped. A table stood in the center of the room, with benches around the sides. She hurried behind it, though the table would be small help.

Crates of iron balls gleamed in the flickering light, with little clock faces strapped to them. Rosalind ran her fingers over one, feeling the thin seam that ran around the middle. There had to be dozens here. Enough to drive a whole horde of blue blood's mad. Just what were the mechs planning?

Another jolt shuddered the door. Rosalind spun, her gaze raking the room for anything to help her. Metal tools hung on the wall, signs of a mech's trade. She grabbed a file and clenched it in her fist, hunting for something sharper. A rack of bottles lined the far wall, the glass gleaming as she lifted the lantern and brought it closer. Taking out the cork, she sniffed at the colorless liquid. The same sickly sweet scent she'd recognized in the cell made her jam the cork back in.

A deafening silence fell, making her heartbeat thunder in her ears.

Then a fist came through the door.

Rosalind screamed, dropping the lantern on the bench and spinning to face him. Her gaze fell on a pile of goods on a small table near the door. A dart gun with the bright blue feathers of a hemlock dart.

Lynch groped for the key, turning it in its lock. Then his hand withdrew, the knuckles bloody. Slowly, so slowly, the handle turned.

Rosalind pressed herself back into the bench. Nowhere to run. Nothing to fight him with. If only she could get to the dart gun.

The door slowly opened. Darkness entered, materializing into a man she barely recognized. His black hair gleamed in the lantern light, the flame flickering off his obsidian eyes. Stark light carved out the refined features of his face and broad shoulders.

"Lynch?" she whispered.

He was breathing hard, his chest rising and falling. Slowly he shut the door. Then locked it. For a moment his head bowed, as if some part of him still fought for control. Then he started toward her.

Each step was mesmerizing, his power and grace so dangerous it stole her breath.

Rosalind swallowed. No point running or fighting. Either would only rouse his hungers. "Would you like… another button?" she whispered, lifting her hands to the tiny buttons that curved up her bodice. Her fingers jerked and the top button tore, pinging away to the floor. The lavender cotton was almost ruined anyway.

Lynch stilled, his gloved hand sliding over the end of the table as if in thought. Rosalind tore another button free, discarding it with haste.

Then another.

"Do you remember the observatory?" she asked, tugging the tiny buttons free desperately.

His gaze dipped, running heatedly over the exposed skin of her décolletage.

"That's it," she whispered, taking a sidelong step around the table. Closer to the door—and the dart gun.

He didn't like that. Rosalind stilled as the muscles in his thighs bunched. Reaching up, she slowly shook out the last few pins in her hair, letting it tumble down over her shoulder in bright, coppery coils. Lantern light made it gleam richly against her pale skin and the hungry look in his gaze hardened.

"You're mine," he said coldly.

Then he was on her. Rosalind barely had time to suck in a sharp breath as his hand sank into her hair and wrenched her head back. She caught a fistful of his shirt and bit back a scream as his mouth slashed down over hers.

Lynch devoured her, slamming her back against the wall. A crate dropped off the bench and those little metal balls rolled everywhere as his tongue thrust, hot and hard, against hers. Rosalind melted against him, her knees giving way as a surge of relief filled her.

"*Yes,*" she almost sobbed, grabbing a fistful of his hair.

Lynch caught her up beneath the thighs, sliding her onto the bench as he kissed her desperately. She couldn't draw breath, couldn't escape him. He was all over her, his huge body wrapping around hers with a possessiveness she couldn't fight. His teeth sucked her bottom lip between them and he bit her, one hand shackling her right wrist.

But at least he hadn't drawn blood. Yet.

Rosalind whimpered, wrapping her legs around his hips as she kissed him back with a fierceness born of relief. She couldn't let him go. Not for a second. If she did, then she might lose him.

The door slammed open and a man burst in, dressed all in black leather.

"No!" she screamed as Lynch tore himself from her arms and leaped toward the stranger. The Nighthawk.

If she didn't know any better, she would have thought he placed his body between them, an almost protective gesture. But then it couldn't be true. He wasn't thinking right now. Only reacting.

Their bodies met, Lynch slamming the Nighthawk against the wall. The man's eyes widened in shock. "Sir?"

"He'll kill you!" she yelled.

The stranger's icy blue eyes flickered to hers, then he shoved an elbow into Lynch's face that snapped his head up. A grim expression crossed the stranger's face—utterly ruthless.

Lynch went for his carotid but the man chopped a fist into Lynch's throat and locked an ankle behind his. They both went down, the Nighthawk fighting desperately.

There was no finesse to Lynch's movements. He was stripped down to the basics of survival, barely protecting himself, intent only on the kill. Yet his rage and strength were unstoppable.

Rosalind slid off the bench slowly, her eyes on the dart gun. Inching toward it, she flinched as Lynch drove his man face-first onto the ground. His head lifted, tracking her movements. Rosalind swallowed, her fingers closing over the dart gun.

He came at her so quickly she could barely see it. Only years of training saved her life. She shot him from three feet away. He took one more step, his knees going out from under him as the hemlock raced through his veins.

"I'm sorry," she whispered as those black eyes met hers, strangely human in that moment. Betrayed. "So sorry."

Seventeen

AWARENESS CAME SLOWLY.

Lynch fought his way toward it, straining, yearning, hunger gripping him so hard he screamed. Something held him back. Men shouting. The hot coppery scent of blood in the air and then the splash of it against his lips. It was never enough. He wanted it hot and fresh, aching to take it from someone's throat. To tear and kill, to rip apart flesh like it was paper and drown himself in blood.

He couldn't find her. No matter how hard he strained, peering past the swirl of faces in the room, she wasn't there. Fear drove him. Fear and a protective fury he couldn't fight. His woman. *His.* And someone was keeping her from him.

A face swam into view, hands gripping his shoulders. "It's me, sir. Garrett!"

The words were oddly distorted. "Where is she?" he screamed, tearing at the metal cuffs that kept him pinned on his back.

A hand slid over the man's shoulder. "He ain't there anymore, lad," an older man said gruffly. "Let 'im go."

"No! Give him more of the hemlock." Light gilded the man's coppery hair and all Lynch saw was the color of blood. "We wait him out. He'll come back."

Then he was slipping into darkness, his body slackening against the steel that kept him pinned. No matter how hard he strained, he couldn't catch even a hint of that familiar lemon scent.

&

Ten hours since she'd seen him last. Screaming and straining in his manacles...

Rosalind wrapped her arms around her and peered through the gloom. Beside her the soft rasp of Jack's breath through the air filter itched over her nerves.

"Where is she?" she murmured, shivering against the cold. She felt it so deeply tonight. As if the fright of last night had leeched into her bones. She'd thought Lynch would be fine when they got him back to the guild. But he wasn't.

"She'll be here," Jack said, his voice smooth and melodious. His throat was the one part of him that hadn't been damaged by Balfour and his steady drip of acid. His lungs were another matter, hence the air filter in the mask. The thick coal-choked air of London was too rich for him, sending him into paroxysms of coughing without it. Sometimes she wondered if he wouldn't be better off in the country, or somewhere along the Mediterranean, where the air was clear and warm. Maybe Italy, where there were no blue bloods and the church ruled supreme. He'd like that.

Rosalind dragged her pocket watch out of the tight waistcoat that cinched her curves and examined it.

The back was a clear bubble of glass, revealing the winding brass cogs and gears within it, while the face was sheeted in pearl. A flicker of gaslight caught the pearl and turned it into a rainbow shimmer.

"Ten," she muttered. As if to spite her, a bell rang nearby, over the rooftop spires of an old half-burned church. Once, twice, thrice… It droned on, cutting through the thick fog.

"I should have gone with Ingrid," she murmured.

Jack shot her a look, his monocular eyeglass gleaming eerily in the low gaslight. "We only just got you back. I'm not letting you out again, not with those bleeders out there." His voice roughened. "I'm not letting you near them ever again."

She had nothing to say to that. If he found out the truth—the reason for the blood on her skirts when she'd fled back to the house and the shaking that she couldn't quite stop in her hands—he'd have gone after Lynch with a pitchfork. As it was, she'd had to make up some story about being accosted on her way home by an anonymous blue blood.

It was the first lie she'd ever told her older brother. Growing up in the grim streets had hardened them both to the world and made them cling to each other. They couldn't trust the world. Only each other. He'd had her back and she his for years, until that fateful day when she'd dipped a pocket and Balfour had seen her.

He'd recognized her as his own, one of the three children her mother had taken from him when she'd broken her thrall contract and fled from him. Rosalind had never truly known why her mother did that, though she could perhaps guess. By that stage, she'd been long dead and both Rosalind and Jack had done what needed to be done to survive. Jack knew her down to the very last inch of her soul.

"I'm fine," she told him. "It was nothing that I couldn't handle."

"Wasn't it?" He opened the small, copper air filter in the middle of his leather half mask and cupped his fingers around the hole, breathing into them to warm them. "You've been distracted of late."

"I'm worried about Jeremy."

"Are you?" The dipping baritone of his voice drew her gaze.

"What do you mean? Of course I'm worried about him."

Slowly Jack lifted a gloved hand, his index finger sweeping a strand of her hair out of the way. His finger brushed against her neck tentatively. "You have a bite mark on the back of your neck. The kind a man gives his lover."

She couldn't breathe. Lynch. In the bathing room. He'd bitten her there, suckling the skin until she bruised and she'd forgotten all about it. Rosalind ducked away from his hand, tugging the collar of her coat higher. "Don't."

"You're troubled," Jack said quietly. "The last time I saw you like this was when you were sent to spy on Nathaniel."

Rosalind turned away, staring out over the narrow alley. The brick was pitted and scarred and sheathed in thick coal dust, but she didn't see any of it. Instead, Nate's face swam into her mind.

Head of the humanist movement in London, he'd

been an irrepressible fool who'd argued in the streets for human rights and had then dared take his arguments to the Ivory Tower. Organizing an interview with him, she'd had him wrapped around her finger before he'd even finished stammering a greeting. A ripe plum for the plucking. A week later, they'd been wed and she was Mrs. Nathaniel Hucker, the snake in his bed, reporting everything she heard back to Balfour.

A dreamer, yes. Naive. Blind. Yes. And the very best of men. Four months for him to melt her heart and make her start questioning everything Balfour had ever told her. She'd kept her doubts secret from Balfour, but not from Jack. Slowly the tides turned. She reported back to Balfour but only enough to ease his suspicions. And as she'd started listening to what Nate preached about human rights, she'd started to believe.

The conflict of loyalty had torn her in two. She'd fallen hopelessly in love with her husband, but by that time, Balfour had owned her body and soul for eight years. She'd killed for him. Spied for him. His little falcon. She'd have done anything for him.

Except kill Nathaniel.

"Who?" Jack asked simply.

Tears burned in Rosalind's eyes. She shook her head and kept her gaze turned irrevocably away. What would he think if he knew what secret thoughts her heart kept producing? Nathaniel had been human but Lynch was not. Lynch was the very creature that Jack most feared.

"Lynch?" he asked, a hint of anger warming his voice. "Did he do this to you? Did he force you into his bed?"

"For God's sake Jack, do you think any man—blue blood or not—could ever force me to do something I didn't want to do?"

His gaze sharpened and she realized her mistake. "So you wanted him to bed you?"

Scraping a hand over her face, she looked for Ingrid. "He can help me find Jeremy. I need to lure him close, to—"

"To seduce a blue blood? You could let him actually touch you? To lay his blood-soaked hands on you?"

"He's not like that."

Jack fell silent. "This is exactly like Nathaniel."

"No." She shook her head. "I loved my husband. This is nothing like that, but I can't deny…Lynch is… He's nothing like the rest of the blue bloods. He tries to fight it."

"Don't forget what he is."

"I know better than anyone what he is."

"And what the hell does that mean?" Jack grabbed her arm.

"Nothing." She pressed her lips together. This morning she'd stopped by the guild to see if he was recovering, but he still couldn't recognize anyone. Garrett had refused to let her see him, stating that all Lynch wanted was her.

It scared her. She'd thought at the time that the worst thing he could do to her would be to drink her blood and drain her dry, but she'd been wrong. Instead, the demon inside him had claimed her as his own.

Mine, he'd snarled.

Imagine his fury when he discovered how she'd

played him. Imagine…his hurt. Rosalind swallowed hard. She felt like she'd trapped herself in her own sticky spider web of lies and the weight of it was crushing her. She didn't want to hurt him. He was too good for that.

Jack watched her, no doubt drawing his own conclusions. "You shouldn't go back there. He's making you stray from your course."

"Is it the right thing to do?" she whispered, thinking of the silent Cyclops army sitting in the dark in Undertown.

Jack stiffened. "Don't doubt it. We made this pact eight years ago, after Nathaniel was murdered. Anything to bring them down—to destroy them."

"Is it worth Jeremy's life?" she snapped, turning on him. "Is it? Because if that is what is has cost me, then I cannot do this."

"Are you certain it's only Jeremy you're worried about?"

She groaned under her breath. The truth. If she continued as she was, one day she would have to go up against Lynch. Was it worth it? Could she truly strike him down for her cause?

No. The answer was a sickly whisper in her mind. A betrayal of everything she had stood for over the last eight years. But how could she avoid him? He stood between her and the Echelon and she *knew* that his sense of duty and honor would force him to move against her.

"I'll deal with it." *How?*

"See that you do," Jack said. "Don't forget where your loyalties lie. With your family, with your own people—with the humans who live in this wretched city and look to us for the only cursed hope they have."

"I know where my damned loyalties lie," she snapped.

"Devil take it, I can hear you two all the way to Limey," someone cursed. Ingrid materialized out of the fog, dragging a young lad with a missing eye and three iron fingers.

The tightness in Rosalind's chest eased. She stepped forward as Ingrid shoved the lad to his knees in front of her. "Found 'im in the Pits, betting on the blood sport," Ingrid said. "Couldn't take him there so I had to wait till he'd blown his quid."

Rosalind knelt down, resting her elbows on her knees. "Hello, Harry."

The mech grimaced, dragging himself up into a sitting position. Blood dripped from a slash in his forehead. Ingrid hadn't been gentle, then.

The youth was of an age with Jeremy and the pair had always gotten along smashingly well, even if Harry'd looked to Mordecai for leadership, rather than herself. His lips thinned as he scanned Jack's menacing form behind her. "Don't know nothin'."

"Yes, you do." Rosalind smiled, then held up a finger to stall his protests. "Let's not pretend that you won't tell us everything you know. The question is, whether you will do it now and be sent on your way unharmed, or whether Ingrid must break every bone in your body first."

His blue eye rolled to Ingrid and he swallowed.

"Firstly, I want to know if you've seen Jeremy. Or gotten word from him at all."

Harry's shoulders relaxed, as if realizing he wouldn't

be asked to betray his fellow mechs. "Ain't seen 'im since the tower," he admitted. "Thought 'e were dead—or taken by the Nighthawks."

Her eyelashes lowered as she fought to control her emotions. Her last hopes were drying up. If none of the mechs had seen him... "Why would you think the Nighthawks took him?"

Harry shrugged. "I were kinda 'opin', you know? They were all over the tower after the bomb went off."

He knew nothing then. Rosalind sat back on her heels, her throat dry and tight. Jack's hand slid over her shoulder and she clutched it, squeezing his gloves gently as the world dissolved around her. The last hope she had lay with Lynch, and she wasn't sure if he would recover from his bloodlust.

Ingrid sighed. "Be off with you then—"

"Wait." Rosalind looked up. "Wait," she added softly, forcing her thoughts to focus. "Tell me about the clockwork balls. The ones you use to drive a blue blood mad."

Harry's face paled under his mop of dark hair. "I don't know nothin'."

"Ingrid," she said. "Cut his thumb off."

"No!" Harry squealed, scrambling back on the cobbles—directly into Ingrid's legs.

Ingrid grabbed his hand and dragged an enormous knife from her belt. "Which one?" she asked Rosalind. They'd played this game many times.

Rosalind shrugged. "It doesn't particularly matter. Your choice."

"This one then," Ingrid said, yanking the lad's hand back.

"No!" he screamed. "No, stop! I'll tell! I'll tell you anythin' you wanna know about the Doeppler Orbs!"

Rosalind gestured Ingrid away and leaned closer. "Then tell me," she said. "What is in the orbs that drives a blue blood mad? Is there a cure?"

"There's a Dr. Henrik Doeppler in the East End," he blurted, staring at Ingrid's knife. "Some kind of nutter but 'e was tryin' to come up with a cure for the cravin', and found this formula instead. Don't know if there's a cure. We don't let 'em live long enough after…"

"After the tests," she encouraged.

He looked at her.

"Yes," she smiled. "Be careful that you tell the truth, Harry. You don't know how much I know."

"We done tests," he said quickly. "Just a few down below. It were 'ard to get our 'ands on a blue blood, you see?"

She nodded.

"So Mordecai thought we oughta try it on the Echelon. Get 'em runnin' scared and see 'ow well it works before we attack."

Her instincts had been right. This was bigger than it had seemed. "And where's the final attack going to happen?"

Harry stared at her helplessly. "I don't rightly know." He jerked his hands up in front of him as she frowned. "I don't! I swear it! Mordecai only tells me what I need to know."

Rosalind frowned. "I saw crates filled with the orbs. There were enough there to drive half the Echelon into a frenzy. He has to be planning an attack on something big, somewhere a lot of the Echelon will be trapped together."

"Only thing I know is its 'appenin' in two days' time," Harry added helpfully. "Started shipping the crates out to the gangs tonight."

Two days time. None of her spies in the Echelon had mentioned anything important.

"Let him go," Rosalind murmured, then narrowed her eyes on Harry. "If I were you, I wouldn't breathe a word of this meeting to Mordecai."

"Believe me"—he gave a shaky laugh—"I won't."

⁓

The next morning found Rosalind on the guild steps after slipping out without waking Jack or Ingrid. Yesterday morning they hadn't let her in. "Please," she whispered under her breath. "Please let him be himself again." Whether the plea was to a God she'd never prayed to before, she didn't know.

Rapping sharply at the main door, she waited with bated breath. The minutes dragged by and she was just about to rap again when Doyle jerked it open.

His glare faded when he saw her, a soft sigh in his throat. "Ain't no change, Mrs. Marberry. Garrett dosed 'im with 'emlock again. You'd best be on your way, its may'em round 'ere."

She shoved a hand against the door as he sought to close it. "Do we know what the long-term effects of hemlock will do to him?"

"Mrs. Marberry, we don't even know if 'e'll be 'imself again. 'E's been wild this mornin'." Again he moved to shut the door.

"Can I sit with him?" she blurted, shoving herself between the narrowing crack. "Just for a half hour. Please?"

"I don't 'old as that's such a good idea."

At the top of the stairs a dark figure distinguished itself from the shadows and Garrett leaned on the railing. "Let her through."

Doyle scowled. "You know what's 'e's been like. Ain't the done thing to let a lady in there with 'im like that."

"Isn't it? Nothing we've done has made one ounce of difference. He doesn't recognize any of us; indeed, he sees us only as threats." Garrett's expression softened as he looked at her. "But he's called for you, many times. Maybe she can do what we can't."

Rosalind pushed past before Doyle could say another word, feeling breathless. "Is he dangerous?"

Garrett's lashes brushed his cheek as he looked down. "We have him restrained. He only becomes violent when we enter the room."

She swallowed the hard lump in her throat. That moment in Undertown where he'd pinned her to the wall had frightened her. She shouldn't even be here; both Jack and Ingrid had argued against it until she'd agreed not to go, if only to placate the pair of them.

But she couldn't leave it alone. She needed to see him, needed him to be all right.

She missed him.

Gathering her skirts in her hand, she swept up the stairs, falling into step beside Garrett.

"I remembered something," she said, "about the attack. They mentioned a Dr. Doeppler—the man who created the drug that...that did this to him. Perhaps he has an antidote?"

Garret shot her a sharp look. "Dr. Doeppler?"

"In the East End," she replied, her gaze narrowing on the door to her own study. She felt light-headed, each step deliberately laid.

"I see. I'll send someone to see to the doctor." His gaze dipped to her clasped hands. "Don't be scared. I don't think he'd hurt you or else I wouldn't allow this."

Garrett opened the door and ushered her inside with a cool hand in the small of her back.

"What if he doesn't want to see me?" she whispered suddenly. The silence in the rooms was almost deafening. "What if it sends him over the edge again?"

"There is that risk," Garrett admitted. "That's why he's bound. He can't get to you, Rosa." A hesitation. "But I fear you might have to do this alone. If he sees me—He doesn't react well to the sight of any of us, and I fear if he sees me by your side...he'll perceive a threat."

"He's afraid of you?"

Another odd hesitation. "Not quite."

"Garrett, please." She actually laid her hand on his arm. "Tell me what you're not saying."

"The darkness inside him—his demons, whatever you wish to call them... They're focused on you, Rosa."

A frisson of fear—and something else—traveled over her skin.

"Sometimes it happens with a blue blood," he added quietly, "when he desires a woman beyond all else. It's a possessive, driving force within him. To protect you, to have you with him, to—" He actually colored. "A need to claim you as his own. I believe it's the only thing that saved your life in Undertown. His bloodlust was stirred, but with it roused the darker side of his nature, the part that recognizes you as his." Something bleak traveled through those pretty blue eyes. "We all have the capacity for it, Rosa."

A disaster. She could never escape him if this was the truth. And Lynch would demand more of herself than she could give. "What would happen if I don't go to him?"

"If we can't find a way to bring him back, then we—I—will have to kill him."

Pain filled his eyes and with it came the realization that Garrett was a better man than she'd ever suspected. To do such an act would hurt him beyond reparation. But he would do it if he needed to—that ingrained sense of duty that she suspected Lynch had had a hand in instilling.

"I'll try." The part of her that had been trained by Balfour was screaming at her, forcing her to look at this strategically.

Heat burned behind her eyes and she gathered herself and stepped to the door of his study. Her careful strategies be damned. No matter how much she'd tried to deny this, she felt something for Lynch. Something strong. Something that almost made her feel human again.

She couldn't leave him behind if she was the only chance he had of recovering.

Eighteen

ROSALIND KNEW AS SOON AS SHE TOUCHED THE door handle that Lynch was awake. She could almost hear him listening and sweat touched a damp hand to her spine.

Courage.

Resolutely, she turned the handle.

The sight of him stole her breath. Spatters of dull, drying blood flecked his chest and the bed sheets, his arms yanked high above his body and bound with enormous iron manacles that someone had driven into the wall with what looked like railway spikes. The sheet covered his hips, but they'd bound his feet in much the same way and from the vial and pair of needles on the bedside table, they were dosing him regularly with hemlock.

She slowly closed the door behind her. Lynch watched her, those black eyes gleaming in the flickering dance of candlelight. A predator's eyes. Not the man that she longed for. Not her clever adversary, her dearest enemy.

"Hello," Rosalind whispered, trying to still her

racing heart. "I've missed you, my lord." Her voice sounded loud in the room, silence broken only by the slight shifting of sheets as his head turned to track her.

This was what she had hated and feared for so long. Balfour's eyes had been like that, black and emotionless, when he'd cut Nathaniel's throat in front of her. *You are the devil*, she'd screamed at him then, and she'd believed it.

Rubbing at her chest, Rosalind crossed to the window and jerked the curtains back, unable to stand the dark anymore. What did she believe now?

Behind her, the low exhale of his breath caught her ears. When she turned, Lynch twisted his face away, hiding from the almost-blinding light. Of course. Blue bloods tolerated sunlight, but they preferred darkness, with their overly sensitive eyes and pale skins. The higher their CV count, the harsher they felt it and right now, with the bloodlust ruling him, he'd be even more sensitive.

Rosalind tugged the curtains half-shut. "I'm sorry. But I can hardly see." Her nose wrinkled up. The room smelled like blood. She opened the window and a cool breeze stirred the curtains.

"Have you eaten?" she asked, her voice strengthening. She eyed the rusty stains on his shirt. "Have they bathed you at all?"

The answer of course was no.

Crossing briskly to the door, she reached for the handle. It was only then that she realized how relaxed his body had been, for he jerked to attention, the manacles cutting into his flesh.

"No!"

Rosalind paused. Their eyes met. "I'm not going anywhere," she said. "I'm only going to send Garrett for some fresh sheets and water."

Breath heaved in his chest, his eyes glittering dangerously. Rosalind slowly turned the handle. "I won't leave the room," she promised.

Garrett waited in Lynch's study, leaping to his feet with a desperately longing expression as soon as he saw her.

She shook her head, not daring to step over the threshold. "I need warm water and soap," she told him. "Fresh sheets for his bed too, and some blud-wein."

Garrett nodded, his shoulders slumping in relief as he sprang toward the door. Rosalind didn't have the heart to tell him there had been no change.

Closing the door, she turned back to Lynch. His lip curled and he glared through the wall, an angry purr sounding in his throat.

"That's enough," she said, stepping between him and the door. His gaze lit on her and she shivered. *Dangerous*.

The corded muscles in his throat clenched and he strained against the manacles that bound him. Rosalind hurried to the bed. "Stop it," she said, laying her hands on his chest. "You'll hurt yourself."

The reaction had been instinctive. Hard flesh flexed beneath her gloves and her lips parted as she looked down. Those eyes watched her again, but the look was no longer dangerous. Stark primal need crossed his expression, desire burning in the black heat of his eyes.

It lit within her, her body reacting as if he'd put flame to oil. Rosalind lifted her iron hand tentatively, stroking her other hand over his bare chest. The buttons on his shirt were torn, gaping over hard flanks and the rippled muscle of his abdomen. Instantly she was transported back to that night in the bathing room, not so long ago. The feel of his teeth on the back of her neck and his hands cupping her breasts and sliding lower, into the vee of her thighs. His hips thrusting against her, warm lips tracing the curve of her shoulder…

A little shiver ran over her skin, her nipples hardening behind the thin lawn of her chemise. Fear died a short death in her breast.

He didn't want to hurt her. He never had. To claim her as his own yes, to sink his teeth into the smooth skin of throat and drink her blood. Whether he could have stopped himself, she didn't know, but he had no intentions of hurting her.

Just of claiming her.

Pain she could deal with—the idea of belonging to him, to anyone, so completely, sent a nervous thrill through her. Not entirely unpleasant, almost the same play of nerves that she enjoyed in dangerous situations—and yet so much more terrifying. Her feelings for Nate had been the warm joy of friendship and shared respect, a love that didn't challenge her yet left her feeling safe and protected. Whatever this was—whatever she felt for Lynch—was a maelstrom in comparison, and she wasn't sure if she could hold herself together through it.

She didn't know what to do, but she did know that she had to try and help him through this. The idea of losing him to the bloodlust almost choked her.

"My lord," Rosalind murmured, kneeling on the bed and leaning over him. "I know you're in there."

Her whispered breath traced his ear. Lynch turned his head with a snarl, breathing hard as he drew her scent into his lungs.

Her heart thundered in her veins. Slowly, Rosalind brushed her silky glove over his lips, leaning closer. Lynch stilled beneath her like some enormous jungle cat, violence bunching in each muscle. But she wasn't frightened anymore. He was bound and chained and she had the upper hand.

The thought was almost titillating.

Leaning down, she traced her gloved finger over his lip, dipping wetly into his mouth. Then lower, down the cleft in his chin and then the smooth hollow of his throat. The muscles beneath her hardened like marble, but he held still, a fine tremor in his arms. Reined in by her touch, the look in his eyes darkly curious. As if warning her that he was by no means tamed, he turned his face into her hand, his teeth sinking into the fleshy pad of her palm.

A gasp wet Rosalind's lips, the sensation seeming to tug all the way through her, right to the heart of her sex, until she throbbed with liquid fire. The pleasure of his bite was almost painful, almost a little too harsh. She rocked onto her knees, biting her lip, her fingers curling helplessly around the side of his face.

"Please," she moaned. Begged.

His teeth released her skin and feeling flooded into the flesh, making her eyes clench shut and a shudder run through her.

A knock on the door tore her head up, a hot flush

of heat burning through her cheeks. Had Garrett heard her? Tension rode through the hard body on the bed and she stroked his face, turning it toward her.

"I'll be back," she whispered, leaning down to brush her lips against his cheek. The rasp of his stubble roughened her sensitive mouth. "Then we will finish this."

Dark lashes hooded his eyes. He liked that.

Rosalind hurried to the door. Jerking it open just wide enough for her body, she saw Garrett's gaze lift over her shoulder. Some protective urge almost made her straighten, as if to block Lynch from his sight.

"Thank you," she murmured, accepting the bundle in his arms. A pair of sheets, with a bowl of water balanced on top and a butter-yellow bar of soap to the side.

"Is he—"

"Go," she told him, pushing the door shut with the toe of her slipper. "He's not going to hurt me."

The door shut in his face.

"Mrs. Marberry," Garrett called through the door.

Rosalind glanced over her shoulder as Lynch stirred, staring malevolently at the door. "You're making him worse. Leave us alone. I'll send for you when I need to."

"There's blud-wein in the liquor cabinet in the corner." Then Garrett's footsteps echoed on the other side of the door as he walked away, the sound vanishing as he shut the other door between them.

Steeling herself, Rosalind turned around, her arms aching from the strain of the sheets and the water basin. She put them down, then swiftly tore the shirt from his arms. There was no point in retaining it; it was quite ruined.

"Come closer," Lynch commanded, his voice a harsh whisper as his gaze locked on her throat.

"No," she replied, dragging the sheet out from under him. Her expression softened when she saw the helpless fury cross his face. "Please. Let me take care of you." Her lashes lowered. "Perhaps you'll even enjoy it, sir?"

Stillness. He watched her though; she could feel it prickling over her scalp.

Once she'd stripped and remade the bed, she tucked towels around his body and then placed the basin on the chest of drawers by the bed. As she washed him, he seemed to calm, his eyelids drifting half-closed. She knelt over him with the washcloth, dragging the sheet lower.

Lynch's black eyes locked on hers and his hips gave a suggestive thrust as he sucked in a sharp breath.

"Not until you come back to me," she whispered.

Those eyes narrowed dangerously. "I never left."

His dark side tempted her. Rosalind slid the soapy washcloth beneath the sheet, her hand cupping the surge of his erection. Lynch froze, his back rigid.

"You know what I want," she whispered, fisting his cock. Heat speared through her abdomen...and lower.

"You know what I want."

"To claim me," she murmured, unable to tear her gaze from his. Twisting her wrist, she drew another snarled gasp from him. Her nipples hardened and Rosalind swallowed. "Perhaps I'll claim you?" she suggested, the thought burning through her with wicked intensity.

Tossing aside the washcloth, she dried him with the

towel, taking her time and paying taunting attention to his straining erection. She'd thought the expression in his eyes couldn't get any darker, but he was almost writhing now, fury and need choking him. The manacles rattled as he yanked against them.

"Let me go."

"Let him go," she countered, grabbing a handful of her skirts and straddling him.

Those merciless eyes locked on her. "I am him."

"You are all the darkness in him," she corrected, leaning low and pressing a kiss to his chest. The combination of fear and power made her feel frightfully dizzy.

"What do you think he is?" the demon inside him whispered.

Rosalind reached out and traced her tongue over his nipple. Lynch jerked. "He is good," she whispered. "And loyal and honest and brave." She took her time, her teeth sinking into the delicate flesh of his nipple.

"And the rest? The darkness," he demanded with a snarl. "You belong to me too. Don't ever forget that."

His hips thrust beneath her, hot flesh driving against her thigh. Rosalind gasped, her own hips flexing. Somehow the end of his cock rasped against her, riding the wet silk that clung to her quim.

"Take me," he whispered. "Give yourself to me. Need you... Want you..."

She couldn't think. Rosalind groaned, then shook her head. "No. Not until you let him surface."

"Not...stopping him..."

The tip of his cock breeched the slit of her drawers. Rosalind sank her nails into his rippled abdomen. She could feel him now, silky slick against her wetness. Those wicked black eyes met hers and then the broad head of his cock dipped inside her.

She'd thought she was in control. She was wrong. A gasp tore from her lungs and Rosalind flexed involuntarily. She wanted this, needed it. But she wanted to be here with him.

"Why?" she whispered, her thighs burning as she held herself above him. "What is he—are you—afraid of?"

Lynch smiled, a dark, wicked look that made her melt. "He's afraid of me." He gave a thrust. Earned another hot inch. "He's afraid of letting me go."

Rosalind clenched around him, riding just the head of his shaft. She took a calculated risk. Lynch's darkness, his hungers, were just another part of him. If she couldn't accept it, then how could he?

She threw her head back and sank down, embedding him to the hilt. Her skirts flowed over his stomach and chest and Lynch cried out in need as she took him.

So long since she'd had a man. So long since she'd wanted one. But she'd wanted this one from the start and that thought had terrified her. Rosalind met those black eyes and slowly, slowly arched up until just the tip of him penetrated her. A blue blood. Her worst fear once, but she was starting to realize that he was just a man, like any other. She sank her teeth into her lower lip with a groan and sank back down.

"Hell." Lynch arched, his back jerking. "You feel so fucking good."

"So do you," she whispered, riding him slowly, firmly.

"Want to touch you…" His fists clenched and he tore at the chains.

Dare she? Rosalind's eyes narrowed as she rolled her hips. She wanted his hands on her. Needed them. Reaching up, she tugged a pin from her hair and gave him a smoldering look.

Short work to undo the manacles around his wrists. Lynch grabbed her by the hips, jerking his body down the bed so that his knees bent and she was driven forward, impaled on his cock. The darkness in his eyes looked back at her, captured her.

"Yes," she whispered, riding him faster, harder, as his hands on her hips urged her on.

Deft fingers slid beneath her skirts. "You look so prim," he whispered. "I like it." Then they were parting her drawers, stroking the hot, wet flesh that trembled so desperately.

"I like you," she groaned. "Like this. I like you out of control, uninhibited."

Doubt assailed the darkness. She saw it and moaned at the victory, even as his fingers wrought such delicious damage. They froze.

"I hurt you," he said, as if remembering. "In Undertown."

"No." She rubbed against his fingers, urging him on. Grabbing his wrist, she pressed him harder against her. "You never hurt me. You never wanted to. All you wanted was this. To make me yours."

Lynch shuddered, slivers of gray creeping into his eyes. Rosa sensed her victory and slowed, grinding herself against him. "I can't remember," he gasped. "I see… flashes of it… Of shoving you up against the wall—"

"Sometimes," she whispered, "I like it when you're rough with me. Besides…" Biting her lip on a groan. "What makes you think I can't handle you? All of you?"

She came with an explosive jerk, her entire body singing with need. A soft scream died on her lips, her gloved fingers digging into his chest as she slumped over him.

"God," she whispered. "Oh God."

Somehow she met those wide eyes—gray eyes. Rosalind almost cried out again, her hand sliding over his cheek in tender desperation as he grabbed her hips and took control. She couldn't move, could barely breathe. All she could do was gasp as he thrust into her, driving them both to the edge…and over.

This time there was no coming back. Rosalind collapsed over his heaving chest, her body molten as the fingers on her right hand laced with his.

Lynch lifted his head, gasping. "Rosa?"

She sensed the difference in his tone and knew she'd won the battle. "I'm here," she replied softly, then kissed the cool skin of his chest. His cock gave a little teasing clench inside her.

His hand slid into her hair and held her there, his other arm sliding around her in panic. "Don't leave me. Don't let me go."

Rosalind nuzzled closer, her eyes closing sleepily. "I'm not letting you go. You don't ever have to fear that again."

Nineteen

A KNOCK ON THE DOOR WOKE HIM UP.

Lynch dragged himself into a sitting position, the sheet pooling in his lap. Darkness skated through his vision and his fist clenched in the mattress before he took a deep breath. How long would it be like this? Every sudden move and sound stirring the hunger inside him? It terrified him that he was still so close to the darkness within. One wrong move and he could be lost in the shadows again, seeing nothing but prey.

Looking at his own men as if they were the enemy and as for Mrs. Marberry... He looked around then. There was no sign of her, beyond the faint, elusive scent that lingered on his sheets and his skin. Last night had been a revelation, both of the flesh and of herself. In the dark, he'd made love to her twice more as the hunger rose in him, sating himself on her flesh. In between, she'd curled in his arms, whispering with him. Quiet words. Little secrets. Bits of herself and some of the life she'd led on the streets before her father had found her. Of him, she said very little, and yet the not saying was telling enough.

She must have left him sometime during the night. *No*, the darkness inside him roared.

Scraping a shaking hand over his jaw, Lynch swallowed. "Come in."

Doyle backed into the room, bringing a breakfast tray with a flask of warmed blood and the *Standard* neatly folded atop it. Lynch's gaze narrowed in on his friend's throat and he looked away, his face draining of color.

How long, damn it?

"My lord." Doyle stared at him, as though searching for signs of it in his face. "You're lookin' better this morn."

Lynch nodded brusquely. "I feel it too." Awkward silence descended and he gestured to his side table. The scent of the warmed blood spilled his vision over into tones of gray again, and his nostrils flared as he took tight rein of himself.

"Got the paper, sir." Doyle rambled on, the same as any other morning. Or not quite the same. Tension stiffened his shoulders. "And your letters."

"Anything of interest?"

"Two of them. The Council wishes a progress report—and to remind you that you got only two days left."

"How kind of them." His mood soured, black heat spilling through his eyes. Perhaps he should accept a meeting and show them what he thought of their solicitousness.

"And this." Doyle held a scrap of paper up between his fingers, his brows arching. "One o' your little pigeons, no doubt."

Lynch took the folded note, eyeing the frayed edges and the stained parchment. None of the boys he paid for information could read or write. Anticipation became a sharp edge within him. He tore it open, gaze raking the few lines.

"*I know something you don't. Meet me at the Dog and Thistle, Shoreditch, at twelve.*"

He didn't recognize the writing, but he knew who it was from immediately. Tension coiled in his gut muscle, the thought of Mrs. Marberry springing to mind. Her husky laugh as she lay in his arms last night, her eyes sparkling with teasing humor as she lifted her lips to press a tender kiss against his pectoral muscle. By going to meet Mercury, he was effectively pretending nothing had changed when the entire world had shifted around him.

But the letter… Dare he ignore it?

He crushed it in his fist. If he didn't find a way out of the looming jaws of the Echelon's trap, then either way, it wouldn't matter. He had to do something to appease the prince consort. "Get my body armor."

∽

A pair of Coldrush Guards in nondescript clothing tried to follow him, but he lost them at the wall, ducking into the thick weave of the East End. This was his world, not theirs, and he knew it like the back of his hand.

The Dog and Thistle bustled with drinkers; working class laborers and grizzled old seamen. Lynch dragged the collar of his coat up around his throat and pushed between them, the press of bodies arousing his predatory instincts. He could hear the steady pulse of every man's heartbeat, the sight of the barmaid throwing back her head with laughter arresting him for a moment. Her carotid throbbed thickly with blood, a flush of color staining her cheeks. Lynch tore his gaze away, his eyes locking on a solitary figure across the bar.

Mercury watched him as if she knew exactly what he was thinking. Glancing down, she peered into her mug of ale, waiting for him.

Lynch choked down the thick need, shoving past a burly man who reeked of sardines. A haze of tobacco smoke hovered in the air above his head, tarnishing the heavy beams that supported the roof. Someone cheered as a dart launched itself into the heart of the dartboard and a few lads clapped the thrower on the back with good cheer.

Mercury trailed her gloved fingers in small circles, stirring the sticky ring of ale that lingered on the bar. It was dark back here, shadows pooling across the heavy coat that she wore and the mop of thick close-cropped curls around her head. Someone had pasted a very authentic moustache to her lip and there was enough coal dust—or grime—shadowing her jaw that he almost mistook it for stubble.

"You're late," she said, thick, dark lashes fluttering against her cheeks as she slowly lifted her gaze.

He stared into a pair of the bluest eyes he'd ever seen.
Blue eyes.

Somehow the thought struck him as wrong, as if he ought to recognize her from somewhere. Lynch frowned, leaning on the bar beside her. "You deserve to be up on stage."

She lifted her mug to him, taking a heady sip. "Per'aps I were once."

That set his mind racing. Until he saw the faint gleam in her eyes. She was toying with him, knowing that the mystery of her identity fascinated him.

"Is that where you came into contact with blue bloods?" he asked coolly, gesturing the barmaid for another ale. Folding his arms on the bar, he observed the room. Mercury had a good view here. She could see everything while few could observe her. And from the draft at his back, there was a door somewhere behind in case she needed to get out in a hurry.

"Whatd'ya mean?"

"People don't just decide to join a cause," he replied, slipping a pound note toward the barmaid as she handed him a foamy mug. "Keep the change."

Sipping at the ale—it wasn't what he wanted but it would do—he turned his head to look at Mercury.

The humor faded from her face and suddenly he felt the room narrow around them, as if someone had slammed an invisible window shut between them and the raucous laughter.

"You ran afoul of a blue blood once," he told her. "That's why you do this. Whoever it was, his face haunts you, night after night, or you wouldn't feel this way."

The color drained out of her face, her fingers clenching around the heavy mug. She jerked her gaze down, staring into the foamy dregs. "You don't know a damned thing about me."

"What did he do to you?"

She hissed between her teeth, shoulders stiffening.

"Let it alone, me lord Nighthawk. Ain't no bloody business o' yours."

"Of course it is. You made it my business the moment you kissed me."

"A fact I still regret, me lord."

"Liar." Reaching out he brought his fingers to her cheek. He could feel her trembling.

She laughed bitterly. "I do. Every day I regret meeting you."

"Why?" It wasn't his imagination. The cockney accent had faded there for a moment. Her voice sounded almost familiar.

She looked up, blue eyes gleaming. The flicker of light off the irises made his breath catch. An occipital lens, if he wasn't mistaken. Designed for spies by the Echelon—by Balfour himself, the prince consort's spymaster. How the devil had she gotten her hands on a set?

And what color were her eyes if they weren't blue?

His heart was beating so fast he suddenly realized that shadows washed his vision. Her distress beat at him until the devil inside roused. A craving. A fierce need to protect her.

He shut his eyes and breathed through it. He had two days. Two days before the executioner's blade descended on one of them. A sick feeling invaded him and as he opened his eyes and saw the fine trembling of her lips, he knew what his choice was going to be.

Lynch let her go, the taste of regret like ash in his mouth. He couldn't do it. He barely knew her, but he could no more hand her over to the Council than he could have plunged a dagger in her heart. The wave of regret that swept through him was almost intense enough to buckle his knees. *Rosa... All the missed opportunities.* For years he'd wanted to find someone and now he had... And it was too late.

"You know why I regret it." Sucking in a deep breath, Mercury reached out and pressed her iron fingers against the center of his chest, a tortured expression on her face. "You were right. I do picture 'is face every night. I 'ate 'im so much I wanted to burn the whole Echelon, but—" She hesitated, her eyes lifting to his. "What if I were wrong? What if they weren't all bad?"

The last few words were a whisper.

Lynch's heart constricted in his chest as if she'd punched him. "Do you take me for a fool?" he asked harshly.

Those stricken eyes stared at him without recrimination. "No." She wet her lips with her tongue, emotions battling their way across her face. "I should never have kissed you. Never."

Then she was on her toes, her hot little mouth seeking his in the shadows. The taste of her exploded through him, his hand coming up unconsciously to cup the base of her scalp. *No.*

Yes, the demon in him purred. *She is mine.*

Lynch dragged his mouth away with a gasp, turning his face so that her lips brushed his cheek and not his own. Her heart thundered in his ears, matching the racing gallop of his own, and for a moment, the memory of holding Rosa in his arms rose to the fore. Both of them fit so easily there and both of them kissed as though seeking to drown in it. He could almost taste Rosa on his lips but that was...insane.

Lynch shook his head. Ridiculous. No doubt it was guilt that brought the image of Rosa to mind. Guilt that left the taste of her in his mouth. And that revealed his heart's intentions more than anything else. The shock of it pushed him away from her, so that he could find some sense of breathing room. Some sense of distance.

"Me lord?" Mercury whispered, hands stroking the shuddering planes of his sides.

"I can't," he said hoarsely. "My heart lies elsewhere." The confession burned through him and he caught her wrists and held them away from him. The shock on her face was almost tinged with hysteria as she pulled at her hands.

"No," she said, voice getting stronger. "No. You can't."

"I'm sorry."

"Who?" she demanded.

"It doesn't matter," he replied, letting her wrists go. "You don't know her."

Taking a step back, she leaned heavily on the bar. "It's the redhead, ain't it?" She looked up, her expression so lost. Then it hardened. "You don't think I can make you forget her?"

He caught her wrist as she reached for him. "For a few minutes, yes. But I'm not that type of man."

A sound of faint regret whispered through her throat. When he opened his eyes, she was staring up at him again, helplessly.

"This," he told her, "is just need. Just desire. She

is more to me. She is…everything that I thought I'd never feel again."

Slowly, she dragged her arm back to her chest, clutching it as if he'd hurt it. "You can't have her. You know that?"

"I know." *Two days.* He smiled bitterly down at his untouched ale. "But I won't betray her."

"There you go again, shatterin' me perceptions." A hurt smile ghosted over her lips, but her cheeks were still white. She took a deep, shuddering breath. "It were easier when the blue bloods were just monsters. You oughta know, me lord Nighthawk, that I won't move against you. I couldn't." Her fists clenched and she shook her head. "All this plannin' and you destroyed it in the matter of a few weeks."

Her lashes fluttered against her cheeks. "I know what the mechs are up to. The massacres in Mayfair were just a test. They're plannin' on goin' after the Echelon with their Doeppler Orbs, creatin' a widespread massacre. Lettin' you blue bloods rip each other apart."

Lynch stilled. "When?"

"Tomorrow."

"Where?"

"I don't know." She held up her hands when she saw his expression. "I don't. Mordecai's keepin' 'is cards close to 'is chest. But it'll be somewhere where a lot o' blue bloods are gathered. Somewhere as'll make the biggest impact."

Where? His mind raced. There were no major political events planned nor even social ones. The Season was winding down, most of the thrall contracts signed.

A commotion caught his ear and he spun, sighting a pair of immaculately shaven gentlemen shoving their way into the pub. His gaze caught Sir Richard Maitland's, though the man was lacking his distinctive Coldrush livery. Fury flared white-hot in him and Lynch stepped in front of Mercury, shielding her with his body.

"Go," he told her. "Out the back. Don't get caught."

She stared at him, then back to Maitland. "Who is 'e?"

"Go," he repeated, harshly this time.

Her eyes met his. "This is good-bye then?"

Lynch nodded, the hunger in him screaming its rage. A vein in his temple throbbed, his color dipping to shades of gray, then flashing back through color again.

"Good-bye, me lord Nighthawk," she whispered.

"Good-bye," he repeated, then he turned and shoved into the crowd, not looking to see her go. The hunger in him, his inner demon, roared its silent fury.

No! Take her!

Lynch ignored it, shoving the thought deep. Neither of them could be his.

He had a date with the executioner.

Twenty

"Roz?"

She jerked her fingers away from the window guiltily.

Ingrid's expression was watchful as she stepped over the threshold of the bedroom. "Did you get any sleep?"

"No." Rosalind's eyes burned, her thoughts chasing themselves around and around in her head, the same way they had done all night. Those devastating words he'd spoken in the pub, as if there could be a future between them.

There was no future. Not without her brother. And if Lynch found out her secret, he would never look at her—at Mrs. Marberry—the same way.

It isn't me he loves! It was a person who didn't exist, a role that she had played all too well it seemed over the past few weeks. The hurt knifed through her. She was finding it difficult to keep herself separated from Mrs. Marberry. Balfour had taught her to place as much truth in her lies as possible, and that lesson had been her downfall.

For Mrs. Marberry was everything that she secretly

wished to be. Unburdened by hate, by the violence of her past, the subject of a good man's love. She touched her lips lightly, as if she could still feel the phantom touch of his caress there.

"What's going on?" Ingrid demanded, her eyes narrowing in suspicion. "You ain't been acting like yourself lately. You been lying to us, avoiding us…"

"I didn't lie—"

"Where were you yesterday then? You said you were only stepping out, getting some fresh air."

Rosalind saw the truth in her friend's eyes. "You followed me."

Shaking her head in disgust, Ingrid stalked to the window and yanked the sash up. "Aye, I saw you at the Dog and Thistle. I saw *him*. And the day before, when you were supposed to be sleeping all day?"

"I was with him," Rosalind admitted, feeling tired of all the lies. "I went to help him recover."

"Why?"

"Because I couldn't bear to see him like that," she whispered.

Ingrid's brows drew together. "I don't understand. What changed? You hate them—or you did. Fact was, once, you would never have let one of them lay a hand on you."

"I don't know. He wasn't as I expected him to be. He's…nothing like I expected."

The sound of footsteps on the stairs broke the standoff. Ingrid breathed deeply. "Jack," she said.

"Don't tell him. Please."

Ingrid gave her an uneasy look, then nodded.

By the time Jack reached her door, he was

winded—a residual effect of the scarring. He paused by the door, gaze darting between the pair of them. "Did you tell her?"

Ingrid shook her head. "Didn't get a chance."

"Tell me what?" Rosalind demanded.

"The next shipment came through," Jack said. "Including a mech to do the work for us."

"A mech from the enclaves? They've changed their mind and will work for us?"

"This one will," he replied.

"Why?"

Ingrid looked up sharply. "Said he was paid good money."

Her contact in the Echelon. Rosalind turned and stared out the window. She'd always thought her contact had ties to the Humans First Party that spoke in parliament—perhaps Sir Gideon Scott himself, the head of the party. They provided the money and she created the Cyclops.

The hairs on the back of her neck rose. "Scott doesn't have the sort of money we've been receiving this year. None of the party does. Steel's expensive."

"A lot of people donate to the cause." In the reflection, she saw Jack shrug.

That was true. Still, she didn't like the feeling that itched its way down her spine. "I think it's about time we discovered precisely who is donating to this cause." When she'd first taken over Nate's work, she'd found most of his contacts in place already. The money had been a trickle then, until she'd come up with the Cyclops plan. Then it had become a flood. Too much, in fact, for her suspicions not to be roused.

Someone wanted her to create a metal army and she'd been too preoccupied with Jeremy lately to wonder why.

"What are you planning to do?" Ingrid asked.

"Get some of our humanists in place—the ones we know are loyal to us—and have each member of the Humans First Party watched. If there's a money trail, we should be able to find it."

"That'll take months," Jack said.

Rosalind nodded. "Yes, it will. But I want answers."

"And in the meantime?"

She met his gaze boldly. "Get the mech started on the next Cyclops," she said. "We'll continue as is for the moment, so that no one grows suspicious."

"And you?"

She thought of Lynch and the threat of attack. "I am going to go see that my lord Nighthawk thwarts the mech attack."

And make sure that he wasn't injured in the midst of it.

Ingrid's gaze shot to her, but Rosalind pretended she didn't see. "Ingrid, would you help me into my corset?"

❦

"This is everything, sir." Garrett tossed a variety of newspaper clippings and invitations on the table.

Lynch snatched them up, raking through them. "A few soirees, a poetry reading, Lady Callahan's charity dinner…" He paused, unfolding a pristine sheet of parchment. "*The Baiting of the Wolf.*"

"The opera," Byrnes murmured, leaning closer to see. "Last showing of the Season. Everyone will be there."

"This is it." It had to be. The prince consort himself was most likely to attend, as would anyone of influence.

"It's an enormous building," Garrett said. "They could already be inside and we would never know it."

"And they'll never let *us* inside," Byrnes said quietly.

Lynch looked up, tapping the parchment against his hand. Byrnes was right. Only the purest of bloodlines would have an invitation. No rogue would be allowed in, no matter what Lynch said—especially when Maitland's men would be guarding the opera house.

Someone rapped on the door to his study.

"Come in," he called.

Perry stepped through the door, her short-cropped dark hair pomaded closely to her scalp. Rosa followed at her heels, wearing dark green cotton that swished around her ankles. Her gaze met his, then flickered away, a faint pink flush rising in her cheeks. It reminded him of the wicked pink flush in her cheeks as she'd sat astride him, her small white teeth worrying her lip as she slowly, slowly lowered herself down over his cock.

The sensation shot through him, dashing his control and his wits. She was shaded with shadow now, the pinkness of her cheeks lost to the monotony of the predator's vision. A hand pressed into his chest and he looked down in surprise as Garrett pushed against him, a warning look on his face.

"Your eyes," his second murmured. "Control it."

And just that suddenly, he recognized the fierce need surging through him and the intent way in which he'd moved toward her—a movement that he could not remember beginning.

They were all looking at him. Byrnes's eyes narrowed in thought and he glanced at Mrs. Marberry as if suddenly realizing what Garrett's words meant.

Lynch swallowed hard. "Rosa." He inclined his head politely.

She returned the salute and he realized that she was pale this afternoon. The light had drained from her creamy skin, leaving her faintly ashen.

"What have I missed?" Perry asked.

"We think we know where the mechs are going to attack," Lynch replied, snapping his gaze back to the opera notice. He didn't dare look at Rosa—not even to wonder why she looked so strained. Was it him? Did she regret what had happened between them? "We know it's going to be today. The only event of any social import is the opera."

"So what do we do?" Garrett asked. "Call it off?"

"No." He rubbed his knuckles. "I've spent months playing this safely and—" His voice caught. "I'm running out of time. If we call the opera off, then the mechs will simply fade back into the populace and we won't be able to bring them before the court…" He almost added *in time*.

"Then how do we get inside?" Byrnes asked.

"You don't," Lynch replied. "The only one with any chance of being accepted at the door is myself. The rest of you—"

"No."

The word was soft and came from behind him. Lynch glanced over his shoulder. "We're all rogues, Mrs. Marberry, but at least my knighthood might finally provide something of use."

"No," she replied, stepping forward with her fists balled. "You're not going in alone. If they're planning on releasing the orbs, then I won't have you there. You know what happened. I won't allow it! Not again."

Lynch stared at her, feeling everyone's eyes upon them as he struggled to find the words. She wouldn't have said this if she didn't care for him, would she? Elation soared in his chest, but he choked it off ruthlessly. He had nothing to offer her. No hope of anything beyond today, no matter how much he wished it.

Because he couldn't bring himself to betray Mercury to the Council.

"You are not in a position to deny me," he reminded her quietly, though the words spoke of so much more. He hated having to do it—hated watching the furious flood of heat surge through her cheeks as if he'd slapped her—but this was for her own good. If he let her have hopes, then he would only cruelly dash them. Let it end now. Before the damage became too great.

Garrett winced but Mrs. Marberry tipped her chin up. "You're correct," she replied. "I have no authority—no…no right to deny you. Do as you will, you stubborn fool, but don't doubt this. You won't be going alone. I'm a respectable widow with a—"

This time it was his turn to start. "Absolutely not!"

"And how do you propose to stop me?" she replied, lacing her arms across her chest. "Let me assure you that I can and will find myself a ticket to the opera if you try to keep me out of this. I can be extremely ingenious when I wish to be."

"I'm aware of that," he replied. "But that should be rather difficult—even for you—if I chain you up in my bloody bedroom!"

"Sir, really," she drawled, a glint of humor warming her dark eyes. "A gentleman never reveals his intentions in public as such."

He gaped.

Rosa took a step toward him, her smile growing victorious. "Besides, what makes you think I won't simply pick the lock?"

"I will remove all of your pins." That vein in his temple was starting to throb again. Did the woman have no sense? This was dangerous.

"*All* of them? My lord, you *are* thorough."

It couldn't have sounded more like innuendo if she'd tried. Garrett coughed, and Perry's lips were pressed so tightly together she looked like she was going to burst.

"I believe you are being outmaneuvered." Garrett murmured. "I'd suggest a healthy capitulation now, before you say something you truly do regret."

"Fine." Lynch narrowed his glare toward Garrett. "I am not taking her into the opera alone. You at least look the part. I want you in court clothes within two hours. You don't stray an inch from her side."

"I don't need a nursemaid," Rosa protested.

Perry grinned. "Those pretty looks have come in handy again, Garrett."

Lynch's gaze cut to hers. "And you can find a dress."

Perry's jaw dropped. "Not a chance, sir."

He stabbed a finger toward her. "I'm not asking. Find a dress and a wig or else I will find one for you. Then I will stuff you into it myself if I need to!"

Silence greeted this outburst. Even Garrett—who was struggling to suppress his laughter—didn't dare say a word. Lynch straightened. "Byrnes, I want you to have men in place surrounding the building. I also need a contingent sent to each of the other events on the list, just in case we've picked the wrong one." He knew he hadn't, but there were enough Nighthawks to cover each place.

"Have a man sent to Barrons and alert him to what is happening. He can get the queen and the prince consort out if matters go awry." He started picking at his cuff links. "Garrett, on your way, send Doyle up to help get me ready."

"Aye, sir." Garrett snapped a salute.

"And what about me?" Rosa asked.

He looked down at her. "If you think you're coming, you need to look the part. It's going to be difficult enough convincing the doormen to let us through as it is."

"Take Perry," Garrett added blandly. "You may have to show her what a dress is."

Perry's sudden glare was one step short of murder. "I hope you choke on your cologne," she snarled, stalking toward the door and grabbing Rosa by the arm.

Twenty-one

THROUGH THE DOOR, LYNCH BARKED ORDERS, SNAP-
ping one last briefing to his men. Rosalind took a deep
breath, smoothing the trim skirts over her hips. The
gown fit almost too snugly, her breasts threatening to
spill over the top of the peach-colored silk's square
neckline. Bands of chocolate brown chenille passe-
menterie foliage trimmed the neckline and the soft
drapes of her skirt. A cream foile hip scarf spilled to
the ground behind her, making a rustling sound every
time she moved.

Perry raked her with an experienced eye. "You'll
do. Turn around."

Perry herself was almost unrecognizable. Gone was
the cold-faced woman in harsh black leather with her
pomaded hair. Instead, a white ostrich feather danced
in her hair, the curls of the black wig trailing over
her shoulder. She wore red silk, the bias-cut panels of
the bodice creating slight curves out of the woman's
slender figure. An underskirt of Point d'Angleterre
lace peeked out from beneath the drape of her train,
and she wore pearls wrapped thrice around her throat.

Rosalind knew all of this, because Perry had explained it in quite explicit detail while they raided the French couturier that afternoon. One flash of Perry's leathers and the madame had been most accommodating, no doubt for fear of incurring the wrath of the Nighthawks.

A strip of black velvet ribbon circled Rosalind's throat and Perry tied it. A single teardrop-shaped pearl hung from the center, warming against her skin.

"Lynch is going to have an apoplexy," Perry muttered with a nasty smile as Rosalind stared into the cheval mirror.

"You're very good at this," Rosalind noted, meeting the other woman's eyes in the mirror.

"I prefer to wear pants. It doesn't mean I don't know what a dress is for."

"I wear dresses," Rosalind pointed out. "And I don't know what half of this is called." She pointed at the lacy frill that draped her shoulder.

"Do you know how to use a knife?" Perry asked, ignoring the question in her words.

"Better than I know how to use that fan."

"This?" Perry grabbed the fan off the bed with a sharp flick of her wrist. The copper-plated blades fanned out, creating a deadly half circle that looked like it could be thrown.

For the first time that afternoon, Rosalind leaned forward in interest. "Are the edges sharp?"

"Sharp enough to shave with," Perry replied, folding it back into itself. She hung it from her own wrist and took a small six-inch shape off the bed. "This is a bodice dagger." Drawing the small blade from its velvet sheath, Perry flipped it in her fingers with a dexterity Rosalind almost envied. "Do you want it?"

Rosalind nodded and accepted the blade, tucking it between the fine boning of her corset, the handle sitting snugly between her breasts.

"And this"—Perry grabbed a thin shiv off the bed—"is designed to be worn in the hair. See how the handle is ornamental?"

"Very pretty."

Perry grinned, handing it toward her hilt first. "Don't let Lynch lure you into any dark corners. He might cut his fingers off by the time I'm through with you."

Rosalind glanced at her beneath her lashes. She was almost starting to like the other woman. "I thought he looked more likely to throttle me."

"Interesting. I was expecting you to deny it."

❦

"Black suits you, my lord."

The sultry voice came from behind. Lynch's fingers jerked on his cuff links and he turned around…then stopped.

Rosa sauntered down the staircase, fanning herself with a scrap of white lace as her skirts trailed behind her. His breathing quickened. Hell. Someone had poured her into that dress. If she took a sharp breath buttons were going to suddenly become a fatal hail around her.

His gaze dipped. Buttons trailed down the nipped in waist of her gown and vanished into the gauzy fabric bunching at her waist. He couldn't breathe all of a sudden, an image of her clever little fingers working on similar buttons springing to mind.

"You look like your collar's too tight." A little smile flickered over her lips as she reached up and gently toyed with the white bow tie around his throat.

"You look amazing." His gaze dropped again, a faint darkening shadowing the edges of his vision. Every man at the opera was going to be staring at her…buttons.

"Don't scowl." Rosa's smile faded, her fingers lingering on his collar for longer than was appropriate. She stared at his throat, a small hint of nervousness flickering through those dark eyes. "I want you to be careful tonight, sir."

The thought that she was worried about *him* drew a harsh laugh. He'd spent hours trying to work through his own arguments about why she shouldn't attend.

Slowly her hands slid down to his chest, resting lightly against the lapels of his coat as if she couldn't quite bring herself to stop touching him.

"Rosa," he murmured.

Her dark lashes fluttered against her smooth cheeks and those luminous eyes hit him with all the power of a punch.

"Rosa, I wanted—"

"Don't." A bleak word. Her gaze dropped, her hands fluttering helplessly against his chest. "Please, don't."

Light gleamed over the coppery shine of her hair. Lynch took a deep breath, drawing in the lemony scent of her as he closed his eyes. He felt as if they stood alone, the world a thousand miles away. Silence fell over them like a mantle, and he simply listened to the soft sigh of her breathing, the racing, throbbing beat of her heart… The sound of it was its own form of communication and he felt it echo deep within his chest.

Reaching out, he traced his fingertips over her lips. He'd sworn he wouldn't do this. It would only hurt her if he failed at his task tonight, yet he was as helpless as a moth drawn to flame. Slowly his head lowered, his forehead leaning against the soft silk of her hair. He could taste her breath between them and as she shifted, her own face lifting ever so slightly, he felt the stir of it against his own lips.

Lynch couldn't move, couldn't press closer. Instead he lingered, drawing her breath into his lungs, where it belonged. Feeling her so deep inside him, as if she had wrapped chains around his heart and bound them together.

Rosa tilted her face, a soft whimper sounding in her throat. Her mouth brushed his. Once. Twice. Silk rasping over his sensitive lips. His hands fisted at his sides and he brought them up, stroking the backs of his knuckles against the velvety skin of her jaw.

I wish that it didn't have to be this way.

Again their mouths brushed against each other, more of an inhale than a kiss. Rosa's body surrendered to his, her hips pressing hard against his thighs. Yet despite the softness of her body, her hands still curled around his lapels as if she was afraid to let go entirely.

"Be careful tonight," he whispered, tracing her mouth with the words. "I could not bear to see you hurt."

She licked her lips, her tongue wetting his own. A groan echoed in his throat and he took a deep breath and pulled away. The world spun. When he met her eyes, they held the same unfocused breathlessness he himself felt.

Slowly, her pupils focused on him. "I won't let you be hurt," she said, swallowing hard. Her voice strengthened. "No matter what I have to do."

The edge of ruthlessness was so at odds with what he'd known of her, yet he could remember the dark shadows in her voice the other night when she lay in his arms and told him of her life. Rosa was sunshine and smiles, yet an edge of hardened steel existed beneath the exterior. She had known pain and she had survived it. As she looked up at him, he realized then that he had underestimated her.

She *would* do whatever was necessary to protect him.

He saw in her eyes the truth of what she wouldn't tell him, the truth she wouldn't let him tell her. Fear wouldn't allow her to give voice to it, yet it existed between them, as heady as opium.

Lynch nodded slowly and stepped away, her hands falling helplessly from his coat.

"I have something for you," she murmured, her pulse still throbbing in her throat. Reaching down, she drew a leather mouth mask out of her reticule. "I know someone who makes them and I bought as many as I could while Perry and I were out…shopping."

Easier to speak of this than everything that remained unsaid. His gaze cut to her face, noting the stiffness of her shoulders. Something had changed between them that night they'd been taken to Undertown, and though self-doubt told him it was because of what he'd almost done to her, his gut clenched with instinct. It had happened before that; the moment she told him he couldn't kiss her again, the moment panic had edged its way across her face.

For so long he'd been afraid to let another woman close after Annabelle's betrayal. It had hurt so badly, though the ache of it was like an old scar now. He'd never wanted to feel that way again.

Somehow Rosa had gotten beneath his skin. He hadn't even realized what was happening until it was too late. And now he was falling for a woman who was afraid to love him back.

Oh, yes, he recognized the deliberate distance she kept between them. The only time she'd ever come close to revealing herself—that secret core she kept hidden—she'd been in his arms and his bed, and neither of them had been focused on speaking.

He knew she had secrets. He simply didn't care.

The taste of her fear rode over his tongue, despite the weak smile she flashed him. If she wanted to pretend that nothing had happened, then he would let her—he had to. Anything else would only prolong the pain of his death if he couldn't figure out a way to give the Echelon what they wanted without betraying Mercury.

So he didn't push her to face this fear. He didn't ask what it was that she was keeping from him. Instead, he took the half mask in dubious fingers and examined it. "What is it?"

A small round disk centered over the mouthpiece, bound with mesh that roughened the pad of his thumb as he scraped it over it.

"It's a filtration mask. It helps those suffering from

the black lung, or other lung diseases, to breathe without the choke of London air."

"You think it will stop the bloodlust from affecting me?"

"I don't know. It might. It's supposed to filter out all noxious gases and pollutants."

She knew. Knew the fear that lurked in his own heart. The vulnerability should have concerned him—he hated having anyone know his weaknesses—but Rosa was different. He trusted her implicitly, despite the secrets that lurked between them. This meant more to him than any gift. "Thank you."

"I have three more." The look in her eyes told him she knew exactly what he was thinking. "One each for Perry and Garrett and one left over for whoever you feel needs it."

"Byrnes," he said instantly. "He'll be leading the outside contingent."

Footsteps intruded. "I heard my name," Garrett announced, striding out of the shadows and into the light, his attention focused on his cuff links. He straightened them and looked up, light gleaming off his chestnut hair and the stark white shirt beneath his black coat.

One would think a member of the Echelon had arrived; from the pristine folds of the white scarf dangling around his neck to the crisp white gloves Garrett tugged into place, he looked like any other dashing young rake.

His body was focused however, stillness radiating through sleek muscle. A weapon at Lynch's side and one he had to trust enough to use. Garrett would survive, he had to believe that. Lynch couldn't protect them all, especially not when this time he was the one who needed help.

"Where's Perry?" Garrett asked. "Still trying to figure out which end of the dress goes where?"

"Oh, I managed," Perry drawled, from the top of the stairs.

Even Lynch's eyebrows shot up when he saw her. Languidly waving a fan, Perry slid her blood-red skirts into her other hand and started down the stairs. Her natural predatory grace made it seem as though she were stalking them, a small triumphant smile on her painted lips as her blue eyes locked on Garrett.

"Do you think I'll do?" she asked in a surprisingly girlish voice as she reached the foot of the stairs. Glancing at Garrett beneath her lashes, she gave a little twirl that flared the skirts around her trim ankles.

At his side, Rosa pressed her gloved hand to her lips and coughed. Lynch looked down sharply. That had sounded suspiciously like a laugh. When he saw the smile she couldn't quite hide, he raised a questioning brow.

She tilted her head toward Garrett, who was frozen in the act of straightening his coat.

"Well?" Perry repeated, coming to a halt, with her red skirts wrapping around the bottom of her legs and an excited, breathless flush in her cheeks.

Garrett cleared his throat. "Good God. Mrs. Marberry you work wonders."

"I had nothing to do with it," Rosa replied. "Perhaps you're not giving Perry her dues. It seems she's been hiding more than a knife or two under that body armor all along."

The color drained out of his second's face. A
dawning suspicion began to grow on him and Lynch
glanced between the pair of them. Rosa's face came
into view as she straightened his coat and she winked
up at him as if she knew precisely what he was thinking.

"*Don't ruin it*," she mouthed silently.

"Quite," Garrett said in a crisp, distant tone that
sounded not at all himself. His eyes were wild.
"Shall we?"

Light gleamed over the heavy Grecian columns that
supported the opera portico. Dozens of brightly
dressed ladies littered the marble stairs that led to the
doors, fans fluttering like ghostly wings in the night.

Lynch stepped out of the plain black steam carriage,
raking the crowd with a ruthless gaze. Blue bloods
thronged all around him, some of them casting
curious glances at the carriage as if wondering what
he was doing there. He'd earned a knighthood over
twenty years ago for finding the kidnapped cousin of
the queen, but he rarely moved amongst them. They
might call him "sir" to his face, but they still considered him little better than a rogue. Indeed some of the
younger members of the Echelon didn't even bother
with the "sir," too young to remember a time when
he'd walked amongst them with the same rights and
dues as they owned.

He offered his hand to Rosa. Her glove rested on
his, then she slid down from the carriage with effort-
less grace, fanning herself. The bored expression on
her face perfectly matched every other lady there, as

though they didn't dare reveal too much emotion for fear of appearing gauche.

Her eyes however raked the crowd with the same attention to detail as his—almost as if she were looking for someone. Lynch slid his hand into the curve of her back and urged her toward the opera house, bending low to murmur, "Don't be nervous. I won't allow anything to happen to you."

"I know."

Her spine was steel, reluctance tight in each muscle beneath his fingertips. "Do you expect your father to be here?"

Rosa stopped in her tracks. "How did you—" Then she stopped and he had no difficulty deciphering her thoughts.

"I know he's of the Echelon. And I know he hurt you. One of these days, you will tell me what he did—" At the sudden jerk of her head, he lifted a soothing hand. "But not now. Just rest assured that you will come to no harm. If you wish to wait in the carriage, you may."

"If I see my father, then I know I shall not come to any harm." Her expression tightened. "I cannot say the same for him."

Cold foreboding traveled down his spine. "Do you have your pistol?"

"Of course. It's strapped to my thigh." She pasted an impressively convincing smile on her face. "Fear not, my lord, for I don't intend to hunt him down." She reached up and trailed the edge of her fan over his lips. "I also have no intention of waiting in the carriage." This time her smile softened with genuineness.

"It was worth a try."

She laughed under her breath, low and husky, the sound stirring over his skin like soft fingers.

"Can you see Garrett or Perry?" he asked, looking around. "I wish I could wear the aural communicator."

"Garrett is probably still gaping like a breeched cod," Rosa murmured, catching a handful of her skirts as she smoothly took the first stair at his side. "They'll have to leave the hackney out of sight and walk on foot. I shouldn't expect them very soon, not with this crush."

More people turned to glance at them as they reached the top of the stairs, whispers sprouting.

At the door, a pair of Coldrush Guards gave him an uneasy glance. The prince consort and queen must be in attendance then. Lynch's gut clenched. As if tonight wouldn't be difficult enough.

Handing over his tickets at the door, he and Rosa slipped inside the marble foyer. A black-and-white checkerboard of tiles extended all the way to a gilded pair of spiral stairs.

"Where to?" Rosa whispered, looking up at him. She was almost breathless with excitement, her eyes sparkling in the candlelight.

"Upstairs," he murmured, shielding her from the buffeting crowd with his body. Dozens of gold-plated servant drones wheeled through the crowd and he snatched a pair of glasses off the flat tray on one of their heads. Offering her the champagne, he sipped at his own blud-wein. The crowd was starting to move, and across the foyer he saw Garrett protectively ushering Perry inside.

If the mechs were here, they'd know him on

sight. They wouldn't, however, recognize the pair of Nighthawks unless he did something to draw attention to them. Lynch glanced away, focusing on the liveried servants that mingled with the crowd. None of them looked as though they'd led a hard life and he could see no sign of a distinctive mech limb anywhere.

"Not the servants," she murmured. "These men are from the enclaves. There's no way they could blend in enough for the Echelon to mistake them."

She was right. They'd be somewhere deep within the bowels of the building, perhaps posing as workmen behind the scenes or maintenance workers.

A blue blood minced past with a pale young woman on a leash, her gaze downcast and a thin, gauzy white robe revealing inches of decadent skin. Rosa's eyes hardened and Lynch steered her away with a hand to the small of her back. One glance told him she knew exactly what he was doing; that diamond-sharp gaze scored him and for a moment he felt a flush of shame, as though by his very complicity, he himself had put the golden shackle around the young blood slave's throat.

"There's nothing I can do about it," he told her. "Nor you."

"So we simply ignore it?"

Swallowing her champagne, she slammed the glass flute down on the tray of a passing servant drone and jerked away from his touch.

"*We* keep our minds on the business at hand." He grabbed her elbow in a hard grip and Rosa stilled, her back rigid with barely suppressed fury. Lynch sighed under his breath and stepped closer, lowering his face close to her ear. "I have no influence here. I'm as much an outsider as you are, Rosa."

One look at Rosa's face, at those implacable black eyes told him she wasn't swayed. "If you could, *would* you help her?"

Something about the stillness of her figure told him the answer was deadly important to her. She looked right through him, as though seeking to bare his soul, to find something inside him that she desperately needed to find.

"Do you have to ask?" His hand gentled on her arm. Hell, he couldn't believe what he was thinking, his mind branded with shock. She'd admitted her brother was a humanist, but her own thoughts on the matter were dangerously revealing. "Rosa, you need to keep such thoughts close, especially here. If anyone overhears…"

Rosa sucked in a sharp breath, her entire body quivering beneath his touch. "They would think I had humanist tendencies. Perhaps I should say something. Perhaps this eternal damned silence—this hold-your-tongue-or-die attitude is what keeps women like that in shackles. This lack of a voice—it's the very reason we are here. The reason there is a war going on, played out in secret beneath the Echelon's very noses."

She was shaking so violently he could barely contain her. Darting a look over his shoulder, he pressed her against the wall, using his body to screen hers. For once, he was relieved at the oppressive laughter and gossip nearby, for it kept Rosa's damning words from common ears.

Their eyes met. She was angry and he didn't quite understand.

"If I said something—"

"Then you would die, and I with you," he said curtly.

Rosa's lips parted, her eyes widening. He watched thoughts racing in rapid emotion across her face, like the shadow of cloud cover over the ground.

"They would have to go through me first," he explained. "But I would die, and you too, and perhaps there would be some to cry 'martyr,' but in the end it wouldn't matter. Nothing would change. That girl will go home with her collar and leash, and her master will take as much blood from her as he desires." The back of his gloved fingers trailed over her jaw. She looked so lost, so crushed. "That is why I must stop these humanists, these mechs. They will bring war and death down upon the Echelon, but they will trample the innocent in their path just as much as the enemy. If we don't find them, theirs will be a hollow victory, earning them nothing but hate and fear. And when the Echelon fear something, they destroy it."

She quivered, her lashes drifting shut—but not before he saw the diamond glimmer of a tear in her eye.

"Thousands will die," he said. "You know I'm hunting humanists, but the Echelon shall not be as discreet. They'll simply round up whoever they can and execute them all until they get what they want."

"That's not true," she whispered hoarsely. "There has to be a way. We have to have some way to fight—"

His mouth tasted like ash, his worst fears springing to life. *We...* She'd named herself amongst them as surely as if she'd claimed it directly to his face. Doubt assailed him—a moment where he wondered just how deeply she was involved, how much trouble a spy in the Nighthawks could cause.

But she couldn't feign everything, could she? If she was a humanist, then she never would have kissed him, never would have…

Mercury did.

That was different. That was lust, a burning brand between them. A flickering match thrown on a puddle of oil. Whatever lay between he and Rosa, it was more than that.

Or it could have been, if he let it.

Still, his thumb stroked over her chin, doubt crippling him. He had to know. Was this real, or was she the greatest actress to ever grace a stage?

He took her mouth, capturing a gasp. Rosa's hands fisted in his coat instantly, her body pressing against his as she kissed him. This was madness to take such liberties here. The corner was in shadows, weak golden light dripping down the red and white wallpaper throughout the foyer, but he knew this would be noticed and remarked upon.

Still…the taste of her set the darkness roaring inside. A need to claim, to take her as his. Damn her. His hand fisted in the base of her elegant chignon. He was losing himself in her, no matter what he promised himself.

Just once he cursed duty and pushed it aside. Fuck the Council. The prince consort could go to hell. He wanted this—he wanted her, with all his heart. A lifetime would never be enough.

And he only had one more night.

Lynch dragged in a shuddering gasp, breathing hard against her mouth. With barely an inch between them, he could see the wild hunger gleaming in her eyes. It tempted him but he fought it, licking the taste of her from his lips. He could lose himself here, lose himself in her, but if he did, if he took her home and let the mechs do whatever they wanted, then he knew that no matter how frantically he kissed her, he would hear the clock ticking slowly in the background.

"I need you to know something," he breathed, fingers trembling on her jaw. "No matter what happens…I need you to know."

"What?" She clutched at his coat as if some sense of premonition shivered through her.

"I lied when I said that I wasn't sure what I felt for Annabelle. I lied when I said that I didn't once think of revenge," he said roughly. "I did. Losing her hurt a great deal, so much so that I swore I'd never let myself feel that way again." Lynch's gaze cut to hers, forcing her to meet his eyes, no matter how much she stiffened. He didn't care if she was afraid of this; he needed her to know, before it was too late. "You make me forget the hurt. You make me wish that there were more days ahead of me. So that we could—"

Rosa put her finger to his lips, stilling the flow of words. Horror rounded her eyes. "No," she whispered. "No, you barely *know* me." Hysteria laced the last two words.

"I know you're frightened—"

"You don't know anything!" She pushed past, pressing her gloved fingers to her lips.

Lynch followed, hard on her heels, ignoring the sudden scattering of curious debutantes. They couldn't say this here. It was too crowded, every ear and eye suddenly turning their way.

He caught her wrist, his fingers locking around something hard. Rosa spun like a scalded cat, yanking at his grip and clutching her hand to her chest. Lynch's fingers rubbed slowly together, as if his mind sought to assimilate the sensation of that touch.

Hard.

Like iron.

She froze like a trapped animal, a vicious, desperate look on her face. "And now, *me lord Nighthawk*? Do you still feel that way now?"

The noise and laughter around him drained away, the world narrowing in on the woman in front of him as she stared at him, almost daring him. He barely saw it. Everything in him turned to lead, darkness obliterating his vision as the hunger surged.

No. It couldn't be.

Me lord Nighthawk...

As if a veil had been lifted, everything he knew about her—everything she'd explained away so well—crashed together. Her hands—*don't touch my hands*—the pistol she carried, and the way she could pick a lock with barely a thought. *No!* He'd seen her hand, seen Mercury in the park while Rosa sat in the carriage beside him... Or had he? The truth hit him like a bucket of icy water, washing away the willful blindness, making him feel sick at the deception. The way she'd fooled him and so easily too.

Or perhaps, if he were honest, he had let himself be fooled.

"Mercury," he whispered, and realized that she had been right.

He knew her not at all.

Twenty-two

Rosalind panicked.

What had she done? The look in his eyes—*oh God, his eyes*—like little black pinpricks of blazing fury. But she couldn't cope, couldn't face the oppressive weight of his declarations without ruining it. She had to. Before he said something she wouldn't be able to forget. Before the sickening bite of her own secrets strangled her with guilt.

Rosalind couldn't face him anymore. Couldn't stomach the look on his face, as if she'd punched him in the chest with a knife. Betrayal. That's what she saw and it hurt her so much she couldn't breathe.

Heart thundering in her ears, she turned and ran toward the staircase. All around her blue bloods pressed close in their powdered wigs and extravagant velvets.

Rosalind sucked back a sob, the world blurring around her in a golden haze of melted candlelight. Why the devil hadn't she kept her mouth shut? Let him profess his undying love for her; it meant nothing. It shouldn't.

Why had she blurted out the truth?

She'd wanted him to know. So he wouldn't love her anymore. So he wouldn't torture her with these false declarations. So she'd never have to see him again, never feel the aching pain of her secret gnawing like a tumor within her. Never let herself wish for something she couldn't have…

This felt like a nightmare. The stairs were endless, as if no matter how hard she ran they would never end. She kept waiting for a hand to yank at her skirts, for him to grab her by the shoulder and wrench her to her knees. Finally! The top. She pushed into a pair of blue bloods and came to a staggering halt, trapped by the crowd. *Where was he?* Why hadn't he grabbed her yet?

Rosalind risked a glance. Her eyes met Lynch's, dark brown clashing with icy gray and something in her chest constricted at the way he stood at the bottom of the steps, staring at her as if she'd ripped his heart out and fled with it.

Her pulse thundered raggedly in her ears. As if he shared the same nightmare, he shook his head, shaking off the spell. The expression on his face hardened and something hurt deep within her at the sight of it.

Why? This is what you wanted!

His first step was slow, deliberate. Light gleamed in the polished shine of his boots, the blackness of his coat absorbing every shadow. Somehow the crowd gave way to him as though sensing the danger that prowled within its midst.

Rosalind's lungs caught until she could barely breathe. Panic flared. She took a step back and Lynch's gaze flattened. He was furious. Beyond furious.

Sudden terror made her turn around in a swish of skirts and press into the crowd.

An elegant little bell rang and the doors to the theatre opened. Laughter echoed, so rough and raucous against her skin that she felt as if it rubbed her raw. The swarm of the crowd pressed through the doors, heading for their seats, and she was dragged along in the tide, trapped by the current of people. Buffeted on all sides, panicked, almost blind to the world around her, she shoved and pushed her way through, not caring what they thought anymore. Lynch was the danger. If he got his hands on her...

She sucked in a sharp breath. Nearly clear of the crowd. Just three more steps and then she was going to grab a handful of her skirts and flee across the blood-red carpets for the exit.

Two steps. One. A hard hand gripped her elbow, the other settling on her waist. She was shoved free of the crowd, then the grip on her tightened.

Rosalind stiffened.

"Don't," Lynch murmured, leaning close to her ear. His hard body pressed against her back, driving her against the wall.

Rosalind spun, the bodice knife clutched in her gloved fingers. Lynch pressed her against the velvet embossed wallpaper, examining the crowd around them with a dangerous glare. As if he felt her gaze on his face, he slowly looked at her.

"Are you going to use it?" That voice... So cold.

"Use what?" she whispered, unable to break the hold of his gaze. *I'm sorry.*

"The knife," he said, enunciating each word with

a diamond edge. He let her go, his nostrils flaring and his gaze black with fury. "Go on. Use it." His arms dropped to his sides, presenting the vulnerable expanse of his abdomen and chest.

Rosalind stared at him. She had barely realized what she'd done; drawing the blade was always her first instinct. Only there was nothing to fight here. She couldn't knife the brutal crush of feeling in her chest, the weight that made her feel like she was slowly drowning. Her fingers opened nervelessly and the knife fell to the floor.

If anything, his gaze narrowed further.

Then he was hauling her toward the next staircase—the one that led to the boxes. Trapped by the ruthless steel of his grip, Rosalind could do nothing but stumble along in his wake. Her mind was blank. No clever escape routes, no witty rejoinder. She was numb all the way through.

They staggered into the hushed foyer that led to the boxes. Gilt soared up each column and the roof was mirrored in small tiles of glass. An image of the pair of them, locked together in a horrific embrace, danced through thousands of tiny glass shards. A red liveried servant stepped forward. "Sir, you can't be up here—"

Lynch shot him a deadly look and Rosalind grabbed his arm in desperation as the darkness within him looked back.

"Don't," she said shakily. "Take your anger out on me. Not him."

The servant swallowed hard and bolted out of the way. Lynch raked a glance at the heavily gilded sigils on each door: a griffin, a swan, three roaring lions, a serpent... He yanked the door open, the scarlet snake seeming to hiss in her face as she was wrenched through.

The House of Bleight's box. Bound to be empty so soon after the death of the duke's son.

Plunging into darkness, her knees hit one of the chairs and she tripped, clutching at the velvet seatback. The theatre spread before her, golden light basking over hundreds of pale faces as the blue bloods took their seats. The dull roar of conversation echoed in the cavernous theatre, a monotonous drone that masked the harsh pant of her breathing.

Rosalind spun.

Lynch pressed the door closed with a quiet, controlled click, his head bowing for a moment as if he fought for control. The line between his shoulders was rigid with tension. Taking a deep breath, he pushed away from the door and turned to face her.

Gray eyes met hers, devouring her face as if he'd never seen her before. "Did you enjoy it? Making me a fool? Laughing at me behind my back?"

"It was never about that—"

"No?"

The harsh word stopped her. Rosalind tilted her chin up defiantly. "Maybe at the start I enjoyed it a little."

A bitter smile curled over his mouth. "And what happened? Come, entertain me with some story about how it started to change—how I began to matter to you. How long did you intend to carry out this charade? Until you'd broken me? Until you'd won whatever game you thought you were playing?" He stepped closer, looming over her, each word cutting and precise. "You should have left me in that cell, my dear. I'm certain the mechs would have taken care of me and then you wouldn't have had to dirty your own hands eventually."

Rosalind's fists clenched, pain razoring through her. In defense, she felt her own anger rise. "You had nothing to do with it. I would never have risked such a charade if I didn't need to, if I...if I could find my brother. You arrogant bastard, stop thinking this was about you! You were never supposed to happen, this..." She choked on the words. "You ruined everything."

Silence. Lynch stilled, his heavy-lidded eyes examining her. "You expect me to believe the story about your brother was the truth?"

"I don't expect you to believe anything. I don't care whether you do or not. It doesn't matter one whit to me." The words would have been so much more believable if her voice hadn't broken at the end.

A shiver of strings whispered through the air, then a mild percussion as the orchestra encouraged everyone to their seats.

"So your brother was the only reason you infiltrated the guild? Or were you planning something else?"

"Believe what you will, but Jeremy was my only concern. I've had no hand in anything since he went missing."

"And the boiler pack from the enclaves?"

Not a lie, not precisely. "Something that was set in motion years ago."

"Fitz suspects it's similar to the model used to power the Echelon's metaljackets." His gaze sharpened.

"What are you planning, Rosa? Or is that even your real name?"

She had nothing to say to that. Each word only damned her further.

"Hell," he swore, slamming a hand against the wall beside her head.

Rosalind flinched.

"And your husband?" he demanded. "Was he real? Was any of it fucking real?"

"Almost all of it." She closed her eyes, unable to bear the demand in his own. "The best lies are based in truth."

The cool rasp of his breath stirred against her cheek as he leaned closer. Rosalind's breath caught and she steeled herself. A blow she could tolerate. But not this... Not his gentle cruelties.

"Don't," she whispered, meeting his eyes. "Please."

"Why?" A stark demand, laced with harsh longing. "Or do you only use your body for the sake of the cause? You kissed me once, gave yourself to me. Was that real, Mercury? Or just another way to bring me to my knees?" His hand lifted, hesitated by her face. He wanted it to be real; she read it all over his expression.

Rosalind turned her face aside, letting out the breath she'd been holding as she pressed back against the wall. Anything to stop him from touching her. From destroying her.

"Please..."

"You do that so well. It almost makes me think some part of you gives a damn. But as you say, the best lies—especially this—are based on truth." His fingers caught her chin and tilted her face to his. His other hand brushed against her mouth and he leaned closer, a cold, almost fanatical light in his black eyes. "Don't you dare look away. You owe me this."

Owe him or not, this was no lie. This was her only real truth, but she'd never convince him of that, even if she found the words to say. She never had the words—to bare herself so completely went against every harsh lesson she'd ever learned—but this…this she could do. Only with her mouth, her hands, her body, could she tell him what her heart could not.

With his body so close to hers, Rosalind could barely think. Anger vibrated off him, burning her with its intensity. He'd not forgiven her. He probably never would. But he was as trapped by this as she was, desire weaving a thick net around them. In the darkness of the theatre box, with the shivering hiss of the orchestra strings swelling in the background, getting louder, almost angry themselves, she could nearly pretend that they were alone. Somewhere else. Somewhere where the lemon verbena perfume of Mrs. Marberry stained the air and the rustle of sheets shifted beneath them.

Rosalind wished desperately she could go back to that. To be Mrs. Marberry again, a woman whom he had admired and respected, a woman he'd loved.

But she wasn't and he didn't. There was truth again, so painful that she wanted the lie that he offered as he stroked his fingertips across her mouth.

Rosalind looked up. The naked desire in his eyes was fueled by anger. She didn't care. Not anymore.

For a long heated moment they simply stared at each other. Lynch's face lowered, his eyes half shuttering and her breath caught. *Yes. Please.* Her hands fluttered near his chest, not quite daring to touch him.

He stopped, his face barely a half inch from hers, his breath cool on her moist lips. *Just another inch...* Lifting onto her toes, she reached for him.

"I never make mistakes twice," he whispered harshly, his lips almost brushing hers. Then he pushed away, dark shadows flickering through his eyes. Looking at her as if she were a stranger. "It hurts, doesn't it? To be played for a fool."

The ache in her chest solidified into something heavy. Rosalind slumped back against the wall, hope dying a short, painful death. This was the end. She'd lost him. Truly lost him.

"You bastard," she whispered without heat.

"Now that, I cannot claim."

Silence reigned throughout the theatre, thick with anticipation. The red velvet curtains swept back with a whisper, a circle of light highlighting a buxom shepherdess on the stage. As the opera singer opened her mouth to sing, a coughing eruption barked from the orchestral pit and the shepherdess flinched, glaring at the conductor before resuming.

Steam curled up from the orchestral pit. Some of the crowd clapped, no doubt thinking it an effect.

"Lynch," she called sharply.

He looked, then strode to the edge of the box, his white gloves curling over the balcony. Another coughing roar echoed in the theatre below. Steam poured from the gaping gilt mouths of the gargoyles that lined the walls and whispered out from beneath chairs. Several of the blue bloods exclaimed in surprise, looking beneath their seats curiously. One of them fell into a paroxysm of coughing, landing on his knees in the aisle.

It would be a massacre.

"They must have set a timer on them," Rosalind said, her gaze darting around the theatre.

Lynch shot her a hungry look, then swore under his breath. He ripped his coat off and threw it aside, tugging at the white bow tie around his throat until it eased. A pistol was tucked into the waistband of his trousers in the small of his back, but no other weapon seemed visible.

"What are you going to do?" she asked.

He stepped up onto one of the plush velvet chairs, then leaped lightly to the edge of the rail. "What I always do," he said coldly. "My duty." Glancing over his shoulder, he surveyed the crowd below and the curling wisps of steam. "Consider yourself fortunate the mechs are the greater threat at the moment."

Rosalind swallowed. He was retreating behind that distant, efficient mask, pretending that nothing in the world was the matter—steel walls closing around his already guarded heart. The taste of shame was so thick she almost choked on it.

The theatre looked like the bowels of hell, frightened screams echoing through the darkened chamber. The singer strode to the edge of the stage and began arguing fiercely with the conductor.

Lynch's weight shifted. Rosalind darted forward and grabbed the leg of his pants, making him look down in surprise at her.

"Where's your mask?"

"Does it even work?"

She wanted to hit him she was so furious, but a part of her couldn't blame him. She'd lied to him all along, why would he trust her?

"It works. Why would I send you in unprepared? I want to set you against the mechs, remember? I wanted you to destroy them."

"So you did." With a tight little smile, he straightened and stepped to the edge of the rail. "It's in my coat."

Rosalind fetched it swiftly. He hesitated for a moment and she couldn't stop herself. "If I wanted to hurt you, I'd push you off the damned balcony. Take it!"

His white gloves curled around the tan leather. "You would be wise to use this opportunity to flee. If I see you again, I won't be so remiss in my duty."

Then he bowed tightly, a slight tilting of the head to an adversary—to a stranger—and stepped backward off the rail.

Twenty-three

A FRIGHTENED SCREAM PIERCED THE THEATRE.

"What's happening?" a woman called shrilly. "Robert, what's going on?"

And then, from further back, near the doors. "We're locked in!" A man yelled. "Someone's locked the doors!"

Rosalind's fingers tightened on the rail. A perfect opportunity for her to get away... Why then did the ache in her chest intensify? She didn't owe him anything. She didn't owe any of them, but it was Lynch she was suddenly frightened for.

Yes, run and you could get away, a little voice whispered. *Run while you still have the chance...*

A sweet scent drifted past her nose as the steam rose. The sound of coughing and choking began below. Rosalind hesitated.

Hundreds of blue bloods in the theatre. Lynch didn't stand a chance by himself. And knowing the man as she did, he wouldn't back away from the challenge. He'd risk his own damn head at the best of times and now... Now, wasn't one of those.

Walk away now and she'd never forgive herself.

Rosalind wrenched her reticule open, fighting through the contents until she could drag out her opera glasses. They'd been modified with several different lenses: one that made everything black and white, so that she could view the world as a blue blood did; one that minimized distance, so that it seemed like she stood next to the soprano on the stage; and a phosphorus lens that amplified light, so that one could virtually see in the night, highlighting the faces in the audience below. That was for those theatregoers who were more interested in viewing what was going on around them in the darkened theatre than on stage.

Rosalind snapped the handle off the opera glasses and yanked at her skirts. Dragging her garter down her thigh, she looped it through the edges of the glasses, creating a makeshift pair of goggles. Yanking them over her head, the garter tugging tight at the back of her scalp, she slid the phosphor light-amplifying lens into place and peered over the rail.

The theatre was a green-tinted melee; ladies wilted in the aisles and blue bloods shoved their way toward the door as if escape could save them. One of them leaped onto the stage and rode the opera singer to the ground, her frightened screams piercing the air and then dying abruptly. The bright light from the stage left Rosalind momentarily blind.

Where was Lynch? Her vision blurred, her stomach fluttering with fear. She'd felt this way before: the helplessness, the fear, the guilt… Chained in the darkness while Balfour knelt in front of her and told her that she had five minutes to save her husband.

Taking a deep breath, Rosalind tore her skirts down the sides to free up her movement and then slid her legs over the balcony. Grabbing hold of the polished mahogany, she twisted and let her body fall, the weight dragging at her hands. It was barely a drop for Lynch, but if she landed this wrong, she'd twist her ankle...or worse.

Glancing down, she let herself drop, catching at a gilt gargoyle at the base of the balcony. The goggles skewed perception of distance and she found her fingers slipping. Somehow she turned the fall into a drop, landing on the plush velvet seat of one of the chairs. Thrown off balance, she tumbled into the aisle and rolled out of the way as a blue blood rushed past.

The air was humid here, the taste of the sweet scent stronger. Shoving to her feet, she found herself almost hip-deep in a dense fog. There was no sign of Lynch anywhere. An enormous mob of blue bloods hammered at the heavy bronze doors, cringing away from the steam. They might not know what it was, but they could see the effects clearly enough. Several of them had already succumbed and were hunting debutantes through the seats.

A figure in a white shirt and gleaming silk waistcoat leaped lightly onto a chair back as though it were solid ground and tackled a maddened blue blood lord to the ground as his frightened prey escaped. Lynch. Her breath caught in her chest, but she hesitated, glancing again at the main doors. The steam was rising. If the blue bloods didn't get out of here, they'd all be stricken with the blood thirst.

Rosalind had to trust that Lynch could take care of

himself for the moment. Better one maddened blue blood than an entire theatre full of them.

Lifting her foot onto a chair, she slid her skirts up high enough to retrieve the ladies pistol she kept strapped to her thigh. It was barely the size of her palm, but the firebolt bullets within it were packed with enough chemical to make a blue blood's head explode on impact.

Shoving grimly into the pack of blue bloods, Rosalind made her way toward the doors, unafraid to use her elbows or wave the pistol in a few faces. Three men strained against the heavy brass doors, stripped to their shirtsleeves.

"Get out of the way," she snapped, aiming the pistol. "It's obviously barred from the outside."

A clever move. Rosalind's gaze fell on the hinges and she took aim, then fired twice. The hinges, a large section of the door and half the door frame vanished in a small explosion of brass slivers and splinters.

Covering his face with his sleeve as he coughed, one of the men rammed his shoulder against the door. Someone had shoved a heavy bar through the handles on the other side. There was no way to open it, but somehow a pair of the blue bloods managed to pry the outer edge open just wide enough to slip through.

"Hurrah!" one of the lords cheered, clapping her on the back.

"My thanks," another blue blood said sincerely, his pale blue eyes wide and frightened.

I didn't do it for you. But then she stopped, watching as he helped a frightened young woman through the narrow gap. She of all people should know that sometimes the monsters were just as human as the rest of the world.

Rosalind didn't bother to watch as the first of the crowd slipped through the gap. She had to find Lynch or, barring that, Garrett or Perry.

Something caught her eye as she glanced around the darkened theatre. A tall man flashed through the green-tinted lens of the opera glasses, his rough-hewn face watching something in the chairs intently as he stalked forward.

Mordecai.

Her blood went cold when she realized who he was staring at.

❧

Lynch ground his teeth together and wrenched the blue blood's head sharply to the right. A faint crack. Then all of the fight drained out of the man and the body slumped to the floor beneath him.

A thrall in buttercup yellow lay on the carpet between the seats, staring up at him in shock and horror. Blood splashed her skirts and there was a bite mark on her shoulder that would leave a scar. Her lips parted as the blue blood collapsed, then she scrambled to her hands and knees at his side.

"Epson?" she whispered. Her hands began to shake and she looked up at Lynch with wide blue eyes. "You've killed him."

"It was either yourself or him," he replied, struggling to assuage the bloodlust that roared through his veins. The mask helped. Each breath tasted like sugared buns, but though it stirred his heartbeat, he could control himself.

"Look out!" a woman screamed.

Lynch spun low, ducking between the seats as a man behind him lifted a pistol. The shot went over his head, an enormous chunk of plaster exploding on the wall.

The pistol lowered and Lynch stared down the barrel. The man's face was rough with stubble, his eyes cold and merciless as he thumbed the hammer back. "Fare thee well, Sir Nighthawk."

A blur of cream silk came out of nowhere just as the pistol retorted. The pair of them tumbled out of view, but he knew who that had been as surely as he knew his own name.

Rosa.

What the hell was she doing here? And where the hell did that bullet go? There was no sign of struggling, no sign of movement... The anger that had consumed him at her treachery lost its fire, a cold hard knot twisting in his chest.

Leaping over the row of chairs, Lynch skidded to a halt in the aisle. The stranger reached for the pistol on the ground with grim determination—an enormous brute in a workman's shirt that strained over his enormous shoulders. Scrambling to her knees, Rosa launched herself past the stranger and kicked the pistol under the chairs.

"Curse you," the stranger snarled, rolling to his feet. "Who's damned side are you on?"

Rosa straightened, her cool glance shifting past him to settle on Lynch. Just a moment, one that burned him right through. "You want to know what I am? Who I am? Then stay out of this."

The stranger shot him an uneasy look.

"Where's my brother, Mordecai?" she asked.

So she had been telling the truth.

If she thought he could stay out of this, she was mistaken. She'd betrayed him, lied to him, made him think there was more between them than there was… But to watch her get hurt was beyond him.

"Ain't seen 'im," Mordecai retorted, turning so that he could keep them both in view. "Probably the same place as mine."

Rosa's lips thinned. Her expression was tight and focused, so far removed from Mrs. Marberry's saucy cheer that Lynch suddenly realized he was seeing the reality of who she was. Not Mrs. Marberry. Perhaps not even Mercury. She stood with a self-assurance and determination that were but echoes of the other two women.

Herself.

"I'm sorry about that," she admitted. "But Mendici went for his gun. I was faster."

"Aye." Darkness shadowed Mordecai's eyes. "But are you faster 'an me?"

He lashed out with a meaty fist. Lynch leaped forward, then stopped as Rosa ducked beneath the blow as if she'd expected it, her elbow locking Mordecai's arm in place as her metal hand chopped down in a brutal blow against the fellow's neck. Mordecai roared in pain and drove her into the seats with his shoulder in her midriff.

Rosa drove a knee up, bringing her elbow down between his shoulder blades. Each movement was sparse and economical, lacking the flamboyancy of someone who did this to prove his skill. She could have drawn this out, but instead she aimed for blows that would cripple and maim—the swifter to finish this.

So quick. Mordecai staggered to his feet and Rosa hopped up lightly on the chair to get height, then kicked him in the face. Her skirt tore at the extension of her leg, high and graceful. Mordecai stumbled backward, blood dripping from his nose, but he didn't go down.

Lynch's vision dripped between color and black and white. The Doeppler Orbs had dissipated, but he didn't dare take off the mask. He wanted to step in, to end this, despite the fact that Rosa had matters well in hand. The darkness in him was a gathering storm. For a moment his vision dulled, fury riding through him. *This was his woman.* His. *And he wanted to kill anyone who threatened her.*

Their eyes met.

Just long enough for Mordecai to lash out.

Rosa staggered back several steps in the aisle, grinding her teeth against the blow. Lynch dug his fingernails into his palms, fighting every instinct he owned.

Mordecai swung the enormous metal fist of his right arm. Rosa blocked it with her own bio-mech hand, but the force staggered her back into the seats. Light from the stage backlit them as Lynch took a step closer then stopped.

Mordecai flexed his metal fingers. "You hit like a girl."

Rosa looked up, her eyes black as night. Kicking

out, she drove her heel into his kneecap and Mordecai screamed as it shifted.

It should have been the end. But even Lynch was surprised when the huge mech lunged forward in an awkward lurch and drove his enormous body directly into Rosa.

For a moment they hovered on the edge of the orchestra pit, Rosa's wide, startled eyes meeting Lynch's and then they were gone. An enormous cacophony of noise drifted up.

"Rosa?" Lynch scrambled to the edge of the pit.

She lay on her back amongst the strings section, wincing as she lifted her hip. Her groping hand found the edge of a brass cymbal and she clenched it in her mech fingers, the edge a dangerous weapon.

Mordecai groaned, flat on his face beside her. Rosa scrambled over him, driving a stockinged knee into his back as she jerked his head back by his hair and pressed the cymbal to his throat. It wasn't sharp but with enough force…

Lynch leaped down beside her, catching her wrist. "Enough."

She looked up, black eyes gleaming. In that moment, he saw the coldness in her. She'd have done it. Not because she wanted to, but because it was what she should do—The next step to this.

A trained killer.

He recognized it, even as the coldness faded from her expression, replaced by breathless misery. Because of him. His hand slid from hers, unable to reconcile the woman he saw in front of him with the woman he'd known.

"I need him alive," he said.

Rosa let go of the cymbal, as if seeming to see it for the first time. Color flooded into her cheeks, emotion heating her expression. He couldn't read what she was thinking, but at least she was no longer the ruthless assassin he'd caught a glimpse of.

She knew it too. Her dark eyes flickered to his, saw everything he couldn't hide and looked away. "Of course."

Ripping out the strings on several violins, he knotted them together and then bound Mordecai's hands behind his back. The man groaned but didn't fight it. From the angle of his knee, he wouldn't be fighting anything soon. Then Lynch sat down and scraped his hand over his face.

What was he going to do?

Fury had died. He felt numb. Numb and so very, very old all of a sudden. The brightness he'd felt whenever he'd been around her had seemed to leech out of him, as if she'd sucked the very soul from him.

I loved you. He looked at her, waiting patiently on her knees, with her hands pressed so tightly together, he felt as if he'd somehow struck her a mortal blow. Dark lashes fluttered against her cheeks, but she couldn't—or wouldn't—look at him.

"Why?" he asked hoarsely. "Your brother? Only your brother?" *Was there ever anything for me?*

She toyed with the fingertips of her gloves, a move so reminiscent of Mrs. Marberry that his lungs arrested. Then he shook it off. He couldn't keep looking for things that weren't there.

"I swear," she whispered. "I only ever wanted to find my brother."

The dull truth of that made the fluttering hope in his chest die. He couldn't stay here anymore. Shoving to his feet, he buried everything deep inside. This was worse than that moment when he'd realized that Annabelle had played him false. Perhaps it was the healing balm of all those years dulling the memory, or perhaps because he'd finally dared to let himself feel something for someone, only to have it happen again.

Lesson learned.

Face expressionless, he yanked the groaning mech to his feet. At least he had something to show for this night's efforts, though he knew it wouldn't appease the prince consort. No, the Council wanted blood. Wanted the woman at his side.

He shoved the mech out of the pit. Jumping up, he caught the lip of it and hauled himself out, ignoring the way she watched him, as if waiting for him to speak.

He had no more words. *Only one more night.* And he couldn't see any way out of it for himself. No matter how much she had hurt him, he could never hand her over. His feelings, at least, had been true.

"Lynch," she whispered, looking up at him. "I'm sorry. I know...I know nothing I say could ever—"

But he wasn't listening to her. A figure stepped slowly out of the darkness, coalescing into a tall man in the aisle, leaning on an ivory handled cane. Strands of white dulled his coppery hair until it was a faded strawberry blonde, and lines fanned out from the corners of his small, black eyes. He wore the crisp black of a long-tailed coat, the stark white of his shirt gleaming in the shadows. A typical uniform for any man attending the opera, he was so unremarkable that the eye begged to skip directly over him.

As he no doubt intended. Nobody looking at him would know that this man was one of the mighty powers behind the throne, second only to the prince consort in manipulating the events of the realm. Lips thinning, Lynch reached down and offered Rosa his hand.

He yanked her to her feet beside him, ignoring the man in the aisle. The prince consort could damn well wait. He'd had enough of being played with for one night.

"Thank you," she murmured, blinking against the sudden glare of the spotlight.

Lynch ignored her, stepping down out of the light and meeting Balfour's gaze. "What do you want?"

Balfour wasn't looking at him.

A sudden coldness seemed to trickle down his spine. Lynch had seen that expression before—the faint smile, the piercing blackness of Balfour's narrow eyes as he'd watched an enemy humbled before him.

Lynch might as well not even have been there. He followed Balfour's gaze, his hand reaching for the knife that was no longer at his hip.

Rosa hovered just out of the spotlight, so still, trembling, like a deer caught in the sight of the hunter's gun. Her dark eyes—so similar, now he saw them together—narrowed. A thousand emotions crossed her face. Hate, fear, and finally...rage. The cold tremor down Lynch's spine grew. *If I see my father, I know I won't come to any harm... I cannot say the same for him.*

Lynch moved before the muscles tensing in her legs could even shift her. He caught her around the waist, swinging her in tight against his own body. Rosa snarled, shoving at his chest. She didn't even look at him, fixated solely on Balfour.

"Let me go!"

Lynch caught her back against his chest, his arms locking around her. "No."

He knew what she didn't. There was a shadow behind Balfour. One of his falcons no doubt, disguised as a bodyguard. The man wore black and hovered with seeming indifference in the darkness. Rosa would never get close enough, even if Balfour wasn't half as dangerous as he truly was.

For the first time, those dark eyes lifted from Rosa's face and Lynch met them. He tilted his chin up, extending a silent challenge. *Rosa belongs to me...* The thought took him unaware, but he didn't fight it. Not now. His own fractured pride was nothing compared to the dread that filled him.

"You have something of mine," Balfour murmured, his accent so haughtily elite that it spoke of years of breeding. A faint smile played over his lips. "I thought you dead, Cerise. All these years I thought I had lost you."

Cerise.

Rosa jerked, fighting his grip. "You did! I don't belong to you anymore. I haven't for years."

"I made you," Balfour said gently. "One only had to watch that fight to realize that you have forgotten nothing that I have taught you." He took a step forward. "I thought I saw you earlier tonight, but you are much changed. It wasn't until I saw you fight that I realized I wasn't merely feeling maudlin."

Rosa launched herself at him. Lynch swung her back behind him, stepping between the pair of them. He shot her a dark look. "No."

"Stay out of this," she hissed.

"He's more than you can handle."

"You don't know *what* I can handle."

The disturbing truth was that she was probably right. If she was Balfour's—if she'd ever belonged to him—then she had been created to be a weapon. His gaze dropped to her hands and memory flickered. *My hands…don't touch my hands.* What the hell had the bastard done to her?

"I can't let him get away," she whispered. "Lynch, please. He took everything from me."

"You made your choices," Balfour corrected.

Rosa glared at him. "I chose Nathaniel. And you killed him because you couldn't bear for me to have loyalties to anyone else."

A slight twitch on that expressionless face. Balfour tugged slowly at his gloves, as if thinking. The move was dangerously reminiscent of Rosa. "You should have known not to push me in that mood. I had given you *everything…*" His voice hardened. "And you threw it back in my face for that naive fool." He clutched the gloves in one hand, finally meeting her eyes. "I gave you a new hand in the end."

"You chained me to the wall, gave me a sword, and told me I had five minutes to save him." Her eyes were wet with furious tears. She held up the gleaming steel of her fist. "You *did* this to me."

"You did it to yourself," Balfour replied. "I only gave you a choice. Him. Or me. You didn't have to take it."

Somehow she'd found a knife. "You broke your word. You said if I got there in time, you wouldn't kill him."

Silence. Lynch held a hand out, warning her not to do this.

"You were late," Balfour finally said. "I gave you five minutes."

Lynch saw the surge of fury in her eyes a second before she went for Balfour. He caught her. "Fifteen seconds!" she screamed, kicking and fighting in his arms. "Fifteen seconds late! You cut his throat in front of me!"

Balfour's lips thinned. "You only have yourself to blame, Cerise—"

"I'm not Cerise! I'm not! My name is Rosalind."

At that Balfour smiled. "Rosalind Hucker, the humanist's wife? That was only a role, my dear. A mission I gave you." He took another step closer, as if sensing that he'd beaten her. She was crushed by grief and rage, unable to do what she wanted so desperately. And Balfour, the viper, knew it.

He reached for her.

"Give me the knife," Lynch murmured, taking it from her lax grip. He turned her, putting more distance between her and Balfour's outstretched hand.

The prince consort's spymaster noticed it. Those black, devil's eyes lit on him as if marking him as a potential adversary. "Don't do something you'll regret, Lynch."

He still had her knife in his hand. Easing her into a chair, curled up upon herself, looking so much like a lost child at that point, Lynch slowly straightened. "I never regret anything I do."

In the next second, he had Balfour's back to his chest, the knife against his throat. The falcon took a sharp step forward, then froze.

Lynch eyed him. "Don't move or I'll cut his throat."

"It won't kill me," Balfour murmured.

The pressure of the knife increased. "Don't ever doubt me, you smug bastard. If I want to kill you, then I'll do it."

"And what will the prince consort say?"

Lynch leaned close enough to put his lips to the older man's ears. "I don't see any witnesses, do you?"

"There are eyes on us," Balfour replied. "Always."

His own little network of spies. Lynch glanced at Rosa beneath his lashes. She stared up at him with wide, tearstained eyes, as if she'd never seen him before. As if he were something more than he was.

"Go," he said softly.

"What are you doing?" she whispered.

He didn't have time for this. He could see the muscle working in the jaw of Balfour's man. Only so long before the falcon came for him.

"Go," he snapped.

She flinched, her gaze darting between the three men. "I'm sorry." A whisper for him alone.

"So am I," he replied, the words emotionless.

Then she was gone, disappearing through the back of the stage, her footsteps echoing in the darkened theatre.

"I never took you as a man who'd ever show a weakness," Balfour murmured.

Lynch let him go and gave him a shove in the back. "I never took you as one either."

Balfour didn't bother to rub the thin line of blood at his throat. "What do you mean?"

"She might have belonged to you once, but you'll never leash her again, Balfour. She was meant to fly free, and she'll never succumb to your will this time. She hates you. You pushed her too far."

Thought raced behind the spymaster's eyes. "She was the most like me." A faint tremor of pride traced his words.

"No," Lynch replied. "She was nothing like you. You would never have cut your own hand off to save another." He sheathed the knife at his belt before he was tempted to use it. "Let her go. If you have any sense of feeling for her, then let her be."

"You'll never have her either," Balfour said. He knew. Knew that tomorrow Lynch would be called before the Council to either present Mercury—or himself.

Lynch nodded slowly. "You're right. I won't."

"I could intercede."

"At what price?" Lynch replied, knowing Balfour would ask for her. "You can't buy me, Balfour."

"That's what makes you so very dangerous," Balfour replied. He glanced down at the groaning mech on the floor by Lynch's feet. "You do realize that this has nothing to do with the revolutionary?"

Lynch paused.

"You have four hundred and fifty Nighthawks," Balfour murmured. "And you insist on doing the right thing, no matter who you defy. Some might say that's a dangerous combination. Enough to make...certain people...fear you."

The prince consort. "I would never have moved against him."

Balfour smiled. "*I* know that. I never feared you, Lynch. You're predictable. I know which way you'll move before you even make it. Honor is such a weight around one's neck." He gave a terse nod, his gaze flickering to the door. And the pair of blue bloods who slid through it. Garrett and Perry. Balfour straightened, gesturing to his man to fall in beside him. "Even if you could somehow find Mercury by the morning, there would come another demand. And another. Until you eventually gave him an excuse." Balfour saluted slowly. "I will see you in the morning, then?"

For a second, Lynch thought about using the knife. "You're attending?"

With one last smile, Balfour gave him his back and smiled at Garrett and Perry as he passed them. "I wouldn't miss it for the world."

Twenty-four

LYNCH SCRATCHED OUT SEVERAL WORDS WITH THE pen, then his eyes slowly lifted. The candle flame in front of him danced as if someone had opened a door somewhere.

Putting the pen down, he rubbed at the tired line between his brows and glanced at the clock on the mantel. Three in the morning. There was no point trying to sleep. He needed to put his affairs in order and see that certain events took place as he willed them.

A slight whisper of sound.

He cocked his head. Silence. Still, the unnerving sensation of a presence filled the room, itching over his skin. Lynch shoved to his feet and crossed toward his bedroom on quiet feet, the candle in hand.

Turning the handle, he edged it open. The curtains to his bedroom fluttered in the breeze, the window cracked halfway. Before he even took a step into the room he knew; he could scent her, clean and fresh, stained with the faint sickly sweet scent of the orbs. And then he could see her, moonlight gilding that porcelain skin with a loving touch.

Rosa.

"What the hell are you doing here?" he whispered harshly, bringing the candle up.

Rosa lifted her chin, staring at him as if she herself didn't know. Long tendrils of coppery hair clung to her shoulders and hung around her tearstained face, the torn scraps of the gorgeous dress she'd worn still clinging to her legs. With her red hair and pale skin, she wasn't the type of woman made for crying, but there was something about the defiance in her eyes that made his breath catch. "I wanted... I needed to speak to you."

Lynch swallowed the hard ball of emotion in his throat and strode past her to the window, placing the candle on the tallboy beside his bed. "I believe everything that needed saying was said." He peered out, hunting the shadows for hidden eyes. "Do you think I let you escape for nothing? Damn it, woman, I have no doubt Balfour has eyes on the guild. He'll be expecting me to do something tonight."

Slamming the window shut, he drew the curtains across with a harsh jerk and took a steadying breath. Hell, he hadn't expected her here. His fingers trembled slightly on the curtains. A part of him didn't want to face her.

"Why tonight?" she asked. A note of doubt crept into her voice. "Did he threaten you? What did he say?" The rustle of skirts swept closer. Then stopped. "He didn't hurt you, did he?"

Would she care? His fingers tightened on the sill, then he slowly pushed away and looked at her.

A faint flush of color crept up her cheeks and her

gaze dropped. Toying with the tips of her gloves, her shoulders slightly hunched, she managed to draw in a deep breath. "You shouldn't have let him live." Quiet words. "If you'd let me go, I could have—"

"Gotten yourself killed," he replied, with just a touch too much vigor. Hell, if she knew what she was doing to him... His hungry gaze ran over her slender figure and despite himself, his body yearned for her. Just one touch. He knew if he went to her, she'd turn her face up to his eagerly, but would it mean anything? He didn't know. He'd thought himself a great judge of character once, but now she'd shattered his perceptions with the web of lies she'd woven. He couldn't see the truth anymore and it made him doubt each and every one of her actions.

"Why did you come here tonight?"

Rosa shrank a little, as if the weight of his gaze drove her shoulders down. "I wanted to say...I'm *sorry*." That last was a whisper. "I couldn't—I had to see you."

Running his hand over the back of his neck, he crossed to the liquor decanter and poured himself a generous glass of blud-wein. *Hell.*

She took a deep, shuddering breath. "I know you won't believe me. I can't blame you for that, but I wish—I need you to know that I never meant any of this to happen." She took a step closer, her skirts swishing. "I'm not good at this. I never have been. It was easier when I was Mercury, easier...as Mrs. Marberry."

"Easier to lie?" he asked, tossing back the blud-wein.

"It wasn't all a lie."

Lynch put the glass down with a ringing sound. He

turned—and then wished he hadn't. Those vulnerable eyes burned him. He wanted to believe her. Gods, he hungered for it.

Just let go, whispered his darker side. *Take what she's offering. You'll never get another chance.*

And a part of him hated her for that, for the fact that his heart and body still wanted what it wanted, regardless of her betrayal.

"You should go."

His quiet words lifted her head so sharply he might as well have slapped her. Determination stared back at him. "No," she whispered. "I won't. I know that I lied to you. I know you'll never forgive me, but please, what I felt for you—"

He couldn't stomach it anymore. Turning away, he crossed to the grate and stared into the ashes. Her letter was still there, a forlorn crumpled note in the powdery fine ash. "It meant nothing. I'll forget it." His own lie. "And no doubt you will too."

"That's not true."

Lynch glanced over his shoulder darkly. "Isn't it? Which part?"

"All of it. You want me. I know you do—"

He turned then. His body was as tight as a fucking violin string. "Maybe you're wrong."

"I can make you want me," she declared, giving a little shimmy that slipped her capped sleeves over her shoulders. Her bodice softened, her plump breasts threatening to spill. "You wanted me once."

"Whether I want you or not, it doesn't change the fact that I don't even know who you are!" he snapped. "I thought that I loved a woman, but she didn't exist. I've had enough of betrayal to last me a lifetime."

Rosa flinched. But she didn't back down. Instead, her fingers went to the bodice and the little row of buttons that ran down the front of her finely tailored corset-dress. The light gleamed off the metal of her left hand; she'd taken her gloves off, no doubt to force him to admit to himself that she wasn't Mrs. Marberry.

"You want to know me?" Rosa asked. "Then so be it. I was a thief. On the streets as a child. Then Balfour's spy and later…later his assassin. I let my husband die because I couldn't save him in time and I can't tell my brothers how much I love them because I never have the words. Not when it means something." Licking dry lips, she continued, "I'm not good, I'm not kind, I don't seem to be able to feel such things that other people do—as if I can lock a box inside my mind and hide all of the…emotions inside it. But I can't do that now. Not with you. I *hate* feeling like this. I hate being so uncertain. I hate the guilt, knowing that I was wrong, that I should have told you." She struggled with a button, fingers trembling, cursing under her breath. "I don't know what to say. All I have is this, to show you—"

"I'm not your husband," he said, a brutal reminder of the one man she *had* loved. "You might have fooled him, but I won't make that mistake again."

Another arrow in the dark. Her skin blanched, still her trembling fingers began tugging at the little row of buttons. And no matter what he said, he couldn't tear his eyes away.

"You're right. That was the mistake *I* made.

Pretending to be someone that I'm not. Twice."
Uncertainty stilled her fingers. "I loved him, but…he
didn't know me. Not until the end, when Balfour told
him what I was, what I'd done." Sorrow shadowed her
eyes. "I couldn't go to him. I never got that chance.
That's why I'm here now." She stiffened, as if waiting
for a blow. "You said that your heart belonged to me,
but you never truly knew me. All the…the ugliness…
Now you do. And…if you want me to go, to truly go
away, all you have to do is tell me that you don't love
me. Tell me that I'm not the woman you cared for.
That there's nothing in me that you could ever love."

Her whisper cut him, her fingers trembling on the
next button as she stared at him and waited for the
guillotine to fall.

He couldn't do it. He wanted so much to believe
her. He wanted *her* too much.

Two steps and Lynch was in front of her, his hands
reaching for her face. Cursing himself. Cursing the
weakness in him that made him desperately long for
her words to be true. The silk of her hair slid around
his hand as he cradled the base of her skull and then
her mouth met his and he was lost.

"God," he whispered, yanking her hard against
him. "Rosa—I wish—" Her tongue, hot and wet. Her
hands grabbing him by the shirt so that he couldn't get
away. "I wish I could give you forever."

"I'll take tonight."

Then her mouth met his and all thought scattered,
except for the desperate desire to have her.

❧

For a second Rosalind thought she'd failed, that he would turn away, not want her. But even as her lungs deflated he was moving toward her, his mouth swooping down to capture hers. The kiss was hard, desperate. For the first time, nothing lay between them and she couldn't stop herself from clutching at him, her heart thundering in her ears and hope rearing its head.

He wanted her. Despite what she'd done. Despite her lies, the betrayal... Knowing everything that he knew about her, he still wanted her. This was what she'd never gotten a chance to see in Nate's eyes. Instead, he'd died before she could dare ask if he could ever forgive her.

Forgiveness might not be so swiftly earned, not with Lynch. She'd hurt him so badly... But at least this was a start. At least he hadn't thrown her out the window like she probably deserved.

Rosalind drew back for a breath, gasping, her fingers darting under his shirt. Greedy. So greedy for his skin, his body... To show him how she felt when she couldn't find the words. He slid a hand through her hair, tilting her head back, and then his cool lips were running down her throat, the feel of it echoing between her thighs. Her back hit the wall, his other hand cupping her lush bottom and then she could feel the hard edge of his cock pressing against her stomach.

Grabbing the back of her thigh, he dragged her knee up, pressing hotly between her legs. Rosalind moaned, her nails sinking into the smooth skin of his back, trailing up the long, lean muscles. Somehow, her hand found his, then she was pressing it lower, over her abdomen and down, hot desire racing through her veins.

A soft gasp as he found her, wet and ready, his fingers sliding between the slit in her drawers. Her gasp or his, she didn't know. Her head dropped back, nails digging into him as she bit her lip. He knew exactly where to touch her, exactly how to make her scream. But then this was the only thing she had never lied to him about. He knew her here. Knew every little place to stroke to drive her crazy.

Hard fingers sank inside her, his thumb stroking hard over the nub at the heart of all this pleasure. Rosalind couldn't think, couldn't see. Her body moving against his, desperate for this, to assuage the ache in her chest, and now the ache between her thighs. It rose with choking swiftness—maybe because she wanted this so much, maybe out of sheer relief that he was touching her, giving her what she needed—and then it overwhelmed her with shocking suddenness.

Her cry echoed in the room, her body convulsing around his fingers as she clung to him, trying to ride it out. Somehow this was purer and sweeter than anything she'd ever felt before, as if the purging of all that emotion that had been choking her let her body sing.

Teeth rasped over her throat, biting at the soft skin over the vein. Rosalind's eyes shot wide, knowing what he wanted, knowing the dark hungers that drove him. But if she dared ask him to trust her, then she had to give him the same trust. He wouldn't force this on her, wouldn't take directly from the vein. He never had.

Her eyes widened further, fear thick in her throat at the idea that sprang to mind. She couldn't. Could she?

The thin stiletto rasped in her hair. The more she tried not to think of it, the more she couldn't help herself. It terrified her. To give such control to another person, even Lynch. Her heart throbbed in her chest. Lynch lifted his head, his eyes half-lidded and dazed, his cheeks flushed with desire. He'd felt her withdrawal and looked to find the cause.

Rosalind grabbed a handful of his hair and kissed him, trying not to panic. She couldn't let him go. Not now. Fingertips trailing down his chest, she felt the hard press of the hilt against the base of her skull.

"Rosa?" he asked.

She had the knife in her fingers before she could even think about it. Swallowing hard, she caught his own hand and wrapped his fingers around the hilt.

Lynch froze. His smoky gray eyes met hers, heat spilling through them until they were black with fierce need. His gaze dropped to her throat, his lips parting with a little quivering jerk. He wanted it. So much. Too much.

Closing his eyes, he tried to breathe through it and she watched the harsh emotions chase each across his face. "No," he said softly. "No, you're frightened… I won't—"

She dragged his hand to her throat and pressed the edge of the blade against the throbbing vein. Their eyes met. "I *want* you to claim me. I want to be yours."

Another shuddering moment. Then the hot sting as the blade sliced through skin. It clattered to the floor and then his hands cupped her arse and his mouth closed over her throat as her hips nestled around his.

The surge of feeling shot straight between her legs, igniting her body. Each pull of his mouth, each hot swallow tugged on her clit as if his mouth were *there* instead. She came, clutching at his shoulders, crying out, her hips rubbing against his, *desperate*, desperate now to get him inside her... Hands sliding between them, tugging at his breeches and then he was free, the hot surge of his cock filling her hands, rubbing against her wet-slick skin. She came again, crying out, whimpering... It felt like her heartbeat sped up, beating in time to his as his mouth took her blood into his own body, his own veins.

One hard thrust. Rosalind's eyes went wide, drugged, candlelight melting into a puddle around them. Firm hands cupped her breast, sliding the buttons free, the very same ones she'd struggled with... Then his clever fingers slid over her nipple, tugging, teasing, his hips pumping as he thrust deep within her.

A rasped curse. Then Lynch was licking at her throat to close the wound, his hips thrusting her against the wall with furious desperation. His mouth caught hers, and she could taste the coppery tang of her own blood as their tongues clashed.

Rosalind's heart thundered in her ears. *I love you.* She screamed the words inside, where he couldn't hear, her eyes flooding with heat. Why couldn't she do this? Why was it so hard to give so much of herself? It shouldn't be this way. He deserved so much better, but she was so afraid, afraid that a part of him would look at her and not see anything deserving of those three little words.

"God, Rosa... Need you so much..." He gasped, fingers digging into her hips, his face tightening with fierce need. "Taste...so damned good..."

She cupped his face and kissed him, feeling the pressure building within him, within her. She wanted to explode, but she had to get this out before it was too late.

"I love you," she blurted, a harsh whisper in the gasping stillness. Not what she'd intended but...enough...

He kissed her. Hard. Capturing the words on her lips as he drove her into the patterned wallpaper. Fingers slid between them and then she was lost, crying out, anchored only by the feel of his hands on her hips as his body shuddered against her, a harsh cry torn from his own throat.

Heat spilled within her. She held him through it, his face tucked against her shoulder and her hands sliding through his hair. Gasping, trying to catch her breath again, she felt each tiny shudder as it went through him.

Hers.

She understood then why he'd longed for her blood. This was the same. Not to own him, not to bind him to her with ties he couldn't break, but to exist in that moment where the pair of them were one. To give—and to receive.

To be claimed.

Completely and utterly.

She knew that there was still so much between them, so many damned words that hadn't been said, but for the first time tonight, she felt a tiny little bud of hope swell in her chest. Resting her chin on his shoulder, she pressed a small kiss against his throat.

She was never going to let him go now.

Twenty-five

LYNCH ROLLED TO THE EDGE OF THE BED AND SAT UP, scrubbing his hands over his face. Soft dawn light crept through the window and he could hear pigeons cooing on the roof above.

Panic surged through him and he dragged his shaking hand down over his mouth. So much he hadn't been able to get through last night. And so much he had...

He glanced down, at the slumbering woman on the bed beside him. Rosa's warmth lingered in the sheets, her breath shifting the cotton sheet that wrapped precariously around her, caressing the lush curves of her bottom. His heart stuttered in his chest. The memories of last night hammered at him like pinpricks of image shoved red-hot into his brain. Everything she'd admitted to, everything she'd said, those last whispered words he'd pretended not to hear... The ones that did so much damage to his heart.

He wanted them to be true. Wanted this to at least be worth it. But could he trust them? Trust her?

The answer to that was easy; if he believed that they were true, then he wouldn't even be questioning it.

Lynch felt utterly drained. Judging by the clock on the mantel, he had only three hours before he was due to present himself before the court. His chest caught again, panic clutching at him with greedy fingers. He couldn't breathe. His lungs simply refused to open. Reaching out, he grabbed for Rosa's hand, felt her warm fingers tighten around his as she stirred with a soft moan. He didn't want to be alone. Not this morning.

Somehow he sucked in a breath. It was easier, with her hand in his, but not enough. Lynch turned to her, sliding his other hand down over her bottom as he kissed her shoulder. Her eyelashes fluttered against her cheeks as he kissed her, stole her own breath.

This was good-bye. Those dark eyes met his as she woke and then she slid her iron hand into his hair and yanked his mouth to hers as if she felt the need, the fury that rode him. "Jasper?" she whispered, but he didn't wish to speak. Not now.

He pushed her onto her back and came over her desperately. The heat of her body drove away the last of the panic as he thrust into her with fierce need. Each soft gasp from her lips anchored him, fighting off the last of his fear. If he could protect her, if she lived because of his sacrifice, then that would be enough.

It was fast, furious, desperate. And when it was over, she smiled up at him with dazed eyes, one hand still linked with his, and those iron fingers drifting tenderly over his cheek. His heart squeezed again and he buried his face in her shoulder, holding her beneath him as he fought one last wave of panic.

"Lynch?" she murmured, shifting as if to look at him. "Are you all right?"

His throat was dry. "I'm fine." Lynch wrapped his arms around her and shifted her so that her body tucked into the curve of his hip, his face buried in that glorious red hair. So that she couldn't see him. "Go back to sleep."

She brought their linked hands to her lips and pressed a kiss to his white knuckles. "I think I will," she murmured, in her husky Mrs. Marberry voice. "You've quite worn me out."

Her soft laughter echoed through her chest as he held her. For a moment all felt right with the world. He breathed in the scent of her hair, so familiar and yet so uniquely hers.

The minutes stretched out, each tick of the clock sounding like the clang of a jail cell. Rosa softened in his arms, her breathing becoming slow and even. He wanted to stay here all day. Forever. But the hour hand struck nine and he knew there was too much to do if he wanted to protect her.

Untangling himself from her body, he slipped from the bed with careful grace and made his way to the door.

He didn't say good-bye.

He didn't even leave a note, though he lingered over his desk for long moments in indecision.

In the end, they'd said everything that needed to be said.

⚜

There was a knock at the door. Rosalind lifted her head off the pillow, feeling the aching bruise of that fall into the orchestra pit. She winced, then realized she was alone.

Jerking the sheet up to her chest, she looked around, her heart hammering a little faster. There was no sign of Lynch and from the sunlight streaming in through the window, she'd slept half the morning away. Little wonder, what with the emotional and physical exertion of the night before.

"Mrs. Marberry?" Perry called. "May I come in?"

Scraping her hair behind her ear, she called out an assent. Her eyes felt tight and puffy. Vanity compelled her to admit it was probably a good thing Lynch had left early.

Or was it?

She couldn't help feeling nervous. So much had happened between them in the last day, and yet not all of it had been resolved. He'd forgiven her? Hadn't he?

Perry swept in with Rosalind's green dress from the previous afternoon over her arm. Dark circles lingered beneath her cerulean eyes; she looked almost as poorly as Rosalind felt.

"Here," Perry said, thrusting the dress toward her. "Garrett said it was time for you to get up. He wishes to speak with you."

The abrupt tone of her voice made Rosalind's chest tighten. They didn't know. They couldn't. "Is Lynch here?" she asked. "Is he…did he want to see me?"

Perry stiffened, her gaze darting to Rosalind's— then away. "You'll have to ask Garrett."

Perry left her to dress. Rosalind made swift work of the gown and stockings, butterflies starting to tickle in her abdomen. Instinct—ever a curse—was starting to make her nervous. Something was wrong. Perry had been warming to her last night but this morning they might as well have been strangers.

When she jerked open the door to Lynch's bedchambers, she found Garrett drumming his fingers on the desk in Lynch's office. The fingers stopped, his gaze examining her with an obliqueness that wasn't normal. One could always gauge Garrett's thoughts by the expressions that flickered across his face. There was no sign of his usual, slightly self-mocking smile as he stared at her.

"What's going on?" Rosalind asked.

He eased to his feet, white lines straining around his mouth. "Mrs. Marberry." Those blue eyes were watchful. "I've been instructed to escort you to the dungeons."

The blood drained out of her face. "What?" He wouldn't. Not Lynch. Damn it, last night had to have meant something. She'd given him everything, until she was almost wrung dry. Unless…she had hurt him so badly that she had destroyed even the glimmer of affection that he'd had for her.

Garrett gestured her in front of him. "Shall we?"

She wouldn't break. Not here. Not in front of Garrett or any of the Nighthawks she might see on the trip to the cells below. Her vision white with shock, she preceded him through the door, seeing none of the twists and turns they took. All too soon, she was standing in front of what looked like a pair of doors made entirely of interlocking brass cogs.

Garrett stepped past, his hands darting over the display. Each cog gave a click as he turned them, though she couldn't fathom by which order he moved them. Then he stepped to the side and pressed a small button concealed beside the doors.

The whole display began to move, the cogs in the middle beginning to grind, then each subsequent cog turning and shifting the others at its peripheral until the whole door was a whirling rotation. A heavy clunk sounded within. Then another. And a final, dull throb that sounded as if it were low within the door. The cogs ground to a halt, and then the thin crack in the middle began to separate.

"A clockwork door," Garrett murmured. "You must move the pieces correctly the first time, or it grinds to a halt and can't be resurrected until the entire thing is reset. Lynch and Fitz came up with the idea. Nobody can get in without the first piece of the puzzle—and nobody can get out."

The doors parted to reveal the inside of an elevation chamber. Rosalind swallowed hard and stepped inside.

"He has an extraordinary mind," she replied quietly.

Garrett stepped beside her, then pressed the button for the doors to close. The boxcar began to move, the steely rasp of the heavy winch sounding above her.

"He has an extraordinary heart," he corrected, shadows darkening his vision. "He told me who you are and what you had done."

The words were polite; the tone held a core of steel however.

Each jerk of the elevation chamber reminded her that there was no way out. Worrying at her gloves, she tried to keep her breathing steady. Already little white dots danced in her vision. "Does he intend to speak to me?"

She could feel him looking at her, his gaze burning through her. "You puzzle me, Mrs. Marberry—or whatever your name is—"

"Rosalind. My name is Rosalind."

"Rosalind." He seemed to be considering something. "I'm not quite certain if you are playing games or if you truly do care. I thought you were rather enamored of him."

She kept silent, despising the probing nature of his question.

He let out a low breath. "As impenetrable as a damned sphinx. I see. You don't give a damn what I think of you, do you?"

The boxcar came to a halt, its doors opening to reveal another set of clockwork doors. Rosalind met his gaze. "Not at all, sir." After all, she'd been hated and feared and worse in her time. She'd grown used to the sensation, to the thick callus that seemed her only form of protection.

Or had been once.

The only one whose opinion mattered wasn't here.

Garrett turned several of the cogs in the door—she tried to watch this time—and the mechanism swept into a whirling, dizzying dance again.

"We don't often keep prisoners," he said, gesturing her through the doors. He wouldn't stop looking at her, as if trying to puzzle out some mystery. "Only the five of us who make up Lynch's Hand know of the existence of this one—and have the code to the doors."

"Are you trying to suggest that there's no one here to help me escape?"

He stopped in the middle of the corridor, a row of

gaslight's gleaming on the shiny black leather of his body armor. A moment of surprise, then he bowed his head. "My apologies. I hadn't realized that you don't understand his intentions. We're not here to lock you in a cell, Rosalind."

"Though your opinion differs from his."

"No," he said. Again he seemed on the verge of saying something, then shook his head with a frustrated expression. "I'm hoping that I was correct. I'm hoping that some part of you did care for him. Here." He stepped toward one of the cell doors. They were all made of interlocking clockworks.

Garrett set one in motion and stepped back to wait. Rosalind held her breath, watching the cogs glisten and gleam as they ground slowly through their transition. Whatever was on the other side of this door was going to change her life, she was certain of it.

The locks clicked. The doors began to part.

Rosalind found herself staring into a small, dark cell with no windows, a single gaslight shining down on the occupant within. The boy sitting on the single cot winced at the sudden brightness, his arm held up before his eyes. Rosalind's heart dropped through the floor of her stomach. She knew him—knew him so well she'd practically been his mother.

"*Jeremy*," she whispered. There were hands on her shoulders, helping to hold her up. Clinging to Garrett, she blinked, trying to orientate herself, but the world was still spinning and she had the feeling it would never stop.

"Rosa?" Jeremy lowered his arm, the color blanching out of his face. He jerked to his feet, horror painting itself across his expression. "Damn it, I wouldn't tell 'em nothing. What happened? How'd they get you?"

She took a step forward. Then another. Then he was in her arms, and she was crushed against his chest, her hot tears staining the rough cambric shirt someone had provided for him. So big now. Tall and lanky and pale for lack of the sun.

"Oh God," she whispered. "You're alive. You're... not hurt." Clutching at his arms, she felt his chest and shoulders, dashing at her tears with her gloves. She couldn't stop crying. He was real. He was there. All this time... all of the hours she'd spent worrying and searching and he was alive.

"What happened?" A hiccup took her. "How long have you been here?"

He shot a glare over her shoulder. "They got me just after the tower. The Nighthawk's been hammerin' me with questions, but I swear I didn't tell him naught. He don't come so often anymore. Only this mornin'. Didn't say much but he knew me name this time. Didn't figure he had you." His hands caught her upper arms. "What happened? How'd you get nicked?"

"I didn't. I'm not—" She looked at Garrett, who lounged in the door with his lashes half-masted over his eyes. "What happens now?"

"I escort you to the exit and you leave."

"Just like that?" she asked, wiping her face. Surely there couldn't be any more tears left. But with her fingers clenched through her brother's, she felt it bubbling up again: anger, joy, disbelief... How? How had this happened? She could remember that night in the alleyway and Lynch's reticence once he discovered her brother was a humanist.

He'd known.

Known and promised her he would do his best to give her brother back to her. No doubt he'd fought his own instincts, knowing that Jeremy had been part of the bombing and wondering if it were the right thing to do. Yet, he'd still given her what she longed for the most.

Her heart swelled...and broke. Despite her treachery, he'd given her the one thing she desired most in the world.

"Where's Lynch?" she asked. "Would I... Could I thank him. Please?"

"He's gone to court." Garrett pushed away from the door. "I'd suggest we get your brother out of here. Quickly. Before someone with less nobler intentions than I realizes what's going on."

She hurried behind him, dragging Jeremy in her wake. "I thought you said only his Hand knew his mind."

"I did." Garrett ushered them into the elevation chamber. "You have to remember that he took us off the streets or the execution block and gave us a way to live. Not all of us think you should go unpunished for this."

The doors shut and the elevation chamber started upwards. "Byrnes," she guessed.

"Byrnes is our biggest problem," Garrett admitted. "Though not the only one. Doyle thinks you ought to be whipped."

"How fortunate that you obey Lynch's commands still."

He met her eyes then. "I'm still undecided."

"Rosa?" Jeremy asked. "What's going on?"

She stilled him with a hand. Urgency settled heavily on her shoulders. She had to get Jeremy out of here. Then she could deal with Lynch. This was all starting to confuse her. Her nerves—which should have settled—were stretching tighter. What wasn't Garrett telling her?

Once they reached the ground level of the guild headquarters, Garrett ushered them down several dark corridors and halls. She kept expecting Nighthawks to leap out from behind each corner, but the halls were strangely silent.

"Perry's keeping the others busy," Garrett murmured, pausing before a heavy-set steel-bound door. When he swung it open, sunlight flooded in, revealing the back entrance to the guild and the alley behind it.

Rosalind's spirits lifted immediately. She looked at Jeremy and met his astonished gaze before giving his hand a tremulous squeeze. She was free and Jeremy was safe. Jack and Ingrid would be so happy. And she—her elation died slightly.

She would speak to Lynch. Last night had to have meant something, didn't it? She wouldn't let this be · the end of it.

Jeremy dashed through the door, tugging her after him. "Come on, Rosa. Let's get the hell outta here."

But she paused in the alley and glanced back at Garrett, Jeremy's fingertips sliding through hers.

"Tell him that I'm sorry," she said. "And thank him for this."

"I can't." Garrett folded his arms over his chest and stared at her. This was what he'd been waiting for, she suddenly suspected, from the hungry, desperate look he gave her.

The hairs along the back of her neck lifted. *Something was wrong.*

"Why?"

That stare. As if it tried to peel the protective layers off her. "I promised I wouldn't tell you. But I think you should know. There was a price for this, Rosalind. And he is going to pay it."

"I don't understand. What did he do? What price?"

"The Council gave him three weeks to find Mercury. Or he would share Mercury's fate."

The world went white around her. She thought she staggered, but she wasn't sure. No. *No!* "When?" A whisper.

"Today." Garrett was merciless. "It was him. Or it was you."

And that was when she finally noticed the gleaming epaulets of the Guild Master on his own shoulders.

Twenty-six

ROSALIND HAD NEVER FAINTED IN HER LIFE, BUT SHE came close that afternoon in the alley. Garrett's words took her like a harpoon in the chest.

It was him. Or it was you.

Stupid, stupid man! This was exactly what she'd been afraid of. Not of loving—it was far too late for that, it had been for days—but of being loved so much that another man lost his life before hers.

She couldn't do this. Not again. Clapping her hand over her mouth, she groaned in pain as she bent at the waist. Her fault. All her cursed fault. She couldn't watch another man die for her. She wouldn't.

Don't be weak. Lynch needed her to be strong, especially now.

Biting on her fist, she swallowed the hard bubble of emotion in her throat. Distantly, she realized that Jeremy was patting her back, his voice rising in increments as he demanded to know what was wrong with her. And she was suddenly so grateful that he was alive and well—that Lynch had given him to her. Yet another debt she owed him.

Her brother was safe. She'd done what she came to do. And Jack… Ingrid… It was their turn to look after him.

She looked at Garrett, throat dry and hoarse. *Focus.* "What are you going to do to free him?"

"Nothing." Garrett shifted. "If it were just I, I'd take the chance. But I've had it explained to me very clearly that if I make one move, then every Nighthawk under my command will be cut down by metaljackets. All the young lads in training… Doyle, Byrnes… Perry." That last name seemed an oversight but the way his voice softened, she knew exactly which face he was picturing now. "I can't undo this. Not without starting a war between the Nighthawks and the Echelon. Besides, I'm running out of time. They threatened to execute him today."

"How long has he been gone?" she asked, thinking furiously.

"An hour. I came to wake you as soon as he left."

Of course. Because Garrett's hands were tied and hers were not. She knew what he was asking. All of this had been a ploy to test her feelings for Lynch, the length she would go to save his life.

"I want you to go home to Jack," she said to Jeremy, the words sounding as if they came from mechanical lips. "There is something that I have to do."

Jeremy grabbed her hands, panicked. "What the hell's goin' on, Rosa?"

"Your sister is going to help me rescue Lynch," Garrett replied, his shoulders slumping in relief.

Jeremy shook his head. "Aw, no. Ain't no way I'm letting you do this. You're goin' up against the Echelon, ain't you?"

"You can't stop me," she said wearily. "If I need to, I'll have Garrett put you back in the cell until it's done."

"Till what's done?" he demanded.

She couldn't tell him. Her eyes met Garrett's and she glared at him. *Don't you dare.*

"I'm going to free Lynch," she said. *His life or mine.* Curse the man. Curse him for a fool. Why the devil hadn't he told her what he was planning? Or had he suspected this might be her reaction?

Of course not. He'd doubted her, doubted everything that lay between them. But the only reason he wouldn't have told her was if he was afraid that she hadn't been lying about how she felt.

"How?" Jeremy demanded, his eyes narrowing. He looked so mature all of a sudden—a man grown, not a boy. Then his eyes lost their worldly look. "And why?"

"Perhaps if I give them what they want," she suggested, pasting a smile on her lips. "Or some part of it. We captured Mordecai last night. In the wake of the opera attack, I'm certain they'll be after blood. We give them what they want."

It wouldn't be enough—not if Lynch hadn't tried it himself. But Jeremy's narrowed eyes lost their edge. He believed her. She almost choked on the lie.

"I'll go," he warned. "I'll tell Jack what you're doing."

Jack wasn't nearly as easy to fool as Jeremy. Rosalind kept the smile on her mouth. "Of course," she said. "Give him...give him my love. And Ingrid too." Reaching out, she stroked her hand over Jeremy's arm and the fine red hairs there. *Tell them to forgive me.* "I'm so grateful to have you back." At that she couldn't help herself. She dragged him into her arms and hugged him tight, the smile dying as she pressed her face against his chest.

"I love you," she whispered.

"Love you too," Jeremy muttered, clearing his throat and shooting Garrett an embarrassed glance.

She stepped back. "You'd best go. Before one of the other Nighthawks realizes you're missing."

"I'll fetch Jack," he warned again. Perhaps not entirely fooled at all. Then he backed away, glanced up over the grim building, and spun toward the mouth of the alley.

She watched him go, her fingers curling into small fists. The rush of feeling was sweeping back into her now. The breaking point.

When she thought she had herself under control, she looked at Garrett. "Well?"

"An excellent performance." He bowed his head slowly. "I'll keep the Echelon off their trail."

"Thank you." Her mouth was dry. "You play a dangerous game."

"I wasn't entirely certain," he admitted. "Whether you cared enough."

"And now you know."

Garrett scrubbed a hand through his hair. "Now I know. And so will he."

She swallowed. She hadn't thought of that. Lynch was going to be furious. "He'll hate you for this."

"I know." Garrett offered her his arm. "That is my price to pay. I intended to present Mordecai to the Echelon but…I don't think it will be enough. I'm sorry to ask this of you."

"You don't have to ask," she replied. "Just tell him that I made the decision myself as soon as I heard. Tell him... Tell him that what I said last night... I meant every word."

∽

The prison cart was stuffed with straw, a biting wind creeping through every minute crack. Rosalind found herself shoved up into it ungracefully and spun to bare her teeth at Byrnes. He arched a cool brow at her, met Garrett's challenging look, then turned and strode out of view.

"Sorry," Garrett muttered, reaching up to help her to her feet. "He's a cold bastard, but he looks on Lynch like a brother."

Rosalind shrugged, sinking onto the narrow plank of wood that served as a seat. Slowly, she looked up and met the eyes of the man sitting opposite her. Mordecai shifted in his chains, squinting at her through a black-ened eye. His gaze dropped to her unbound wrists. Not quite sure what she was doing here.

Garrett shut the door and the light faded. By the time the steam engine throbbed to life, her vision had adjusted enough to make out Mordecai's grim expression.

"So we're both dancin' today." He smiled, revealing a split lip. "Guess we'll be findin' out soon if that brother o' yours is still alive."

She didn't bother to correct him. Instead, she curled her hands into her lap and looked down at them. Her stomach was a mess of nerves. The thought of being executed terrified her. For a moment she thought was going to be sick and shifted in her seat, unable to sit still. Her lungs seized.

Don't think about it. Shove it all in that nice safe box where you don't have to think about it.

Mordecai's hot gaze drilled into the top of her head. "How'd they catch you?"

She didn't particularly wish to speak to him, but at least it took her mind off what lay ahead. The prison cart lurched forward and she grabbed the seat. "I let my weaker emotions get the better of me."

He laughed softly. "Emotions? You don't got none. Most coldhearted bitch I e'er met."

"I wish that were true."

Silence. "So they got you an' they got me. Who's left? I assume none o' me boys made it out o' the opera alive?"

"Some," she admitted. "The Nighthawks had the place surrounded however."

He grunted. "And that brother o' yours?"

She didn't want to think of this either, for this meant she'd failed. There was a reason she'd led the cause and not Jack. "He and Ingrid are still unaccounted for by the Nighthawks."

"Don't mean shit," he snorted. "Jack talks a treat, but I know he's hidin' somewhat beneath them clothes of his. He don't lead no action, far as I saw."

"He can't," she said. "His entire body was burned with acid." By Balfour. When she'd chosen Nate over him. By the time she'd woken with a new hand and a fever, it had been too late. Balfour's temper had cooled and he'd actually admitted some remorse over the action, but the damage had been done. "His skin's too tight now. It hurts him to move quickly, though he can if he needs to."

"You think he and that verwulfen bitch can 'old it together?"

Rosalind looked up. "I thought you hated them?"

A slow shrug. "Never liked you lot much. Still don't. But 'ere we both sit. Ain't no more o' my mechs. We went at 'em 'ard—'arder than you e'er did—but the truth's the truth. All the 'umanists left belonged to you and I 'ate the Echelon more than I e'er 'ated you."

So many times she'd fought and argued with this man.

"We both made mistakes," she admitted. "I should have included you and your brother in my schemes when you asked." She took a deep breath. "I let pride and mistrust make my decisions, instead of thinking them through rationally."

Interest flickered in his dark eyes. "That an apology?"

"The only one you'll ever get," she replied tartly.

A soft laugh. "And now you want me to admit I shouldn't a gone against you? Bugger that."

"I understand why you did."

"All them years…" He shut his eyes and tilted his head back against the timber slats of the walls. "Locked in the enclaves, servin' me time for a limb I never e'en wanted." Bringing his iron fist up, he clenched it, staring at the shifting metal. "They said I owed 'em fifteen years for this. Fifteen years in that hell." A harsh laugh. "Then you with your pretty promises. All I e'er wanted was some action. Some way to even the score. And you kept urgin' us to wait, build yon fuckin' metal army." He spat to the side. "I worked metal for o'er ten years. What you wanted would 'ave taken at least another three. I couldn't wait that long."

"If you did, perhaps we wouldn't be sitting here now."

"Aye." He rubbed at the bruise on his face absently, then winced. "Got a mean right 'ook, you do. Never seen you in action afore. You could 'ave done some damage." Scraping his thumbnail against his mouth, he looked considering. "The Echelon, they want Mercury bad, don't they?"

She nodded.

"Then answer me this; why you given 'er to 'em?"

The look in his eyes was surprisingly astute. "I don't know what you mean."

"I saw the way that dandy 'anded you up in 'ere. Whatever you're plannin', 'e don't like it none." Narrowed eyes. "What are you plannin'?"

He thought this a ploy. Rosalind looked away. "I'm planning to give myself up in exchange for Lynch. They want Mercury, so I'll give her to them."

"*What?*" Mordecai looked incredulous, then a canny expression crossed his face, a smile. "Tole you a woman ought not be in charge. Them weaker emotions be the death o' you."

"I know."

He shook his head. "A blue blood, eh. A bleedin' Nighthawk."

"*The* Nighthawk," she corrected.

"Aye. And still a bleeder."

"So I used to believe." She closed her eyes and leaned her head back against the wall. "They're not like the Echelon."

"No?"

"No." A small smile crossed her lips. "If it makes you feel any better, I quite suspect the greatest threat to the Echelon won't be you or I. It will be the Nighthawks. They've already got an army; they don't have to build one."

Silence greeted this statement. When she opened her eyes, he was staring at her. "You believe that?" No matter his bravado, she sensed the need in him. The desire to know that this wasn't all for nothing.

"I do."

"You ain't so bad," he muttered. "When you ain't so cold. A pity. We coulda worked well together."

A humorless smile touched her lips. "I set the Nighthawks on you," she reminded him.

Despite the bruises, he almost smiled back. "That were clever. I ain't never suspected that."

The words trailed off as both of them peered through the barred window at the back of the prison cart. Her stomach fluttered. Getting closer now. They were nearly at the tower. She could almost feel the looming shadow of it over the prison cart.

"What would you 'ave done, if this 'adn't 'appened?" Mordecai suddenly asked. "If 'is lord Nighthawk were free and you weren't facin' the guillotine?"

She had to think about it. Indeed, she'd had so much time to think lately—about everything she'd done wrong or right, everything she might have done differently. "I wouldn't start a war," she said. "Not in the streets. Not the way I planned. There was something Lynch said…about war not being the way to win. The Echelon are so strong because they are feared, because no one dares to speak against them."

"You'd speak against them?"

"I'd find a way," she said. "Perhaps I'd join the Humans First Party."

"Join?" He laughed, a rough burr. "You wouldn't follow. Not for long. You'd want to lead."

"Perhaps I've learned my lesson," she replied. "Or perhaps not. Who knows? The point is moot."

The prison cart slowed down, someone shouting in the background. Then Garrett's voice, cutting through the shouts as he proclaimed, "Prisoners. For the tower."

Their eyes met. Mordecai paled beneath the swarthy layer of grime. "Do you think they'll call us 'eroes out in the streets?"

"Anything is possible." Rosalind's breath caught. She could taste fear, see it in his eyes and knew he saw it in hers.

"Always wanted to be a 'ero." He took a deep breath as the lock on the back of the cart rattled. "Guess this is it. A damned shame—after all we did— that it ends 'ere."

"With nothing gained," she agreed hoarsely.

Their eyes met. Mordecai nodded slowly, thought racing behind his eyes. "They don't even want me, do they? All they want is Mercury."

Rosa nodded.

Mordecai licked his lips and shifted in his seat. "Guess I'm dead then and the bastards won't even remember me name. Curse 'em. Curse 'em all to 'ell."

Twenty-seven

"THIS IS RIDICULOUS," BARRONS SNAPPED, STEPPING TO the front of the dais in the closest he'd ever come to confronting the prince consort.

"You dare defy your prince?" The Duke of Bleight asked.

Of course that vulture would be here. They all were, Balfour taking the place left vacant by the demise of the House of Lannister. He drummed his fingers on his chair, the only sign of movement apart from the eagle dart of his eyes.

Lynch stood with his shoulders squared and his head high. He couldn't quite control the racing beat of his heart. Death would never have been his choice, but then he had no choice. He could have handed the mech leader over in some attempt to sway the prince consort's mind but that was dangerous. Too many people knew who Mercury was and Mordecai was the only one whose tongue he couldn't control.

"I offer *council*," Barrons replied icily, "when the rest of you would rather bite your tongues and bob your heads for fear of offending." He turned to glare at the prince consort. "I know I'm not the only one who thinks this is foolishness. I'm just the only one who dares voice it."

The prince consort cut him a sharp look. "You're very close to crossing the line, Barrons."

"And then we would be down two council seats. Perhaps you would prefer a dictatorship?" Barrons replied.

A dangerous move. But Lynch saw the thoughtful flicker in several of the councilors eyes. They were clinging to power and they knew it. All it would take would be for them to unite against him and the prince consort's stranglehold would be over. But that would never happen so long as every councilor served his own purposes first.

As if he couldn't control it, Lynch looked at Bleight. The duke was getting older, perched like a vulture in his chair as he glared at Barrons. Firmly in the prince consort's pocket. For the first time, Lynch wondered what it would have been like if he hadn't refused to duel his cousin. If that were him sitting up there, trying to hold the Prince Consort at bay.

His breathing quickened. He didn't regret a thing, not truly, no matter how much heartbreak both Annabelle and Rosalind's deceptions had wrought, for to have done things differently would have meant he would have been a different man.

Yet perhaps it would have been better for others. For the humans, the mechs, and the rogues, the ones the Echelon ignored as inconsequential. He could have held a position of power, of influence.

The lack of power irritated him now—to live or die by this man's whim.

The prince consort finally turned his attention on Lynch, ignoring the speculative looks between his councilors. Or perhaps not fully aware of them. The queen stood at his side, her pale hand resting on his shoulder and her vacant eyes wandering the room. The fact that she stood while her husband sat was indicative of the power shift between them. Slowly her gaze settled on Lynch.

One powerless puppet to another.

"Do you think this is wise?" she asked quietly of her consort. "Sir Jasper has served us so very well over the years. Remember when he found cousin Robert for me?"

The prince consort shook her off. "Nearly two decades ago. He has not served us so well since. The city is almost overrun with humanists." He glared at the Council. "Or has anyone forgotten that mayhem last night? Is nowhere safe? I can't even sign a damned treaty in these halls or attend the opera in peace! No." He turned back to Lynch. "I gave you a chance and you failed. I swore then that you would share Mercury's fate and you will. Guards!"

Sir Richard Maitland took great pleasure in kicking his knees out from under him. The man had been stripped of command for failing to find Mercury and wore the ordinary epaulets of a lieutenant.

Lynch hit the marble hard, a fist in his hair wrenching his head back and the tip of a blade against his throat. Light streamed through the glass ceiling and Lynch suddenly couldn't breathe.

This was it.

The doors slammed open. "Wait!"

His heart plummeted. Garrett's voice. What was he doing here? Lynch jerked off balance, Maitland's blade pressing hard against his throat. At least one other person didn't want the disruption.

"Who is this?" the prince consort demanded.

"Lynch's second, Your Grace." Barrons sounded almost relieved. "Temporary Guild Master, Garrett Reed."

"And your companions?" The prince consort's snarl was lethal.

"You said he had three weeks to the day to deliver Mercury," Garrett announced. "Let him up. I've come to bring you what you want."

No. No. *No.* Lynch grabbed the knife and shoved it away, slicing his hand in the process. But he had to look. Landing on his hands and knees, his gaze went straight to the door.

Garrett stepped aside, revealing a hesitant pair in the doorway. Lynch barely saw the tall mech in chains, with the iron brace holding his knee in place so he could walk. All he could see was Rosa, standing there quietly, swallowing hard as her gaze darted around the room. Their eyes locked. Proud and beautiful and defying him with her knowing gaze.

Don't.

But it was too late. The council's breath caught, seemingly at once, as attention turned to the pair in the door.

There was only one reason she could be here. She loved him. Truly loved him. He saw it in her eyes as her weight shifted forward. *No!* The irony of it tore through him, that she was giving him everything he'd wanted from her—only for it to be the last thing he now desired.

"Where is Mercury?" the prince consort asked coldly.

"Right here," Garrett shot back.

And Rosa took a deep breath and prepared to step forward.

Twenty-eight

"YOU WANTED MERCURY?"

The voice startled her as Mordecai shoved past, pushing her out of the way roughly as he stared cockily at the Council. "Well, 'ere I be."

Shock tore through her, freezing Rosalind in place. All she could see were Lynch's furious eyes as he glared at her. He froze too, turning his gaze on the sturdy mech.

"Afraid o' just one man." Mordecai laughed. "Look at you all. Perched up 'igh in your Ivory Tower. And 'ere's me, got to you even 'ere."

The prince consort shoved to his feet, his eyes glittering with icy rage. But at least they were no longer resting on Lynch.

"I want his head," he snapped. "Bring me his *head*!"

The Master of the Coldrush Guards gaped at the prince consort, shooting Lynch a disappointed look. As Maitland moved toward Mordecai, Garrett stepped between them.

"You'll honor your word?" Garrett dared to ask. He looked nervous; no doubt he was. None of them had expected this. "Lynch brought down Mercury. You said it was his life or the revolutionary's."

"Then get him out of here." The prince consort's hungry gaze never shifted.

Lynch slowly pushed to his feet. Garrett bowed and stepped out of the way, his hand finding hers in the shadows of his body. She squeezed it back.

Mordecai glanced over his shoulder. She stared at him, an almost inexplicable sense of sadness sweeping through her. How truly she'd underestimated him.

He gave a loose one-shouldered shrug before turning back to the Council. "Aye, kill me then. And know that I'll die a 'ero. They won't ever forget me, out there in the streets. And they'll finish what I started, what we 'umanists started. Your days are numbered, you pasty maggots." His laughter bounced off the roof. "You think this ends this?" he shouted. "You think my death will stop us 'umans from risin'? This is just the start!"

"Seize him!" the prince consort screamed.

Mordecai's words echoed in the chamber, but she knew who they were aimed at. *Use it. Use this chance. Do what neither of them had managed so far.* His sacrifice floored her. He'd already been dead, but at least this way he earned them a chance.

The Coldrush Guards grabbed his arms and yanked him to the brass circle cut into the marble floor. His knees were kicked out from underneath him, the whites of his eyes flaring as they yanked his head back. Rosalind jerked, her fist tightening around Garrett's. She couldn't look away, couldn't find that inner cold-ness that protected her at times like this. She felt it as the sword rasped over Mordecai's throat, and swallowed hard against the lump in hers.

"Mount the head on the tower wall," the prince consort said coldly. "Let the masses see what happens to those who dare defy me." His voice rose. "Let them come at me and see how defiance ends! I will not be cast down. Not by you. Not by that horde of filthy unwashed humans! You are cattle!"

Then the sword slashed down, blood spraying over the marble floor. Mordecai's body jerked, blood fountaining from his throat, then it hit the ground.

So quickly. Without even a formality. Rosalind stared at the spreading pool of vermillion on the alabaster tiles, as they dragged the body away. That could have been her. Should have been, except for this one small act of mercy—of heroism. Heat sprang up behind her eyes.

You won't be forgotten, she vowed. And neither would her own pledge. He hadn't given her this chance for nothing.

Garrett squeezed her fingers. She was shaking so badly she could barely stand. But Lynch was alive. And so was she and somehow they had pulled the wool over the prince consort's eyes.

She could hardly breathe for the lump in her throat. And then she saw Balfour.

He watched her with those emotionless black eyes, his lashes so colorless they were almost white. Not a fool. He never had been and he *knew*; she saw it in him. He alone of the Council had watched her foot shift as she made to step forward, to claim the name of Mercury. She watched swift expression dance across his face as he made the connections. He was the one who'd sent her to spy on the humanists, on Nathaniel. After years of believing her dead, she had suddenly shown up, just as the name of Mercury was on everybody's lips.

One word and he could condemn them all.

But he didn't say it. The moments ticked by and he glanced down, toying with the signet ring on his finger. Strain tightened his face. He'd never once betrayed his prince, yet at what cost would this take? What would he demand of her?

She looked for Lynch, frightened and unsure. Their gazes locked and she knew that he understood her fear.

"You're lucky your man has your best interests at heart," the prince consort said to Lynch with an oily smile as he settled in his chair. "If he'd stayed his arrival another minute, he would have been able to cast aside the label of *temporary* Guild Master and replace it with *permanent*."

"Perhaps you don't understand loyalty then, Your Grace?" Garrett again.

Lynch cut him a look and shook his head in warning.

The prince consort stared at Garrett for an uncomfortable minute. "Oh, I understand loyalty." His smile vanished. "Lynch, you may go."

Rosalind let out a breath. *Please. Let them get away from this awful place.*

But Lynch paused, turning to face the council, his boots almost in the puddle of blood Mordecai's body had left behind. "I do believe you promised something else, Your Grace. Some incentive, should the revolutionary be brought to justice."

Silence.

Barrons stepped forward, clad entirely in black velvet with a ruby dangling from his ear. "You swore that you would revoke Sir Jasper's rogue status and name him one of the Echelon."

The prince consort's smile died. "So I did. Thank you for reminding me of that, Barrons."

"My pleasure."

"And so I declare it. Sir Jasper Lynch," the prince consort called. "I officially revoke your rogue status and name you one of the Echelon." A nasty little smile twisted his mouth. "As such, I strip you of the title of Guild Master of the Nighthawks. No blue blood could remain amongst the rogues."

"I agree." Lynch straightened.

He was up to something.

Drawing all eyes, Lynch took a step back, his boot heel cutting over the brass circle. Then another, until he stood fully within it. He met the Duke of Bleight's gaze and gestured with a mocking little twitch of his fingers. "This has been a long time in coming, Uncle. I challenge you for the duchy of Bleight. First blood."

The prince consort's grip tightened on his chair, his face going white with fury. And Rosalind understood what Lynch had planned. Her heart leaped—then fell. If he won this fight, he became a duke and would join the council. There would be no place for her at his side.

But he would be free of the threat of the prince consort's power. Safer perhaps with power of his own. She couldn't—wouldn't—deny him that.

The Duke of Bleight slowly levered himself to his feet, his ancient face expressionless. Most duels were to the death. Not only was Lynch offering a reprieve, but in the Echelon's eyes, an insult. Would his pride overcome his fear of mortality? They all knew how uneven this match would be, even Bleight.

The rest of the council waited with bated breath.

"I accept, you little cur."

Twenty-nine

Three days later...

THE WIND TORE THROUGH HER HAIR AS SHE STEPPED down from the front door of the brownstone manor and Rosalind clamped her gloved hand to her hat. Her heart was still hammering in her chest. She'd done it. Without a shadow of a lie or even omitting a single detail. Everything she'd just won had been with the truth.

Her burgundy skirts flipping around her ankles, she crossed to the plain black steam carriage that waited at the curb. It was rented, of course. Jack blew warm air into his palms through the open hole in his respirator and then stepped forward to open the door for her. People stared. He'd tugged the collar of his coat up to hide the half mask, but still their eyes lingered and women grabbed their children by the arms and dragged them away as if afraid whatever contagion he had might spread.

Rosalind reached for him and squeezed his hand. Asking him to step out of the dark shadows he'd hidden in for the past eight years was an enormity she didn't underestimate.

"So?" he asked, ignoring the crowd as if he didn't give a damn.

"Sir Gideon has agreed to have lunch with me on Friday at the Metropolitan Hotel. He's cautious, but he certainly seemed interested in what I had to say." Excitement bubbled up in her chest. "Oh, Jack. You should hear some of his ideas. I always thought the Humans First party to be nothing but hot air but he's not. He's actually quite clever."

"You think this will work then?"

For the first time in days, her smile softened, losing its hard, false edge. She hadn't realized how unfocused her dream had been lately. Everything she'd done had become reactive, rather than taking initiative. She'd done what she had to, but she'd done it mechanically, without any real feeling for it. A chore. Something she owed Nate, for what she'd cost him. But now, a thousand ideas sparked through her breast. "I do. I really do. I had thought that giving up my plans would hurt more, but it doesn't. We're going to draft a bill to put before the Council about the increased rights for mechs. Mordecai's Bill. That's a start."

"You think they'll approve it?"

Her smile was vicious. "Of course not. Not at first. But unfortunately for the Council, I'm not going to go away. I'm going to keep at them until they are weary of my voice."

Calculation gleamed in his gray eye. The other was covered by an eye patch. "I think you'll have at least one of the Council votes in your pocket."

The reminder shattered her smile. She'd been trying not to think about it ever since Lynch won the duel. There'd been so much to do and she'd gotten swept aside in the chaos after that swift battle. Standing in the doorway, watching as Barrons swept him up with a hard thump to the back, she'd slowly edged back through the door. He'd won. He was safe and the Duke of Bleight banished to a country estate, his titles stripped. If Lynch had wanted to see her, then she wouldn't have sat up for the last three nights alone, watching her candle burn down as the night slowly passed.

"I wouldn't presume," she said stiffly.

"I would." Jack tipped his head toward the open door of the carriage. "Perhaps you'd best step in."

The expression on his scarred face was unreadable, but she could detect the faintest of lines around his eyes. A smile perhaps. Her eyes darted toward the carriage, her chest squeezing just a little tighter. That tickly sensation in her stomach multiplied a thousand times over, burning through her until she thought everyone would notice.

"Jack, what have you done?"

He held his hands up in surrender and stepped back onto the curb. "Why nothing, Roz. Some gent approached me and we had us a little chat." From the sudden sharp gleam of his eyes, she had a feeling the discussion might have lasted at least one of the several hours she'd been inside.

It was then that she noticed the driver sitting up on the seat of the carriage. Perry glanced at her, a cap pulled low over her eyes. Rosalind swallowed hard. As much as she was blindingly desperate to see Lynch, she didn't want to get in the carriage.

"Be brave," Jack lowered his voice, taking her hand by the fingertips to help her inside. "You deserve to be happy." A faint grimace. "Even if *he's* what makes you happy."

She thought that somewhat presumptuous. So much had happened between her and Lynch in the last week, yet nothing had been resolved. And he was a duke now. As the Master of the Nighthawks he'd been somewhat within her reach, but the Echelon would be expecting him to take a consort or begin making thrall contracts. No matter how much she loved him, she could not be a thrall.

"How are you getting home?" she asked.

"I've a mind to walk." Jack shrugged. "See if I can convince Ingrid out of her sulk."

Not all of them had been so happy to hear her confession about her feelings, both for the cause and for Lynch.

"She'll come around." Jack saw the expression on her face. "She loves you. She just doesn't like change. And she's scared that there's no place for her here, out in the light."

Rosalind nodded. The carriage door loomed open, revealing nothing but shadows within. Steeling herself, she gave her brother a kiss on the cheek, grabbed a handful of her skirts, and swept inside.

The sudden plunge into darkness left her blind. Jack slammed the door shut and somehow she found her seat, the shadowy shape of long legs starting to form in front of her. Following them up, she noticed the tight frock coat Lynch wore and the stark white spill of a cravat. Not his usual uniform then. It only reminded her of the distance between them and the small, hopeful part of her stuttered in its exhilaration.

Rosalind finally met his gaze, twitching at her skirts to straighten them. Beneath the dark curve of his lashes, his eyes gleamed an intense gray—watchful but giving nothing away. His only awareness of her showed in the stiffening of his body and the sudden clenching of hard muscle in his thigh. Seeing him again made her heart twist as though some enormous hand were squeezing it. She barely had the control to comport herself. She wanted to throw herself at him and drag his mouth to hers. To touch him. Assure herself that he was really there.

But why was he here?

"Hello, Your Grace," she said quietly.

At that Lynch grimaced. "I've had enough of that to last me a lifetime."

"You'd best get used to it as I believe you're going to have a lifetime of it."

A sigh. Then those canny eyes found hers again. "You've been busy."

Rosalind folded her hands neatly in her nap. Nothing. The dratted man was giving her nothing. She was so tense she felt as if she were going to fly apart. "I've had nothing to do for three days." Censure crept into her voice. "And someone once told me that I would never win a war, not in the streets."

Lynch glanced toward the window and the brownstone, as the carriage lurched into motion. His fingers drummed a slow, steady beat on his thigh. Restless.

"So now you're going to go after them in their own hallowed halls. Beard the lion in its den?"

"I'm going to dabble in politics," she said. "Sir Gideon Scott is interested in several of my ideas and I…" Her heart quickened. "I admit I've grown somewhat excited about some of his. He's not the fool I took him for, but he knows how far he may extend at each step."

"It's a dangerous path," Lynch said bluntly.

"Less so than my previous one." She took a deep breath. "Do you remember that boiler pack I was trying to smuggle from the enclaves?"

He nodded.

"It's designed to power an automaton. We call them the Cyclops. They're built large enough for a man to sit inside them and manipulate them and they've enough firepower to handle four of the Echelon's metaljackets."

Lynch's eyes narrowed on her. "How many do you have?"

"Not enough. Not yet," she admitted. "And most likely I won't pursue the project. You were right. This can't be won by outright war."

He scraped a hand over the back of his neck. "That doesn't ease my mind one whit."

"What would you suggest? That I pursue a hearth and home, perhaps take up knitting?"

The sudden smoky intensity of his gaze unnerved her. "That's not quite what I had in mind. Besides, you would probably stab someone with your knitting needle."

Rosalind couldn't help herself. Her heart began to

quicken, her fingers toying uselessly with each other. Her gaze dropped to them. Damned hands. Always betraying her. "I see. And what did you intend for me?"

"Damn it, Rosa. Do we have to be so formal?"

Again she lived in uncertainty. Looking up, she found the hard line of his jaw clenched. He had never been a man given to much emotion, but she saw it, gleaming in his pale eyes and pinched nostrils. A man holding himself so tightly he was afraid to let go.

But one of them must. Or they'd exist in this exquisite politeness until the carriage pulled up and then he would help her down and offer some platitude and she would probably accept it, watching as he left.

To take that next step scared her. But she wasn't as afraid as she had been. She'd thought once that to love again would be the worst that could ever happen to her, but it wasn't. To come so close to losing him had shown her how small such a fear could be.

"I waited for you for the last three nights," she said in a small, choked voice. "I was so certain you would come for me. But you didn't. I had to do something with my time. I was going out of my mind—"

"Hell, Rosa. I wanted to come. I thought—you weren't there. When I turned around you'd gone and… There were things I desperately needed to take care of."

"Oh?"

"Balfour," he said gruffly. As she stiffened, he reached out and took her hand. "He won't bother you again, Rosa. Indeed, he has no desire to hurt you. He's almost as intent as I in seeing that the prince consort never hears the truth of Mercury."

Heat flashed through her. "Why?"

"I believe he regrets what happened. No matter what you may feel, he seems fond of you and quite proud."

Rosalind tore her fingers from his. "It's a ploy."

Reaching out, Lynch tried to touch her again but she was too agitated. What was he saying? That in his fury, Balfour had done something he'd regretted? She shook her head. *No*. He'd killed Nate and crippled her brother. That was unforgivable.

"If it is a ploy, then I am prepared for him," Lynch said quietly. "You mentioned that he asked you to assassinate several persons for him. I would like the details, when you are ready. I want to prepare a full case against him, in case he decides to manipulate you. I've spoken to Barrons about it and he's prepared to press the case for me."

"Blackmail?" she asked, swallowing the hard knot in her throat. "I would never have expected it."

"Leverage," he corrected. "Balfour once said I am predictable. Maybe I was. But not anymore." His expression darkened. "I have had enough of being manipulated by those in power. I won't be threatened anymore—and I won't have those I consider mine threatened either."

The look he gave her left her in no confusion as to whom he referred to.

"And us?" she whispered. "What of us? You said—"

"I know what I said." His face darkened, his eyes going black with heat and need. "Rosalind… When you walked into that chamber…" He shuddered, each word said so precisely that it was clear he was barely holding on. "I know what you intended. I could see it all over your face. Don't you *ever* do that again."

"What was I to do? Let you die in my place? It nearly killed me when Garrett told me what you were planning." Everything that she'd been holding inside for the last few days boiled up. Heat raced behind her eyes. "You stupid man! You should have told me what the prince consort was demanding! I can't believe you... You—you didn't even say good-bye..."

She couldn't help herself. She was so angry. Or hurt. Or...something she couldn't quite explain, even to herself. Leaping toward him, Rosalind balled her fist and drove it into his arm. Lynch caught her wrists, dragging her forward.

"Damn you," she snapped, then his mouth took hers and the words were lost.

She slid her hands into his hair and yanked his face closer to hers. The hard edge of violence rode him, the muscles in his arms quivering with restraint as she raked her hands down them. She didn't want restraint. She hated it, hated the distant politeness, the way her emotions sat in a hard ball in the center of her chest. She let it all out, biting at his tongue just enough to sting.

As if the move goaded him into action, he growled deep in his throat, one hand fisting in her hair as he arched her back, his other hand grabbing a handful of her arse and hauling her closer. Rosalind's knees drove into the hard leather seats, her skirts bunching between them as he settled her firmly in his lap. Too many damned skirts. She caught a fistful of them and wrenched them out of the way, and then she could feel the hard steel of his erection between them, separated from her own flesh by his trousers and the barest silk slither of her drawers.

Lynch swept her bustle out of the way, and then his hand drove low between the back of her legs, fingers sliding over the delicate puckered rosebud of her bottom and deeper still, where the silk pressed wetly against her flesh. Rosalind's head spun, a gasp tearing from her bruised lips.

"Oh God," she whispered, grinding against him. Suddenly she couldn't hold herself back anymore. She needed to feel him against her, feel his cool-as-silk skin, taste it on her tongue. Shaking fingers found the buttons on his black waistcoat and then Rosalind was tugging, frantic in her haste, buttons tearing free from the lush velvet—hot and shivery and so close to coming apart that she couldn't breathe.

The fingers between her thighs slid mercilessly between the thin slit of her drawers. Against her wet flesh. She groaned, grabbed a handful of his waistcoat and tore it open.

"Easy, my love, easy…"

Rosalind kissed the smile from his lips. She didn't want easy. She wanted now. Somehow she had his shirt open and then she was dragging her mouth down his throat, her teeth rasping against the flat disk of his nipple. Lynch's hand fisted in her hair, and he sucked in a sharp gasp. He couldn't quite reach her now, his other hand clenching in the mound of her arse. She needed the respite. She wanted him to be with her this time, and if he kept it up, she'd have come in seconds.

Her hand slid down between them, grasping the straining length of his cock through the tight material of his trousers. Kissing her way down, Rosalind started tugging at his laces, her lips brushing through the line of hair that arrowed south from his navel...

"Enough," Lynch rasped, grabbing her hips and swinging her around so that she straddled him backwards.

Shoving through the layers of skirts, he found her wet and wanting. One hard jerk and her drawers were gone. Then he fumbled between them and suddenly she could feel the silky-soft brush of his erection. Grabbing her by the hips he eased her back, sheathing himself inside her with one firm thrust.

Rosalind threw her head back, biting her lower lip until it hurt. Her bottom nestled against his lap, his breath harsh and cool against the back of her neck. Firm hands caught her hips, eased her into a rocking motion. Then they were sliding up, cupping her breasts from behind, thrusting them high.

"Faster," she whispered, her thighs burning as she rode him. Strands of her coppery hair tumbled down around her face as her head fell forward, her lip held fast between her teeth.

Lynch's fingers found her and she cried out, her body slowing on his, unable to move, her thighs quivering as she hovered there. It was too much. She grabbed at his knees, holding on, his hips moving beneath her...slowly...torturously... As if he wanted to feel every last second of this.

The world went white. Rosalind jerked, her body clutching at his greedily as pleasure washed over her.

She couldn't hold her balance anymore. All she wanted was to wilt over him like a flower, bonelessly, blissed out on pleasure. He wouldn't let her. One hand thrust out, shoving aside the small curtain, and then she could feel cold glass beneath her touch, fingers spread and grasping for something—anything—to hold on to.

"I missed you," he whispered in her ear. "I was so angry at you, yet the thought of not having you… It did something to me. Tore something deep inside."

His words set off another cascade of pleasure within her—this time of the soul.

"I missed you," Rosalind admitted. "But I couldn't stand it anymore. I needed you to know the truth."

"Aye." He kissed her shoulder, slowly grinding against her again. "I'm glad you told me." She felt his lips twitch against her skin. "Though the timing could have been better."

Another slow grind. Rosalind shifted, rolling her hips. Pushing away from the window, she arched her back and lay back against his shoulder, sliding a hand up his throat. Clenching her inner muscles, she heard him curse softly, under his breath.

"You like that?" she whispered.

"Minx." But his hands were quivering on her hips and he urged her faster. Each squeeze drew a sharp intake of breath from him. "You drive me insane." He groaned and pressed his lips to her shoulder. Teeth sank into the soft muscle there as he thrust hard against her. Hoarsely, "Want you so much, so damned much…"

He pressed her against him, one hand on her abdomen as he gasped. Rosalind squeezed hard, feeling his body shake around her as he climaxed. She loved this feeling, the power she had over him, the way the world seemed as though it belonged to just the two of them.

Lynch collapsed back against the seat with a groan, dragging her with him. Long minutes ticked by as she lay back in his arms. She didn't want this to ever end.

"I never thought I'd miss the mask," he murmured, kissing a blazing trail across her trapezius. "But I like this too. Having you so vulnerable beneath me—atop me. Knowing that it's you. That it was always you." His teeth sank into her skin and she gasped.

A little uncomfortable now. "It wasn't always me. Not... Not the true me."

"You don't think I see her?" he whispered, nuzzling her throat. "The true Rosalind? Cerise?"

Rosalind pushed away from him, turning in his lap to face him. "I'm not Cerise."

"She's as much a part of you as Mrs. Marberry was. Or Mercury. I can see pieces of them all in you. You shouldn't be ashamed." His hand came up, cupped her face, his thumb stroking over her mouth. Those glorious gray eyes dropped too. As if he were thinking of tasting it again. "All of those pieces are you, Rosa. They made you what you are. Even Cerise...the girl who hurt...the girl who didn't want to exist anymore... You wouldn't be you, who you are, without her."

Tears stung her eyes that he should see it so clearly. She swallowed hard, wanting to kiss him again. But that was the coward's way out. A way to hide herself, to express herself without speech. "I wanted to destroy her," she whispered. "Because she didn't deserve to live after what she'd done. I wanted to be Rosalind. A new start. Away from all of the guilt. All of the hurt. If I finished what Nate started... It was a way to make things right, to find...forgiveness..."

That cool hand cupped her face, made her feel safe.
So safe. Rosalind tilted her cheek into the touch, like
a cat. Nothing had ever felt better than this, than being
in his arms. A wet tear slid down her cheek.

"He forgave you," Lynch said gently.

"You don't know that."

"I do." He insisted. "That is what it means to
love another."

The words stole her breath. With them came hope.
Then his arms crushed her against him, holding her so
tightly it were as if some part of him were afraid she'd
be torn from his grasp.

The words bubbled up in her throat, tickled against
the roof of her mouth. Clutching at his ruined shirt,
she pressed her face against the bare skin of his throat.
But she couldn't say it, as if a part of her still felt
unworthy. Pushing against his chest, she looked up.
"I lied to you."

"With your lips, yes." His eyelids lowered, almost
hiding those luminous eyes, but his hand kept on
stroking her cheek. "I should have paid more attention to my instincts, to what my dark half was telling
me." His thumb paused in the middle of her lip and
he looked up, capturing her gaze. "It knew who you
were no matter what guise you wore. It claimed you
long before I did." He took a deep, shuddering breath.
"And did you ever lie to me...here?" Tentative
fingertips pressed between her breasts, directly over
the thumping beat of her heart.

Rosalind shook her head, swallowing hard. "You
know I didn't," she whispered, cupping his hand and
holding it firmly against her chest. She could feel the

heady pulse of her heartbeat through his touch. "It belonged to you long before I knew it." Another heady swallow. She had to say it. He deserved it and she wanted him to know. "I love you."

"I know." He said the one thing she needed to hear the most. This time he believed her. Slowly his lips curled up, and she thought she might die for the joy the sight elicited in her. His smile—so rare—was a thing of wonders. "I knew the instant you walked through the doors of the atrium." The smile began to fade.

Rosalind quickly pressed her fingertips to it, as if to capture it. "Don't think about it."

Lynch kissed her fingertips and took a shuddery breath. "I won't. That is done. However, there is one last thing we must discuss."

"What now." It wasn't a question.

His fingers laced between her iron fingers and held them up. "I have had Fitz design something special for me." Reaching into the pocket of his waistcoat, he drew out a small red velvet box. "Considering that no normal ring would fit—"

Rosalind sat up and nearly lift her head. All she could see was that box, her heart pounding so swiftly she almost swayed with dizziness. "What are you saying?"

"I asked your brother if I had permission to make you my consort." He flicked the box open. "I want you to share the world with me. Forever, Rosa. No more secrets between us. Nothing but you and me, till death do us part."

Nestled within was a gleaming steel ring, burnished so brightly that it shone. An enormous square diamond was set into the top, with a lattice of tiny, filigreed silver holding it in place. No lady of the Echelon would wear it, but it suited her, so perfectly he had obviously designed it himself. And the fact that he had asked Jack—who had given his blessing—meant so much more to her than any diamond.

"Yes," she whispered, her hand trembling as she held it up.

Lynch slid the ring from the box. "You can never take this off, Rosa. I intend to have Fitz solder it to your finger."

"I don't want to take it off." She bounced impatiently. "Hurry up and put it on."

He slid it down over the iron knuckle and settled it in place. "Well, duchess... How do you feel?"

"I feel as if you have given me the world." Her throat was dry and tight again as she looked at him. How could one have so much feeling inside and not drown in it? She would have to learn to cope with this. "I wish I could give you half as much."

"You have." He kissed her iron fingertips. "You have given me a future and joy in it too. Before I met you, I was only existing. I wasn't living life. The last few weeks...as tumultuous as they've been, at least I've lived them." Leaning down, he kissed her lips lightly.

"Besides," he whispered against her lips, "we have so much to do together, you and I. A whole world to change." The words caught her breath. "You are the only one I trust to watch my back."

"Well, it is *almost* my favorite part to look at," she whispered.

Lynch smiled. "And there is my wicked Mrs.

Marberry. I do believe I have one last request though... Something I would like to ask of you in exchange for the ring."

"Anything," she promised, smiling at this amazing man: her future, her hope, her heart...

"Keep the mask," he breathed, and leaned down to kiss her again.

In case you missed it, check out an excerpt from Bec McMaster's debut

Kiss of Steel

Now available from Sourcebooks Casablanca

HONORIA PUSHED THE DOOR OPEN AND WHISKED inside. And stopped dead in her tracks—

Blade spun on his heel at her shocked gasp, swiftly wrapping a towel around his hips. It wasn't quite big enough and gaped over one heavily muscled thigh as he tucked the end into itself at his waist. His eyes widened in surprise when he saw her, then he scowled.

She couldn't stop herself from staring. Acres and acres of wide, muscled chest. The barbaric band of tattoo around his left arm and down his ribs. An arrow of hair trailing from his navel down into the edge of the towel. And the tented suggestion of what that towel was hiding, proving that Blade didn't find this intrusion entirely disagreeable.

Honoria turned away quickly. This wasn't what she'd planned at all, but how could she go about her revenge when he was practically naked?

"Well," he drawled. "I guess you ain't 'ere to tuck me in."

"Of course not," she threw over her shoulder. She caught a distracting glimpse of him in the mirror and turned her burning face back to the wall. "You know exactly why I'm here. Put some clothes on. This is indecent."

"I ain't the one as just barged into a gent's rooms without knockin'."

The sound of the towel hitting the floor made her mouth go dry. Oh, my goodness. He was naked. And her mind's eye was most enthusiastic about supplying her with a vision of what that might look like.

It would be very easy to confirm whether her vision was accurate. *Don't you dare*, she told herself.

"I'm afraid you've got me at a loss," he replied, leisurely moving around behind her. Sheets rustled and then she heard the unmistakable sound of leather sliding over skin.

"Are you decent?"

"Rarely," he said, with an ironic drawl.

"Are you clothed?"

"Aye."

He was going to play games with her. Her fists clenched and she turned to look him in the eye. At the edges of her peripheral vision, she could just see him tugging the leather breeches into place, but she didn't dare look lower.

"I need those diaries," she said firmly. "This isn't a game. You know how important they are to me."

"The diaries, eh?" He feigned surprise. "You're 'ere to fetch your diaries. I thought you took 'em 'ome last night."

"You swapped them while I was getting dressed! I opened the bag and found *The Scarlet Letter* and *The*

Taming of the Shrew—no doubt you had a good laugh at that."

He crossed his arms over his chest and gave her a steady look. The muscles in his forearms bunched.

"Aye. I were so desperate for your company that I stole your precious diaries. What's in 'em that's so important, Honor?"

"That's none of your business."

"Then you ain't gettin' 'em back."

The ring on her finger seemed to burn. "Yes, I am." She started toward him.

"You goin' to turn me up sweet, luv? I got news for you—I'm tired o' playin' games." He took a step forward and glared down at her. "And you already owe me a kiss which you ain't paid."

He was in her space again, using his size and height to intimidate. A little flutter started, low in her stomach. "I thought you didn't want me to kiss you unless I wanted it too."

"Maybe I changed me mind."

A little flick of her fingernail opened the toxin-smothered needle. The thought of kissing him did horrible things to her willpower—and her knees—but it would also get her close enough to render him at her mercy. Honoria tilted her chin up and stared him directly in the eyes.

Go ahead, you bleeder. Force a kiss and it shall be the last thing you're capable of doing for some time.

His eyes widened imperceptibly, and his voice was low and husky when he said, "Is that a dare I see in your eyes?" He took another step closer, so close that her skirts brushed against his legs.

"I can't stop you," she said. "But I promise you shall regret this."

Blade reached up and slowly, slowly stroked her cheek, his gaze following the path of his fingers. They dipped over the lush pillow of her top lip. Tasted the wetness of her mouth. And then lingered at the center of her lower lip. She was shivering by the time he'd finished.

"Aye," Blade murmured, his lips curving in a satisfied little smile. "A bleedin' martyr till the end. I think not."

He stepped away, giving her his back. Honoria's jaw dropped as he turned and held up his shirt as though examining whether it suited him for the day or not.

"I beg your pardon?"

Blade knelt on the edge of the bed, with its rumpled sheets and mounded red cushions. His leather breeches molded faithfully to the lean curve of his buttocks, revealing a healthy amount of muscled thigh. He reached for his daggers, the thick black ink of his tattoo riding up over his ribs.

Her mouth went dry.

"You 'eard me." He straightened and slung the belt around his waist, pulling the buckle tight. Only then did he look up at her, with that mocking little smile playing over his lips, as though he knew precisely what was going through her mind at the moment. "If you think I'm goin' to steal a kiss just so as you can cry protest, you can think again. You want me, then you're goin' to 'ave to make the move yourself."

"I don't want you."

"Aye. That's why your scent changed. You smell all plump and lush, my little dove. I knows when a woman's got 'er eyes on a man. One of the advantages o' bein' a blue blood." He held his arms out, displaying his magnificent body to full effect. "Do you want to touch me? Is that what's got your heart poundin' in your ears and your breath thick in your throat?" A little smile touched his lips. "I'll let you, you know. You can run those pretty little fingers *all* over me if you want. Or that sweet little mouth, if you'd prefer." He took a step closer. "Do you want a taste o' me, Honor? Do you want to lick the sweat from me body, taste the salt o' me skin?"

He leaned closer, looming over her. It was only then that she realized she'd backed up against the wall, her gaze locked to his wicked mouth and all of the sinful things it was saying.

"I don't want to touch you. I don't want to taste you," she whispered and shut her eyes. It was no good. She could still see him, that lean body caging her in, the muscles in his arms rippling as he pressed both hands flat against the wall on either side of her hips.

"Liar."

A silky whisper. In her ear. A curious, whimpering sound came from her throat.

He took her hand. Pressed it against the ripple of his abdomen. Honoria's eyes shot open and locked on his.

It was the perfect opportunity. All she had to do was turn her hand just so and press the tip of the needle into his body. But something stopped her. Perhaps the silky-cool feel of his skin beneath her hand. Or the look in his eyes as he stared down at her.

His mouth was close to hers. She barely felt his fingers trailing through her hair, tugging a soft curl over her shoulder. All she could see was that mouth, with its sensual lips, and the slight lopsided dimple as he smiled. A sinner's mouth. A demon's mouth. Tempting her with all manner of ungodly acts. His breath stirred over her face, caressing her cheeks.

Honoria could barely breathe for the pounding of her heart. This was madness. She'd never felt like this before, not even with the exquisite, practiced flirting of the blue bloods she'd encountered at Vickers's house. Blade was nothing like them. Rough. Raw. Virile. The kind of man who would steal a kiss and not take no for an answer. The kind of man who could capture her heart…and crush it in his fist.

This was dangerous. And yet for the first time in her life she wanted to throw caution to the wind and simply take what he offered. To just be a woman who wanted to forget about all of her burdens, her worries, and simply be young and carefree for once in her damned life.

I want to know what he tastes like. I want to be kissed.

She stared up at him. And all at once, the willful part of her nature erupted from its cage. Damn it. What harm could one kiss do?

Acknowledgments

Thanks as always to wonder-agent Jessica Faust and all of the folks at Sourcebooks who helped to push this manuscript into something resembling a book. To my editor Leah Hultenschmidt, who cuts right to the heart of the matter and sees what I can't, to Danielle for all the PR efforts and my poor copyeditors who have to deal with the cockney.

A huge debt of gratitude to the ELE for keeping me sane, especially my font of wisdom, Kylie Griffin, and my CPs Dakota Harrison and CT Green who get to wade through the manuscript before anyone else ever sees it. To all of my local supporters and family, who continue to put up with my hermit-like ways and proudly support the book. And to Byron, who makes all of this possible and gets excited over the little things with me.

And finally, to my readers. Thanks for coming on the ride with me.

Kiss of Steel

by Bec McMaster

When nowhere is safe

Most people avoid the dreaded Whitechapel district. For Honoria Todd, it's the last safe haven. But at what price?

Blade is known as the master of the rookeries—no one dares cross him. It's been said he faced down the Echelon's army single-handedly, that ever since being infected by the blood-craving he's been quicker, stronger, almost immortal.

When Honoria shows up at his door, his tenuous control comes close to snapping.

She's so…innocent. He doesn't see her backbone of steel—or that she could be the very salvation he's been seeking.

For more Bec McMaster, visit:

www.sourcebooks.com

Heart of Iron

by Bec McMaster

❦

No one to Trust

Dangerous. Unpredictable. That's how people know the hulking Will Carver. And those who don't like pretty words just call him The Beast. No matter how hard Will works to suppress his werewulfen side, certain things drive him beyond all control. And saucy Miss Lena Todd tops the list.

Lena makes the perfect spy against the ruling Echelon blue bloods. No one suspects that under the appearance of a flirtatious debutante lies a heart of iron. Not even the ruthless Will Carver, the one man she can't wrap around her finger and the one man whose kiss she can never forget. He's supposed to be protecting her, but he might just be her biggest threat yet...

❦

"Edgy, dark, and shot through with a grim, gritty intensity, McMaster's latest title adds to her mesmerizing steampunk series with another gripping, inventive stunner."—Library Journal *Starred Review*

"McMaster's second London steampunk book dazzles and seduces...will leave readers breathless."—RT Book Reviews *Top Pick of the Month, 4.5 Stars*

For more Bec McMaster visit:

www.sourcebooks.com

Forged by Desire

by Bec McMaster

────────── ❧ ──────────

***Look for the fourth book in Bec McMaster's highly
acclaimed London Steampunk series, coming in late 2014***
The captain of the Nighthawk guard has a deadly mission:
capture a steel-jawed monster who's been preying on women.
Capt. Garrett Reed hates to put his partner Perry in jeopardy,
but she's the best bait he has. Little does he realize, he's the
one about to be caught in his own trap…

Perry has been half in love with Garrett for years, but this
is not exactly the best time to fall in love—especially when
their investigation leads them directly into the clutches of the
madman she thought she'd escaped…

────────── ❧ ──────────

Praise for Bec McMaster:

*"Bec McMaster brilliantly weaves a world
that engulfs your senses and takes you on a
fantastical journey."*—Tome Tender

*"[McMaster's] descriptive powers are flawless
and her ability to draw the reader in is
unparalleled."*—Debbie's Book Bag

For more Bec McMaster, visit:

www.sourcebooks.com

A Lady Can Never Be Too Curious

by Mary Wine

❧

**Beneath the surface of Victorian life
lies a very different world...**

Hated and feared by the upper classes, the Illuminists guard their secrets with their lives. Janette Aston's insatiable quest for answers brings her to their locked golden doors, where she encounters the most formidable man she's ever met.

Darius Lawley's job is to eliminate would-be infiltrators, but even he may be no match for Janette's cunning and charm...

❧

"This fast-paced, unique steampunk story has introduced me to a whole new world that I can't wait to read more of."—Night Owl Reviews

"Filled with action, intrigue, and a small twist of humor, **A Lady Can Never Be Too Curious** *is for the true lover of romance—some of the scenes are sure to peel the wallpaper right off the walls."*—[Book Loons]

For more Mary Wine, visit:

www.sourcebooks.com

A Captain and a Corset

by Mary Wine

There's trouble in the skies…

For Sophia Stevenson, there's no going back to the life she knew. She never asked for the powers that make her a precious commodity to the secret society of Illuminists—and their archenemies.

Captain Bion Donkova would give anything to possess the powers that have fallen into Sophia's lap. If only the beautiful, infuriating woman could stay out of trouble, he wouldn't have to keep coming to her rescue…

Bion and Sophia have friction to spare—and nothing fuels a forbidden passion better than danger…

Praise for **A Lady Can Never Be Too Curious***:*

"A fun, distracting, and entertaining read with plenty of racy moments."—RT Book Reviews

"Steampunk fans will happily embrace the altered history offered by this escape into 1840 Great Britain as Wine steps away from her Scottish series."—Booklist

For more Mary Wine, visit:

www.sourcebooks.com

Prince of Shadows

by Tes Hilaire

—⁓—

It's forbidden for a warrior of the Light to love a creature of the Dark...

Valin has never quite fit in with the rest of the Paladin warriors. His power to manipulate shadow has always put him at odds with their purpose of using heavenly Light to eradicate evil. His warrior brothers have no idea how close he is to being lost to his dark nature.

But maybe he was never all that Light to begin with

When Valin meets the vampire Gabriella, she awakens within him something he thought long buried. But as he watches Gabriella's need for vengeance threaten to drag her down into the same dark hell that he's living, he knows his only chance at redemption is bringing her out of the dark...

—⁓—

Praise for the Paladin Warriors series:

"This world and series is great. If you love the warrior series books along the line of J.R. Ward or Sherrilyn Kenyon, I highly recommend that you pick these up."—*Smitten with Reading*

"Hilaire has created a unique blend of mythology and fantasy... a scorching read."—*Fresh Fiction*

For more Tes Hilaire, visit:

www.sourcebooks.com

Tall, Dark, and Vampire

by Sara Humphreys

—〰—

She always knew Fate was cruel...

The last person Olivia expected to turn up at her club was her one true love. It would normally be great to see him, *except he's been dead for centuries*. Olivia really thought she had moved on with her immortal life, but as soon as she sees Doug Paxton, she knows she'd rather die than lose him again. And that's a real problem...

But this is beyond the pale...

Doug is a no-nonsense cop by day, but his nights are tormented by dreams of a gorgeous redhead who's so much a part of him, she seems to be in his blood. When he meets Olivia face-to-face, long-buried memories begin to surface. She might be the answer to his prayers...or she might be the death of him.

—〰—

Praise for Untamed:

"The characters are well-developed, the twists and turns of the plot are well-crafted, and the situations are alternately funny, action-packed, and sensual."—*Fresh Fiction*

"An excellent paranormal romance with awesome world-building and strong leads."—*The Romance Reviews*

For more Sara Humphreys, visit:

www.sourcebooks.com

The Outcast Prince

by Shona Husk

—◊◊◊—

Just one taste is all it takes…

This was no ordinary mirror. Caspian caught a hint of color, a whirl of a waltz just past his reflection—a glimpse into the decadent Fairy Court of Annwyn. The home he could never have. It called to him, whispering temptation after temptation…if he would only reclaim his rightful heritage.

To be forever lost

Caspian has an even stronger reason to stay in the world of humans. He's just met a woman who captivates him like no other. But loving him has proven to be dangerous. And he will do whatever it takes to protect Lydia from the vicious, seductive world of Court—even if doing so requires the ultimate sacrifice: his soul.

—◊◊◊—

"Brilliantly unique, beautifully sensual, *The Outcast Prince* had me spellbound from the first page! Shona Husk's engaging voice and vivid, creative world-building make every one of her books a must-read!"— *Larissa Ione,* New York Times *bestselling author*

For more Shona Husk, visit:

www.sourcebooks.com

About the Author

Bec McMaster lives in a small town in Victoria, Australia, and grew up with her nose in a book. Following a lifelong love affair with fantasy, she discovered romance and hasn't looked back. A member of RWA, she writes sexy, dark paranormals and adventurous steampunk romances. When not writing, reading, or poring over travel brochures, she loves spending time with her very own hero or daydreaming about new worlds. Visit her website at www.becmcmaster.com or follow her on twitter @BecMcMaster.